Al

# The ONE MONTH Boyfriend

USA TODAY BESTSELLING AUTHOR

# ROXIE NOIR

Editor: Edits in Blue
Proofreading: Honey Palomino
Cover: Najla Qamber Designs

*For all the unlikeable heroines.*

# CONTENT NOTE

PLEASE BE aware that this book contains: discussion of anxiety, on-page panic attacks, on-page PTSD, on-page racial micro-aggressions, discussion of past drug use and addiction, past emotional abuse, and past death by suicide.

# ONE
## SILAS

IT'S LATE AFTERNOON, the first Friday of August, and I'm making a vow.

I, Silas Flynn, hereby vow to always ask about stairs before agreeing to lift anything heavy. I vow to say no to things once in a while. I vow to use any of a plethora of excuses—busy at work, existing plans, bad back—next time Javier needs help moving his sculpture collection.

Right now I could be anywhere, doing anything, but I'm sweating myself to death in a downtown parking lot, trying to get a seven-foot-tall Mothman up a set of narrow concrete steps.

"Higher," Gideon grunts from below. "I don't want to—"

*Clang.* Mothman's flank hits the metal banister and something falls off.

"Fuck," Gideon swears under his breath as I switch my grip, managing to get it about two inches higher. "Hope he didn't need that part."

"He can come get it himself," I mutter. "Okay, I think we need to tilt—yeah."

The two of us haul Mothman up the stairs, one precar-

3

ious step at a time. It's like moving a couch, only the couch has sharp edges you can't see, pokes you every time you move the wrong way, and is three times as heavy as any couch has ever been. By the time I get to the top step I'm sweating even harder, Gideon's swearing under his breath nonstop, and my back feels like I'll regret this tomorrow.

And the door's shut. The wooden stopper we'd stuck in there is gone, so I balance the statue on one hand and one knee, pray, and turn the knob.

It's locked.

I swear and re-balance Mothman. Something sharp digs into my thigh, and three steps below Gideon makes a noise of weary-yet-inevitable irritation, shifting his stance.

I skip knocking and pound on the door with the side of my fist as hard as I can, the dull thud swallowed by the humid August air.

"Hey!" I shout, already out of breath. "Javi, where the— where are you?"

It's fucking heroic, but I don't scream curse words in the middle of a family-friendly event. Gideon makes up for it by muttering a few more.

There's no response. I wait about five seconds, then pound again, because this thing is heavy and if no one answers this door soon, it'll be broken.

"That fucking idiot slacker," Gideon growls. "The fuck did he go?"

Swearing is pretty much Gideon's love language.

"Probably found the snack table and forgot he was having an art show," I say between my teeth, then take a deep breath. "HEY, SOMEONE COME OPEN THE DOOR!"

"I swear to God, if he shows up with a bag of fucking Doritos in one hand—"

4

"This is the fire door!" a voice shouts from the other side of the door. "Go around!"

My blood pressure spikes. I swear to God I can feel my veins constricting at the voice on the other side of the door, the very last person I want to deal with while carrying this son of a bitch and sweating my balls off.

"No!" I shout back, Mothman slipping a little against a slick palm. "We've got one of the sculptures for—"

"If I open it, I'll set off the—"

"It's fine!" I roar. "Just open it!"

"What the fuck," growls Gideon from below.

"IT'S A FIRE DOOR," she shouts back, enunciating each word at top volume as though I'm a mentally deficient sea cucumber. "IF I OPEN IT, THE ALARMS WILL—"

"FUCK THE ALARMS!" I shout back, forgetting not to swear because Kat Fucking Nakamura sends me from zero to ten in half a second. "OPEN THE DAMN DOOR BEFORE WE DROP THIS THING AND—"

The door shoves open and hits me in the shoulder.

"Shit, sorry," Javier's already saying as I swear, Mothman wobbling dangerously. "Sorry, I got hung up with Linda, she wanted to make sure she'd spelled my name right on the plaque and next thing I know she's telling me how excited everyone is to meet your girlfriend tomorrow and asking whether I think it'll be a spring wedding."

I'm only half paying attention as he holds the door open and I carry Mothman past him, into the slightly cooler dark of backstage, doing my damnedest not to run into a wall or let my sweaty palms slip on the metal. I blink, willing my eyes to adjust faster as the door swings shut again behind Gideon.

God, I love air conditioning. The pinnacle of human achievement.

"Where'd you want this?" I hear him ask Javier as faces coalesce from the darkness.

Then I realize I'm staring at her.

She's just inside the door, a glasses-wearing oval with dark eyes and dark hair in side-swept bangs. She's glaring at me, exasperated, arms crossed, like I'm a cat who can't decide whether he wants to be inside or outside. Her entire stance—her entire *being*—gives off *I can't believe I have to deal with this jackass* energy.

My attention snags on her like a loose shirt on a thorn. I can't seem to pull it away.

"I don't hear the alarm," I say.

Kat doesn't respond. She doesn't do anything, except maybe glower a little harder.

"Silas. Move your ass," Gideon says. "This thing is fucking heavy."

"That way," Javier tells us. "Next to Bigfoot. There's no podium this time so it's just gonna go on the floor..."

Javier keeps talking instead of helping as I shuffle backward.

Behind him, Kat narrows her eyes, somehow gives me a look even more disdainful than the look she was already giving me, and then stalks off into the darkness.

I back into a wall.

"Silas," Gideon says, and I turn my head so I can see where I'm going.

· · · ★ ★ ★ ★ ★ · · · ·

"I WISH I could've made Bigfoot bigger," Javier says, staring up at the sculpture, arms crossed in what I've come to recognize as his thinking stance. "He really ought to be towering over the other two, you know. King of the gods! Raining down lightning and thunder, all that."

"I think any bigger would have killed us both," Gideon says, voice low and deadpan. "We nearly died getting that into the freight elevator to begin with."

"It wasn't that bad," Javier says.

Gideon lets his silence speak for him. I wasn't there when he, Javier, and our other buddy Wyatt got a seven-by-three trunk of oak up to his fourth-floor studio, but I sure heard about it later.

And heard about it. And *heard* about it.

"I think he's majestic," I offer.

"Thank you."

It's the first Friday of August, which means that tonight is the last Sprucevale Summer Night until next year, and the town went all-out. They closed a couple blocks of Main Street to traffic in favor of food trucks, pony rides, folk singers, a performance stage for the Sprucevale School of Ballet, and a street magician named The Incredible Dwyane Wayne who pulls empty beer cans from a camouflage baseball hat with a fish hook on the brim.

I'm not sure who approved that last one. Maybe he'll switch to Coke cans for a family-friendly event.

The three of us are on the stage at the Irene Williams Historic Theater, which is currently hosting the Burnley County SPCA Fundraising Carnival, Silent Pie Auction, and Art Show. The carnival—which is just basic games like Pin The Tail on the Tortoise—is set up where the seats used to be, the pie auction is right in front of the stage, and the art show is on the stage. The walls are lined with artistic black-and-white photos of animals up for adoption, and there's a cash bar in the back.

The SPCA adoptions are really Gideon's thing, and the

art show is Javier's. I'm just here because I'm a helpful, supportive guy who'd get into a fistfight over that blackberry pie. I shove a hand through my hair, the roots stiff with dried sweat, and consider the art.

"Aren't there supposed to be twelve?" I ask Javier, not for the first time. "If it's Appalachian Olympus?"

"Sure, everyone's a mythology expert."

"There *are* twelve Olympians," Gideon says. "Everyone knows that."

"Look, I'm working on it," Javier says, and shifts his stance, one hand going through his shaggy dark hair. "We'll get there. Right now there are three. Deal with it."

I give Javier shit, but honestly? These are good. He has a whole spiel about backwoods-cryptids-as-Greek-mythology that he's told me more than once, but when you're standing in front of a seven-foot-tall oak Bigfoot wielding a lightning bolt or Mothman made from junked car parts, you don't need all that. You just need eyes.

The three of us just look at the sculptures in silence for a minute before another thought crashes into me.

"Javi," I say. "Why does Linda think I'm having a spring wedding?"

"Oh, yeah," Javier says, casually, tweaking something on Mothman. "That was weird. She thinks she's meeting your girlfriend tomorrow?"

On his other side, Gideon makes an ungainly noise that is very definitely a laugh.

"Fuck off," I tell him.

"Don't tell me to fuck off, you're the idiot," he says, still laughing.

"She's really looking forward to finally being introduced," Javier, who's now grinning, adds.

"And to being invited to your wedding," Gideon adds. "In the spring."

"Such a lovely time of year, spring."

"You're both assholes," I tell them. "*Fuck*," I add, mostly to myself.

"Yes, but neither of us told Linda Ballard that we had a girlfriend," Javier points out. *Gleefully.*

"Why does she think—" I start, but don't bother finishing the sentence because it doesn't matter. I swallow hard against the knot of anger and resentment that's formed in my chest, take two deep breaths and stare up at Bigfoot-as-Zeus while the old urge to punch something slowly fades.

It's not Linda's business whether I'm dating someone or not. It's not anyone's business but mine—and, I guess, whoever I'm dating or not dating but for some godforsaken reason, everyone in Sprucevale seems to think it's their business, not least Linda Ballard, the office manager at Hayward & Marshall, Attorneys at Law.

Because it's odd and unnatural to be closing in on forty without a romantic partner. Because if I don't have a wife or a girlfriend—the possibility of *boyfriend* or *husband* doesn't seem to have crossed anyone's mind, though it doesn't apply here—I must be desperately sad and lonely and lacking.

Because there's no way I could be perfectly happy to be single. No way that, after years of failing to find that special someone, I'd prefer it.

Still, telling Linda that I was seeing someone just so she'd stop asking was dumb, impulsive, and I've already lived to regret it.

"I need a reason to break up with a girlfriend," I say.

"I think you two should try and make it work," Javier offers, grinning like an asshole. "Have you considered couples' counseling?"

"Try bringing her flowers," suggests Gideon. "Maybe a love sonnet."

"She doesn't even exist and you two assholes assume I'm the one who fucked up?"

"If she's not real, can't be her fault, can it?" says Javier.

Gideon shrugs, his hands in his pockets. I think he's trying not to smile, but it can be hard to tell behind the beard.

"Tell Linda and your boss that she can't make it because she's busy rescuing a bus full of orphans that's about to fall off a cliff," he says. "Or... she has a work thing."

"My girlfriend has had *a work thing* for almost three months now," I point out.

"And Linda still believes you?"

I glance over the edge of the stage at the people on the floor below, all setting up cardboard carnival games, dragging coolers around, putting pies on a table, and hanging glamour shots of various cats and dogs. I should probably be down there, helping, but instead I'm here trying to untangle this damn mess I've made.

"For now," I say. "Which is why I need to break up with *this* girlfriend, and then maybe be so heartbroken about it that I can't possibly think about seeing someone new for at least a year."

That might get Linda off my back for a while, and by extension, half the Sprucevale gossip machine.

"I'll just tell her I work too much and my girlfriend left me," I say.

"For another man," Javier offers.

"A billionaire playboy with a superyacht," adds Gideon.

"Who's also an underwear model and a firefighter."

"There was just no way you could compete," Gideon says, and claps a hand to my shoulder. "Sorry."

"You think I couldn't compete with that?"

"You have a yacht?" asks Javier.

"I don't need a yacht to be a better boyfriend than some rich asshole," I point out.

"You kinda do."

"*Guys,*" interrupts Gideon in his most imposing Oldest Brother voice, even though he's younger than me. "Silas, stop fighting with Javier over whether you're better than fictional people. Javier, stop baiting Silas into fighting over fictional people, you know how he is."

"Sorry, Dad," Javier says, grinning. I flip them both off, then remember I'm on a stage at a family event and shove my hand back in my pocket.

"Fine," I say, and fold my arms over my chest. "I guess I'm getting dumped for a Greek shipping heir or something."

"Aim high," Javier agrees.

"You think she'll believe me?"

"That you've conveniently been dumped for a billionaire by a woman who you've refused to give literally any information about? Why wouldn't she?" Javier says.

"Javi," warns Gideon.

"No, he's right," I say, and scrub my hands over my face. "Fuck. Maybe she's busy with work again tomorrow."

Javier makes a noise that clearly means *that won't work but I can't be the one to say it aloud.* Gideon contemplates the art, frowning.

Silence falls between the three of us.

"Or," Gideon says, slowly.

I turn and look at him, hands in his pockets, looking stern and backwoodsy as ever with his dark hair, dark beard, and eternal frown.

"Just get someone to be your date tomorrow and break up afterward," he says. "Same end result, less suspicious."

"That's a terrible idea," I tell him.

"Why?" says Javier.

"Because," I start.

They both look at me expectantly as I grasp at reasons.

"I can't take a first date to dinner at my boss's house?"

"Obviously your date is in on it," Gideon explains, as if to a child. "You get a girlfriend for a night, she gets free drinks and, I don't know, a gift card and flowers or something. Make it worth her while."

I look away and swear under my breath because I can't believe it's come to fake dating for gift cards. Jesus, what's wrong with me?

Problem is, I still can't find a reason it's a *bad* idea, or at least not a worse one than anything else.

"I'll think about it," I tell them. "I should go help set up."

"Think fast," Javier says, as I walk off the stage.

# TWO

## KAT

I GRIND my teeth and slam the bottom of a wine bottle into the ice bucket. The giant piece of ice that was there falls apart under the glass onslaught, but the bottle doesn't break.

Not that I wish it would. Not really, because then there would be chardonnay and maybe also blood everywhere, and I'd be causing a scene, but God I want to break something right now and this wine bottle is the best candidate.

But no, I don't even get that satisfaction. The bottle remains stubbornly whole, so all I can do is load more wine bottles into the bucket to sell them for $5 a glass to people looking at art and bidding on pies.

"Everything okay?" asks Anna Grace, who's materialized behind the bar with me. You wouldn't think that someone so loud all the time could also be so sneaky, but Anna Grace contains multitudes.

"Great," I say, and do a thing with my face that's supposed to be a smile. It might be a grimace instead. "Everything is going very great."

"Uh huh," she says, and stops, tilting her head to one side, her blonde curls rearranging themselves.

13

I sigh, take a deep breath, and try to collect myself. Thankfully the bar is at the back of the theater, so at least I don't feel like I'm being stared at.

The pie auction, on the other hand, is right next to the stage and there are lights and tables and signs and oh holy hell, what did I sign myself up for?

"It's been a week," I tell Anna Grace, who already knows it's been a week. "I just. You know."

She puts her clipboard down on the bar and engulfs me in a big, warm Valkyrie hug.

"You don't have to stay," she tells the top of my head. "Go home. Fuck the pies, they'll auction themselves."

"I don't want to go home," I mutter into her shoulder. "If I go home I'll just lie on the couch and *think* and that's even worse."

She responds by hugging me tighter.

"Work was the one thing that was going well," I say. I'm telling Anna Grace stuff she already knows, but I feel like I have to say it again or I might crack apart into a million pieces from nerves. "And now even that has been cruelly taken from me."

She pets my hair.

"He *emailed* me today," I tell her, not for the first time. "He wanted to make sure I could put my *personal feelings* aside and *remain professional* since I'll be sharing his office."

"Fucking asshole," she agrees.

"He wrote that to me! *His office*. It's my office, you self-important ass-goblin."

"They can't put him into another office?" she asks, because I love Anna Grace but she's the kind of person who can't resist offering a solution.

"I didn't try," I admit. "I've only been there for six

14

months and I don't want to be difficult, you know? Especially not when things were good at work."

Anna Grace just makes a soothing noise, thankfully not offering more solutions even though I can tell she wants to.

"And I yelled at Silas Flynn about the fire door and everyone heard me and now they all think I'm a lunatic," I say. "So. You know."

"Kat, I promise everyone in this building has yelled at Silas for something or other," she says, and I just snort.

"He's such a dick."

"Mhm."

I finally pull back, since we're just sort of embracing behind the bar and it probably looks weird, then adjust my glasses on my face.

"Why do people like him?" I complain. "Do they not know what an asshole he is? Or do they just not mind?"

"Your problem with Silas is its own thing," she says, very diplomatically.

"He made me cry in front of the dean!"

Anna Grace just gives me a look that says, very clearly, *that happened over a decade ago and we're not discussing it right now.*

"Do you need more ice?" she asks instead.

I take a deep breath and look around at the various coolers and ice buckets I've set up behind the bar, filled with wine, beer, sodas, water, and a handful of juice boxes for the kids. I remind myself that I'm here because I am *being social* and *making acquaintances* and *dealing with my anxiety in a healthy and normal way*, not so I can explode at people for using the wrong door.

"I think we're okay for now," I say, perfectly neutral. "Thanks."

I must look weird, because Anna Grace hugs me again

and even though she's a hugger in general, this is a lot of hugs. I wonder if it looks strange to anyone else in the building, especially after I yelled at Silas about a door, even though I was right about the door because there's a huge sign on it that says FIRE DOOR, DO NOT OPEN so of course I thought all the alarms and sprinklers were going to go off —

"It sucks that you have to share an office with your ex for a whole month," Anna Grace says, in her most validating voice. I do, in fact, feel validated. "Your boss should've handled it differently, and if you want me to break into his car and put shrimp paste under the floor mats, I will."

Now *that's* the kind of friendship I need.

"In August, no less," I say.

"Can you imagine?"

"I don't want to."

"My cousin's friend's roommate said someone did it to her once when she left her car somewhere for a whole weekend, and it smelled so bad she called the cops because she thought there had to be a dead body in there," she says, comfortingly.

"Wow," I say, my chin digging into her shoulder.

"One of the cops puked. She had to sell the car for scrap. Hey, thanks for hanging all the art up, it looks great."

"No problem," says Silas Flynn's voice behind me, because I can't have peace and quiet for more than five minutes. I release Anna Grace from her supportive, sympathetic hug to see Silas casually opening a cooler and grabbing a bottle of water.

"Those are a dollar," I tell him.

"I'm a volunteer," he says, shaking the ice off of it.

"That doesn't make it free."

Silas straightens, still holding the bottle, a half-smile on his face.

"Hey, what's that over there?" he asks, tilting his head vaguely to the left.

"You can't just steal from homeless dogs and cats," I say, not falling for it.

"C'mon, Nakamura. I'm thirsty. It's one bottle of water."

My arms are folded in front of my chest. Nervous sweat prickles on the back of my neck and that spot right between my boobs. My glasses have slid down a little, but I resist the urge to push them back up because I think he might be fucking with me, and that pisses me off even more than the thought that he's too cheap to spend a dollar.

"There's a water fountain near the bathrooms in the entry hall," I say, not budging an inch. "That's free."

Silas looks at me. I look at Silas. He's still got a slight smile on his face, that aw-shucks-I'm-just-kidding-you-can't-you-let-me-get-away-with-it-just-this-once expression that people in this town always seem to fall for.

The longer we stand here, the more that expression fades, until Anna Grace finally sighs.

"It's a dollar," she says. "Aren't you a lawyer or some shit?"

That gets a laugh and another easy smile from him, though this one doesn't quite reach his eyes. I think. Maybe. Who the fuck even knows with Silas, a man who thinks he's weaponized his charm.

"You've got a point," he drawls, reaching for his wallet. He puts his still-unopened water down on the bar, pulls a bill out, gives me an indecipherable look. "Got change for a twenty?"

Of course, he can't make this easy and pay in exact change. Wordlessly, I hand it over. He gives me that look again as he puts it in his wallet and his wallet back in his pocket.

"So," he says, twisting the top off. "Anna Grace, what are you doing tomorrow night?"

"I'm not coming to your open mic night," she says, leaning against the bar, hands next to her hips. "Or your improv group. Or your improv open mic night."

That gets a real, honest-to-God grin out of Silas, his whole face lighting up, one hand going through his hair.

The problem with Silas—one of many, let's be real—is that he is technically attractive. If there were a kit for creating a handsome male human being, Silas would be what you got in the White Guy package.

In other words, he's tall and broad and blue-eyed and square-jawed with a nice smile and nice teeth and cheekbones that are almost too pretty and medium brown, almost auburn hair that's always the exact right degree of almost-but-not-quite unruly. He clearly works out and would probably be happy to bore you with the details of his routine. There are a lot of muscles. He looks good in the suits he wears to work, which I'm forced to know because our offices are on the same floor of the building.

"What about a dinner party?" he says, still grinning.

"Whose?" Anna Grace asks, suspicious.

"Elmore's."

"Elmore, your boss?"

"You know any other Elmores?"

"I had a great uncle," Anna Grace says. "Though he passed before I was born. I think."

"Yes, Elmore, my boss," Silas confirms.

Anna Grace narrows her eyes.

"Are you *asking me out?*" she finally says, as if he's just presented her with a weird bug in a jar. "To a dinner party with your boss? *Why?*"

Silas just laughs at that. His laugh is a whole *thing*: his head goes back and his face lights up and I can see the lines of the tendons in his throat, the way he runs one hand through his hair and his biceps sort of do something nice under his t-shirt.

I turn toward the wine bucket so I stop looking at him.

"Wow, okay," he says, then casts a look over the bar and toward everyone else in the theater. "Because I need a favor."

"A plus-one for a work dinner party?" she asks, still suspicious.

"Sort of," he says, and sighs. "I may have accidentally told Linda Ballard that I have a girlfriend."

"How do you accidentally tell someone you have a girl-friend?" I ask, pretending to adjust a wine bottle.

"It's a long story."

"So you need someone to come be *your girlfriend* at Elmore's dinner party tomorrow night," Anna Grace says. "That is not a plus-one situation."

"It doesn't have to be a big deal," he says. "Come to a dinner party, we'll hold hands or something, we can break up Sunday morning."

"Definitely not," she says.

Silas has the nerve to look surprised, because of course he does.

"I'm that bad?" he says, already covering it up with that dumb, cocky grin he has. "C'mon."

I snort. They both ignore me.

"Look, you're fine," Anna Grace says.

"Thank you."

"Do you know what would happen if people thought we were dating and I hadn't told anyone?" Anna Grace asks. "I would never sleep again for the phone calls. My grandmother would cry with relief. My mother would start planning the wedding."

"I'm that popular?"

"Well, you're male," she says.

Silas just sighs and runs a hand through his hair, somehow making it look even better. Ugh.

"That's a good point," he admits.

"Of course it's a good point, I made it," Anna Grace says, half-grinning.

"Yeah, yeah," he says.

"Maybe you shouldn't have made up a girlfriend," she goes on.

"I told you it's complicated," he says, but now he's smiling.

"Tell them she's in Canada."

"Like you did in seventh grade?"

Anna Grace laughs and casually flips him off.

"Logan, my Canadian boyfriend, was the love of my life," she says. "And totally not someone I made up so people would think I was cool."

The front doors to the theater open, and Anna Grace looks at her watch.

"It's time," she intones, glancing around. "Kat, you still good for the pie auction?"

I push a very normal smile onto my face.

"Of course," I say.

"Good luck tonight," Silas says, backing away, toward wherever he's actually supposed to be. "And if you think of anyone..."

"I'll warn them that you need weird favors," she finishes his sentence, grinning, and he walks away.

"Ugh," I say, quietly, once he's out of earshot.

"He's fine," Anna Grace says, patiently, clipboard in her hand once more.

I make a face, because I disagree.

"You know, you *could* stop being mad about college sometime this decade," she points out, still going down the list. "Just a thought."

"Or I could stay mad forever," I counter.

"If you really want to," she says, shrugging, because this is not the first or even the fifth time we've had this conversation. She shoves the checklist back into her pocket and puts her hands on my shoulders. "Okay. I love you and respect your choices even when I think they're bad and doing you harm."

"But how do you really feel?" I deadpan.

"Like it's time for you to go auction off some pies," she says, nodding at the pie table as she gives me a final smile, then walks away.

I take a deep breath, prepare myself, and head toward some pies.

· · * * ★ ★ ★ * * · ·

THE VERY FIRST chapter of *The Most Popular Person in the Room: Unleashing Your Inner Extrovert and Mastering Every Social Dynamic* says that the first step to all that is getting out of your comfort zone, so here I am. Very, very far from my comfort zone. Supervising a pie auction in the front of a theater full of people I don't know, but who all seem to know each other. Just in case I didn't feel enough like an outsider as the dorky, awkward, Japanese new girl in a small, Southern town where I'm pretty sure everyone else has known each other since kindergarten.

They're all milling around and making small talk with

each other while I stand here behind the pie auction table, trying to figure out what normal people do with their hands. At any moment one of them could turn the blinding beam of their small talk on me, the deer in this small-talk-as-headlights metaphor, and I'd have to respond.

Of course, *The Most Popular Person in the Room: Unleashing Your Inner Extrovert and Mastering Every Social Dynamic* has advice for that as well. Prepare topics of conversation, it says. Smile a lot. Be an active listener. Ask questions. Act interested. Act normal.

As if anyone who purchases a book with that title can simply act normal. If that option were available to me I wouldn't have memorized every day topics of conversation, like *do you have any pets?* or *I heard it's supposed to rain soon.* Small talk leaves me feeling like I've found myself unarmed in the middle of a Nerf gun fight, foam projectiles hitting my face while I wonder why I'm here and where everyone else got a weapon and whether trying to leave would make it worse.

Also, I shouted at Silas through a door earlier because he thinks he can do whatever he wants all the time and rules only apply to other people, and now I have to stand here and hope no one knows that was me, so yes, I feel a little like a rubber band stretched way too far and like I might snap if anyone fucks with me.

At the other end of the table, an older man with gray hair and glasses walks up, looks at the sign, and folds his arm over his chest.

"Is the auction silent, or are the pies silent?" he asks. I have no idea if he's asking me. Shit. Is he asking me? He's not—

"They're both silent, Harold," a woman says, coming to

22

my rescue and not even realizing it. "Should we bid on the blackberry or the strawberry-rhubarb?"

"Blackberry," he says, after a moment. The woman frowns. After a moment, she looks at me.

"Which one do you like?" she asks.

I didn't prepare an answer for this question, and I have no idea why. This is, like, the first question I should have had an answer for, and I'm already blowing it.

I look at her. Then at the pies. Then back at her. I cannot recall ever eating a single pie in my entire life. Oh God.

"They're both good," I finally say.

"I can never decide," she confesses. "I like the blackberry, but the strawberry rhubarb is really something special..."

"Strawberry rhubarb, then," Harold says, supportively.

"You could bid on both," I say, even though the back of my neck is starting to prickle with sweat.

"Giving us the hard sell," Harold says.

"Haha," I manage.

"Well, you've convinced me," the woman says, grabbing a pen and writing her name and a bid on the two pies. "Not that I needed much convincing, of course, Clara's pies are always absolutely divine—"

Something snags at my attention. Even though I'm totally focused on this woman and her pie discussion, mind already racing as I try to figure out what I'm supposed to say next, what manner of baked good discourse is the right thing to say, something else pulls me out and away and I'm standing there, blinking behind my glasses, heart thudding as I try to figure out what it was.

"—just offer to trade her a pie for your famous pickled

okra," Harold says. I scan the crowd, listening, mostly focusing.

"But this is for charity," the woman says. "It's such a good—"

It's Evan. He's standing there, in the middle of the theater floor, staring up at the oversized cardboard thermometer that shows how close the animal shelter is to its annual donation goal. He's wearing boat shoes and Madras shorts and a polo shirt, collar mercifully unpopped, holding a beer, looking for all the world exactly the same as he did the last time I saw him six months ago.

I thought I had time. Greg, my boss, said he'd be here *Monday*. I thought I had the weekend to prepare myself, do some breathing exercises, and maybe also set a couple of minor traps in the office we'll be sharing.

But no. He's here, holding a beer and staring up at this big thermometer like he owns the whole place, standing there while people flow around him looking entirely unbothered at being a stranger in a strange town.

I wish I hadn't had a granola bar thirty minutes ago, because my stomach clenches and wobbles. I take a deep breath as that bright, twisty feeling courses through me. My heart thumps. I'm already sweating. I want to hide under this table and also smash through a wall and run three miles, but that would definitely make everyone look at me, so I don't.

'Thank you, dear," the woman says, finally laying the pen down on the table. I think she might have bid on all the pies. I wasn't paying attention because I was too busy panicking.

"Good," I say. What? Wrong response. I clear my throat. "Thank you for bidding!"

I wonder if it sounds too much like *thank you,*

*forbidding*, like I'm telling her she's forbidding but I'm the only one who thinks that because they walk off, smiling. Opposite them, Evan's headed my way.

I consider running. Seems cowardly, maybe is cowardly, but I know I'm supposed to be *professional* with him and I'm unprepared to do that right now. I'm not sure what I *am* prepared to do, but it's not smile and say, *so glad to see you! Can't wait to work together!*

He steps up to the table. He's smiling. He looks down at the pies, picks up the ballpoint pen, looks at it like he was hoping for something better. I hold my breath so I feel less like puking.

We look at each other. I'm not speaking first. Fuck that.

"Pies, huh?" he finally says, smiling a smile that doesn't quite reach his eyes. "They any good?"

"Sure," I say, letting my face and my voice go as blank as I can.

"You haven't tried them?" he asks, eyebrows going up. He spins the pen around one finger without looking.

I say nothing.

"Seems like false advertising," he goes on, giving me that smile that means *I'm kidding exactly enough to claim later that this was a joke, but you and I both know it isn't, not really.*

"It's for charity," I say, still perfectly flat.

"I'm only messing with you."

I look him dead in the eyes and do not smile like I know he wants me to.

"I know," I say.

Evan looks down at the table, then up at me. He takes a small step forward, leaning in a little, like he's about to share a secret in this big room filled with people. At the other end of the table someone bids on a couple of pies, glances at us,

25

walks away. I'm thrumming with so much unspent anxiety I must be radioactive.

"Listen, Kat," he says, and he smiles at me in that way he thinks is charming and slightly bashful. "I know things ended badly between us."

I say nothing.

"And your feelings were hurt," he goes on, using the passive voice as if it's something that just happened one day instead of something he did to me.

I keep saying nothing.

"But since you're going to be working for me for the next month, I really need you to put those feelings aside and be professional," he says.

"*With* you."

"I understand completely if you still haven't moved past our relationship," he goes on, like I didn't say anything. "But I'm with Olivia now, and if you tried to act on your lingering feelings for me, I'd probably have to talk to my bosses at B&L about it."

My face goes hot. My lips go cold. My body is somehow every temperature at once, I can't feel my fingertips, and I think I might pass out from the sheer, all-consuming blinding *rage*. It feels like someone hooked my brain stem to a car battery, it's so forceful, so palpable that I swear if I move at all I'll send shockwaves through the room.

I've moved past our relationship. Of course I've fucking moved past our relationship. I drove over it and backed up and then drove over it again, for good measure, and now I'm so far away that I can't see it in the rearview mirror any more.

I wish I had a comeback. All I can manage is to stare at him, trying not to shake, for a good five seconds while I try to shape my rage into words and he looks at me. I don't even know why he's saying this here when I already got his obnoxious email.

"It won't be a problem," I finally manage, my voice not even shaking. "Trust me, I have no interest whatsoever..."

He's already not listening to me. He's already looking away, somewhere else, gripping his beer bottle a little tighter, the muscles in his jaw working. He doesn't seem to notice that I've trailed off, mid-sentence, and I have the sudden, wild urge to hit him in the face with the nearest pie and see if the fucker pays attention to *that*.

"Are you fucking serious?" I ask, low enough that in the hubbub of the room, no one else can hear me.

"What?" he says, swinging his attention back to me, only now he's distracted.

"I *said*," I say, a little louder, loud enough to be heard but not loud enough to cause a scene. "I have zero intention of—"

"Meckler!"

Evan turns as Silas comes through the sparse crowd, walking like this old theater is his own personal fiefdom. There's a grin on his face, wide and easy and probably charming to other people, and a beer bottle dangles from his fingers.

"Flynn," Evan says, the word flat. His head is turned to the side, his jaw tight, his hand suddenly fisted on the table.

He remembers to smile once Silas is even with him, but it's forced and angry and doesn't reach his eyes.

"Didn't know you were in town," Silas says. He holds out a hand.

Evan takes it.

"Just here for a few weeks for work," Evan says, and I see his knuckles go white in the handshake a second before they're pulled together in a violent, back-slapping hug that's over as soon as it starts. I swear Silas's smile goes wider, like he's baring his teeth. He cocks a hip against the pie table.

I... this got weird. They hate each other. Right?

Yes. Definitely. I would know. Neither one of them likes me either, and I don't like them, so we're even.

Except, of course, I dislike Silas and would be fine with never seeing him again, and I'd happily launch Evan into the sun. Twice.

"Still doing logistics for Homeland Security?" Silas asks, and perfectly casual except there's an edge to his voice that's bright and sharp, like waves crashing against rocks.

"Nah, I went corporate," Evan says with a smile that doesn't reach his eyes. "Energy sector."

They keep talking, but it feels more like I'm watching two wolves snarl at each other, ready to fight for territory. I wish they would leave. I want them both gone—Silas to somewhere else, Evan to, ideally, outer space—and...

Evan glances over at me, and maybe I'm reading into it, but it's somehow dismissive and possessive all at once. He thinks I *still have feelings*.

I want to punch him. I want to *throttle* him.

I... have an insane idea. It comes to me on a tidal wave of rage and adrenaline. It's a better idea than punching or murder.

I reach out and put one hand on Silas's shoulder before I can think better of it.

"Hey, babe," I say, and move my mouth into a smile. "I didn't know you knew Evan."

Both heads swing toward me, faces frozen. Silas doesn't react for a long moment, smile firmly in place, blue eyes staring me down with an unnerving friendliness, but Evan does. Evan's smile disappears and he looks from me to Silas and my heart jumps into my throat and in that moment, I feel *powerful.*

Evan and I were together for eighteen months. I know what jealousy looks like on his face. I smile right into it, heart thudding with the adrenaline high. I can feel a trickle of sweat on the back of my neck.

"This is Silas," I tell Evan, like he doesn't know. "He's my…"

My pulse is beating and skipping like the tracks under a runaway train and my face is hot and my breathing is shallow and fast and there's a word that I want to use, a good word, the *right* word and I can't think of it, not to save my life.

" —lover," I finish.

Both men just stare at me.

# THREE

## SILAS

I'M HARDLY EVER LOST for words, but Nakamura calling me her lover does it.

I'm not. Obviously. Since she moved here I think she's said five entire sentences to me, at least four of them under duress, because she's an uptight ice queen who can barely give me the time of day. Her fingers digging into my shoulder like claws is the most we've ever touched, and I can't say I'm a fan.

I open my mouth to ask her what the hell she's talking about, but Meckler gets there first.

"Lover?" he asks, all disdain, his mouth twitching down in a snarl. He can't look me in the face. "Flynn?"

Nakamura laughs, tossing her hair back, hand tightening on my shoulder. The hairs on the back of my neck prickle.

"You know what I mean," she says, still squeezing. Jesus, her hand's like a vice. "What's the word I'm looking for, babe?"

She turns her head and looks at me, face hard as stone behind her glasses. She puts me in mind of animatronics, jerky movements with no grace and no soul. I want to ask

THE ONE MONTH BOYFRIEND

what the fuck she's talking about, except there's one problem: this is clearly pissing off Meckler, and anything that pisses Meckler off can't be all bad.

So I hesitate, and she looks up at me. Her face is stone except for her eyes, wide and dark and... pleading?

Fuck. *Fuck.*

"Boyfriend?" I ask, and pluck her hand from my shoulder, putting a smile back on my face. She laughs again, the sound still not quite right.

"That's it," she says. "Don't you ever forget a word in the middle of your..."

I drape her fingers over mine, fold my thumb against them, brush my lips along her cold knuckles. Nakamura's cheeks are faintly pink under the gold of her skin, her lips red, strands of black hair stuck to her throat.

"Sentence?" I supply. I turn to Meckler, shit-eating grin on my face, Nakamura's hand still in mine. "I know. I can't believe it either, but here we are. I'm a lucky son of a bitch, huh?"

"*Babe,*" she says, squeezing my hand too hard. "Haha, stop it!"

"Why? I can't say how lucky I am to be your lover?" I ask, and in the corner of my vision Meckler's face goes from dark to darker.

Nakamura gives a huge, dramatic eye roll. Her hand in mine is sweaty. She sounds a little strange, like she's out of breath. I've got no idea what's going on but here I am, in the middle, between a high-strung Nakamura and a furious Meckler, holding her hand and calling her my lover where dozens of people can see us.

It feels like careening downhill toward a blind curve on a motorcycle that might fall apart under me at any moment, gaining speed and bumping over rocks, wild and reckless and... not bad.

"Glad you feel that way," Meckler says. His hands are in his pockets but he's puffed up, chin high, practically bouncing on the balls of his feet. Ready to fight. "Lucky. Sure. Look, I'll let you get back to selling pies."

"It's an auction," I correct him, still smiling. Always smiling. "For charity."

"Great," Meckler says. "That's adorable."

"You bid yet?" I ask. "You ought to. Delicious pies, and for a good cause."

He clears his throat, glances over at the pie table.

"What's good?" he asks.

"They're all good," I say. "Every last one is a culinary wonder, I guarantee it. Babe, you got a pen?"

She holds one out, and Meckler takes it before I can.

Then, in angry silence, he bids on every single pie at the table. He presses down so hard he nearly rips the paper in front of the blackberry pie, and I swear he growls under his breath.

"You don't have to bid on *all* of 'em," I say, folksy as fuck. "That would be a pretty penny."

He doesn't answer, just throws me a look while bidding on all twelve pies, then tosses the pen on the table.

"See you Monday," he says, nodding at Nakamura. And then: "Flynn," before walking off.

I watch him as he disappears into the crowd. When I look back, Nakamura's eyes are deadlocked on me. I hold her gaze for a minute, then drop it and her hand, pick up a pen, cross off Meckler's name on the bidding sheet and write my own for five dollars more.

"You got a minute to talk?" I ask without looking up.

"Not right now," she says, voice stiff.

I don't look up, move to the next pie. It's coconut creme, a pie I don't like, not even when Clarabelle Loveless makes it. I bid on it anyway, just to cross his name off.

"Are you fucking kidding?" I ask, voice low.

"I'm guarding the pies."

"It's a small-town fundraiser for an animal shelter, not Fort Knox."

"That doesn't mean I can leave. I have a job."

Jesus, she hasn't changed at all in twelve years, not since she nearly made me drop out of college. I bite my lips together and force myself not to respond, but I want to shout. I want to get in Nakamura's face and ask why she thinks she can call me her lover—and what the fuck is that, *lover*, is she serious?—in front of half of Sprucevale when so many of the people in this town are dangerously over-invested in my relationship status.

I already know I should regret it, and there's a part of me that does. I was supposed to be fixing a damn mess, not creating a bigger one and yet here I am up to my neck in it, and I'm not even mad at myself. I should be.

Instead my blood feels like it's fizzing with trouble and the sheer glee that comes from reckless, impulsive decisions.

I make Nakamura stand there and watch me while I outbid Meckler on every single one of these pies. When I'm done I walk around the table to where she's standing, staring her down the whole way. She doesn't move.

I drape an arm over her shoulders, and I swear I can feel her tense.

"Take a break, babe," I say, keeping my voice low. "You deserve it."

"Silas," she says, through her teeth. "I am guarding. The. Pi—"

"Please tell me she made her pecan pie," says Gladys

Dawson, who's just walked up to the table and interrupted us without so much as looking up. "I was devastated last year when there wasn't one. Something about a pecan shortage?"

"Right over there," Nakamura says, pointing helpfully. "Plenty of pecans this year!"

Gladys finally looks up, a small polite smile on her face, and I can practically see her taking notes before she responds.

"Thank goodness," she says. "I guess I ought to bid on the blackberry and the lemon meringue as well..."

She steps away, crossing out my name and writing her own with the zeal only a southern retiree raised on passive aggression and hush puppies can muster, commenting politely on baked goods the whole way before she finally leaves, huge purse slung over one shoulder.

I pull Nakamura a little closer, turn my head.

"Fuck guarding the pies," I tell her hair, closer to my face than I'd expected. Why did I think she was short? "You called me your lover in front of that asshole, half of Sprucevale, the office gossip, God, and everyone, and I want to talk about it."

"You said you needed a girlfriend," she says, voice quiet and controlled.

"Yeah, and I asked—"

"Are you looking for pecan?" Nakamura asks a couple who's just walked up. "That one's the chess pie, and then peanut butter is right next to it."

"—Anna Grace, not you," I finish once they've moved away.

"Well, you're standing there with your arm around me so it can't be too bad," she says.

"The fuck else was I gonna do, Nakamura?" I hiss. "The

34

only way I could've made more of a scene would've been to fight you on this. Hi, Mrs. Edwards, enjoying your night?"

Connie Edwards' eyes are on my hand, currently draped over Nakamura's shoulder, like she's already thinking about how she'll report this to her friends.

"Yes, it's lovely. And you?" she asks, pointedly.

"It's great," says Nakamura exactly as I say, "I'm having a fantastic time."

"Can we talk in an hour when I'm done here?" Nakamura asks when Connie leaves.

"An hour? It'll be front page news by then," I say, still stiffly frozen in place, the two of us looking like a bad approximation of American Gothic.

That gets her to turn her head and glance up at me, through bangs and glasses, with a look that could saw through bedrock.

"You think your dating life is that newsworthy?" she asks, voice clipped, precise, as the movement of her head slides her hair over the backs of my fingers.

I take a strand between index and middle, twirl softly, smile down at her like she's told me a charming joke.

"Babe, I *know* my dating life is that newsworthy," I say, mostly because it'll piss her off more. "I'm kind of a big deal around here."

Nakamura mutters something so low I can't hear it, only imagine.

"As soon as I'm done here," she says, pulling her hair from my hand. "I agreed to run the pie auction, which means I need to be here and make sure it all goes smoothly and no one harms or absconds with a pie."

"Jesus," I mutter, head turned.

"Sorry."

It's almost as surprising as the word lover.

35

"Are you?"

"Absolutely."

Of all the high-handed nerve.

"See you in a bit, babe," I say, loud again, and give her shoulder a squeeze. "Good luck with the pies."

"Thanks, babe," she says, and tries a smile, that edge back in her voice, and I kiss the top of her head, hair warm beneath my lips. I do it to piss her off and to look right in public, but mostly it's the adrenaline and the sheer pleasure of white knuckling a problem that makes me.

Then I walk away, equal parts annoyed, irritated, and giddy with the recklessness.

# FOUR

## KAT

SILAS MATERIALIZES the moment the last person goes through the doors at the front of the theater, leaning in the dark rectangle that leads backstage, arms crossed, watching. Waiting to reckon with me, and I don't think I've ever looked forward to anything less.

That's not true. Evan's mom insisted on throwing me a bridal shower. That took two Xanax and I still called Anna Grace from the bathroom, hyperventilating.

"I win anything?" he asks when I step into the doorway, feeling like it's the Tower of London.

"Coconut creme, I think," I tell him, my voice coming out wooden, the way it always does when I'm nervous. "Pecan went for close to nine hundred."

"Lord have mercy," he says. "Meckler get any?"

We're a few steps backstage, in a hallway next to a set of steps, dimly lit from the stage and the door.

"No," I say, and a smirk works itself across Silas's face. The two of them spent the last hour alternating trips to the pie table and outbidding each other, Evan never saying a word, Silas never shutting up. I'll admit it: I'm curious.

"Good," he says, and leans back against the wall, one foot propped on it behind himself as he flattens his back to it, arms still over his chest. He looks different alone, in the low light, at the end of the night. There's less bluster and superficial charm, more humanity. Not too much more, but some.

I take a deep breath and find the opposite wall with my own hands behind my back, prepping the thing I've been practicing for the past hour.

"I'm sorry," I say, voice steady.

Silas waits a beat, watching me.

"Go on," he finally says, and I have to look away as irritation flares inside me.

"I'm sorry that I panicked and forced you into telling Evan, and by extension everyone who was present tonight, that we're dating," I tell him, focusing on the steps to our left because if I make eye contact, I'm certain I'll sound insincere, and I'm not.

I'm sorry that I claimed to be dating Silas just to piss off Evan, even if the way his eyes glinted and his jaw tightened and his face darkened brought me pure, crackling glee, an unparalleled high.

Mostly. I'm mostly sorry.

"Forced?" he says, a low drawl with fight running underneath it. "You didn't force me, Nakamura."

Behind my back, I make a fist against the wall and press my knuckles into it. Of course Silas can't just accept an apology.

"You said it yourself," I say, sounding remarkably calm. "I didn't give you many options."

"But you did give them."

"Then I coerced you," I say, over-pronouncing the word as if I think he's never heard it before. "I'm sorry for *coercing* you into being nice to me for five minutes, can we—"

"When you called me *your lover* you gave me options and I picked one," he says, cutting me off. I press my knuckles harder into the wall. "You don't get to act like you're some all-powerful puppet master pulling the strings and making me dance."

"*Puppet master?*" I say, sarcasm now on full blast. "Are you serious?"

"You didn't force me into shit. I picked an option, and I picked the one that did you a favor." He says, tone not shifting in the slightest. "And now, you owe me."

"I already apologized."

"Thanks. That's not what you owe me."

I'm tempted to tell him to go fuck himself and then walk away, because I don't want to be in Silas's debt for anything. I don't see what he could possibly want me in his debt for, what he could need from me that he can't get on his own.

There's a long, long silence in the hall, the sounds of people on the other side of the wall drifting dully through.

"This is the part where you say *so, Silas, what do I owe you?*" he says in a terrible imitation of me. "And then I say, *thanks for asking, Nakamura, it's so kind of you to acknowledge both my existence and the fact that I helped you out earlier.*"

I set aside *acknowledge his existence* for another time, because I can only deal with so much of his bullshit.

"What do I owe you?" I ask, perfectly steady, even as my blood feels like sludge in my veins. I think of The Godfather and hope the favor isn't murder.

"Thank you for asking, Nakamura," he says, and smiles a big, wide smile that only gets partway to his eyes. "You owe me a date."

There's one single, horrifying, world-turns-on-its-side moment where I think he's making a romantic overture, and it must show on my face because he snorts.

"To the dinner party at my boss's house," he says, after a moment. "You know, the thing I asked Anna Grace to?"

"Obviously," I lie.

"Was it?"

"Is that all?" I ask.

"Is that not enough?" he asks, tilting his head slightly. "If you really want, I bet I could come up with—"

"No," I cut him off. It's harder and meaner than I meant it to be, but the thought of going to a dinner party full of strangers and the silence makes the sound of my own pulse overwhelming, makes this back hallway feel far too tight, makes politeness a remote impossibility.

"Okay, then," he says as I breathe.

"If anything, an evening of charming your boss and coworkers sounds like you're getting more out of this deal than I am," I say.

He's laughing by the time I get halfway through the sentence: a fake, demonstrative laugh that sets my teeth on edge. Fucker.

"The favor isn't for you to charm anyone," he says, like he's still trying to sound amused. "The favor's for you to be *present* and not bite anyone's head off. I'm not about to bargain for impossibilities."

"Four hours of politeness is a lot to ask in exchange for five minutes of small talk," I point out, ignoring the rest. I'm aware that charm isn't one of my strengths and don't wish to discuss it further.

"Consider it an exchange for springing it on me with no warning in front of that jackass," he says.

More silence.

"How do—"

"Why was—"

We both start and stop at the same time. Look at each other. Silas makes an irritated *you first* gesture, and I press my knuckles into the wall again.

"He's my ex," I say.

"Didn't end well?"

"No," I tell him. "You?"

He looks like he might ask another question, then decides he doesn't care.

"We served together," he says.

"You did?" I ask, and I'm surprised despite myself. I knew they were both in the Marines, but I never realized it was at the same time and I never realized they knew each other. Evan refused to talk about it in anything other than bland, patriotic platitudes, and it's not as if I've exchanged more than a handful of sentences with Silas since college.

"Unfortunately," he says.

Fine. I'm curious. I'm curious enough that I consider asking one more question, but then decide to return his favor.

"All right," I say, because someone has to say something, but apparently that's not it because silence falls between us again until Silas sighs.

Then he tosses his phone toward me, and instead of catching it I accidentally bat it toward the steps.

"Jesus," he mutters.

"You can't just throw things at people," I snap. "The hell did you think would happen?"

"You'd catch it like a normal person?"

Luckily, the phone is fine.

"Why do I have this?"

"Why do you think? Give me your number," he says, as

41

if throwing something at me was the obvious way to get my contact information. "I'm picking you up tomorrow at five."

"Silas," I say, very slowly. "I am not going to this dinner—"

"I'm picking you up at five or telling Meckler what's really going on."

We stare at each other in the low light, and I'm tempted to throw his phone down, walk up to him, and put my hands around his neck. Of course Silas is going to get what he wants, because he always does. He's a handsome white guy who gets to disregard whatever rules he wants and run roughshod over anyone else, and he doesn't even know it. He thinks I owe him.

I'm so angry I want to cry, but instead I put my number into his phone and throw it back.

"Great," he says. He doesn't sound like he thinks it's great, but a moment later my phone is buzzing in my pocket, and I assume it's him. "Text me your address tomorrow."

"Silas," barks a voice, and I jump. We both turn to see Gideon leaning in through the door. "You done here? We still gotta get the art back to Javi's. Hey, Kat."

I nod, because I've got no idea how to act.

"Hey."

"Thanks for overseeing the pies."

"Of course."

He nods, then looks over at Silas.

"You coming?" he asks.

I like Gideon. I don't know him that well, but he doesn't bother much with small talk and he likes animals, so we're good.

"Course," Silas says, pushes himself from the wall, nods at me. "Five. Don't forget the address."

He walks away without waiting for confirmation as

Gideon looks from him, to me, and then back, face filled with questions but none of them getting to his lips. The two of them leave and I finally take a deep breath, put my hands over my face, curl my fingers into my hair.

Maybe I could launch *myself* into the sun.

· · · · ★ ★ ★ ★ · · · ·

THE NEXT AFTERNOON, I stand in front of the eye makeup selection and consider my options under the fluorescent lights of Sprucevale's most comprehensive drug store. That's not saying a whole lot, since the only other drug store is mostly an old-timey soda fountain that also has, like, two boxes of Sudafed on a shelf, but here I am. Looking at eyeliner.

My conundrum is this: I left my apartment with the explicit intention of buying the most expensive eyeliner I could find, because fancy eye makeup soothes me sometimes. Yes, I already have at least ten pencils, sticks, jars, and pots of black eyeliner, but what if none of them are the right one for tonight? What if I go to put one on and it smears everywhere and I look like a raccoon but I'm already running late and then I not only have to go to this awful dinner, but I have to go while also looking like I lost a fight with a chimney sweep?

Clearly, twenty-dollar eyeliner is the solution to every problem I have right now. It'll make me look polished, professional, and like I got more than two hours of terrible sleep last night. It'll fold the five loads of clean laundry that I can't even look at without feeling like I want to crawl out of my skin with pointless, endless anxiety. It'll quiet the endless babbling monologue in my brain of everything that could go wrong. It'll call my psychiatrist and ask about possibly increasing my Lexapro dose because the life I had almost rebuilt for myself feels like it's imploding around me.

See? Twenty dollars well-spent. It might even do the first thing and make me look more awake. Now the only problem is deciding whether I want the waterproof version or not; on one hand, waterproof formulations sometimes make my eyes itch.

On the other hand, there's a non-zero chance that I'll burst into furious tears at some point tonight, given that I'm going to be with Silas Fucking Flynn for several hours, so the waterproofing might be necessary.

After more deliberation, I buy them both. And a shimmery gold eyeshadow pencil, just for fun. And some deep red matte lipstick, in case I ever need it. And some electric blue nail polish, because I can.

And some gum, and some breath mints, and some peanut butter cups, and a jar of something that promises to 'instantly reverse aging,' and also a ten dollar bluetooth speaker for my shower that I'm sure will stop working after a week. I don't really need any of it, but I feel like shit and I've got the money, so I do it.

Afterward, I sort of feel better. I don't feel *good*; I still feel like my skin is stuffed full of writhing snakes and like no matter what, I can't breathe quite deeply enough, but I feel good enough to go get ice cream instead of heading back home to hide out between piles of clean-but-too-stressful laundry. Besides, if I have to look at the laundry that I physically cannot make myself fold for much longer, I might have a breakdown about it.

Much better to have a breakdown while eating a waffle cone, so I head to Walter's.

Walter's Ice Cream Shoppe—the *e* on the end is necessary—is the kind of place that people are thinking of when they talk about how great small towns are, a little ice cream stand that's only open from February through November, only takes cash, always has a line, makes three flavors of ice cream, and has not changed one single thing about its recipe, presentation, or process since about 1955. Also, the ice cream is really fucking good.

I'm sitting on a bench in the courtyard, eating a large chocolate cone in peace and actually starting to feel better, when my phone buzzes and all the dread comes rushing back.

**Silas:** I need your address

I could lie. I could refuse. So what if he tells Evan that he barely knows me and went along with me calling him my lover because everyone in town knows I'm the new, crazy girl and it's better to indulge my weird whims or I might really freak out and oh, God, that raw, crushing anxiety feeling hits me right in the chest when I think that.

I take a deep breath and eat some more ice cream, focusing on how creamy and chocolatey it is. How crunchy the cone. How hot the day. Et cetera.

**Silas:** You've got read receipts on

I close my phone and leave him on read, just to give the asshole something to think about, because someone needs to tell him off once in a while, and also because if I give him my address this will all suddenly become real.

I do not, in the least, want to spend any amount of time pretending that I am Silas's girlfriend. Yes, it was my idea in the first place, but that was a very bad idea borne of panic and desperation and I really shouldn't have done it because

Silas is intolerable. He's always smiling and slippery. He laughs too much. He acts like everyone's his best buddy. He ignores the rules he doesn't want to follow—like the ones about fire doors or paying for water—and somehow seems to get away with it every damn time, simply because people like him or something.

He made my last year of college a total nightmare.

I was a senior in the geology department, and since something happened with one of the graduate students who was supposed to be teaching a section of Earth Sciences 101, the job got offered to me. I jumped at the chance to put it on my grad school applications and also get a head-start on teaching experience. It was great.

And then Silas Flynn happened.

I was already nervous about teaching, about talking in front of a classroom, about whether I'd be taken seriously being young and female, and the first day of class he sauntered in five minutes late with sunglasses on and proceeded to noisily search through his backpack for a pen for another ten. Then he borrowed a pen. Then he borrowed paper. Then he came to the table at the front of the class where I was standing, grabbed a syllabus, and sat back down.

The semester went downhill from there. Most non-traditional students—he was twenty-five, three years older than me, and (I'd learn later) fresh out of the Marines—were studious, hardworking students who took their studies seriously. Silas showed up hungover half the time and still drunk the rest. He reeked of whiskey even though he sat in the back. He had black eyes on two separate occasions and a split lip once. He hardly ever bothered with homework, routinely turned quizzes in half-blank, and seemed to absolutely delight in asking me questions about whatever I'd just finished explaining.

The worst part was that the other students liked him. They'd happily chat with him while I was trying to teach, smile as they lent him pencil and paper, sometimes laugh at the dumb bullshit he said when my back was turned. By mid-semester I was barely sleeping the nights before I had to teach and throwing up before class, because I had no idea what to do. The lead professor told me to fail him, but that wouldn't solve the continued problem of his existence.

It got really bad near the end of the semester. At that point I'd been warning Silas for weeks that he was failing, but suddenly he seemed to notice. He showed up at my office hours and tried to charm me, and when that didn't work, he tried to bribe me.

When that didn't work, he suddenly got the Office of Students with Disabilities involved, claimed mental health accommodations he'd never once mentioned before, and the whole thing ended in a disastrous meeting with the Dean of Physical Sciences where I burst into unprofessional tears.

So yes, I'm leaving his text on read and he can suffer. I finish my ice cream in peace, crunching the cone and trying not to think about anything but how blue the sky is today. I sit there until I feel a little better; not like I can actually fold my laundry, but maybe like I can consider folding the laundry without crying. It's progress.

I'm walking back down the sidewalk, feeling lighter than I have all day, when the people heading toward me come into focus, and I slam to an awkward stop right in the middle of the path.

Evan doesn't stop. He walks right up to me, a pretty, smirking redhead at his side.

"Kat," he says. "You remember Olivia, right? She came down for the weekend to see me off."

And there it is again, the crushing weight that I thought

I'd escaped. The snakes beneath my skin, the bright sickly feeling that I need to escape my physical being and I can't. I want to throw up. Instead, I take a careful breath and hold out my hand.

"Of course," I say, and my voice doesn't even sound weird. "Kat. Good to see you."

"Same," she says, her hand a delicate offering in mine, like she thinks I might kiss it or something. "I didn't know you'd moved here."

"Yep. Did," I say. I pull my hand back, nod, step away because I'm not prolonging this one second longer than I have to. "See you around, I guess!"

Then I'm off, and whatever Evan says, I don't hear it. Instead I open my phone as I power-walk away, sweat already gathering at my hairline, and send Silas my address.

# FIVE

## SILAS

"TELL YOU WHAT," Elmore says, gesturing with a Scotch in one hand. "I remember when Route Thirty-Nine was nothing but farms, all the way down the valley, and the only stoplight in town was the one at Main and Caroline. Every summer we'd leave the house in the morning and not come back 'til dinner, running wild. No video games. No reality TV."

He pauses and looks at the knot of people around him, like he's waiting for impressed murmurs. They come, and he looks pleased, the portrait of a magnanimous white man bestowing his wisdom upon younger generations, and doing it without a single gray hair moving out of place.

I murmur some sort of approval noise, because I'm supposed to, but next to me Nakamura—Kat, dammit, *Kat*— is dead fucking silent, staring ahead like she's some sort of creepy statue and not a person, tense as a suspension bridge.

For at least the fifth time in thirty minutes, I fight the urge to kick her foot and tell her to *smile*. Or speak. Or, I swear to God, just *blink*. There's no point in her being here if she's going to make all my coworkers think I've kidnapped her and threatened her family.

"Hear, hear," my colleague Pierce is saying, because his primary skill is assholery. "To the good old days."

He says it with a smirk and a glance at Elmore, because it's common knowledge that Elmore's not far from retiring and it's common presumption that Pierce and I are the favored candidates for the promotion to partner in his place. Pierce is handling this knowledge by shoving his nose so far up the boss's ass it's a wonder he can breathe at all.

I'm handling it by lying about my relationship status, so I probably don't have a leg to stand on. Elmore smiles indulgently at Pierce, then shakes his head gently, and here comes another mini-speech.

"Family used to mean something," he intones. "Nowadays, it's only about what we can get from each other..."

I look at Nakam—at Kat again and wonder if she's got an on switch. She's managed to look the part—black cocktail dress, heels, black hair in a low bun, sparkly earrings that dangle above her shoulders and brush her neck if she moves her head just the right way—but she may as well be a robot for all she's helping the situation. Jesus, at least a robot would be programmable. I could probably get her to say *nice to meet you* or *yes, I'm Silas's girlfriend* if she were a robot.

Elmore's still going, so out of desperation I finish my drink and put one hand on her back.

To her credit, she doesn't scream or jump or punch me in the face, just looks over at me like she can vaporize me with a glance. I press my hand to her back a little harder because she's wound so tight I'm afraid she'll snap her spine, but she doesn't relax. She keeps giving me that look from behind glasses and bangs and a thick swipe of eyeliner that ends in a point so sharp I think it could make me bleed.

My attention snags there for a moment, like it's caught. That same clothing-on-a-thorn sensation as yesterday, and then it's gone, Elmore is wrapping up whatever story he was telling, and I clear my throat.

"I think I need another drink," I tell Pierce and Elmore when there's a break in conversation, holding up my glass as if for proof. "You want anything, babe?"

Under my hand, her back muscles tense even more, steel cables against my fingertips.

"Martha assures me the 2014 Château de Marmotte Écarlate is excellent," Elmore says.

"I think I'll come with you, babe," Kat says, and lo and behold, she nods at the group. "Lovely to meet and talk. Very pleasant!"

Maybe she is a robot. Jesus.

We turn away and walk toward the bar at the other side of the room, my hand never leaving her back. If this were a normal house, I'd probably call it a living room, but Elmore's place is a spectacularly ugly new-build mansion, where everything is in the wrong proportion and then they slapped some columns on the outside to give it that look of *grandeur*. I'm sure this room has some other name, with its expensive, uncomfortable sofas and chairs I wouldn't dare to sit in.

"Refill?" I ask, holding up the bottle of white wine without quite looking at her.

"No," she says, and shakes her head, and the earrings sway and bump into her neck. My attention snags there for a blink of an eye, and then I refill my own glass. Take a sip as she stands there, statue-like, no movement except those earrings, staring at the backlit liquor cabinet full of things to be discussed rather than drunk.

"You can relax and *pretend* to be human," I tell her, after a moment. I'm trying for levity and probably failing. "No one's gonna bite."

Kat doesn't answer. I look over at her, only an inch or two shorter than me with heels on, and get back an unholy, unnerving glare.

"*What?*" I grind out, keeping my voice low so no one can hear.

"Fuck off," she says matching my tone exactly.

I face the liquor and take another drink.

"Jesus," I tell the aged rum.

"That's your advice?" she goes on, voice low but cutting through the background noise like a scalpel. "*Relax?*"

My temper surges, quick and hot, roughshod over everything else. A dust storm fit to blot out the sky.

I focus on the rum and take a deep breath, hold it a moment, exhale. Let it settle. Unclench my jaw.

"You could stop acting like a party with free drinks, good food, and interesting company is akin to getting your eyeballs scooped out with a rusty spoon," I tell her, never taking my eyes from the bottles.

We exchange glances. Kat glares like she'd do the scooping herself.

"Excuse me," someone says behind me.

I take Kat's elbow and say some polite words and even manage a smile, then pull her away. At least she doesn't shake me off, but she doesn't exactly concede, either, as I guide her through a wide doorway and into another room. I don't know the name of this one, either, but it's got bookshelves and windows and more uncomfortable-looking chairs, a very large deer head mounted over the fireplace.

I wander over and stand in front of it, looking up into its glassy eyes, while she goes into standby mode or whatever the hell she does.

This is some of the dumbest shit I've ever done, and I've done some dumb shit. Lying to piss off Meckler was one thing, but trying to convince all my coworkers that Kat's even human, let alone my date, is clearly beyond my powers of persuasion.

I stand there for a long time, staring up at a dead animal with my back to her. She's so silent that I wouldn't even swear she's still there until she speaks.

"I told you this was a bad idea," she finally says.

"Are you doing this so you can say *I told you so?*" I say in the direction of the deer, voice still low.

"Doing what?"

I turn my head and look at her. She's staring ahead at an ornate bookshelf filled with perfectly matching leather-bound books that I'd bet have never been opened.

"*This,*" I say, pointedly looking at her. "Pretending you're some sort of alien ice robot who's never interacted with humans before."

Kat snorts. It's the loudest noise she's made all evening.

"Sorry, did I tell you I didn't want to come to a party and now you're finding out why?"

"If you can't manage more than two sentences, could you at least gaze up at me adoringly or something?" I ask. I can't keep the sarcastic edge out of my voice. "Flutter your eyelashes and sigh when I talk. Something besides the laser glare of death, for fuck's sake."

I'm looking at the deer head again, away from her, and there's a very long silence. When I finally look back at her, she's openly staring at me.

"Doubt it," she says. "I'm a shitty actress."

"Yeah, you're not acting *human*."

"I have bitten zero heads," she says, voice low and sharp,

and she says it like she's making a point. "That was the criteria. Bite no heads."

"The criteria was *act like my girlfriend*," I say, and glance back at the doorway, to make sure no one's overhearing our very un-couple-like argument.

"That's not what criteria means."

I take a deep breath, because otherwise I might pull a bookshelf over and slam it to the floor.

"The whole point," I get out, my voice low and dangerously soft, "is to convince these people that I'm the sort of stable, responsible man who a nice girl might want to be with, who'd make an excellent partner at a law firm sooner rather than later."

We're now face-to-face, three feet apart, her knuckles white on the stem of her wine glass, her eyes flashing up at me.

"Are you?"

"That's not the point. The point is for them to think I am."

"So you couldn't get an *actual* person to date you and now you're here trying to pass me off as the real thing and failing miserably," she says, and for the first time there's a slight tilt to her head, the tiniest angle to her shoulders. "Which makes it my fault and not because you have a shitty personality."

I pause a moment, eyes narrowed.

"Did you just admit to being an android?"

That gets a long, still silence where she clearly thinks I'm insane and I wonder what the hell possessed me to say that out loud.

Then she says, very quietly: "Beep boop."

I stare. She stares back, and then I have to look away because if I don't, I might... smile? At her joke?

54

"Do you think," I say very slowly, because I need to get this back on track, "you could manage a smile and a nice to meet you in the next five minutes?"

Kat takes a long swig from her wine glass before answering, her earrings brushing against her neck, her throat working as she swallows, and out of the heat lamp of her gaze, I realize she... looks nice. Even if she's an android, Kat dressed the part: a classy sleeveless black dress, black heels, and a necklace with green stones that make her skin extra gold.

She even looks... good?

"*What?*" she asks, and that's when I realize I was staring at her in confusion.

"You look nice," I tell her, the most lukewarm compliment ever given to a woman.

"Did you think I was gonna show up in a Nine Inch Nails t-shirt and ripped fishnets?" she asks, but her voice isn't quite as sharp as before.

"I didn't think you weren't."

"Well, the night is young," she says, and closes her eyes. Tips her head back. Takes a deep breath. I watch it heave her shoulders and carve out the hollow of her throat, and I feel like she's made of thorns, sharp little hooks into my thoughts.

I've probably had enough wine.

"Listen," she finally says. "I could use a game plan. Give me something to say to these people, please, because I have no fucking clue. Do I ask about their golf game? Their preferred country club? Their interpretation of the Second Amendment?"

"Definitely not that."

"The Third?"

"About quartering troops?"

"I don't know! What do lawyers talk about, Silas? I need a script. I need *something*."

"Okay," I tell her, nodding. I try to think of what lawyers like to talk about but I can only look at her and feel like I've seen a statue come to life, stone turned to warm flesh and blood. She *does* move. She *does* talk. Sometimes she even asks nicely. "Baseball and football are a pretty good bet with most of the men. The Washington teams. In general, ask if they've got any vacation plans coming up, everyone likes talking about that. You can also ask about their kids, but only if you think you can fake interest."

"That probably depends on the kid," Kat says, a little too honestly.

"I'll try to give you hints," I tell her, glancing over her shoulder and at all my colleagues, milling around the living room. "You know, 'this is Billy Bob and he loves hot dogs and claiming he fixes up classic cars.'"

Kat's lips move in something that might almost be a smile. Her shoulders have descended from her ears, and I spent a moment too long looking at the curve of her collarbone, the places where it's transected by her necklace, the wings that disappear under the shoulders of her dress. It moves a little when she breathes.

"Thanks," she says, and looks over her shoulder as well. "I *did* tell you—"

She doesn't finish her thought because she goes sideways with a yelp and I grab her waist, wine sloshing out of her glass. A little goes on me, most on the plush carpet.

"Shit," she says, and looks down at herself, then up at me. I make sure she's upright before I take my hand off her, just in case. She looks at the carpet like it's a snare. "This is why I never wear these things."

I assume *these things* are her shoes, black spindly-looking high heels, bottoms sinking into the thick rug.

"Where's the kitchen?" she goes on, turning toward the door and making no other move. "I should go get some paper towels or something."

"Nah," I tell her, and rub my shoe over the patch of wine on the carpet. "I won't tell if you won't."

She looks from me to the rug very, very skeptically.

"That's what they're for," I point out, the spot now invisible. "It was white wine. It'll dry. It'll probably improve the room. I doubt you're the first person to spill something on it."

"Right," she says, but she's still looking at the carpet like she doesn't believe me. "Still—"

She's interrupted by the sharp sound of silverware on glass, coming from the main room.

I swear I can see her turn to stone, her whole body going rigid: knees, spine, shoulders, face. She stands taller, swallows hard, white-knuckles the stem again.

"Football," I remind her and offer my arm. "Vacations. Kids."

She gives it a suspicious look and pushes up her glasses with her free hand, but she takes it.

"Right," she says. "Thanks."

We walk back into the main room. Her hand is warmer than I expected.

· · · · · ★ ★ ★ · · · · ·

OF COURSE ELMORE wants to make a speech before we sit down to eat. He's allowed, of course; it's his house, his food, his wine, and his parlor or sitting room or whatever he calls it. He's already started talking as Kat and I enter the room and stand in the back. There are maybe ten other people here, and at least two turn to look at us when he comes in.

Kat may as well be an ice sculpture.

"...so the judge looks at him, sittin' there in the witness box like he's just seen a frog jump out of his mouth, and looks at me feeling about the same way, and before I can so much as think of a response he says, 'Counsel, please control your client,' and we keep going."

There's a polite sprinkle of laughter through the room, and I stop listening. I learned a lot of things in the military—some valuable, some practical, some ugly—but if you'd told me at age eighteen that the skill I'd use the most at thirty-eight was the ability to stand still and stare straight ahead for any length of time, I'd never have believed you.

I use it now, until I hear my name.

"...who decided last-minute to grace us with his new lady friend," he's saying, and he nods at Kat and I, standing in the back.

Every head turns, and I swear even the air around Kat goes brittle, like if she moves it might all shatter. Her hand isn't on my arm any more, so I put mine on her back, smile and lift my glass. I think of the dinosaurs in *Jurassic Park* who could only see something if it moved. Maybe I can distract them.

"We've all been quite eager to meet this mysterious young lady," Elmore goes on. "Glad you've finally brought her around."

I keep smiling, tamp down a quick thump of anger.

"I wasn't sure I wanted her to know I worked with lawyers," I say, and I can hear my accent shine through, like I'm imitating Elmore. They all laugh politely, because no one likes lawyer jokes better than lawyers.

"Well, now you're good and found out," he says. "Welcome, Miss Narumoto."

Her spine goes even straighter under my hand as I open my mouth to correct him.

"Nakamura," she says instead, voice pitched high, not quite loud enough.

He leans in, frowning, bends one ear forward with a finger.

"Sorry?" he says, pleasantly enough.

I can hear her swallow, see the tendons in her neck like cables.

"Nakamura," she says, louder this time.

"Namukur—"

"*Nakamura*," she says, slow and loud, the air around her practically vibrating.

Elmore smiles, then gives the tiniest of shrugs.

"What she said," he says, and there's a rustle of agreement and laughter as he brushes this off. "I'll get it sooner or later, you just make sure she sticks around, all right? Anyway I won't keep you all any longer, dinner is served."

Kat takes a long, deep breath. Ten feet away, Linda sights us and starts heading over with her husband, waving one hand decked with rings.

"That's Linda and her husband Chuck," I tell Kat, keeping my voice low. "She's got three grandkids and—"

"I can't," she says suddenly, her voice a harsh whisper like she's breaking a spell. "Sorry—I just—give me a—"

She doesn't get the sentence out before she crashes to the floor, upright one second and gone the next. The wine glass she was holding smashes and Kat yelps and Linda gasps and I'm already kneeling down, one knee on the carpet and one off, heel stuck in the pile, Kat twisted funny on her hands and knees over the broken glass—

"Fuck," she gasps, and then she's up and gone.

# SIX

## KAT

I DON'T KNOW where I'm going, I just bolt. I know I've broken a glass and spilled wine and caused a scene, and somewhere in the back of my mind is a voice that won't stop telling me those things, over and over, like a song played too fast. I shouldn't run but I'm running a little, dangerous in these goddamn shoes, but it feels more dangerous not to run.

I turn left, then right. Half-jog down a hallway, one hand trailing along the wall so it doesn't tilt too much. Fight the feeling that my vision is bubbling around the edges like an old film reel that's caught fire, that there are a thousand rubber bands around my chest and every breath feels like almost enough air. No plan except *leave*.

The first two doors are closets. The third's a bedroom, but the fourth is a bathroom and bathrooms are Alone Places and I sit on the toilet and put my head between my knees and try so hard to breathe it feels like I might crack a rib with the effort.

*Everyone saw you look like an idiot and trip over your own feet and break a glass and freak out and run away*, the voice says. *Can you breathe? It's bad that you can't breathe.*

*Maybe you're dying. Maybe it's a heart attack this time. Don't pass out, you'd hit your head. Good thing you wore the waterproof eyeliner. Don't bleed on the floor, the tile looks nice. Can you believe you did that? One little micro-aggression and you flip out? Do you think everyone will know soon? You're gonna get weird looks at work. I bet they'll tell Evan. You sure it's not a heart attack?*

I'm not sure. I'm never sure, because even though this has happened a dozen times in the past year it always feels like I'm dying. Fuck. *Fuck.*

I sit up, dizzy. Clench my teeth against it, still panting. I put all my will into not passing out and grab some toilet paper, hold it to the bleeding heel of my left hand.

*"Fuck!"* I hiss when it hurts in a new, twisty way I wasn't expecting and the gray bubbling film feeling comes back. My fingers are cold. My lips are cold. Do your lips get cold when it's a heart attack?

*I bet they're talking about you right now, eating dinner, getting your name wrong again and Silas is—*

There's a knock on the door. I startle so hard I almost fall off the toilet.

"Inside!" I manage to say after a long moment.

"Kat?"

It's Silas. The person whose night I'm currently ruining.

"I'm fine!" I shout, still gasping for air. My voice sounds weird. I bite my lips together, try to force air into my lungs through my nose, still gripping one hand with the other.

There's a long pause, and over my own fast, ragged breaths, I can hear the sound of a hand touching a doorknob.

In theory, I know what to do right now. It's not my first panic attack or my fiftieth. I've walked through this with therapists and had plenty of practice, but that's worth fuck-all right now because I can't think of a single thing

I'm supposed to be doing besides not passing out on this toilet.

"Can I come in?" he asks, and now it sounds like his face is right up against the door.

I shake my head *no*. I'm dizzy and the rubber bands are still there, tight around my chest, and I bite my lips together and close my eyes and shake my head *no* and the door opens.

"Ah," he says, and the door clicks shut. Footsteps and then he's right in front of me, the rustle of clothing, the quiet pop of a knee joint. "Okay."

"Don't."

"Can I see your hand?" he says. He has the calmest voice I've ever heard, and I don't answer. I don't know the answer.

Silas reaches for me, slowly, so slowly I have all the time in the world to pull away or punch him in the face or scream. His fingers slide over knuckles and along the bone until he's cradling my hand in his. Both hands. It's more okay than I expected.

"I've got you," Silas says, and I believe him. I don't know why, but I believe him. "Tell me five things you can hear."

I can't breathe and I can't move and I *can't* open my eyes and look at him. I can't do that more than anything.

"Nothing," I gasp. "I'm fine, I'm good, I just—"

"Five things."

"I don't fucking know," I hiss. I suck in a breath, swallow, keep my eyes shut.

"Then start by telling me one."

My inhale is too sharp.

"My breathing," I get out. "My heartbeat."

"Good."

There's a moment of stillness, between breaths.

"The air conditioning."

62

"Three."

A faint hollow click from far away, the ghost of an echo.

"A door," I say. "Shutting."

"Four."

I swallow hard, my mouth suddenly sticking to itself.

"You. Breathing."

"Good," he says, and his hands flex around mine, and—it's not so bad.

"Four things you can feel," he tells me.

I swallow again and try to breathe and shift gears, like I'm wrenching a massive wheel around to point in the right direction. I can practically hear the screech of metal on metal, gears grinding as the machinery lurches around. Around my chest, a few rubber bands pop off.

"My hand hurts," I say.

"One."

"My feet are sweaty."

"Two."

"Cold toilet seat."

"Three."

I pause. Breathe. That bubbling, graying feeling has receded, and I know what the fourth thing I can feel is but I don't want to say it, somehow don't want to acknowledge it for reasons I can't enumerate so I resist. And resist.

Silas shifts on the floor in front of me, and I feel it in the slight shift in pressure of his thumbs on my skin. A sway. A pull.

"Your hands on mine," I finally say, and as I do my eyes open and Silas is right there, a foot away and holding my gaze as he kneels on the bathroom floor. His eyes are the clear, deep blue of mountain lakes at sunrise. The churning blue of the sea after a storm.

He nods at me. Holds my gaze. Comforting and unnerving, all at once. I clear my throat, then swallow.

"White towel on the rack behind you," I say, glancing up at it, moving on to three things I can see without needing to be told. I've done this exercise a hundred times, I know how it goes, and I glance around, breathe a little deeper. The cacophony of panic retreats further. "A white shower curtain."

"Keep going."

I look at him again, only to find it's hard to look away.

"Your laugh lines. And freckles," I finish.

"Now you're imagining things," he says, but the laugh lines deepen even as he says it.

"Have you looked in a mirror?"

"The freckles at least," he admits, the lines still there, the smile still there. "My sister's always after me about sun damage."

"You do. Almost," I say, and I can mostly breathe again and I'm mostly not shaking, but the panic attack loosened something in my brain, the same way it always does and I'm saying things I never would otherwise. Call it a temporary lack of oxygen. Call it the sickly euphoria of having made it through another one.

Silas is on his knees in front of me, sitting back on his heels, my hands palms-up in his. A supplicant's position except for the way his thumbs are pressing into the bones of my wrists, like through that one small, firm touch he can keep me from floating away.

There's a slice on the heel of my left hand, blood oozing out, and jagged cuts on my forearm where I tripped onto my wine glass. Silas has blood on his thumb, a single drop on the pretty marble tile below us.

And he has freckles, almost. I've never seen them before

64

but I've never been this close to him. Why would I? We're unfriendly acquaintances at best, but up close his skin has flecks of deeper color across the bridge of his nose, his cheeks, his forehead, barely there and undetectable from any further away. I could have gone a lifetime without knowing about them, and now that I do, it feels like I know his secret.

Gray hairs, too, a handful shot through the deep golden brown. I wonder what else I've never noticed.

"Keep going," he says, and I take a deep, perfect breath that feels so good I shiver.

"Air freshener," I say. "Bleach, probably. And... chardonnay."

Silas nods. He looks at me for a long time, a lock of hair coming loose from the rest and twisting around on itself, resting against forehead. It makes him look roguish, charming, just the right amount of carefree.

I wonder if he planned it this way.

"Did it help?" he asks, softly.

I sit up straight, breathe in, leave my hands in his for now.

"Yes," I say, formally as I can, my voice sounding oddly distant to my own ears. "Thank you."

"Sometimes the simplest tricks work the best," he says, and leans over my hands, examining. "Let me see if there's a first aid kit here somewhere."

It's under the sink, and Silas pulls out a pair of tweezers as I scoot back onto the toilet, push my glasses back up my nose, smooth my dress against my legs with one hand. At least black won't show blood, or won't show it much.

"I think you've got a piece of glass in there," he says, standing in front of me. "Can I, or do you want to?"

Even though I can breathe again I still feel strange, fizzy

and shaky, like a penny that's been dropped in champagne, and whatever part of my brain might normally go *ugh, Silas*, is smart enough to be quiet right now.

"You don't mind?"

"I wouldn't've offered if I minded."

I hold out my hand and this time he goes down on one knee, steadies the back of my hand against his other kneecap.

"Yes, you would've," I say as one thumb presses down on the heel of my hand, pulling the cut apart. It hurts, but not so much that I react.

"You think I'm in the habit of offering to do things I don't want to do?"

"I think you're in the habit of helping when you know it'll make you look good."

His eyes flick to mine and instantly, I wish I'd kept my mouth shut or said something pleasant and normal like *thank you*, especially to the man who's fishing glass from my cut.

A few moments later, he carefully lifts the shard out and it shines red in the bathroom light. It looks small for something that hurts so much, and he taps the tweezers on the trash can, looks into the slice again.

"Feel like anything's still in there?"

I open and close my hand, press the sides of the cut together and watch red ooze out.

"I think I'm good," I say, and then, finally: "Thanks."

Silas nods. Without standing he puts the tweezers on the sink, grabs a hunk of gauze and a roll of medical tape from the kit, and starts wrapping my hand.

"You're good at this," I say, for lack of something better.

"You're not the first drunk I've had to bandage up," he says.

66

"I'm not—"

"Joke," he says.

I clear my throat and take a deep breath, reveling in oxygen.

"Sorry. Thanks."

I nearly ask if the drunk he had to bandage was him, but I bite my lips together to keep my mouth shut because even if it's true, now's not the time to go dredging up bullshit that's more than a decade past.

"That should do it," he says, tearing off the tape and tamping the end down gently. He gathers the supplies, sees to the tweezers with the alcohol wipes, clicks the first aid kit shut. I breathe in and out, still sitting on the toilet, and wish I'd brought a valium or a klonopin or even some Advil, but at the last second before I left in a moment of panic I opted for the Chic Professional Clutch over my usual purse and there's nary a pharmaceutical in it.

Silas turns to me, and I stand. I only sway a little at the head rush.

"Okay," I say.

"Okay what?"

"I'm ready to head back."

He rubs his hands together slowly. A soft line appears between his eyebrows.

"No," Silas says.

"I have a deal to uphold," I point out.

"You just had a panic attack and bled all over the bathroom," he says, and folds his arms over his chest, sleeves rolled up to his elbow.

*I know*, I want to say.

*This happens*, I want to say. *How many times in the last year have I had a panic attack in the bathroom and gone back to work? How many times a day did I do that in the weeks*

67

*after Evan dumped me and I still had to see his face every day?*

"It's not my first time, you know," I finally tell him.

"I wasn't under the impression that it was."

"I'm fine," I go on. "The edge is off now."

The line between his eyebrows deepens, but the look he gives me is indecipherable. I feel like a tricky bit of legalese, about to be untangled. He shifts his stance slightly as he thinks.

"I'm not having you go back to the situation that gave you a panic attack in the first place," he proclaims. "You can wait in the truck while I make up an excuse."

"Yes, you can, and you can't order me around like—"

"God almighty, stop fighting me on this," he says, loud enough that I wonder if anyone else can hear. "I'm not taking you back there to drop another glass and bleed on another floor, Nakamura."

My stomach curls in on itself at the unbidden thought: *smash, trip,* and my fingertips and cheeks go cold. I fucked this up pretty good, didn't I?

I take a deep breath, counting to four, release to the same rhythm.

"Right," I say, my voice surprisingly even. "The truck, then."

Silas fishes the keys from his pocket, hands them to me, then brushes past me on the way out of the bathroom.

"Ten minutes," he says over his shoulder, and then he's gone.

# SEVEN

## SILAS

WE'RE silent on the drive back to Kat's house, the radio in my truck quietly playing radio hits from ten years ago. She's still as a statue in the passenger seat, hands in her lap, skirt demurely above her knees. She looks a little like if she gets jostled the wrong way the fissures might open up, a feeling I know all too well.

Twenty minutes into a thirty-minute drive, I can't take the silence any more.

"I once had a panic attack because of a crow," I tell her on a dark stretch of two-lane road.

There's a long silence, so long I get a little worried.

"Was it a particularly large crow?" she finally asks.

"No," I say, eyes still ahead, not looking at her. "But it had learned to imitate a car alarm, and it did so while perched on my windowsill at five o'clock in the morning."

"That sounds like an ill omen of myth and legend," she says. "What'd you do to the crow?"

I feel myself smile at *ill omen*, slide my hand around the wheel to the bottom.

"I'd spent the night at my buddy's house, and he has a relationship with them," I start to explain.

"He feeds them and they bring him stuff?"

I glance over. She's looking at me now.

"You know Levi?"

"No, but everyone knows that about crows."

"Not everyone," I point out.

"It shouted at you and you had a panic attack?" she asks, and I brace myself but that question isn't mocking, it's only a question. I lick my lips, move my hands on the wheel again.

"I was dead asleep and thought it was the warning sirens back at Dwyer," I say. "Fell out of the bed and then crawled underneath it until... it stopped."

The panic attack didn't just stop. The day before that I'd been rear-ended on the highway, and even though I wasn't really hurt the shock and the loss of control were enough to send me spiraling, so I did what I'd learned to do by then: I went to Levi's house.

His house was the first place I found solace after I came back home. For years, it was the only place I could find it: quiet, serene, isolated in the woods, built by the man who'd been my best friend for two decades.

When I spiraled I'd call, and he'd say to come over, and then he'd make tea or hot cocoa or water, whatever I needed. He'd sit with me and listen if I talked and talk if I needed to hear something. He'd hold me if I needed it, and I did. More than once I woke up in the middle of the night, the two of us slumped together on the couch, the first time I'd slept in days.

It wasn't sexual, or romantic. Just the bone-deep under-standing and love I needed.

The morning the crow gave me a panic attack, Levi heard the thump, found me under the bed, crawled in after me, and held me until I could breathe again. I don't tell Kat that part. I can feel her looking at me, thinking, her hands folded in her lap, the medical tape bright against the dark of her dress.

"Thanks. At least I've never had a bird-induced panic attack," she says.

"You're still young and there are some fucked up birds out there," I tell her, and she laughs.

It's louder than I'd imagined. It sparkles, more like broken glass than stars, but it's surprisingly pretty all the same and I smile.

"There are some fucked up birds," she agrees. "Geese, for example."

"Bastards," I confirm.

We're silent again until I pull up in front of her building, a duplex on a quiet street near downtown Sprucevale that's a hundred years old if it's a day. I shut off the engine, the headlights, and we're bathed in the orange glow of the streetlight.

"Thanks for the ride," she says, then pauses, her hand on the door handle, fingers tapping. She looks out the wind-shield at the car parked in front of us. "So, uh, how do you want to break up? Do you want to say it was mutual and we were growing apart or whatever, or do you want me to be the bad guy, or do you want to, or...?"

Finally, she glances over, pushes up her glasses with one knuckle. I clear my throat.

"We can't break up yet," I say.

"I'm very sure we can."

"I told my whole office that I was taking you home early because you had food poisoning so bad you fell over and sliced your hand up," I say, matter-of-fact as I can. "If I break up with you before Monday, I'll be the asshole who dumped you because you ate egg salad."

"You said egg salad? I hate egg salad," she says.

"Well, you sure do now."

She sits back against the seat, right hand still on the door handle, looking at me.

"We can tell people that it's been coming for a while, and the egg salad incident was the final straw," she says.

I turn a little in my seat and lean back against the window, left arm draped over the top of the steering wheel, and I look at Nakamura. At Kat. At the way her shoulders aren't around her ears any more, at how her feet no longer look like they're braced against the floor, at the way her glasses shadow her face like she's wearing a mask.

"We're here because you wanted to piss off Meckler," I say, half a question.

She slouches against the seat, exhales hard.

"I'm sorry," she says. "I shouldn't've—I mean, fuck. I can't believe I did that."

Her eyes close, and even from here I can see her tense, the anger leaking into her voice.

"*Lover*," she mutters, mostly to herself. "Jesus."

"Well," I say, slowly. "I'm more than happy to help you piss off the useless son of a bitch."

"That's not the impression I was under this time yesterday," she points out, eyes still closed.

"I've updated my opinion."

"I broke a glass, got blood everywhere, made you leave a party early, and your opinion of me got *better*?" she asks, opening her eyes and looking at me, glasses still shadowing her face.

"I said updated, not improved."

She's silent for a moment, perfectly still, and I have the

strange feeling that right now she could see through my skin to my bones if she tried.

"Your opinion's not improved, yet you're about to ask me on a second fake date?" she finally says.

I give Kat my most charming smile, run my right hand through my hair. Her face doesn't move.

"How long's he in town for?" I ask, sidestepping her accusation-slash-question.

"Until Labor Day," she says. "A month."

For a long moment, we look at each other across the cab of my truck, all shadows and streetlight.

"How mad you want him to be?" I ask.

Kat swallows, the shadow in the hollow of her throat deepening for a split second and she looks forward now, through the windshield, out at the quiet street.

"As mad as you can get him," she says, softly. "Furious, raging, spitting nails, ready to—flip desks and punch through walls and scream impotently at the sky when he sees us together."

Her right hand, the hand that's not bandaged, is curled into a fist in her lap, the cords on her neck standing out, lit orange. Her jaw flexes. Her lower lip twitches the tiniest bit, like maybe she's about to go on, but she doesn't.

"You want him jealous," I say, softly.

"I want him miserable," she counters, turning back to me.

"Jealousy can be pretty miserable."

"Then it'll do."

Kat's anger is something to behold. It makes her shimmer, like hot oil on a frying pan, ready to burst into flame at the slightest provocation. It makes her seem like she's all sharp angles: her bangs, swooping to a point; the rectangles of her glasses; the sweep of her eyeliner; the narrowness of her eyes; the corners of her mouth. I get the sense that in daylight, she'd be slightly pink right now.

I get the sense that if she wanted to, she could slice me to ribbons.

"All right," I finally agree. "We'll get Meckler good and jealous, and as a bonus, I get my coworkers off my back for a while."

Kat takes a deep breath, still regarding me.

"Okay," she says, then nods. "Okay."

"Okay," I agree, and hold out my hand.

Her shoulders square, and she shakes it, her fingers cool even in the warm night, the angles still on her face.

"Pleasure doing business," I tell her, and her dark eyes flick to mine.

"Pleasure's all mine," she says, and I swear she's almost smiling.

# EIGHT

## KAT

THE DOOR to my office dips inward, and I jump halfway out of my seat. A moment later, my assistant Lucas sticks his head around it, face serious, hair parted and tamed like he's been in church.

"Need anything else, boss?" he asks.

I cross my ankles under my desk and try not to look like I'm one minor surprise away from a heart attack, which I might be. My laundry isn't any more folded than it was Saturday morning. I've gotten maybe seven hours of sleep over three nights. I feel scraped out and raw, and the month of sitting across from my ex all day, every day, has only just begun.

"You were supposed to go home an hour ago," I tell him, and it comes out sharper than I mean for it to. "And don't call me boss, I'm not Springsteen."

That gets a blank look, because Lucas is twenty-one and apparently unconcerned with classic rock.

"Sorry," I say in the next breath, because none of this is poor Lucas's fault and I know it. "I'm fine. I got behind today because of—" I gesture at the second desk now in my office, "—but you should go home. I'll see you tomorrow."

"Have a good night," he says, and then Lucas disappears and I put my face in my hands, shoving my glasses into my hair.

Today, I did not cry under my desk.

I wanted to. Just a nice, quick, stress-fueled sob while most people were at lunch, leaving plenty of time to splash off my face and pull myself together before anyone came back.

But alas, no. Not only is crying at work generally frowned upon, I'm one of three women employed by Strati-fite, so not only is it my job to manage the projects of half the programmers here, I also get to prove to everyone that two X chromosomes do not render one incapable of working in tech. If I get caught crying under my desk, I may as well resign my job, put on a frilly apron, and start ironing some-one's tie.

Of course, that might happen anyway, because B&L— the energy conglomerate with more branches and subsidiaries than a whole forest full of rivers—bought Strati-fite last week, and now we're merging. There might be *redundancies*.

And who's overseeing the process? Evan, who has already asked me twice what exactly my job here is, as if he's never heard of a project manager before.

I keep my face in my hands as I hear the main door shut behind Lucas. I finally slump to my desk, forehead on my hands, and I stay like that for a few minutes because giving up feels kinda good.

I don't know how long I've been like that when the main door opens again.

"Kat?" calls Silas's voice.

I pull my glasses back down, brush my bangs out of the way, stand for the first time in a few hours and steel myself.

"Back here," I call, and push my door open to see a bouquet of roses walking across the room toward me. A dozen? Two dozen?

My stomach plummets, and I'm intensely glad we're the only ones here.

"Voila, babe," he says, and holds them out to me with a grin.

I stare, motionless, as anxiety pours into my chest for a reason I can't even name. They're flowers. Only flowers. From someone with whom I have a reasonable truce.

What the hell is wrong with me?

"What are you doing?" I finally manage.

"I can't bring my girlfriend flowers?" he asks, casual and charming in a button-down shirt, no tie, sleeves rolled up. He's a little too loud, a little too much, and it takes me a second.

"There's no one else here, you can turn off the Silas Show," I say.

"This isn't gonna work if you call it a show."

"This isn't gonna work if you—"

I don't have an end to that sentence, so I stand there and gesture with my hands while he watches me. Finally I take a deep breath and close my eyes, squeezing my fists. Well, one fist. The other is still too bandaged.

"Sorry," I say, and push my glasses up. "Thank you for the flowers. They're lovely. Let me find something to put them in."

"I got a vase," he says, tapping it with one finger. "I figured your office wouldn't have anything."

"Right," I say. "Great. Thank you."

"Can I put them down somewhere?"

I nod and walk back into my office, then gesture at my desk. Silas sets the flowers on a corner, then brushes his hands together and looks around.

It's just an office, and it's all very... well, office-y. My desk is mostly clear except for a notepad, a keyboard, my monitor, and some headphones. I've got a pretty nice chair. On one wall is a bulletin board, and on the other, a huge geological map of southwestern Virginia.

And, of course, a few feet away and facing my desk is Evan's. That's a new addition as of eleven this morning.

I lean against my desk, staring at the roses, trying to put the dark, sticky anxious feeling in my chest into words. I wish I could erase Saturday and all the parts of me I wish he hadn't seen.

"Look," I start, and fold my arms over my chest. "Thanks, but I'm not fragile or something. I don't need to be coddled, or romanced, or treated like I'm made of glass. I don't need to be taken care of, I'm fine."

Silas gives me a strange, almost wary look.

"Everyone needs to be taken care of," he says.

"But not me by you."

"It's flowers to make your ex jealous," he says, crossing his arms and mimicking my stance. "Which is what you said you wanted."

"I didn't mean for you to give me things."

"You do realize that couples often give one another tokens of affection, right?"

"We're not—"

All at once, I realize what my problem is, and I stop mid-sentence.

"No, finish, I can't wait," Silas says. "I thought we'd already discussed this, but by all means continue."

"The last time you gave me something it ended with

both of us, our advisors, and Professor Nelson in the Dean's office," I say. "When you were about to fail Geology, so you showed up wasted at my office hours with a six pack of Natty Light and told me it was all mine in exchange for a C minus."

Silas props himself against the desk opposite mine. He sighs. And then he looks away, toward the window and the lowering sun, and actually looks... contrite?

"And *then* drank two before our meeting was even over," I add.

"Would you have passed me for all six?"

"*No*," I hiss, because even though I know that question doesn't deserve an answer, I can't help but give him one.

"The flowers aren't a bribe," he says. "They're just flowers, given freely in a spirit of vengeful fake romance."

The stretching, clutching feeling in my chest has loosened a little, and I shake my head, looking at the roses and wishing they made me feel some other way.

"Right," I manage to say. "The best kind of fake romance."

Silas doesn't laugh at my joke. He doesn't even smile, but something in his face does lighten a little. Maybe.

"Now are you rethinking our breakup?" I ask, and that gets a smile.

"Less rethinking and more counting down the weeks," he says, unfolding his arms. "How much longer do we—"

When he grips the edge of the desk, his elbow knocks over a picture frame on Evan's desk, and he reaches around himself to right it.

Instead, he stares at the picture for a moment. It's weirdly big for a desk photo, probably five by seven, and both Silas's eyebrows go up before he looks at me.

"That's Meckler," he says. "Is this Meckler's desk?"

"It is," I confirm, trying to sound nonchalant.

I fail.

"You didn't say you were sharing an office with him for four weeks."

I want to say *you didn't ask*, but I'm trying not to be bitchy for the next five minutes, so I shrug. He looks back at the picture like he's got a question that he doesn't quite want to ask.

"That's Olivia," I say, still not nonchalant. "They're dating."

"I see."

"She's very nice."

"I'm sure."

"She's twenty-four and works in real estate."

"He cheat on you with her?"

I sigh and look out the window, because I knew we'd get here but was hoping we wouldn't.

"Not just her," I admit, and it doesn't feel quite as bad to say aloud as I expected.

"Goddamn bastard," Silas says, and my eyebrows go up. The picture goes back on the desk, face-down. "And now he's gonna be in your office for a month?"

"It's his job to integrate newly acquired concerns into the B&L corporate culture," I say. "I'm a bonus."

Silas gives me a long, studied look, and it's not sexual but it's not platonic, either. It's assessing. Considering. Curious. I look at him until he meets my eyes again, half a smile on his lips.

"If I had to spend a month in an office with a woman I wronged I don't think I'd call it a bonus," he finally says. "Especially if you were the woman."

"Thank you," I say, the words so sharp they've got blades. "But you're not him. You wouldn't expect me to still be pining away for you a year later. Or maybe you would. I don't know what your opinion of yourself is like."

"Pretty high, but not that high."

"Especially with me?"

"You don't strike me as the pining sort, for starters."

Despite myself, I glance at the roses, ridiculously red in their vase on my otherwise very white desk, like the interior of a particularly maudlin Hallmark card.

"I'm not," I say, and shrug. "If anything, I'm ruthlessly pragmatic and no-nonsense. Which leads me to why I asked you to stop by, actually."

I walk around my desk, open a drawer, and grab some papers from a folder. Silas says something under his breath that sounds like it might be *oh goodie*, and I ignore it.

"Here," I say, and hand him one set of papers. "The guidelines."

Across the top is written FAKE DATING RULES AND REGULATIONS, and when he reads it, Silas gives me a *look*.

"Hurrah," he says.

# NINE

## SILAS

OF COURSE THERE'S A DOCUMENT, and of course it's neatly outlined into three sections, each with bullet points.

I can't believe I ever thought this might be the easiest way out. Across from me, leaning against her desk in high-waisted gray trousers and a white button-down shirt, Kat clears her throat.

"Peruse this and let me know if you have any questions," she says, not making eye contact.

It's only a page long, but there are three sections: *Acceptable, When Circumstances Require,* and *Never.* Within each are several bullet points of various actions that could be undertaken by a romantic couple, described in the same academic tone she probably uses to classify rocks, or whatever she does here.

I feel like an asshole who brought a flower to a knife fight.

"Should be pretty straightforward," she says, still not looking at me. I sneak a glance up at her face, tilted down behind bangs and glasses, her whole posture stiff and angular and screaming mental discomfort.

"It looks that way," I start, and her gaze flicks up. I hold it. "But I think we still ought to go over it verbally. Best practices and all."

"What exactly did you have questions about?"

"Just read it aloud, starting at the top," I tell her, ignoring her last question. "We can confirm agreement point-by-point."

"You can't read?"

"I prefer to discuss." Like hell she's shoving some rules at me and kicking me out without talking about it.

Kat stands up straighter. She tucks her hair behind her ears, clears her throat again.

"Okay," she says, and suddenly she sounds nervous. "Acceptable romantic actions."

I settle in a little more against Meckler's desk, getting comfortable.

"Hand holding," she starts, her voice low, not looking up. "Putting our arms around each other. Touching on the back. Touching on the shoulders and arms. Sitting close together. Quietly talking to one another. Hair caresses within reason. Non-mouth kisses in non-risque regions. Moderate cuddling while clothed."

The list comes out rapid-fire and staccato, and I'm not sure she pauses for a breath until it's over. I lean back and take a pen from the pen holder on Meckler's desk, fully intending to steal it when we leave.

"I'd like a definition of *within reason*," I say, making a quick note.

"I mean don't pet me or something, I'm not your cat."

"I promise you look nothing alike."

83

There's a moment with no response, and when I glance up, she's looking at me.

"You have a cat?"

"I do."

"You don't seem like a cat guy."

In response, I toss her my phone. She drops it, picks it up, and looks at the lock screen. A long-haired tortoiseshell cat looks back at her.

"Cute?" she says, after a moment.

"Her name's Beast," I say. "When I found her in my cabin I thought she was a demon at first."

Kat doesn't respond to that, just leans forward and hands me my phone, as if reminding me I didn't have to throw it.

"Are you going to make me define *moderate* as it pertains to cuddling, or can we both agree to a mutual understanding of the word and move on?" she asks, giving me a pointed look.

"If I were your attorney I'd advise a completely new draft of this document five times longer and a hundred times more specific," I say. "You don't even have a breach of contract clause in here."

Now she's pinching the bridge of her nose, glasses hoisted up.

"I'm sorry that I wrote things down because I wanted to be sure we were on the same page about whatever the fuck it is we're even doing," she says, voice muffled by her hand but sarcastic. "Is there any chance we can get through this and move on?"

Something about the way she says it hits me right below the sternum, in that soft, susceptible spot: Kat with her shields briefly down, human for once instead of the stony, spiky creature who saw me at my worst and drove me down instead of having some mercy. Suddenly there's a bend, some give, an acknowledgement of being made of flesh and blood, same as everyone.

"We can move on to the second article," I concede, and then the glasses are back. "Entitled 'Acceptable actions when circumstances require'?"

"Thank you," she says, and reads. "Touching on the leg. Intense cuddles. Full-trunk embraces. Romantic-style face touching. Any sort of stroking. Mouth kisses. Verbal declarations of attraction. Kisses in moderately risqué locations."

She finishes, and there's a moment of silence during which I'm confronted with the fact that I don't hate hearing her say *moderately risque locations*.

"When, exactly, do circumstances require?" I finally ask.

I get a look, and hold up my free hand.

"Honest question."

"When the situation calls for us to... need to demonstrate our attraction," she says, quickly. I think she's blushing, the faintest of pinks under light gold skin.

"You mean when he's around," I say. "This is a list of things you want me to do in front of Meckler."

She holds my gaze for a long time: three seconds, then five.

"The things that'll get him fired up," I go on.

Kat takes one deep breath, her chest rising, falling under her shirt.

"Yes," she finally says, voice hushed. "This is what he's gonna hate."

"When I hold you close and whisper something dirty in your ear," I say, rephrasing the words in front of me. I say it to get a reaction from her, and her lips twitch like maybe she's trying not to smile.

"I think whispering would defeat the purpose," she says.

"Then I'll hold you close and holler something dirty."

"As long as it works."

I don't hate the thought quite as much as I might like. I wonder how she'd react, whether she'd blush or recoil. Maybe both. Kat seems complicated.

"Home stretch," I say, making myself relax back against the desk, banishing all thoughts of whispers. "The *never* list."

"No touching in the swimsuit zone," she says. "No weird PDA. No entering one another's domiciles. No bed sharing."

"That's it?"

"I'm concise," she says, and that glimmer of amusement is back. "And don't ask for a definition of *weird*. If you're worried it's weird, it's probably weird."

"I promise not to lick your eyeball in public," I drawl.

It gets a dismayed noise out of her, and I try not to grin at it.

"You did forget one very important thing on this document," I tell her.

"The part about who gets to sue who for damages?"

"The goal," I tell her.

She puts the paper on her desk, flips it over, turns back to me. Frowns through her bangs and glasses, dark hair draped over the white shoulders of her shirt. Right now, Kat looks for all the world like the movie version of a stylish lady publishing executive, all glasses and business.

"To make Evan jealous," she says carefully.

"Well, the thing about that is it's amorphous, hard to define, and open to lots of interpretation," I tell her. "I can't read minds. I don't know what he's thinking. We can say *make him jealous* until the cows come home, but when do I get to say *mission accomplished?*"

Kat locks eyes with me and frowns, thinking.

"When he leaves here in a bad mood?" she says.

"You gotta do better than that," I tell her. "Go big. Pie in the sky. Tell me what to push for."

"You're really taking this seriously."

"I'm very mission-oriented," I say, and she nods. There's more silence, her eyes on mine. Her lips part by a few millimeters, but in the stillness, I notice. I can't help but notice.

"I want him to beg for me back," she finally says, so low it's nearly covered by the rush of the air conditioning in the building.

Oh.

"I want him to break up with her—or not, I honestly don't care—and beg for me to take him back. I want him on his knees. Losing his mind. So consumed by jealousy that he can't eat or sleep or think straight, and I want him to plead and shout and *fucking beg* for me to take him back."

I'm motionless. Waiting, drinking in the onslaught of her words: beg. Plead. Knees. I'm quiet until I'm sure she's finished.

"Is that all?" I ask, and she smiles.

"You said go big," she reminds me, pushing a hand through her bangs, shrugging, the intensity deflected. "He doesn't really need to get on his—"

"You think we can't make him beg?" I ask, the words out of my mouth before I can consider them.

"I think he's not the begging type."

"All the better."

"Is it?"

"You said knees," I tell her, with more vehemence than I mean to. "I'll get you knees, Kat. I'll get him squirming on his belly if you want."

87

I offer a smile that I don't quite feel and that she doesn't return.

"Knees would be enough," she says, after a moment. "If you think you can—"

She falls silent at the sound of the main door opening.

"—Cash only," Meckler's voice says, cutting across the rows of desks in the open-plan office space. "When was the last time you saw that? I'm pretty sure half the hillbillies here keep their savings account under their mattresses."

Kat's eyes meet mine, wide with surprise and something else.

"It's—"

"On your desk."

She doesn't move. I push myself to standing and put my printout of the rules facedown behind her on the desk, our bodies briefly a few inches apart. She's gone rigid again, like she's bracing for something.

"You're gonna sit on your desk and I'm gonna kiss you," I tell her. Adrenaline pricks through my veins, jolts my brain alive, spins out a plan without me even having to try. "We're gonna touch each other in pre-approved ways and we're gonna look like we do it all the time. You ready?"

"Yeah," she breathes, giving me a nod I feel more than see, as Meckler keeps talking, voice coming closer.

"Probably four," he's saying. "A little less if I'm lucky, but their staffing situation is such a..."

Kat hops up onto her desk, while he goes on, back straight and stiff as a broadsword. I think she swallows. When I step up to her she parts her knees and I stand between them. My hands go to her hips. Hers go to my shoulders. I feel like a mannequin being posed: hand goes here and head tilts this way and stand like this and lean like this, except my fingers sink into her hips where I'm holding her. Except her knees are on the outsides of my thighs, and if I didn't know better, I'd think she was pressing us together.

Except now one hand skims up my neck, into my hair, fingers sliding through. I close my eyes. A shiver cascades down my spine, like my body doesn't know who she is.

"Don't flinch," Kat whispers, her lips brushing mine.

I don't. All I do is press my mouth against hers.

This is not a kiss. This is an arrangement, two bodies arranged together. It looks like a kiss but it's only a pose. Even though my mouth is on hers, and hers is on mine. If it were a kiss she'd move a little. Tilt her head. Push imperceptibly harder against me, maybe make a soft noise and curl her fingers in my hair.

If it were a kiss I'd *want* those things. I'd want to move in, slide my mouth against hers, feel the give in her spine as she accepts. I'd skim a hand up her back and sink my fingers into her thick, dark hair, and tilt her head back. If this were a kiss she'd make a soft, throaty noise when I did and her lips would part and the kiss would deepen and I'd realize that she smells like vanilla and honeysuckle, tastes a little like ginger.

My fingers curl in her hair. She tastes like ginger.

If this were a kiss I'd like it. I'd be shocked at how soft she is, at how warm she feels under my hands. I'd find myself with my thumb on her jaw, my hand in her hair, and when she tilted her head my teeth would scrape her lip and I'd lick the spot as an apology. I'd make a noise I've never heard before, raw and surprising—

The sound hangs in the air as the door swings open. Meckler's voice stops, but I don't pull back and neither does Kat. If anything, her hand tightens in my hair and there's one last, tiny thrill down my back as I think *I want him on his knees.*

"Sorry to interrupt," he says, and I pull away from Kat like I'm surprised that he's there. I offer him a grin that's half sheepish, half smug, and run a hand through my hair as Kat's fingers fall to my shoulders.

"Didn't even hear you come in," I say, as friendly as friendly can be. "Nice office. You forget something?"

Meckler's trying to look nonchalant, but it's buried under a layer of discomfort and prickling anger. He looks from me to Kat and back. I notice his right hand flexes once before he gives me a cursory nod and walks for his desk.

"Flash drive," he says, careless. "That assistant left it in my inbox and didn't tell me it was there."

He says the words *that assistant* like you might say *the roach I found in the kitchen*.

"*Lucas* left it there because that's where you asked Lucas to leave it," Kat says. She leans back on one hand, the other still on my shoulder. I turn slightly but leave a palm on her back.

Meckler just grunts, frowns at the picture frame face-down on his desk, rights it before rifling through a tray on the other side of his desk and eventually coming out with a B&L-branded USB drive.

"Need anything else?" The cheerful, friendly local yokel thing really seems to be pissing him off. Or maybe it's that I've got Kat on her desk. Maybe it's both.

"This is it," he says, and holds the drive up, heading for the door again. His face is redder than it was a few minutes ago, his phone still held in his other hand. "Have a good night."

"Same to you," I call out as he heads back through the door. "Welcome to Sprucevale!"

There's no response, only Kat rolling her eyes so hard it's nearly audible.

THE ONE MONTH BOYFRIEND

"Dick," she mutters, as Meckler pops his head back through the door.

"Kat, I almost forgot," he says. "Olivia says hi."

Her face doesn't move, but I swear the temperature drops by five degrees.

"See you tomorrow!" he says, and then he's gone, his footsteps heading for the office's front door. Kat glares in his direction, hand frozen on my shoulder, and after the outer door closes she looks at me. Her face is flushed and her lips are slightly parted, her eyes dark and serious and she's still on the desk with me between her knees and for a wild, delirious moment I think she's going to kiss me again.

I might even want her to.

"Fuck," she says instead. Pushes me away, drops her hand from my shoulder, hops off the desk. I settle against Meckler's, not disappointed.

"I thought I did pretty well," I say.

She grabs the two printouts and shoves them into her bag, not looking at me.

"You did. Sorry," she says. "Thank you."

She bends over her desk, clicks her mouse a few times, and her monitor switches off.

"You're welcome," I drawl.

"And thanks for the flowers," she goes on. Still not looking at me. "They're very nice."

"My pleasure."

We both pause, and she pushes her glasses up with one knuckle.

"You hungry?" I ask, but she's already shaking her head.

"I've actually gotta be somewhere."

"We could make it quick," I hear myself say.

"Sorry," she says, and opens the door like she's waiting

for me to go through. I do it before she seems to remember herself. "Raincheck?"

"Deal," I say, and walk through the door as if I haven't noticed a damn thing amiss. "You better be good for it."

"Of course," she says, her voice tight, so I leave Kat's office and go back to my own, wondering why I feel like there's an entire phalanx of spears pointed right at me.

# TEN

## KAT

I DIDN'T PARTICULARLY *ENJOY* that kiss. Not more than I'd enjoy any kiss, at least. That's the whole point of kisses: they're nice to do. For whatever reason, it feels good to smash your mouth against someone else's—which is really strange if you think about it too much—and then move your faces around for a bit.

Which is what happened and why it was kind of okay, because humans are wired to think that mouth-smashing is fun. I could have mouth-smashed anyone and it would have more or less been the same amount of fun, and I'm sure I'd also still be thinking about it hours later while lying awake and staring at my ceiling.

I breathe in while counting to four, hold my breath, breathe out for six. I visualize floating down a very serene river, letting all the tension out of my feet, then my ankles, then my shins—

*But then the way he groaned when I grabbed his hair like he didn't even know he was making a noise—*

"No," I mutter out loud, to myself, because I live alone and sometimes you need to talk to yourself about your horny

93

thoughts. Such as when someone you don't even like tells you to get on the desk and then fits surprisingly well between your legs and kisses much better than you expected, which makes you wonder what *else* he does better than you might expect.

Which is... another horny thought.

Honestly, I don't know why I'm surprised. I'm human. Humans are sexual creatures. It is very normal to have a certain number of sexual thoughts in one's life, particularly when the most sexual contact one has had in a little over a year has been soothing but very platonic hugs from one's best friend.

Which is all this is: I'm frustrated, he exists and is technically attractive. It doesn't mean anything that kissing him was, like, not terrible. Or that the way he said *I'll get him to squirm* was technically sort of hot. Or that I kind of wonder what would happen if I sat on my desk and told Silas to get on his knees—

"Okay, okay, fuck," I say out loud to myself as I roll over, open my nightstand, and grab the very fancy vibrator that was my gift to myself when I moved here.

I turn it on, go to town, and when I come a little harder than usual it's for no reason at all.

· · · · ★ ★ ★ ★ · · · ·

"WERE THEY BAD ROSES?" Anna Grace asks, lining up her swing.

"No?" I say watching the club glint in the lowering sun, her blond ponytail falling over her tan shoulder. "Yes? What makes roses bad?"

"They could be ugly," she says. "They could be plastic, they could be poison, they could be those white roses that get painted red in *Alice in Wonderland*. I could see you as a Queen of Hearts type."

She hits the golf ball and it goes soaring through the air before bouncing off the green expanse.

"Nice," I say.

"Thank you."

"Is a Queen of Hearts type good or bad?" I ask, because with Anna Grace, I'm genuinely not sure.

"Well, she's obviously a misogynistic caricature, but also kind of a boss bitch," she says, finally looking at me under her visor. I'm also wearing a visor. Our visors match. I've never dared come to the driving range at the Blue Ridge Country Club, where Anna Grace's family are members, without a visor because I kind of suspect they'll kick me out for not having the right head gear on.

"I've never actually walked on a man's back or used a bird to play... cricket?"

My memory of the Disney movie is, admittedly, foggy.

"Croquet," she says, plucking another ball from the bucket. "And wasn't there that one time in college?"

"We don't talk about that," I say, and Anna Grace grins.

"So the roses themselves were fine, it was the fact of being given the roses you didn't appreciate," she goes on, placing the ball on the tee.

I consider this for a long moment as she lines up her shot, gives it a few practice swings, and then finally lets fly. I've told her everything, of course, so someone knows the story in case I suddenly go missing.

Except the kiss. I didn't tell her about that, or that I've thought about it every two-point-five seconds ever since, or that I'm pretty sure I can still feel Silas's hand on my jaw where he touched me.

"Yeah," I say slowly as the ball hits the grass in the

distance. "I didn't realize we'd agreed to a gift-giving kind of fake relationship, and I just... it felt like he was making fun of me."

High school wasn't a great time in my life. Neither was middle school. Neither, actually, was elementary school, though I think preschool was all right.

Anna Grace gives me a long, considering, affectionate look.

"You're likable and worthy of gifts," she says, and I scrunch my face.

"It's not that."

"You're also doing him a favor."

I sigh and look away, over the blisteringly green horizon, stuffed with grass and trees and mountains, humidity rising in waves even though it's late Tuesday afternoon and the sun won't be up much longer.

*You think we can't make him beg?* Silas asked, yesterday, the darkness of his voice at stark odds with the fluorescent brightness of my office and fuck, *fuck*, why am I still thinking about that? Why does that thought feel like it settles somewhere at the base of my spine, warm and electric?

"I also don't like the roses because now everyone in the office is going to see them and want to talk to me about them and tell me how they're soooo sweet and soooo nice and I'm soooo lucky to have such a great boyfriend," I start.

"Your office is mostly guys in their mid-twenties who live in their parents' basements and wouldn't notice flowers on a desk if their lives depended on it," Anna Grace counters.

"Rude," I tell her, but I'm grinning. "My team is very perceptive and only some of them live in basements."

I don't actually know where most of my programmers live. They're my coworkers, not my friends.

"So you hate the attention," Anna Grace says, and whacks another golf ball. "What else?"

Soar, bounce.

"Do you ever aim for the guy driving around out there in the golf cart?" I ask.

"Of course not," she says, but she's grinning.

"I do."

"Well, you're an asshole."

"I've never actually hit him."

"Wow, really? With your swing?"

"My swing is fine, thanks."

Anna Grace doesn't dignify that with a response, even though it's true. My dad and grandfather are both very into golf, so I've played my fair share of it, even though I'm decidedly fine at best.

"The roses make me suspicious that he's setting me up for some sort of public humiliation," I finally admit.

Anna Grace, God love her, doesn't roll her eyes and tell me that I'm being paranoid, or that I'm crazy, or that it's a completely ridiculous thought to have even though any of those things might be justified. Instead, she gives me another thoughtful look under her visor.

"I know," I say, answering all the things she didn't say.

"Do you think you feel that way because of him, or because of you?" she finally asks.

I huff, pretending to be annoyed, and lean back against the rail behind me.

"I told you about the six pack, right?" I say.

She plucks another ball, lines up the shot, gives me a look.

"Yeah, you've mentioned it once or twice," she says,

which definitely means I've told her the story about Silas trying to bribe me with cheap beer a thousand times.

"He was a nightmare," I go on, mostly to defend myself. "He was drunk half the time and a disruptive jackass all the time, and then when he failed the class he tried to gaslight me with his whole 'traumatized war veteran' shtick in front of the professor *and* my thesis advisor *and* the dean."

A few stalls away, a white man with gray hair shoots me a glare, so I duck under cover of my visor and clear my throat as Anna Grace hits another ball.

"There are channels," I hiss, even though I know Anna Grace is well aware of everything I'm about to say. "You can't just bring that shit up after you've already failed a class."

"Anyway," Anna Grace says, and I take a deep breath.

"Anyway, I'm not completely unjustified for being suspicious," I say.

"No," she agrees, perfectly mild, and I sigh.

"But?"

"But—and not to go defending men or anything, God forbid—that was over a decade ago and during what I understand was a particularly difficult period in Silas's life," she says. "I think it's very possible that he was a raging asshole then and bringing you ulterior-motive-free flowers now."

"Do you think it's likely?" I ask.

She grabs the final ball from her own bucket, and looks at my golf setup, on the other side of the rail where I'm currently lounging.

"Are you gonna hit any of those?"

"I hit a couple," I say.

"Might do you good to hit some more."

This isn't the first thing Anna Grace and I have worked out at the driving range. Two years ago, when I was still living in Fairfax and dating Evan, I came down because her ex-boyfriend got engaged to her ex-girlfriend, and I think she went through about twenty buckets of balls in a weekend. I like to think my excellent insight and copious swearing on her behalf also helped.

"I can't tell if that's a yes or a no," I tell her, and she leans back on the opposite railing, crossing her arms while still holding her golf club in a very rakish way.

"I don't really know him that well," she starts.

"Now you tell me."

"And he's kind of an asshole, but in a charming, do-stuff-first, ask-permission-later kind of way. Not in a calculated-cruelty-to-a-specific-person kind of way."

She gives me a very pointed look at that last part, and I've at least got the decency to glance away.

"So you think they're just flowers and not a sign that he's plotting my social downfall?" I say, still not moving.

"I think if Silas wanted to do you harm, he'd toilet paper your house and fork your front yard, not embark on an elaborate weeks-long ruse to emotionally ruin you," she says.

This time I meet her eyes.

"Not that I disapprove of emotionally ruinous ruses," she says, a glimmer of amusement finally coming into her eyes. "But he wouldn't think of it."

"Thanks," I say, and she picks up her empty bucket.

"C'mon," Anna Grace says, plopping her golf stick on her shoulder. "The bartender who makes the amazing side-cars is working tonight, and we can put it on my parents' tab."

"We should stop doing that someday," I point out, following her.

Anna Grace laughs.

"Never," she says, and we head to the bar.

# ELEVEN

## SILAS

"TELL me again about the full-trunk embrace," Gideon says, sitting across from me. "But this time tell me all sexy-like."

"And explain which one of you is the elephant, because that part's confusing me," adds in Wyatt, on the couch next to Gideon, grinning like an asshole.

I flip them both off.

"The full-trunk embraces are allowable when her ex is within range," calls a voice from the kitchen, interrupted by some clanging. "And preferably on a direct line of sight, whereas you can caress but not pet her hair any time you like, but you can *never* get weird."

Gideon, Wyatt, and I look at each other.

"So when I say your name twenty times in a row and you don't respond, are you fucking with me?" I call out in response.

"Only sometimes," says Javier, his words followed by the annoyed rattle of a drawer slamming shut. "Sometimes I'm deep in conversation with my muse."

I'm ninety-nine percent sure that Javier refers to his muse as a joke, but not a hundred. You never know with artists. They can be odd, and I've never quite gotten up the courage to ask him in case he's serious about her. It? Them? Do muses have gender?

"You're welcome to let 'er rip with the date ideas," I tell the two on the couch opposite me, gesturing with the cherry soda I'm holding. "Go ahead, thrill me."

Wyatt blows a too-long lock of orange hair from his forehead, and Gideon gives the far wall a consternated frown.

"What's that French joint in Grotonsville?" Gideon finally asks. "Le... something red."

"Being in Grotonsville defeats the purpose," I point out.

"Lainey and I went to that new Thai place on George and Lafayette," Wyatt offers. "It was pretty good."

"Was it a date?" I ask, trying to sound as neutral as possible.

"What? No," he snorts. "Just a good restaurant."

"So you're saying that somewhere you took Lainey would be a good place for Silas to take a date, but you weren't on a date with Lainey when you took her there," Javier calls.

"People have friends," Wyatt calls back.

"Sure," calls Javier, packing a whole lot of meaning into a single word. There's more rattling. "You guys know where my spatulas are?"

The three of us on the sofas look at each other, and Wyatt stands.

"You know this is your kitchen, right?" he calls out as he pads across Javier's loft, bottle hanging from his fingers. "Where do you usually keep the spatulas?"

"I already looked there," Javier says, and then Gideon clears his throat.

Pizza? he mouths when I look over, and I give him a subtle thumbs up, meaning that I've got an order all ready to put in the moment Javier's lasagna turns out to be inedible. Gideon nods approval.

"Pack a picnic, toss some pillows and blankets into the back of your truck, and wine and dine her below the stars," Wyatt says from the kitchen.

"Unless I'm doing that in the middle of Main Street, that misses the point," I call back.

"Take her to a movie," Javier says. "Pick a restaurant, any restaurant. What about that wine bar that opened up down the block from Walter's?"

"The county fair's this weekend and next," Gideon offers.

"Yeah, win her a giant teddy bear," says Wyatt. "Women love giant stuffed animals."

I take the last sip of my cherry soda and try to imagine Kat at a county fair, giddy with pleasure over the prospect of an enormous stuffed toy.

I cannot. I can't imagine her giddy over anything, least of all a teddy bear. All I can imagine is the way she'd push up her glasses as she looked at it, and then at me, and then asked what she was supposed to do with it.

And then I'd ask her if she ever got lonely sometimes, and she'd say she's never that lonely, and I'd tell her that sometimes you don't know what you need until you're already getting cozy with a stuffed animal, and she'd press her lips together the way she does when she's smiling but fighting it and I'd get closer, put a hand on her hip, ask her—

I hit the brakes on that train of thought because I've already spent way too much time thinking about a purely transactional kiss. Maybe I'm the one who needs a giant stuffed animal.

"It's not in the freezer," Javier is saying in the kitchen. "Stop looking in the freezer."

"Your egg timer was in here two months ago," Wyatt responds. "I'm perfectly justified."

"Are you sure the spatula is in the kitchen?" I call out.

"Yes," answers Javier.

"No," answers Wyatt.

"Want us to check the paintbrushes?" I ask.

My only answer is a dramatic sigh from Javier, so Gideon and I both stand and head to the far wall of Javier's loft.

As starving artist spaces go, it's very nice, probably because Javier's less *starving artist* and more *extremely competent graphic designer who sculpts and paints in his spare time*. When it was built, this place was a warehouse or a mill or an electrical waystation or something—I've forgotten the details—but it's big and boxy and brick and has tons of windows. Javier's apartment is one big, open space with a kitchen in one corner, the sofas in the middle, his bed in a loft above the kitchen, a neat desk with a laptop by a window, and the rest of the space filled with what I can only call Art Stuff.

*Appalachian Olympus* is here, huddled against a wall. Next to those the floor is covered in something that looks like very complicated papier-mâché, the walls behind both filled with sketches and half-finished paintings. There's an easel, though it's empty. There's a loom that can't possibly have been functional in the last fifty years. There are crates of what look like car parts and bike parts, several tool boxes, various hunks and sticks of wood, and a stop sign from God knows where.

Gideon and I both head for a table, loaded down with paints, paintbrushes, pencils, erasers, colored sticks, charcoal, and about a thousand other art-type things I don't know the word for, and we start scanning for kitchen implements.

It wouldn't be the first time that Javier decided something he uses to eat would also be the perfect thing for mixing... whatever artists mix. Paint? Plaster?

"La Dolce Vita," Gideon suddenly says, picking up a cup of paintbrushes and looking under it. "Classy, quality, and downtown where you're likely to be spotted by at least one gossipmonger. That good enough for you?"

"It'll do," I say, and Gideon grunts in response, just as Wyatt shouts from the kitchen, brandishing a spatula high above his head.

"What the fuck?" asks Javier.

"It's *the fuck* a spatula," grins Wyatt. "And it was *the fuck* in your pantry behind all your boxes of pasta."

Ceremonially, he holds it out to Javier, who looks resigned as he accepts it.

"Thank you," he says, and Wyatt bows before picking up his root beer.

"At your service."

"Shut up."

"Is that any way to treat the man who found your spatula?"

There's a burble in the loft, and Wyatt and Javier keep good-naturedly bickering as an enormous, fluffy black cat unfurls itself, stretches, and lightly pads down the stairs before going straight to Gideon and rubbing against his legs.

Gideon sighs, then reaches down to scratch the cat's ears.

"Don't you ever bother anyone else?" he mutters, and Zorro meow-chirps in response.

"He knows a sucker when he sees one," I offer.

That gets another grunt, though it's pretty unconvincing since the cat's already in Gideon's arms, well on his way to blissfully rubbing his face against the man's beard. Gideon rolls his eyes and looks annoyed, but he's actively facilitating this. It's his own fault.

"Where else?" I say as we head toward the kitchen.

He frowns. Zorro headbutts his chin, ecstatic.

"Does it have to be a restaurant?"

"It can be anywhere that a whole lot of people will see our romance unfold," I say. "Preferably people who will tell other people."

"There's a ghost tour every Wednesday that starts at the graveyard by St. Bernard's," Wyatt says. "It's on foot, but she can get scared and you can act all protective."

"You take Lainey there, too?" asks Javier, squatting to examine the oven.

"Fuck off," Wyatt suggests.

"The hot springs," Gideon says. His beard is now being vigorously cleaned. He still looks annoyed.

"I haven't been there since high school," I say. "Is it all teenagers?"

"Don't know, I haven't either," Gideon admits, and we all fall silent for a moment.

If there are three people in Sprucevale who don't have any idea where to take a woman on a date, it's these guys. Gideon's been in a bad mood since birth, I think, and doesn't seem to have much interest in forming a human attachment that he doesn't already have. Javier's got more than enough to focus on, between his job, his art, and staying sober, and Wyatt is...

...Wyatt is Wyatt and we don't ask questions.

If I were smart, I'd have asked Levi where to take a woman on a romantic date that'd be sure to get noticed, but I tend to shy away from discussing romance with my best friend because I don't particularly want to know what my sister considers romantic.

For the record, I'm over the fact that she stole him from me, especially because our relationship changed far less than I feared it would. But I also have no desire to learn what gets either of them in the mood.

"The Appalachian Folk Art Museum has an exhibit on taxidermy," Javier says, rising. "Has anyone seen my—"

"There," Wyatt says, pointing at two oven mitts on a counter. Javier grabs them.

"Folk taxidermy seems like more of a third date thing," I say, and Gideon snorts. Zorro makes a weird sound, still going to town on the beard.

Javier opens the oven. Everyone goes quiet as he carefully reaches in, both hands oven-mitt-clad, then pulls a dish out and sets it carefully atop the stove.

He closes the oven door.

Tentatively, we move toward it. Gideon and I exchange a look that asks *is tonight a pizza night?* but Wyatt's the first to the stove.

"Oh!" he says, and there's no mistaking the delighted surprise in his voice. "It's lasagna."

"Come *on*," says Javier.

"I thought it might... not be."

"Just for that, I should make you eat with him," Javier grouses, tilting his head briefly toward Gideon.

"Oh, his manners are *fine*," I put in, and Gideon snorts.

"I meant the cat."

"Sure," says Wyatt, grinning, as Javier pokes the lasagna with a knife.

The lasagna does not respond.

"Go set the table," he says, slicing into it. "You know where everything is."

We do. Our weekly potlucks are coming up on three years old, even older than the cabins at Camp Wildwood, and we know each other's kitchens almost as well as we know our own. Wyatt grabs plates and silverware, Gideon unlatches Zorro from his person and feeds the beast, I get the salad I brought and Gideon's roasted carrots from the fridge, and we all sit down around Javier's table as the evening sun streams through the windows.

# TWELVE

## KAT

I CANNOT BELIEVE I agreed to karaoke. I must be high, or drunk, or both high *and* drunk even though all I've had since lunch was an iced coffee, an apple, and some string cheese.

Maybe the drugs were in the coffee. I left it on my desk a couple of times, as one does, and how hard can it be to sneak into an office and lace an iced coffee with LSD, or peyote, or magic mushrooms, or whatever drug makes someone who hates crowds and watching people make fools of themselves agree to attend karaoke with her coworkers?

"We don't have to go if you don't want to," Silas drawls from the driver's seat as he eases his truck into a parking spot, the lot close to full with people out on Friday night.

"Where was that attitude fifteen minutes ago?" I ask, a little sharper than I intend, but Silas grins.

It's a nice grin and I don't like it.

"Fifteen minutes ago you didn't look like I was leading you to the hangman," he says. "And like it or not, this is more strategic than dinner at La Dolce Vita."

"It's all lethal injection now," I point out. "Though I

think you can still request a firing squad in Utah, or Wyoming, or somewhere else that the laws are more like guidelines."

"Should I be worried about you knowing that?"

"Don't you? You're the lawyer."

I'm delaying the inevitable—that is, getting out of the truck and going into the karaoke bar—and I know it.

"I practice land use and property law," he points out, twisting the key and turning off the headlights. "It's not the sort of thing that sees a lot of people put to death."

"Maybe it should be."

That earns a *look*, and I scrunch my face up in response, adjusting my glasses.

"Not really. Sorry. I'm just saying words out loud because they're there. I actually have a lot of issues with capital punishment," I ramble, my heart thudding faster by the second.

Step one: make idiot of self.

Step two: karaoke?

Karaoke wasn't the plan tonight. The plan was a dinner date at La Dolce Vita, where we'd be seen wining and dining, but mostly we'd sit and eat and chat and drink wine, and it would have been tolerable enough. Maybe even pleasant.

But then Lucas came in when Silas did, and it turned out that he and Evan and "a few other people" were going to karaoke tonight, and then it turned out that "a few other people" was "pretty much everyone else in the office," and of course our plans changed. For our purposes, karaoke makes way more sense, and only has the slight drawback of making me feel like I might sweat myself into a coma.

My eyes are still closed when Silas takes my hand in his, and I jump.

"Easy," he says, and I open my mouth so I can give some devastating retort, but he talks right over it. "Don't sing if you don't want to."

"I know, I know," I confess, leaning my head back against the headrest. "That's not—I mean, of course, obviously, but there's also—people never let it go, you know?"

He squeezes my hand, and I look down at my lap. At his hand on mine, all that's left of last weekend's disaster is a bandaid on the heel of my hand even though the cut's nearly closed.

It's... nice?

It's... *comforting?*

"I say *hey, I don't want to sing*, and they say *okay great so how about you sing as part of a group* and I say *no* and they say *okay you can stand in the back* and I say *no, that is still very much singing on a stage* and they say *oh come on it's karaoke have a few more drinks* and I say *there are not enough drinks in this entire state* and then they finally leave and someone else comes over and we do it all again." I finally take a breath. "And God, I hate it."

I know, somewhere in the back of my mind, that I should be grateful people want to include me at all. I should be praising the Friendly Coworker Gods above that they like me enough to want me drunkenly on stage behind them while they slur their way through *Wagon Wheel* or *Call Me Maybe*, but I'm not.

From the driver's side, Silas makes a noise that I can only call a grunt of understanding. He's still got his hand on mine, and it's long enough that it's starting to feel normal.

"We can still go to dinner," he says with a shrug.

"That's suboptimal," I point out.

"But possible."

"Evan's not gonna get an eyeful of my super-amazing,

super-dedicated new boyfriend if we go to the Italian place,"
I say, and draw a deep breath. "It's fine. I'm fine. I don't
mind repeating *I am not going to sing with you* about five
hundred times and drinking my weight in gin and tonics."

Silas is giving me an odd, sideways look as he undoes his
seatbelt, letting it zip and knock back into place. It's been
days since we kissed on the desk in my office and I've mostly
talked myself into forgetting about it, but that look makes
me... less forgetful.

"As long as you're sure," he says.

At last, something occurs to me.

"Right. As long as *you're* sure," I say, remembering that I
should at least ask about the man's opinions and boundaries.
"You don't hate karaoke, do you?"

That gets a laugh and a grin as he opens his car door,
takes his hand from mine, and I'm oddly conscious of letting
the outside world in.

"Fuck no," he says, grin still on his mouth, halfway out of
the car. "Kat, I love karaoke."

· · · · ★ ★ ★ ★ ★ · · · ·

"COME ON!" shouts Melissa, leaning across the table
between us as she flips through the worn, stained book of
available karaoke songs. "Dinesh and Lucas and Steve are
gonna sing Lady Gaga! Ooh, they have Dixie Chicks! You
could do *Goodbye Earl*."

I tighten my grip around the empty gin and tonic glass,
the condensation dripping over my fingers. It was my third
of the night, and it didn't help nearly as much as I wanted
it to.

"No thanks!" I say, leaning in so she can hear me. "I
don't want to sing!"

"How about some oldies? They've got Destiny's Child!"

"No thanks," I manage. Destiny's Child? Oldies?

"Okay, okay," she goes on. I hold my glass up to my mouth, desperate for the last few drops of gin, because while Melissa nervously sits up straighter at her desk every time she sees me in the office, I can't make her stop talking about songs I should sing.

"Lizzo?" she offers. "What about—"

"I got you another one," Silas says, sliding into the seat next to me.

"Thank you," I say, and I give him a look that I can only hope isn't desperate as I push up my glasses. Then I grab the new drink and gulp.

"Stevie Nicks?" Melissa asks me.

"I don't sing!" I practically shout, and Melissa gives me a look that she probably thinks is conspiratorial.

Silas leans in, elbows on the wooden table.

"How about you?" he asks. "You know what you're gonna sing next?"

Melissa moves a curl off her forehead with one graceless hand—I'm not the only one who's had a couple—and keeps flipping through the book.

"I can't decide," she tells Silas. "Is it better to sing something classic, that everyone will know, or something really fun and new? Do I want a *song* song that I'll really have to *sing* or a song that I can just get away with?"

Silas nods thoughtfully as though he understands the nuances of the question.

"How's your voice?" he asks. "Are you a good singer, or do you rely more on enthusiasm?"

Melissa considers this very seriously.

"About fifty-fifty," she says. "I can carry a tune, but I'm no Beyoncé."

"Probably err on the side of caution, then," he says.

They keep talking karaoke, but I stop listening. I focus on the far wall, trying to get my heart to beat less. My skin feels heated. I'm positive my face is bright red—thanks, Asian glow—but it doesn't matter tonight because I'm sitting in the back of a bar, watching other people sing, and that is *all*.

After a moment, I realize it's hot as hell in here, so I peel off the staid, respectable cardigan I wore to the office over a slightly-less-staid but certainly still-respectable sleeveless black dress. Now I feel oddly overexposed, but I remind myself that it's a bar, for karaoke, and wearing a dress that shows five percent more of my shoulders than usual isn't a big deal.

They're still talking songs and I'm still fighting nerves when Evan walks in.

He's late, of course, not that timeliness really matters. He must have gone home to change because he's not wearing the polo shirt and khakis he had on at the office, but a v-neck t-shirt that's tight around the arms and a pair of jeans that fit him pretty well.

Evan looks good. Evan usually looks good, and I hate it. I hate that it's true and I hate that I think it, because now that I've seen his inner self, shouldn't his outer self also be ugly? At the very least, shouldn't I not find him attractive any more?

But Evan's still attractive, even if I'd rather walk ankle-deep through a literal snake pit than touch him.

I'm still glaring at him when an arm slides around my shoulders, and I jump. A thumb strokes my bare shoulder, like it's calming a nervous cat.

I take another sip of my drink and snort at my pun, because what am I if not a nervous Kat?

"—really nothing but enthusiastic shouting," Silas is saying, the two of them still poring over this karaoke book. "But you'd have to know all the words, I think it's too fast for the teleprompter to be much help."

I make myself relax, and after a moment, it feels almost normal, even if I still suspect there's a neon sign over my head that says THIS IS A FARCE.

They decide on a song for Melissa to sing while I'm half-listening and half-glaring at Evan from across the room, trying to hide behind a gin and tonic. She gets up and walks away, looking pleased with her choice, leaving the karaoke book open on our table.

"I think she may have been drinking," he says, his words easy and his smile easier as he settles back, looking at me. "Took her a while to decide."

"I think you might be right," I say. After a moment's hesitation I settle back, too, his arm still over my shoulders. He's still in the clothes he wore to work, the top button of his shirt unbuttoned, the sleeves rolled up to his elbows, his forearm bare against my upper back. I swear I can feel every ridge in his fingerprint as he thoughtlessly moves his thumb over my skin, and I want to... not.

"What is that, a pint of vodka?"

He laughs and takes another sip.

"I'm pacing myself."

"After one beer?"

"You counting my drinks?" he asks, and he's smiling but there's an edge to his voice. I clear my throat and push my glasses up. If I weren't already tomato-colored thanks to the alcohol, I'd be blushing.

"Sorry, that was shitty," I say. "I swear I know better than to harass people for not drinking."

He takes another drink, the muscles in his throat

working below the faintest five-o-clock shadow, his stubble ruddy and auburn, a few shades lighter than his hair. Or maybe it's my imagination.

"I could forgive you for being surprised," he admits, and I squint at him through glasses. He grins.

"You think my surprise merits *forgiveness?*" I ask. I'm teasing and definitely not too far gone for it to become something else. "Like, all-the-way, Jesus-sanctioned, tell-a-priest-in-a-confessional forgiveness? Because I don't think it was that bad."

He's laughing now, which is good, because I was teasing.

"I could understand your surprise, then, given our last set of interactions," he amends himself, and I nod once. We lapse back into silence for a few minutes, sitting together on a cushioned bench seat along one wall of the bar. A group of three programmers on stage finishes out *Sexy Back,* steps down, and another one steps up and starts belting out *Old Town Road.*

Evan's across the room from us. He's practically holding court, already Mister Popular, casually talking to all the guys who work in the office and the women they brought along, not to mention Melissa and Isabelle, the other two female employees at Stratifite.

That's what makes something dark and familiar twist in my gut: the sight of him smiling at them, flattering two nerdy programmers whose work attire consists of hoodies, flip flops, and graphic t-shirts with *Doctor Who* references, who've probably played through Skyrim more times than they've been kissed, who had braces for way too long and coke-bottle glasses and who always got picked last for dodge-ball, even though they weren't that bad at it.

I take another sip of my gin and tonic and acknowledge that I may be projecting. A little.

Silas's hand tightens on my shoulder, and I feel him lean in. My skin prickles.

"Don't look at him," he says, even closer than I realized, and goosebumps explode on my neck. "Look at me."

I do, and his easy smile is right there, so close it's unnerving. Even in the half-dark of a bar I can see his almost-freckles, an archipelago on his skin.

And God, his eyes.

There are lakes so deep that we've never found the bottom. Lakes that sink further into the earth than anyone knows. Lakes that keep their secrets in cold, still water. The kind of lakes that might still have monsters under the surface. Lurking. Waiting. Moving silently through the depths.

Silas's eyes are that kind of blue.

"You're supposed to be showing off your great new boyfriend, right?" he says, eyebrows going up.

"Right," I manage, trying not to think of sharp teeth and tails with fins and something dangerous swimming through the depths.

"Then don't look at him," he says, and that smile is still there but his voice is low and serious and there's a rasp to it I've never heard before. "Look at me. Tell me something so I can laugh."

His hand is still on my shoulder, his thumb stroking my skin, like he's already developed the habit. I don't want to tell him something. I want to kiss him again and I want to not want that.

"There's a log that's been floating upright in Crater Lake for over a hundred years," I say.

He doesn't laugh, but he does raise his eyebrows again. "Upright?"

"Yup," I say, and grab my glass, thankful for something

116

to do with my hands as I bob the straw up and down, demonstrating. "It's buoyant enough for people to stand on the end."

I point to the relevant part of the straw.

"It's called the old man of the lake, it's a hemlock tree, and it was first referenced in 1896. Just... floating around the lake. As one does."

"I had no idea."

I put my mostly-empty drink back on the table, push my bangs to the side, adjust my glasses.

"Well, you wouldn't if you're not pretty deep in the lake fact community," I say, glancing over the crowd.

"Don't *look* at him," Silas says. His voice goes lower, and there's that rasp again, a quality I certainly don't feel in my skin.

"I'm *not*."

"That was his direction."

"That's everyone's direction," I point out, turning to him, his arm still slung over me. "What, are you jealous?"

"I'm mission-oriented and very focused on achieving my stated goals," he says, and the rasp is gone.

"So it doesn't bother you when I look."

"It bothers me that you might fuck up our carefully-laid plans and render this whole operation moot," he says.

"And that's all?"

He leans in the tiniest bit. My depth perception isn't wonderful at the best of times and certainly not after three drinks in an hour, but I can feel the way the air ripples, the way the pressure of the room changes, the way the space between us turns liquid.

"You getting at something, Kat?"

"Just asking questions," I say, and I sound shockingly calm to my own ears.

A song ends. Everyone claps and cheers. I clap, glad for the distraction, and Silas claps, and I finish my drink, and someone else gets on stage. A song starts, something I don't recognize, and glasses or no I'm too far to see the teleprompter screen.

"Did you put a song in?" I ask.

"I did."

"What song?"

He takes a drink of his water and doesn't answer.

"What *song?*" I demand, laughing.

"You'll find out when I sing it."

"What?"

That gets him a little closer.

"You'll find out when—"

"No, you're supposed to tell me these things as your fake girlfriend."

"You're supposed to keep it quiet that you're my fake girlfriend."

He has a point there. I tilt my head, adjust my glasses, and look up at him.

"If I guess, will you tell me?"

"You won't guess," he says, a challenge if I've ever heard one.

I give him a long, searching look, and he watches me back.

"What's something that a white guy in his late thirties—"

"Mid thirties."

"—Mid-to-late thirties would think is cool to sing at karaoke with a bunch of younger people?"

Silas drinks more water and doesn't acknowledge my very good question.

"Eminem," I guess.

"That requires skills I don't have."

"Michael Jackson."

"No."

"Garth Brooks."

"*No.*"

"That Alan Jackson song about the river."

He snorts.

"No. Are you done yet?"

"I don't know, am I close?"

"Not even."

I sigh dramatically and lean back against his arm, even though it's too warm and too *his arm*, the muscle solid behind my head.

"How much longer do I have?" I ask, and I get a faint twitch of his lips in response.

# THIRTEEN

## KAT

IT'S GODDAMN *SWEET CAROLINE.*

Of course it's *Sweet Caroline.* Everyone here knows it, even if it might be older than their parents. Everyone loves it, especially when they're drunk, and by the end of the first chorus of course Silas is leading the whole bar in a very off-key *ba ba ba!*

*So good!*

*So good!*

Even I find myself singing along, quietly and in my seat with my back against the wall where no one turns around to look at me. Even I—probably because I'm four drinks in and at least that many sheets to the wind—can appreciate the man's stage presence, the way he walks across the small, shitty karaoke space like he owns it, the way people respond because he thinks they will.

I'm not exactly jealous, but there's a space in me for it, a space that holds the knowledge that this is unfair, a tiny tangle of anger that he gets to have this and doesn't even know it.

Then it's over, and he comes down, and they applaud. I

applaud. He grins and runs a hand through his hair, and I can see a rivulet of sweat trickle down his neck in the multicolored karaoke lights, and I sit forward on the bench seat, ready to act the smitten girlfriend with a *good job!* or *that was great!* or, most likely, *that was job!*

Silas is all good-natured swagger, his shirt sleeves rolled up and the top button undone as he walks toward me at my table. I wrap my hands around my empty glass. I sit up straight, make sure I'm smiling, the bright and sunny and proud girlfriend who's not going to say *that was job*.

He walks up, plants his hands on the table, leans down, and kisses me.

There's a second when nothing happens, when I'm too surprised to do anything but go still because we didn't talk about this, we didn't plan this, and it's in the rules but I didn't know it was coming and there are people around and oh, no, what do I *do*—

And then I kiss him back. He's warm and solid and still breathing hard, and it's warm and sticky in this bar and I rock against him, slightly, pressing my mouth to his harder than I mean to as I lever my elbows against the table like I'm asking for more.

There's a noise. God, there's a noise, a single low syllable from Silas that's half-lost in the opening bars of *Shake It Off*. I feel it more than I hear it, from his chest to his mouth to mine, into my spine, down to my fingers and my toes.

It shouldn't feel like this. It wasn't supposed to feel like this.

I'm sure it's not because of him. I'm sure it's the noise, the lights, the too many drinks that make me half-stand, that make me open my mouth under his and deepen the kiss, that get a responding noise from me when he slides the tip of his tongue along my lip.

It's been a year since anyone touched me who wasn't a relative or Anna Grace. A long, lonely, sad year where I uprooted everything in my life and planted myself somewhere new, where I gritted my teeth and bent the world to my will as best I could, where I developed a bad habit of snarling at anyone offering me comfort.

And now Silas is here, and I'm drunk and he's kissing me like he can't help himself, so of course I'm going to kiss him back. I'm starved. I'd kiss anyone.

Then the table shakes under our hands and someone says, "Sorry!" and they're already walking away as we pull back. Fuck, I'm breathing like I was just in a fight, and Silas worries his bottom lip between his teeth, his bottomless eyes staring into mine before he smiles.

"Your hand is freezing," he says, pitching it low, for no one but me. He's not six inches away from me, barely far enough for me to see around him to everyone else in the bar glancing at us.

It takes a moment for me to register that I've grabbed the back of his neck. I pull my hand away, still wet from my glass, and wipe it on my thigh. I try to ignore that we're being observed.

"Sorry," I say.

"I didn't mind."

"Should I put it back?"

Silas tilts his head toward the doorway that leads to the rest of the bar, the lights reflected from the stage playing across his face, his neck, the flushed lips that were just on mine. I'm staring at them. I can still feel the echo.

"I could use another drink," he says, thankfully not answering me, and I'm not disappointed that he didn't say *yes*. "You want anything?"

"I'll come with you," I say, my eyes still on his mouth.

I could kiss him again, right now. I could kiss him and everyone in this entire room would find it completely ordinary except for the two of us, and we have an agreement. I'm already drunk, but the thought gives me a head rush of power.

"I don't mind," he says, but I'm already standing, and I tear my eyes away from his mouth so I don't trip over the table legs or my own feet. He puts his hand on my back as I walk past him, the room not quite steady, and I don't think at all about the shimmering feeling that radiates out from his fingers.

· · · · ★ ★ ★ ★ · · · ·

"WATER'S GOOD," I tell the bartender, since I spent the walk here from the karaoke room trying not to fall off the floor. Easy to drink four strong gin and tonics when you're sitting down and trying not to crawl out of your own skin with nerves, only to realize what you've done as soon as you stand.

The bartender looks like she approves of my choice. Silas orders a beer, and instead of interrogating him about it, I put one elbow on the bar and gracefully cross one leg over the other.

Except I somehow miss, wobble in the chair, and have to redo the whole thing.

"Cheers," he says when our drinks come, clinking his glass against mine. "Here's to not looking at Evan again back there."

"I didn't?" I say, then catch myself and clear my throat and hold my drink up. "I didn't. Excellent work, everyone, mission accomplished."

I take a long, delicious drink of water. Silas sips his beer.

123

I do not notice the way a tiny line of foam clings to the slight stubble along his top lip and I most certainly do not notice the way he brushes it off with his thumb.

"We're not quite there yet," he points out, easy smile in place, his beer on the bar. "There's a way to go between not looking his way every five seconds and the kind of on-his-knees begging I promised you."

If the drinks didn't already have me at maximum flush, I'd probably blush. To hide it I take another drink of my water and focus very hard on not spinning my bar stool at all.

"That's negotiable," I tell Silas, careful with the pronunciation. "I was a little... ruffled... when I told you that."

"Ruffled?" he says, the familiar lines sinking into his face, like he finds this amusing.

"Sure," I say, and adjust my glasses, and try to think of one of the colorful Southern phrases I'm always hearing Anna Grace use. "I had my dander up?"

"You were madder'n a wet hen," he says, his twang suddenly pronounced, a grin on his face.

I suck my lips into my teeth so I don't smile.

"They're quite angry, I presume?"

"Lord, yes," he says. "I sure wouldn't cross one."

"Then that's how angry I was," I say, definitively as I can. "Hence my statements about crawling and begging and knees and whatnot."

"I don't remember any mention of *crawling*," Silas says, his eyes meeting mine.

Shit.

"Whatever terms I laid out," I go on, each word careful. "I won't necessarily hold you to the exact, uh, delineations of the accords to which we both peremptorily... what I said."

I give Silas my most serious look, even though he's clearly trying not to laugh at me.

"*Crawling*, though," he continues. "That's a new angle. You want him crawling to you, or away from you?"

"I regret everything," I mutter.

"To, probably," he muses. "So he can beg you to take him back, right?"

I glance away, at the wall about five feet to my left. The bar is L-shaped and he's in the last seat before the wall, his back to it, away from the crowd so it's just Silas and I and sometimes the bartender.

Slowly, it occurs to me that he did this on purpose: put us in the quietest spot in the bar, with the least eyes, the fewest people likely to overhear us or look our way. Where the crowd is in front of us, not behind us.

It occurs to me that I could kiss him again, right now. Hardly anyone would notice. I don't think Silas would mind. I don't think I would mind, and he's right *there* with his deep blue eyes and his barely-there freckles and the hair that keeps falling on his forehead and his pretty, pretty lips.

I realize I'm rotating on the stool. I realize our knees are touching, and neither of us does anything about it.

"What happens then?" Silas asks, his voice suddenly softer.

My eyes jerk to his, my rambling thoughts derailed.

"Then when?"

"After he crawls to you and begs you to take him back," he says. "You never did tell me that part."

I blink at him. I tilt my head, probably looking like a confused parrot. I push my glasses up my nose, even though they're not falling down, and I realize that I don't fully understand the question.

"He crawls," I say, shrugging so hard that my whole arm

kind of waves in the air. "And he begs and says please, Kat, you're the one true love of my life and I'm an awful mean worm who was terrible to you, and watching you kiss this handsome man has made me realize that I super love you and I will feel very horrible if I don't get you back."

"So it's watching you kiss handsome men that does it," Silas says, a slow smile spreading across his face.

I take a moment to rewind the last ten seconds, when I maybe wasn't thinking a ton about what I said.

"I mean," I start, and then stop because finding my way out of this feels tricky. "Look. It doesn't *matter*. You're, like, a convenient hot face—"

He lets out a low whistle, and I would sort of like to die. Or throw my drink in his hot face. Or... kiss him again, because it was nice.

"Shut *up*," I mutter instead, every inch of my goddamn body bright red.

"So what happens after Meckler wants you back because you've been making out with a total smokeshow?" he asks, and somehow we've both rotated on our stools in such a fashion that there's more of us touching? And my hand is kind of on his knee, and *that* can't be right but also his thumb is tracing across the back of my knuckles and wow, I am never allowed to drink ag—

We both jump at the crash, chairs and shattering glass and the ugly thump of a body against something solid. I nearly fall off my stool but Silas catches me because he's standing like he's at attention, ramrod straight, everything about him at right angles.

"What the *fuck?*" someone shouts above the sudden buzz.

"Don't fuckin' put your fuckin' *drink* there, fuckhead," says someone with a very specific vocabulary.

"Shit," mutters Silas, as he puts a hand on my shoulder. "Stay right there, I'll be—"

"How about I put my drink wherever I fuckin' want!" the first voice hollers. "And if you've got a fuckin' *problem* with that—"

And then, chaos. There's shouting and more shouting and the shriek of furniture moved across the floor, grunting and swearing and *more* glasses shattering and several thumps that I can't identify but don't like, and I can't see a damn thing because I'm in the back of a crowd and Silas is gone.

The shouting gets louder and swearier. I half-stand with my feet in the rungs of the barstool, and it's a very bad idea but for a split second I catch a glimpse of Silas, who's got a shorter guy in a camouflage hat by both arms, looking imposing and also like his biceps might actually rip his shirt or something, and I don't hate it but I do sit back down before I cause a second commotion by falling over.

I have no idea what to do. I have no idea what I, a drunk woman who is unskilled in the art of talking to people let alone de-escalation techniques, should be doing right now, so I take another sip of water and keep an eye out for glimpses of Silas's shoulder muscles which, again, I do not really mind.

It's really his mouth that I mind, though I also don't mind that, though I do. Maybe it's his brain that's the problem, because that's the part that makes the mouth so irritating, right? Except sometimes the mouth is kind of—

And *fuck* more stuff is happening that I can't see, except this time a woman screams and I can see limbs flailing so I jump to my feet, ready to ...I don't know... and try to see over all the people in my way.

"God*damn* it, Jake," someone shouts over the yelling and

the chair-scraping and all the furniture clattering. "Fuck's sake, he's bleeding."

I cannot see a single fucking thing, and my pulse skyrockets.

"What happened?" I ask the nearest human, alcohol making me brave enough to open my mouth.

"Bar fight," he says, very stoically, pointing at the hubbub in the center. "Jake and Dale got into it again, prolly over Jake's sister."

"No *shit* it was a barfight." I hiss, mostly to myself, wobbling on my toes. "But who—"

Between two heads, I suddenly see Silas pop up, wild-eyed and bloody-nosed.

Before I can think a single thought, he bolts for the back of the bar.

# FOURTEEN

## SILAS

I SHOVE the back door open and the night air hits me like a
damp towel. A shiver riots over my skin and I keep moving,
walking fast. I feel like I'm made of ten thousand sirens. I
feel like my spine has grown thorns and they're wrenching
into my chest with every step. I feel like every person in a
ten-block radius is watching me right now and the second I
turn my back, they'll strike.

I walk past the knot of people smoking in the alleyway
behind the bar and keep walking until there's a stretch of
brick wall bare enough to lean against, and I do. My heart
stutters. I force my fists unclenched and I keep my eyes open
because I can't close them, not now.

Blood trickles over my lips, and I let it. I splay my fingers
on the rough wall behind me, digging the tips into the
masonry and dragging them until it hurts because I need the
pain to anchor me here, now, to the brick and the alley and
the orange streetlight above, the dumpster casting a shadow
below. The people standing around the door and hopefully
thinking I'm just drunk.

It doesn't take long for people to come outside after me. I

don't know how long because my brain is retreating no matter how I fight it and time is the first thing to go, but they come out of the door and look around and spot me, standing there, and they make concerned noises and hustle over to me while I grit my teeth and pray I don't do anything I can't take back.

"My goodness, you're bleeding," says the first one. She's tall and weathered and a little unsteady on her feet. "You okay, honey? That looked like it—"

"Don't touch me," I grit out, and her hand stops halfway to my shoulder and feels a million miles away, like I'm watching her on a black-and-white TV underwater.

"You poor thing," pipes up another voice. "Let's get you back inside and put some ice on that."

Another woman, less wobbly. Prickles wash over my body in waves, the sense that the air itself is watching me and waiting to strike. My skin feels nauseous.

"Please," I say, out of somewhere. "I'm fine."

"Sweetheart, you're not fine," the first woman says, and then her hand is on my shoulder and I scrape my fingertips against the wall, wishing they'd bleed. I need to leave but I'm afraid if I move at all it'll be violent and I can't. I can't. She steps closer. I feel like a fuse, burning low. "Don't worry, I'm a nurse. We need to—"

"He said don't *touch* him, are you fucking deaf?"

Kat's voice plunges through the air like a knife, serrated with anger, and then there she is, suddenly at the other woman's side with her wrist in her hand, yanking it from my shoulder. Right there and a million miles away, on some other planet.

"Excuse me," the woman says. "I'm a medical professional, and this man clearly needs care."

"He needs you to back up and fuck off and he has made

that *abundantly* clear," Kat says, the word *abundantly* loud and slow and pronounced with total, drunk precision. "So how about you *abundantly* do that?"

"It sounds like you've—"

"Shoo!" Kat says. "Go! Begone! *Farewell!*"

Now she's pointing dramatically at the door, and even in my state I can see the way the light glints off her glasses, the line of her bare arm, the way her hair settles around her shoulders like a cloak. Kat crackles. She fizzes. The women look at each other and walk back for the door, past the group of smokers now unabashedly staring in my direction.

"LOOK SOMEWHERE ELSE!" Kat shouts, and they all turn away with a shrug.

She doesn't look any gentler when she swings her attention to me, but she doesn't come closer, either. Kat examines me. She sways a little. She pushes her glasses up with one knuckle, which makes her sway more.

The kernel of my brain that's in this alleyway and not far away on the moon notes that Kat is *drunk.*

"Would it help you to tell me five things you can hear?" she finally asks, and I take my eyes off her. I look at the line of the rooftops, at the light, at the few scattered stars visible above. It doesn't feel like a question that needs an answer so I don't.

"Okay," she says after a minute, and now her voice is less sharp, like it's been sheathed.

Little by little, the adrenaline filters out of my body, leaving me empty. I stop feeling like a cornered animal, all claws and teeth, but when that sensation drains from me it leaves me hollow.

There's a noise to my right. It's Kat. Leaning against the wall. Three feet away, her eyes on me, her expression unreadable.

"Talk to me," I hear myself say.

"About what?"

"Anything. Just talk. Keep me here."

There's a long silence and I think she won't, and the part of my brain that can think again points out that I asked Kat Nakamura, of all damn people, to talk, and then she clears her throat.

"In the fourteenth year of the reign of the Psychopomp Fargrath, he issued an edict that made it illegal for anyone but the Designate himself to own any metal but tin," she starts, her eyes far away, her voice... different. "Needless to say, there was unrest."

She goes on, her voice low, the edge gone but still glinting in the undertones. I have no idea what she's saying—it's not what I expected, I thought I'd hear about her day—but it doesn't matter because I fade in and out of listening, surfacing and sinking. Kat's voice bobs on the surface, outlined by the sun, and I try to let myself float toward it.

"...Heliotroth the Fearless, sworn warrior to Unstead the Merciful, was the first to raise her fist and pledge her banners..."

After a long time, I take a deep breath and shift against the wall and when I look over at her, she stops talking.

"Thanks," I say, mouth dry, voice filled with rust.

"Do you think you can handle a car ride?"

I swallow, my throat sticking together unpleasantly.

"Not with you driving."

"Oh. God. Fuck no."

I nod slowly, head still against the bricks.

"Five more minutes, then," I say, and her eyes trickle down my face: nose, mouth, chin, chest. I realize I can feel the stiff pull of dried blood when I speak.

"Let me grab you some ice," she says. "Your nose is fucked up."

"Drunk guy had elbows," I explain. "Thanks."

"Don't leave."

I give her a thumbs up and try for a charming smile. I think I miss the mark. She leaves and I close my eyes: experimentally at first, but then I leave it.

The worst is over. The worst wasn't even that bad this time, compared to what it's been like before. I'll still be up all night, feeling drained and buzzing and too *aware* to sleep. I still feel like I'm watching the world on a screen, but I didn't break anything this time.

Footsteps, and I open my eyes again. It's not Kat. I wish it were Kat.

Meckler stands a couple feet in front of me, arms crossed. I fight a dangerous, bone-deep prickle, the urge for violence. I smash my knuckles into the brick behind, looking for distracting pain and not finding enough. His face is blank, and then he smirks.

"Still?" Meckler asks.

I don't answer. He fucking knows it already and the only response I want to give him is a fist.

"I would've thought it had been long enough," he goes on.

"Fuck off and die," I say, and my voice manages to sound normal. I mean it.

"No, thank you," he says, and he's about to say something else when the door opens with force and Kat's there, ice pack in one hand.

When she sees him, she *sharpens*. It's the only word that makes sense. Then she smiles with more teeth than I've ever seen.

"Evan!" she says, too loudly, as she comes over. "Great!

I'm so glad you're here, because we *really* need a helpful team player right now who can find us a ride back to Silas's house."

"Then—"

"Thank you *so* much!" she says, squeezing his arm with one hand, unsteady on her feet. "Great job finding us a ride. Your leadership in our company is totally inspiring! Everyone's inside. Door's right there. Synergy!"

She shouts the last word as he walks back toward the door, and then she turns to me.

"Here," she says, and holds out the ice pack. "For the swelling."

The cold reels me in a little, biting against my raw fingertips. I hold it for a second, my thoughts like a cloud trying to twist into a tornado.

"Synergy?" I ask, as I put it to my face.

Kat flops against the wall next to me, sways once, rights herself. If I focus hard enough, she seems real.

"I had to sit through one of his Powerpoints in a meeting today," she says. "It sucked."

We stand there in silence. After five minutes someone comes out with keys, and I follow him to a car.

· · · · ★ ★ ★ ★ ★ · · · ·

I MAKE IT HOME: the back seat, the window open, Kat hovering and careful not to touch me. The sun's down, finally, and the breeze is cool against my face, my shirt wet against my chest, the ice melting and running down my neck, and all of it feels like it's happening to someone else.

And then we're at my house, and we're going up the steps and Kat's using my keys to open the door.

"In," she says as she pushes it open, but at least her voice doesn't sound like a blade any more.

"You're not supposed to," I tell her.

"Supposed to what?"

"Come in. The rules."

She stands there and looks at me. Blinking. Like she's sorting through a card catalog of memory, trying to remember what I'm talking about.

"That one doesn't apply when you're bleeding," she finally says, and points at the door, and I go.

Finally, it's familiar. It's my entryway first and my kitchen to one side, the bathroom to the left, the living room beyond. It's Beast thumping off the couch and meowing as she jogs toward me, fluffy tail jerking. It's nudging my shoes off and leaving them where they are and walking into the kitchen and tossing the ice into the sink, gripping the edge, finally taking a deep breath in the quiet.

I don't feel like my skin might split apart any more, but I feel the echo of it. The writhing, pent-up feeling is gone but I'm still restless, jerky, still feel like I'm watching my life projected on a far-away wall.

"Thanks," I tell Kat. "I'm good now, you can go."

Beast rubs against my ankles, meowing. She's probably hungry.

"Want me to feed the cat?" Kat asks from the doorway, her words floating through the air, tangling and untangling. It takes me a minute.

"Beast."

"I'll feed the beast," she offers. "Where's the cat food?"

Kat feeds her, and every clink and clack in the quiet behind me sends shockwaves down my spine, but I don't turn around because I'm afraid that if I lose my grip on the sink, I'll lose my grip on everything.

Finally it's done, only the wet smacking sounds of Beast eating her dinner, and the kitchen goes still again.

"Quit staring at me," I get out.

"How can I help?"

"I'm fine."

She says nothing, but I can feel her standing across the kitchen from me. Watching, her eyes sharp and dark behind her glasses, like she can slice me open with a look. Waiting for me to—I don't know. Fall to my knees, wailing. Have some sort of Rambo-style flashback and paint my face with dish soap and chocolate sauce. Start throwing dishes. Fly into a rage and go after her with a frying pan.

I wish I could be absolutely certain that I won't.

"I'm gonna shower," I say, and turn away from Kat and her goddamn eyes.

· · * * * ★ ★ ★ * * · ·

THERE'S a knock on the bathroom door and I twitch. My eyes jerk open. I brace myself but the adrenaline is sluggish by now, like someone holding a lighter to the already-singed ends of frayed nerves. They glow but they don't catch, and I think if *I don't answer she'll go away.*

Instead, she knocks again, and a moment later the door clicks open.

"Silas?" Kat asks. She sounds very, very casual.

"I'm in the shower."

"Yeah, it's like Dagobah in here. Are you..." she trails off.

"I'm fine."

"You've been in the shower for forty-five minutes."

Jesus. I thought it had been five, my brain sticky and sluggish and slow to respond.

"I'm very thorough."

136

"That's past thorough and into *scrubbing off your own skin* territory," she says, her voice closer than the doorway.

Anger flashes through me. It comes from nowhere and tears into my chest, full-throated rage snarling to get out, and before I've realized what I'm doing I'm pulling the shower curtain back so hard I nearly pull the rod down. At the last second I snatch the bottom and pull it over myself just enough for decency.

"Get the fuck out of my bathroom," I say, and my voice has a raw, ragged edge to it. I swallow. "I know how to fucking *shower*, for fuck's sake. Jesus."

She's got her hands over her eyes, head turned away.

"I'm not dramatically opening my veins in the tub if that's what you're worried about," I go on, suddenly savage. Suddenly thinking of blood and the smell of gunpowder and a bathroom floor covered in hair and dirt and God knows what else. A bark of ugly laughter escapes me. I'm coming unwound. Fuck. "I'd do a better job than that. You'd hear it."

"I wasn't worried about that," she says, face still averted.

"I don't need you to watch over me," I go on. "The fuck would you do, anyway? You couldn't stop me. You'd be forty-five minutes too late."

Kat takes a deep breath, tilts her head back, eyes still closed.

"At least goddamn look at me," I say. "I'm decent."

She opens one eye, then the other. Her glasses are fogged and smudged, like she's wiped them, her bangs plastered to her forehead and she gives me a long, searching look, trying to control her face.

"Stay there," she says, turns, and leaves.

I slam the curtain shut as hard as I can, the sudden flame of rage already guttering. Fuck. This isn't the worst part but I hate it anyway, the *afterward* where I don't feel incandescent with panic any more, where I stop feeling like a cornered animal, all teeth and claws and unthinking instinct. I just feel like a letter that's been folded too many times, ready to split apart at the seams and of course the person here to witness it is Kat Fucking Nakamura, a pair of scissors in human form.

The door opens again, then closes. I stand there, warmish water hitting the backs of my shoulders and flooding down my body, thinking that maybe if I ignore her she'll leave.

Instead, the shower curtain rustles.

"Here," she says, and when I open my eyes, there's a hand holding a pair of boxer briefs in the shower with me.

"The fuck do you want?" I ask, but it comes out defeated instead of defiant.

"Put them on."

"Would you *please* leave me the fuck alone?"

"No."

She pushes her hand further into the shower. The shorts wave.

I stare at them for another moment, and then I grab them from her hand, muttering curses as I pull them up my wet legs.

"Are you decent?" she asks.

"My dick's not out," I say. "Want to tell me why the fuck—"

The curtain pulls back slightly, and Kat steps into the shower with me, still wearing the knee-length black dress she had on earlier. I take a step back out of surprise, the spray now hitting the bottom of my skull and curling around my neck.

"Is this some kind of bullshit shock therapy you read

about in the *PTSD Gazette?*" I bite out. "Like scaring the hiccups out of me, but for trauma?"

Kat gives me a very skeptical look. Her glasses are off. It might be the first time I've ever seen her glasses off, and she looks oddly naked, defenseless, black already smudging around her dark eyes.

"Would that work?" she asks, one eyebrow up.

"No," I say, in a tone that suggests it's the dumbest question ever asked, because it might be.

"Okay then," she says. She takes a deep breath, her eyes locked on mine. She's squinting. "Can I touch you?"

I don't answer, but she reaches out anyway like she's in slow-motion. Like she's petting a tiger and waiting for it to bite.

When her fingers are an inch from my shoulder, she looks at me, questioning.

After a moment, I nod, and brace myself.

Her fingertips slide over my wet skin, and I'm ready to feel spikes, or thorns, that feeling of total body revulsion I've been fighting for an hour now, but there's nothing. I don't flinch, or jerk away, or fight a wave of nauseous adrenaline. Just her bare skin on mine and with it, a relief so palpable it aches.

"That's okay?" she asks, her dark eyes darting around my face.

"Fine." My voice is a rough whisper.

"Tilt your head back and get your hair under the water," she tells me, her thumb stroking the outer wing of my collar bone. I wonder if she knows she's doing it. "C'mon," she says when I don't move, so I lean back slightly and run my fingers through it like I'm in a damn shampoo commercial.

When I open my eyes again, she's still got one hand on my shoulder—warm, and there, and solid, and *there*—and with the other she's holding a bottle about three inches in front of her face.

"This is shampoo, right?" she asks, glancing over at me. I don't answer her for a moment because everything's gone off-balance: she's in my shower, wearing clothes, ordering me around, asking my help. Touching me.

For some reason, I reach out and take the bottle, checking the label even though I know damn well it's my shampoo. Our wet fingertips touch and that's fine, too. That's nothing.

"Yeah," I confirm, and then she's pouring it into her hand, putting the bottle back, turning toward me.

"C'mere," Kat says. "Close your eyes."

I do.

When she touches me again, it's so gentle I almost don't feel it. She's soft. Careful. She strokes my hair like I'm a newborn kitten, tender and protective. Her fingertips swirl over my scalp until I've got goosebumps covering my whole body in a gentle, pleasant buzz. I think I make a sound. I feel like I'm buried under ten blankets, all made from angel wings. Fuck. I'm gone.

"Silas?" she asks, her voice barely audible over the shower. "This okay?"

I try to nod but I can't make it work right, so I swallow hard and say, "Yes."

We don't talk any more. I think I've lost the capability. I lose time. I lose my place. I couldn't swear that my feet are still on the floor. When she tells me to step back into the spray I do it without a thought, tilting my head back, and I let her stroke my hair clean.

Then her hands are on my face, wet and gentle, brushing over my forehead and bruised nose and my cheeks.

My chin. I wonder if the blood's off now, and then she runs one thumb over my lips, softly as anything.

I'm gentle, too, when I catch her wrist in my hand, eyes still closed. Her skin is warm and slippery and wet, and even though she freezes I can feel the pull of every tendon, the bones beneath the skin.

It hits me, all at once, that Kat's as breakable as anyone. I knew it before but right now, right here, I can *feel* her astonishing vulnerability, all flesh and blood and bone. Alone in the shower with an unstable man who's got a history of violence. Washing his hair. Whatever else Kat is, she's brave.

"Sorry," she says, and I see her say it more than I hear it. I slide my thumb into the hollow of her palm, her pulse under my fingertips.

"Thank you," I say, as she closes her fingers over my thumb, eyes flicking to our joined hands before she looks back at me, and something even more astonishing happens: Kat gives me a quiet half-smile.

"Of course," she says, and I feel like the dust that settles after an earthquake.

# FIFTEEN

## KAT

WHEN I CLOSE the bathroom door behind myself, I have to stand there against the wall for a moment to make sure I'm not shaking, that I'm not having some sort of alcohol-poisoning induced hallucination.

I'm, like, ninety-five percent sure it's not alcohol poisoning. I didn't drink that much, right? Unless I've also blacked out and had four more drinks, or gone into an anxiety-fueled fugue state, which might be possible but seems like it would've happened at least once before this.

My hands aren't shaking. Good. Great. What the hell did I just do?

*That was weird,* I think as I push open the door to Silas's bedroom, no less nervous than the first time I did this fifteen minutes ago. *That was maybe the weirdest thing you've ever done and you've done some real weird shit, Kat.*

Carefully, like I could set off a landmine if I step on the wrong spot, I cross his bedroom to the dresser where I got the boxers he's wearing.

*You made a man get dressed in his own shower so that*

*you could also get in, fully clothed, and bathe him. Have you even heard of a boundary?*

*Silas knows everyone in this town and the second he's in his right mind he's going to start telling everyone about the crazy lady who got into his shower and touched him a bunch and then everyone is going to look at you strangely, all the time, because you'll be Weird Perverted Shower Woman.*

I haven't even gotten to how I was a huge bitch earlier to some nice people who were just trying to help Silas, and also to some people who were just standing there and looking at us.

Oh God. Oh fuck. I yelled at strangers in public. The thought makes me dizzy with panic.

When I reach the dresser I take a slow, deliberate breath, imagine that my runaway thoughts are loose pieces of paper on a desk, and then I sweep them all off. In my mind. It helps, kind of.

Of course, this is also a strange thing to do and I'm not sure if I should do it or run back down the stairs and leave his house forever, like a normal person.

But he seemed okay with it, right? He said I could touch him, and he did as I asked, and when I washed his hair he kept making these soft, rumbling noises that I'm not sure he knew he was making. He kept his eyes closed. He held my wrist. He has a long-healed scar across one side of his ribcage, white but uneven, like he should've gotten stitches and didn't.

I suck in a breath and blow it out, because thinking will only make things stranger, and because the only reason I'm thinking about noises and touches and scars is because I am still *pretty damn drunk.*

"Goddamn it," I whisper to myself, then pull some clothes out of his dresser for him: pajama pants and a t-shirt that seems soft, because I can only imagine him getting in here in his current state and just... standing here, staring at the dresser for a good twenty minutes or something.

Then I look down at myself in my mostly-wet dress, and decide: fuck it. I help myself to a pair of gym shorts with a drawstring and a t-shirt with a soccer ball on it.

That done, I more or less flee back downstairs. The cat— Beast? Did he name his cat Beast? The thing's the size of a horse—is bathing herself on the kitchen table, and I busy myself making tea.

Tea is calming. It is possibly un-drunkening, and it's something I can do to not endlessly replay how I *got into the shower with a half-naked man who did not want me there oh God.*

"You're still here," he says from the doorway.

I jump a mile, one hand flying to my chest like I'm an eighty-year-old with a heart condition.

"Sorry."

"You're fine," I say with lots of dignity. "Um, yeah. I made tea? You had chamomile, which is like... soothing."

For a moment, he doesn't move. He stands there, in the doorway to his kitchen, in plaid pajama pants and the t-shirt I got out for him.

He doesn't lean, or cross his arms, or give me some smirky look like he's got something smart-assed to say. He stands there and looks at me, his gaze oddly naked and sincere and distant, all at once.

After a moment I point at the two mugs on the otherwise-bare counter. Silas's kitchen is shockingly clean. He picks one up and blows across the top, so I take the other.

"What now?" I ask, after a moment.

He's still staring at the opposite wall, and it takes him a moment to drag his gaze back to me.

"You should probably go."

He's right. I'm damp, bedraggled, trampling boundaries, being weird, wearing his clothes, and breaking our agreed-upon rules that I suggested.

"Do you want me to?" I ask.

He doesn't answer, just looks at me and takes a sip of tea. I wince, because I'm sure it's still too hot, but he doesn't react. I let the moment stretch out until I'm sure he's not going to respond.

"What do you usually do now?" I ask next, wrapping one hand around my mug, the ceramic so hot it almost burns. My stomach twists. My heart pounds.

Silas relaxes, leans one hip against the counter, looks at me with an expression I can't read.

"Usually I watch movies all night because I can never sleep afterward," he says, and I nod.

"What movies?" I ask.

· · · · ★ ★ ★ ★ · · · ·

THE ANSWER, turns out, is slasher movies, the gorier and lower-budget the better. We watch something called *Castle Freak*, and then something else called *Invisible Maniac*. After the first, Silas goes into the kitchen and comes back with ice cream, cheez-its, and a jar of peanut butter. After the second he gets us glasses of water.

"You ever seen *Attack of the Killer Tomatoes?*" he asks around midnight.

We've both got our feet on the coffee table, an entire couch cushion separating us.

"Maybe?" I say. I push my glasses up and consider the picture on the screen: an enormous tomato with teeth and...

tentacles? "I watched a lot of kaiju movies with my dad when I was a kid."

"I don't think this one counts as that, but I could be wrong," he says. "I forget what makes the tomatoes kill."

It's definitely not a kaiju flick but it's very fun, or at least the first half is because I wake up to the end credits rolling, the room dark, and Silas staring at the screen like he's not seeing anything. There's a blanket over my lap. I didn't put it there.

After a moment, he turns to face me. My glasses are still on, so I straighten them, staring back, lost for words because I don't have a precedent for this situation. It feels oddly like I'm in college, the only time in your life when falling asleep on a couch during a movie with a virtual stranger seems normal and expected and not like things have taken a weird turn you didn't anticipate.

"Did they stop the tomatoes?" I ask.

"Yeah. Humanity prevailed," he says. The light from the TV flickers over his face, grayscale in the dark: freckles invisible, eyes slate, the hair flopped over his forehead barely brown. His nose is swollen and there are deep bruises under his eyes, semi-circles black in the darkness. I keep my hands to myself.

"Do you have a concussion?"

"Nah," he says. "Didn't hit me that hard."

"Are you sure?"

"I know what they feel like."

I don't answer, but I pull my legs onto the couch, fold them under me until I'm on my knees, facing him. Silas watches, his head on the back of the couch, the lines of his neck long and shadowed as they point to the divot between his collarbones.

He doesn't move as I lean forward, one hand on the

146

cushion between us, the other on the back of the couch, awkward and slightly off-balance. I stare into his eyes, feeling like I'm stuck in a dream, like nothing that happens tonight will count in the morning.

I get closer than I should. Silas doesn't flinch, doesn't so much as blink as I study him up close, checking for—I'm not sure. That his pupils are the same size, wide and black in the dark. That his eyes are moving together. That I can be this close without him drawing away, closing off, pulling back.

That I could kiss him.

The thought bubbles up from the depths of my mind like air bubbles escaping an ancient wreck. Something that ought to have sunk that hasn't. It's not the time or the place. It's not within the rules we agreed to, the rules I demanded, the rules I wrote down, the rules we went over with a fine-toothed comb standing in the fluorescent lights of my office.

But I could kiss him, and he might not mind. He kissed me after *Sweet Caroline*, after all. He kissed the hell out of me after *Sweet Caroline*, with tongue and teeth and something that felt a little like desire if I don't think about it too much, but that kiss was a kiss clearly within the guidelines: in front of people—in front of Evan—an ulterior motive at hand.

I'm still staring into his eyes. He's still staring back, his face open and bruised. I swallow hard and trace my finger across a black semi-circle, the thin skin soft under my fingertip. His lips part. I know what I want, temptation hammering through me, and I know not to do it.

I half expect something with sharp teeth and a long tail to swim across the surface. I half expect to fall in and drown. But it's just the two of us, in the dark, staring at each other.

"I think you're okay," I finally say, pulling my hand away. As if I'm qualified to make that call.

"I told you."

"I had to check."

Amusement wanders across his face, and I pull back, sitting heavily on my half of the couch as something like regret slithers through me, and I ignore it.

"Of course you did," he says, and then turns away, gestures at the TV. "What next?"

· · · · · ★ ★ ★ · · · · ·

WHEN I WAKE UP AGAIN, the TV is on but the screen is still and I can't make out a single thing on it. I shift on the couch, ready to find my glasses, only to realize that Silas's head is in my lap and my fingers are tangled in his hair, my other hand draped across his shoulder.

I freeze. My breath catches, and the familiar shards of panic prickle at my chest, because what if he wakes up right now? What if he lifts his head and looks at me and asks what the hell I'm doing, touching him?

What if he finds me stroking his shoulder and winding my fingers through his hair and wants to know why I thought I could touch him, why I thought I could stay the night here watching movies?

Why the *fuck* I thought I could get into the shower with him and wash his hair and order him around, why I took advantage of him in an obviously compromised state?

It doesn't matter that he invited me to stay or that he put his head in his lap, not me, or that at any moment he could have thrown me out and we both know it. Anxiety doesn't give a shit about reality; mine, at least, feeds on long-learned fears and uncertainty.

I tilt my head against the back of the sofa and take a deep breath. I don't count down all the way but I push my thoughts out instead of in: fabric under my palm, the ends of his hair curling around my fingers, the coffee table hard under my heels.

As carefully as I can, I move my fingers through his slightly-too-long hair, like he needs a haircut but has been putting it off. I drift my thumb through the shorter hairs curled at the back of his neck and he moves in his sleep, nudging his face against my thigh.

I very carefully don't think about anything besides this exact moment, about how human touch is healing. A comfort and nothing else.

It takes a long time, but I fall back asleep.

# SIXTEEN

## SILAS

I WAKE up sweaty and uncomfortable. My neck hurts and my back hurts, a twinge in the place where I've got two herniated discs, my right knee starting to protest and oh, fuck, I'm using Kat as a pillow.

Double fuck, it's her leg. Her inner thigh. My face is on bare skin, the hem of the shorts ridden up and thank God, thank *God* I'm facing her knee and not the other way because Christ on a waffle, she'd behead me. Which she might anyway. After last night. After waking up like this. Jesus. Fuck.

I sit up, disoriented even though I know where I am. My tongue feels too big for my mouth. My hands feel oddly far away and I swallow hard, trying not to remember what happened last night.

*At least I wasn't drunk*, I tell myself. *At least I tried to end the fight instead of starting it.*

Neither has always been the case, but it's hard to feel accomplished right now, in the half-dark of right-before-sunrise, trying to fight back the rising tide of anger and panic and disgust at myself after sleeping on the person who had to take care of me last night.

The feeling wraps around me like a tentacle—*what's wrong with you? It's been years*—and I take a deep, shuddering breath before I open my eyes and look at Kat, praying she's still asleep and can't see me like this, still inches from falling apart.

She is, and thank fucking God because I can only imagine the look she'd give me, the way her eyes would flick up and down, first with derision and then—worse—with pity. The tentacle around my chest tightens and I swallow, rubbing a hand over my mouth, looking at her, trying to weigh my options.

There's a red spot on her leg where I was sleeping and despite myself, it snags my attention, my gaze hanging there like a scarf on a bramble. It's barely visible in the pre-dawn, but I can't tear my eyes away: an irregular red spot on the inside of one thigh, midway between knee and hip. A swirl where my ear was. Tiny indentations where my stubble grew in overnight—

No. That's ridiculous. It's too dark to see detail like that so I must be imagining hair-width divots marring her skin. Her soft, pliable skin, where I took advantage of her, of the relationship we're pretending to have by making her take care of me—

*Fuck.*

I grit my teeth and swallow hard and stand. My right knee and hip protest and there's a familiar twinge in my lower back, but I get upright. Kat's half-sprawled on my couch, sitting up and turned sideways, bottom leg bent under her, cheek against the back of the couch. Last night she fell asleep in the middle of a movie so I took her glasses off and put them on the coffee table.

I grab an ugly fleece blanket and spread it over her lap gently as I can, removing that red spot from my line of vision and preserving the rest of her modesty. I wonder if I should wake her up and tell her that her chore is over and she can leave, or whether it would be kinder to let her sleep.

I kissed her last night. Unplanned. I stood up on a shitty karaoke stage and sang *Sweet Caroline* and the whole room sang along with me, a tidal wave of drunken adoration and camaraderie, and when the song ended they cheered and shouted and I let it buoy me to where she sat, and I kissed her. And she kissed me back. And I spent the next thirty minutes wanting to do it again.

But then I had *an episode* and she had to calm me down and get me home and Jesus, she had to wash my hair and dress me and make me tea and the second she wakes up, she's going to regret the kiss. She's going to regret having tied herself to me. She's going to wish she'd conned someone else into being her boyfriend for the month, because if there's one man who's not making a single damn person jealous, it's me.

I put both hands over my face and squeeze until my bruises hurt.

"MROWW!" Beast shouts, and I look up, startled. She's pacing back and forth, between me and her food bowl like some unholy union of muppet and lynx.

"Shh," I tell her as I walk to the kitchen, glad to find that my body still works even though I still don't quite feel like I'm part of it.

"RRRRAWMR," she responds, tail twitching, because Beast doesn't give a single shit for my mental state if her food bowl is empty, and I've never loved a creature more in my entire life.

I would die for Beast. I would stand in front of an eighteen wheeler for her. I'd face down a pack of wolves. There aren't many people I'd say that for—my best friend, Levi; my sister, June; Gideon, Javier, and Wyatt—but I would defend this cat from anything, and she doesn't care. Beast has never pitied me. She's never been disappointed in me, or disdainful. She's never wondered why I can't man the hell up and get my shit together.

Beast just wants breakfast. I wish I'd gotten a cat a decade ago instead of last year.

I go about my routine like an automaton: water, coffee, phone. Levi and Gideon texted, Levi to say that I can come over, I can always come over, Gideon to say he heard my nose got fucked up and he hopes I'm okay. From him, it's a love letter.

I skip the gym. I drink my coffee black because to do otherwise feels too hard. I scroll through my phone by the light over my stove, reading work emails and trying to fight the rising waters of panic and anger and self-disgust.

But you can't stop a flood once it's coming. You can only mitigate the damage. All the tools I've learned are nothing but sandbags, so heavy to lift that they don't always feel worth the effort.

Beast finishes her breakfast, gives herself a bath, and leaves the kitchen. I try a sandbag—breathe in for four, hold for four, out for six—and it doesn't do shit. A few minutes later I hear rustling and see that Kat's now stretched full-length on the couch, Beast in loaf position on the coffee table, staring at her face from a foot away.

Seriously, a whole pack of wolves for that creep.

Before I know what I'm doing I find myself pulling the blanket over Kat and giving Beast a few ear scritches. She blinks slowly, which I've been told is a sign of affection. Sure. I wonder if the same is true of Kat, if the way she

153

stared at me last night was *something*, when I was certain she was going to kiss me between bad movies but then she didn't, just declared me okay.

*Of course she wasn't going to,* I think. *Not after she had to wash your hair.*

Now it's a flash flood, a burst dam, the panic and anger rushing in with a roar, threatening to drown me. The tentacle's back, squeezing me, threatening to pull me into the depths.

Fuck. Fuck. *Fuck*. I'm stripped down to a handful of ugly words to match the ugly feeling, the revulsion and self-disgust coming on hard and God, I have to leave. I need to get out of here, go to Wildwood, spend the day finishing the paving stones around the firepit and collapsing onto my camp bed after dark because I can't be here when she wakes up.

Kat's an adult. She'll be fine. But if I have to see the disappointment on her face when she wakes up, if I have to see *pity*, I'm not sure I can take it.

I get dressed. I run a comb through my hair, not that it does anything. I order an Uber since my truck's still at the bar, brush my teeth, pour my coffee into a travel mug. I write her a quick note. I get my phone and my wallet and I'm almost free, one hand on the doorknob, when there's a rustle behind me.

"Silas?" she says, my name slurred with sleep.

I stop. I could run, but she'd come after me. I stare at the paint on the door in front of my eyes, because I can't turn around and look at her.

"Are you—" she says, and then stops short. I can hear more rustling.

"Coffee table," I tell the door. "Next to the cat, I think."

A brief pause.

"Uh, hi," she says. "Can I have those? Thanks." She clears her throat. "Are you going? Why are you staring at the door?"

For now, she sounds more confused than angry.

"Yeah. Sorry. I've gotta be somewhere. I left a note."

"This just says *I'm leaving*," Kat says, after a moment.

"It's not a lie."

"Wait," she says, and fabric whispers and rustles, the sound of her standing. I wonder if her thigh is still red where I slept on her. I wonder if she hates me for it.

"What?" I ask. I close my eyes even though I feel like I'm drowning in panic and self-revulsion and the fear borne of those two things and of the fact that after all these years, after all the therapy and treatment and support groups and meditation and self-help, I still feel this way.

Now she's walking toward me. Stopping a few feet away. I don't turn around. I can't see her see me like this.

"Are you at least okay?" she finally asks, bewildered.

The flood churns around me, tentacles flailing, but I've been here before. I know this monster. I know it well enough to hold it back for the next few minutes and take a breath and make myself sound as if I haven't got a care in the world, like I've practiced again and again.

"Of course I'm fine," I say, like I'm about to start laughing. I smile at the door. "Never better."

"You got hit in the face and slept on the couch," she says.

"Happens," I tell her.

"Silas," she says.

"That's my name, don't wear it out."

"*Silas.*"

"What?"

"Turn around."

I don't.

"Please?"

I'm fucked if I do and fucked if I don't, so I do.

Kat's standing there, arms over her chest, hair wild. She's wearing my t-shirt and it's too big on her, off-center, half her collarbone exposed. She's got pink lines on the side of her face and the moment she sees me, her eyebrows go up.

"You look like shit," she says, not gently. "Do you want some ice or—"

"I want you to leave me the fuck alone," I say, far more honestly than I'd meant to.

Her eyes search me for a long moment, drifting from my head to my chest to my feet like she's cataloging every flaw and tallying them up.

"What is your *problem?*" she finally asks, the words dripping from her lips like tar.

I swallow my first response—my first five responses—and lean against the door. I make myself smile again. No more fuck ups.

"Right now it's that I've got somewhere else to be and you're making me late," I tell her. My accent sounds like biscuits and gravy with a side of cheese grits, always deeper when I smile too much.

"Where have you got to be at six-fifteen on a Saturday morning?" she asks.

"I wasn't aware that you needed to know all my appointments."

"Were you going to leave me asleep on your couch in your house with your giant murder cat watching me?" she asks. "And if you say you left me a note again, I swear to God—"

"She's not a murder cat."

"She's the size of a goddamn Golden Retriever!"

"Doesn't make her a murderer."

I get a long, flat glare.

"My spine is in a knot from sleeping on your couch last night while you were obviously having a bad time and you weren't going to wake me up and tell me you were leaving?"

"You want a parade?"

"Fuck you. I want to know you're okay before you waltz out of here like everything is hunky dory and nothing ever happened."

Her anger feels like knife points against my skin, and I lean into it because it's not pity. I don't know if Kat's capable of something soft as pity; it didn't seem she was all those years ago in college, and it doesn't seem that way right now. Even last night—whatever happened then, the shower, the couch—didn't have the ugly pastel tinge of pity to it.

The realization is pure relief, like sudden sunlight on bare skin, because Kat's sharp, crackling anger feels a thousand times better than baby-soft words ever could.

"I'm all right," I tell her, and for the first time since I woke up, it's almost true.

"Convince me."

"I will be."

She says nothing, just gives me one of her long, searching looks before she walks toward me. Slow and deliberate, like I'm a tiger escaped from a cage.

Not a tiger. Something more ancient, all instinct and teeth. A crocodile. She stops a few feet away, looks up at me.

"I don't know what you think I'm going to do or who I'm going to tell but I probably won't," she says. "I'm not an asshole."

I snort and feel myself smile, my first real smile of the morning.

"I'm not *that* kind of asshole," Kat amends, rolling her eyes. She's smiling, too, the tiniest movement of her lips.

"I'm going to Levi's," I say. "I'm not quite okay yet, but I will be."

"The guy with the air raid siren crows?"

"They don't usually sound like that."

Kat makes a skeptical face.

"If I have your permission," I amend sarcastically.

"Oh, fuck off," she says. I grin and she frowns, then shakes her head, and then she's trying not to smile. "Sorry. That was the wrong response."

"Telling me to fuck off?"

"No, all of it. I stand by telling you to fuck off. I know I should be nicer but that's not—it's not always my first impulse," she says, dark eyes looking away from me. It feels like half apology and half confession.

"I'm tired of nice," I tell her. "I'd rather have—"

*I'd rather have what you give me.* The thought runs into me headlong, stops my mouth.

"—honest. Unvarnished. I don't know. Just not fucking *nice.*"

"You probably shouldn't encourage me," she says.

"Why, because you were holding back before?"

Kat makes a face, and I have the urge to—I don't know. Kiss her, yes, but take her face in my hand again. Feel her cheekbone under my thumb. Wind her hair between my fingers, see if I can get her eyes to close in a moment of unguarded familiarity.

Instead I lean against the door, put my hands in my pockets.

"I'm about to get a ride back to my truck at the bar," I tell her. "C'mon, I'll give you a ride home."

She regards me for half a second more, like she has to process something, and then she nods.

"Sure," she finally says. "Thanks."

· · · · · ★ ★ ★ · · · · ·

"KAT STAYED OVERNIGHT?" Levi asks. He's got his hands on his hips, both of us facing the forest that surrounds his house. It's a hot day but cooler here, in the woods on the side of a mountain.

"Yeah. We watched movies," I say. "*Attack of the Killer Tomatoes.*"

"That one's a classic."

"Is it?"

"I've heard of it, at least," he says. There's a moment of silence where Levi weighs his words, as if he's hopping from rock to rock across a creek and wants to keep his feet dry.

It's a longer silence than usual.

"She do okay?" he finally asks.

It's not the question I was expecting, and I take a moment to answer. Levi's habit for deliberation wears off on me, sometimes.

"Yeah," I say, still looking at trees, the hot August breeze moving the leaves. I wonder if it'll storm later. Levi would know. "I guess she did."

I get an odd look, then, maybe the hint of a smile behind his beard.

"That's good," he says.

"You looking to get rid of me?"

"Always," he says, and the hint of a smile deepens. "Maybe I needed to find you a woman who could take over."

"She's not—" I almost say *not a woman*, but that's nonsense, and what I really mean is *not a woman the way you mean when you say that*. "She was just being..."

Not *nice*.

"Diligent," I finish. "I did her a favor last weekend."

There's that odd look again, and I'm not sure I want to

deal with it so I point at the forest where there's an old, downed log about thirty feet in.

"Start there?" I ask, and Levi rubs his hands together.

"Good as anywhere," he says, and we enter the woods.

I told Levi the truth about Kat because I've never bothered lying to Levi. Even though he did it to me, once, because he was fucking my sister and thought I didn't know and wouldn't find out.

Things were a little weird between us for a while, but I went to a lot of therapy and finally told Levi the truth once I figured it out myself: I was never really worried for my sister, I was angry that she might take my best friend away. We eventually talked it out and I officiated their wedding a few years ago, so I guess I approve of the union.

For a while, we work in old, comfortable silence, clearing fallen branches and dead wood from the forest around Levi's house and stacking it in a pile. With him, I never feel the urge to fill the silence. Maybe it's because I know he doesn't need it. Maybe it's because, by now, we've said pretty much everything there is to say to each other.

"You're over college, then?" Levi asks, nearly half an hour later, as he stomps around the trunk of a fallen tree, surveying it.

I nudge the trunk with one boot instead of answering.

"If she's sleeping on your couch," he goes on. "That was her, right?"

"That was her."

I complained to Levi a dozen years ago when I was in Kat's Introduction to Earth Sciences class, and I complained about her again the day we shared an elevator in our office building and I realized she'd moved to Sprucevale. I didn't think I complained that much, but maybe I'm wrong.

"I admit to liking her better now," he says, then points.

"Grab that end, I think we can get it out without having to saw anything."

I do as he says, lifting with my legs even though it's not that heavy because my back isn't very forgiving these days. Together, we maneuver it out of the forest and onto the growing pile, and I wait until we're done to speak.

"You didn't like her before?"

"I wasn't inclined to," he says, shrugging. "You didn't exactly endear her to me."

"That's not—" I start, and then stop. "Just because we didn't get along."

Levi looks at me like he's waiting for me to say more, but I don't. I'm still scattered, sleepless; the hard work of clearing brush is helping, but I'm unusually lost for words. I'm especially lost for *this* word, something to describe the subtle wrongness in hearing Levi say he doesn't like Kat.

"You did once call her *the ruthless fucking architect of your goddamn destruction*," he says as we head back into the woods.

"I was probably drunk."

"You were."

"She's a little less ruthless now," I say, even though I'm not sure it's true, and it gets an amused snort from Levi.

I don't remember saying it—I was drunk, likely blackout —but I believe I did. Back then I thought Kat Nakamura was the worst part of the worst time in my life.

My first semester of college I was twenty-five, older than almost everyone else in my classes, and fresh out of six years in the Marines. My classmates had study parties and called their parents to ask how to do laundry; I had nightmares most nights and panic attacks if I couldn't sit in the back row of a class. I stayed drunk most of the time to cope, could only sleep when I blasted sitcoms on the TV, screamed at my housemates for playing *Call of Duty*. I kept getting in fights. I woke up places I shouldn't have been: a stranger's front porch, the roof of a building I didn't know, the front yard of a frat house.

And three times a week, I had to suffer through Introduction to Earth Sciences at nine o'clock in the morning, taught by Kat Nakamura, who was more icicle than human. Her attendance policy was Draconian. God forbid you miss a homework assignment or need to make up a quiz: the rules were there for a reason, she told me more than once. The worst was asking questions, the way she'd look at me for daring to do such a thing in her classroom. Her answers, slow and pointed, like I was some sort of moron.

She never gave an inch. She never let me redo a single assignment, or re-take a quiz, or have an extension, things other professors did without a second thought. Kat seemed bound and determined to ride me into hell, even more so after I missed the deadline to drop her class.

I did try to bribe her into a passing grade by taking a six-pack of beer to her office hours once. Didn't work. One of the dumber things I've ever done. It wasn't until it was all over I realized she was still an undergrad.

Later, Levi and I sit on his front porch and drink iced tea. I'm covered in sweat and dirt but it feels like something's been scoured out of me, like the faint rattle and buzz in my bones is gone.

"You staying?" he asks.

"I'll be all right."

"You sure? You know you can."

"I'm not sure I'll survive another night on a couch," I tell him, and he laughs.

The sun goes down. My sister June comes back home and joins us, trading gossip and news and idle chatter in the warm August night. I drive home in the quiet, get home to the quiet, shower in the quiet. I find myself thinking about Kat in those places: my passenger seat, my living room, my shower.

I have a hazy, sleep-dulled memory from last night: on the couch, my head in her lap, her fingers stroking my hair. I'm not sure if it's real or invented, dream or reality.

I fall asleep thinking of it anyway.

# SEVENTEEN

## KAT

"I'VE BEEN THINKING," Silas says the next afternoon as he starts his truck. I click my seatbelt into place and as the engine turns over, the air conditioning blasts me right in the face.

"Sounds dangerous."

"Great joke. Original," he says, giving me a broad grin. "We've got an agreement, and we've got rules. What we don't have is a plan of attack."

With a flourish, he pulls a slim manila folder from where it was stuck between the seats and hands it to me.

"If this is a literal plan of literal attack I don't think I should look at it, for courtroom reasons," I tell him as I take it.

"The plan is literal, the attack is figurative," he says, pulling out of the parking spot in front of my apartment.

"So when I open this I'm not going to see a map of our office building with, like, sniper vantage points and routes of egress," I say.

He shoots me a look.

"Or whatever a battle plan looks like," I go on.

"Have you ever even seen a war *movie?*"

I think for a moment.

"*Mulan?*" I say. "Oh, and *Star Wars*, of course. That one's got *war* right there in the title."

"Then surely, you've noticed that battle plans rarely fit onto an eight-and-a-half-by-eleven sheet of paper," Silas says. "Let me know when you're ready to have a conversation."

I look from him to the manila folder and try to act like this isn't a little jarring. That I'm not currently somewhat jarred by the difference between the quiet, subdued man who said two words on the drive home early yesterday morning before saying goodbye with the softest kiss I've ever had, and the guy full of loud cheer and blatant charm and effortless bravado.

Then I shove those thoughts aside because apparently I've got a battle plan to look at, and open the folder.

Inside is a schedule that covers the next three weeks. It's beautifully formatted, like he used a Word document template for it, with a header that says *The Dating Plan* and underneath that, a line that says *Objectives: convince partners at Hayward and Marshall that our relationship is serious; inspire jealous rage and subsequent penitence in Evan Meckler.*

"What?" I ask, even though I clearly know *what*.

"You can't start a mission without a memo," he says, a smile in his voice. "I'd've made a PowerPoint, but this seemed better."

Below the heading and the objective is an itinerary. Each entry, starting with today, has a time, a place, an activity overview, and an objective.

Today's reads:

**Sunday, 5pm: Burnley County Agricultural Fair**
**Activities:** see animals, eat funnel cake, ride Ferris wheel.
**Objective:** present selves to wider community as happy, functional couple.

"Did you plan dates?" I ask, still confused that Silas has not only used bullet points, but mixed serif and sans serif fonts to pleasing effect.

"All tentative," he says, shrugging. "If we get better intel about Meckler's movements then obviously, we're positioned to pivot on a dime and re-strategize, but it's a guide to follow in the absence of better information."

"Intel," I echo. "About Evan's movements."

"Up until now, we've been winging it," he says. "And I think we've got a better chance of making the bastard crawl if we stay on top of things. Instead of overhearing that he's considering the county fair and guessing when he might want to go, we choose whereabouts and activities that are likely to put us and our very happy love affair directly in his path."

I scan the schedule: *Coffee Outing, Mountain Grind, 10am. Lunch, LouAnn's, noon.* There are dinners, happy hours, breakfasts, a movie. No: a *play*. An art show. The last thing, on Labor Day weekend, is labeled *Hayward & Marshall Soirée: Cocktail Attire Suggested.*

"How do you know where he's going to be?" I finally ask.

"I don't," he shrugs, both hands on the wheel, eyes on the road. "Those are based on his movements for the week he's been here. Obviously they're not much more than guesses, but I think we've got some solid starting points."

"Have you been tracking him?" I say, then turn toward

him in alarm. "Jesus, you didn't put a tracker or something on his—"

"No," he laughs, and flashes me a grin. "Though I could, if you wanted. It's not hard."

"Please don't."

"These days you don't even have to know the right people," he goes on, like I said nothing. "They market them to civilians who lose their keys, and I'm told that just about anyone can strip the security features."

I take a deep breath and close my eyes, shivering a little in the cool air blasting from the vents.

"Silas," I say. "Don't stalk my ex-fiancé."

"If you insist," he says, and lets it drop.

I peruse the schedule once more, simultaneously delighted and... not horrified, but taken aback. On the one hand, I'm a little surprised that Silas is capable of this much planning, forethought, and care. On the other hand, this is all in the service of emotionally manipulating someone else, and even though I'm pretty sure that Evan is evil and deserves whatever we do to him, that's weird.

I feel a little like I'm looking at some kind of battle plan. Like each coffee date is a sniper lookout, each dinner a tank rolling through town, the whole thing laid out with a precision and directness that make me surprised it doesn't read *0600: Caffeine Duty.*

"Why do you hate him?" I finally ask.

Silas is quiet for a moment too long, staring out the windshield as he drives. I wait.

"Because he's a dick," he says.

I don't say anything, just watch him. He licks his lips. His hands tighten on the steering wheel, his forearms flexing under the soft reddish-brown hairs, the scattered almost-freckles. The white spots of a few old scars.

"We were in Afghanistan together," he goes on, after a moment, eyes locked on the road. "And Meckler... was a dick. Did the bare minimum, like was above work. He'd steal shit out of care packages from back home. He'd find pictures of other guys' wives and girlfriends and look at them."

"Ah."

Silas clears his throat. "*Those* pictures."

"I see," I say, definitely not blushing. I don't ask whether Silas ever got pictures or who they might have been from, because I have no interest whatsoever in knowing.

"Nobody was sorry that he didn't re-enlist. He was an asshole who always got away with it, you know?"

"And that's why you made me a very nicely formatted itinerary and suggested a tracking device," I say. "Because he took your peanut butter cups and looked at naked pictures he wasn't supposed to?"

"Levi's mom made me hand pies sometimes," he says. "And she'd have to ship them special, in a cooler, and pay extra for two-day delivery, and he stole three. *Three.* I didn't mind sharing, but the bastard stole them and then lied to me about it with crumbs on his face."

His hands get tighter on the steering wheel, tight enough that his biceps bunch beneath the sleeves of his t-shirt. His face looks like a mask. I'm not even sure he's seeing the road.

"And," he starts, after a pause, his voice hard. "A couple years after I got out, another buddy of mine, someone we'd served with... died. Michael Hernandez. And since Hernandez and I.." Silas trails off again, staring ahead like he's made of stone. "It fell to me to make those calls," he finally says.

He swallows convulsively, the cords in his neck standing out.

"And when I told Meckler, he just snorted and said he was surprised that Hernandez had lasted this long."

"I'm sorry," I whisper, my stomach clenching, my head spinning.

Did that happen when I knew Evan? When we were dating? Was it before? I don't want to believe it of someone I agreed to marry, but I do. I believe every word.

"And he wouldn't let me post my eulogy to our Facebook group," Silas goes on, the words coming faster now. "He ran it—runs it, I guess, I left—and after the funeral I tried to post and that *fucking* bastard deleted it because he said it didn't honor the spirit of the other fallen warriors, and I know how fucking petty it sounds to complain about Facebook bullshit, but—"

He exhales hard, pushes a hand through his hair.

"But there it is. I'm still pissed."

It's more about Afghanistan than I ever heard from Evan. Even though we dated for eighteen months and I spent plenty of those nights in his bed, he never talked about it, not even if I asked. He had nightmares sometimes, when he'd wake up shouting and wild-eyed, but he'd fling off the covers and stalk out of the room to go play video games. The few times I tried following him he nearly bit my head off.

I wonder, now, in this truck with the air conditioning on full blast and the two-lane road unfurling in front of us, the sunlight strobing through the trees, if I failed him.

"He broke up with me at our wedding," I say, my eyes on the curve of the road.

There's a moment of heavy silence.

Then: "*At* your wedding?"

"Yup," I confirm, and look through the passenger side window because Silas is right, it's ridiculous, straight out of an overwrought soap opera. It's been a year but the shame of it feels like it was yesterday: to be the girl jilted at the altar, the girl who wasn't worth dumping in private.

Silas makes a noise that might be a growl. Maybe it's the car.

"It happened when I came in to walk down the aisle," I tell the window. "He was already at the altar, all the guests stood, and instead of smiling when he saw me he shook his head and walked out. In front of the two hundred guests he'd wanted to invite."

It sounds simple when I put it like that, as if anything is over that fast. It wasn't simple. It took hours: the confused guests, my aunts rushing me back to the dressing room, petting my hair and telling me that all men get nerves. Telling me that surely he'd see reason and come back and want to marry me after all, as if that were my concern. As if I'd still marry someone who talked me into standing in front of two hundred people to exchange vows and then ran.

The wedding wasn't quite the worst part. The worst part was the next Monday, when we still had to work together and I had too much pride to call in sick.

Silas swallows hard, his hand still white-knuckled on the steering wheel. He takes a deep breath.

"You know, I can change our schedule," he says, trying for light-hearted and not quite making it. "There's still time to replace coffee dates with sniper vantage points."

"I don't want to go to jail," I point out.

"We could get away with it."

"Forensics are *very* good these days."

He grins. He actually grins.

"This is Sprucevale," he says. "Sometimes I'm amazed they've accepted the science of fingerprints."

"Silas."

"I could hide a body," he says. "I wouldn't even tell you where. Courtroom reasons."

"I'm sure they'd still tie me back to it," I point out.

We come out of the forest and there's the fair: rides spinning and whirling above a yellow-green field, half-baked in the August sun. We park in the part of the field designated for cars, between two giant trucks. My glasses fog with the humidity when I hop out, and I have to wipe them on the hem of my dress.

When I put them back on, Silas is watching me, his hands in the pockets of his shorts. He's wearing a blue t-shirt that's a little snug around the arms and doesn't quite match his eyes, the sun glinting red in his hair. He watches me as I walk toward him, feet whispering through the dry grass. Up close, under the brightness of the August sun, he's closer than ever to having freckles.

"Ready to present selves to wider community as happy, functional couple?" I ask, and it gets a smile that reaches all the way to his eyes, his head tilting back slightly, a perfect, happy, golden picture. There's a wiggle of pleasure inside me at the knowledge that *I* did that. *My* goofy joke.

"Ready if you are," he says, and holds out his hand, and I take it.

· · · · · ★ ★ ★ ★ · · · ·

"I CAN'T BELIEVE we missed the Prettiest Cow Contest," I say an hour later, nodding at the whiteboard with the day's events on it.

"You're not supposed to call *Miss Blue Ridge* that any more."

"I wasn't!" I protest, shooting Silas a quick glare. "Look, it's right there, *Prettiest Cow*—you're a dick."

He's grinning at me, smile lines sunk into his cheeks, crinkles in the corners of his blue eyes.

"I would *never*," I tell him, lifting my chin and looking back at the white board as I take another bite of cotton candy.

"Just because you don't approve of beauty contests doesn't mean you've got to be unkind about it," he goes on, sounding quite pleased with himself.

"Who says I don't approve?" I ask, firmly tamping down any urge I might have to smile. "Maybe I was Miss Lovely Fairfax five years running. You don't know."

I can feel him turn his head to look at me, his hand adjusting in mine. Our palms are sweaty—my entire body is sweaty, it's at least ninety degrees out in the August heat even though it's past six in the evening—but it's not quite as bad as I might have imagined.

"Okay," he says. "Kat, were you Miss Lovely Fairfax five years running?"

He reaches over and takes a hunk of my cotton candy, popping it into his mouth, then briefly sucking his fingertips to get the sugar off. I watch half a second longer than strictly necessary.

"No," I admit, holding the cotton candy further away from him. "I'd look terrible as a blond, so I knew I didn't stand a chance."

That gets a huff of laughter from him, as if my hair's the sole reason I wasn't a beauty queen and not, you know, also everything else about me.

"Then we're not seeing the pretty cows *or* the pretty ladies," he says, and goes for the cotton candy again, but I pull it away. "C'mon."

"No," I insist. "Get your own."

"I don't want my own, I just want one more bite of—"

"I want *all* the bites of mine."

I bite down on the inside of my lip to keep my face serious, even as Silas's eyes sparkle at me like sunlight on the surface of water.

"Fine," he says, pretending to give up. "You want to visit the chicken tent or the livestock pavilion? Those seem to be our remaining options."

I take a bite from the blue side of the cotton candy, holding his eyes as I chew and swallow.

"Is there anything that won't get fur or feathers stuck in my snack?" I ask when I'm finished.

"Not much," he says. "It's the Burnley County Agricultural Fair, most things have fur or feathers."

"Except Miss Blue Ridge."

"Depends on the year."

I take another bite, staring him down, determined not to laugh because the grumpier I act, the more he tries to prod me into smiling and secretly, I kind of like it.

"There's not a giant watermelon somewhere?"

"Why would there be a giant watermelon?"

Another bite.

"Because it's a county agricultural fair? Isn't that what they're for, showing off your giant watermelons and your overgrown hogs and your award-winning banana cake?"

"First, quit acting like you didn't grow up a couple hours from here in the exact same state as me," he says. "And second, if you wanted to see giant melons, we should've gone to the Miss—"

"You're the worst boyfriend I have *ever* had," I tell him, and he laughs before his face goes suddenly serious.

"Speaking of bad boyfriends," he says, voice going low as he levels a gaze over my head. I turn and follow it, scouring the crowd, heart suddenly thumping because if it's Evan

173

that means it's time to *act*, so I should probably go ahead and mash my face against Silas's right now to get it over—

Then Silas swipes a huge chunk of pink cotton candy, laughing.

"Dammit!" I hiss. There's a gouge in the pink half, and I gesture at it as if enraged. "Look, now it's uneven."

"Here," he says, shoving the rest of his misbegotten chunk into his mouth. "I can—"

"No!" I yelp, yanking the cotton candy as far from him as I can get it, given that we're still holding hands. "This is—"

"Ex*cuse* me," a woman's voice says.

I turn to realize that I nearly whacked someone in the face, and all the blood in my body rushes to my face.

"Oh," I gasp, pulling my arm in. "Shit, I didn't—I mean, sorry?"

Her lips thin and she takes a deep breath, looking at me like I'm a cross between a garden pest and a skateboarding teen.

"So sorry, ma'am," Silas says, and there he is, ducking around me, the smile on his face perfectly combining contrition and handsomeness. "That was my fault. I got a little carried away. Apologies."

I swear, I watch her deflate, and she nods.

"Just watch what you're doing?" she says, shoots me a final glare, and walks off. I clear my throat, take a demure bite of cotton candy, and exchange looks with Silas. Together, we start walking along the well-trodden dirt lane of the fair, a few clumps of near-dead but very brave grass still poking up here and there from the reddish ground.

I wonder what it's like to be Silas. To be able to smile and suddenly have people like you, or at least not bite your head off. To just... do whatever you want and then be forgiven for it so long as you apologize and say ma'am. The same words from my mouth never seem to quite have the same effect.

Maybe it's the resting bitch face I've been assured I have. Maybe it's old-fashioned misogyny, or casual racism, or a fun mix of all three. I just know I never seem to inspire friendliness.

"So," Silas says as we turn to a smaller lane, between two low-slung cinderblock buildings. "If you want to—"

"Ayerp!" I squeal as he practically lunges for the cotton candy. I spin and barely get it out of his reach, fighting back the urge to start laughing. "No!" I exclaim, breathless. "It's *mine*—"

His hand closes around my wrist and then his body is inches from mine and he's grinning down at me and I discover I've got nothing to say. Instead I squeeze his right hand where it's still in my left and tug, as if that'll pull him away from the cotton candy I've still got held aloft.

It does nothing, obviously, except widen his grin and deepen the crinkles next to his lake-blue eyes. I give him my best glare through my glasses, even though we both know there's no heat behind it.

"Please?" he says, his voice suddenly deeper and softer, and God, I'm *aware*. I'm aware that I'm flirting like a four-teen-year-old who's never kissed anyone before, and I'm aware that there's no one else in this spot between the two buildings, and I'm aware of his hand on my wrist and of the fact that we're both a little damp with sweat.

And of the cotton candy thread right below his bottom lip. It's a single soft strand, so small I can't tell whether it's blue or pink, but it's stuck to the spot where his skin curves down from his lip and God, I want to lick it off. I want to lick it off that it's all I can think about: the way my tongue would

175

curl against his lip and the way he would taste salty and sweet and how his skin would be rough and his mouth would be soft and whether it would turn into a kiss or whether he'd release me and back away because licking another human is not a normal thing to do.

"One little taste," he says in that same too-low, too-private voice, his fingers sliding on my wrist as I finally collect my wits.

"*No*," I tell him, chin up, and pull my wrist hard enough that it slides from his grip, turning away with my arm extended. "You already ate half of it without even ask—"

Then his arm is around my waist, my back to his chest, and he's pulling me against him with both our arms extended away from us.

I make an undignified noise, somewhere between a yelp and a squeak while Silas laughs.

"You're not even gonna eat it all," he says, fingers outstretched.

"No!" I squeal. "Noooooo!"

The sound breaks apart into a short, high-pitched laugh, and his arms tighten, and I don't need to look to know that Silas is grinning against my hair.

"Kat," he says, and I inhale sharply because oh *fuck* his mouth is close to my ear, his voice even lower and rumblier than before and there's no one else around and therefore no reason for us to be acting like we're in our teens, not our thirties. "Did you just giggle?"

My hand's over his where it clutches my waist, his arm even warmer than the blistering summer day. I wonder if he can tell how sweaty the back of my neck is or if he cares. The hem of my sundress rises slightly with the pull.

I wonder if he'd let me feed it to him. If he'd lick my

fingers after each bite the way he licks his own. The thought leaves me breathless.

"Of course I didn't giggle," I finally say, mustering all the dignity I can.

"That sounded... giggly," he says and sweet fancy Jesus he's even closer to my ear, close enough that goosebumps shiver down my spine despite the heat.

"Cotton candy is no giggling matter," I say, and plunge my fingertips between his fingers against my waist. "Unhand me, you scoundrel."

He laughs as I squeeze my eyes shut against the fact that I said something straight out of a bodice ripper from the eighties instead of something flirty and cute and girlfriendy. For one moment he pulls me against him even tighter, his heat soaking into me, his shirt sticking to my bare upper back.

And then he unhands me and I whirl away, facing him as I back up and praying that I don't look anything like I feel.

"Fine, you win," he says, brushing his hands together in front of himself as he smiles and I take an enormous bite of cotton candy, because now I'm determined to eat it all, even if I regret it later. "C'mon, giant watermelons are this way."

He nods at a door leading into the cinderblock building. On it is a sign that says NO FOOD OR DRINK IN THE HANDCRAFTS AND GARDENING PAVILION, with a helpful illustration to the same effect underneath.

"I *know* you can read," I say around the cotton candy in my mouth. "We can't—"

"Oh, for fuck's sake," he says through a smile, and before I know it he's snagged the cotton candy and disappeared through the door.

"What—" I start, but the door swings shut behind him and then I'm standing there, in this blank spot between two buildings as the sun beats down and the far-off cows moo, looking at this door. I consider proving a point by walking off and leaving him to whatever fate awaits him, but I don't even know what point that would be.

In any case, the door swings open again and he's standing there, taking a bite from my cotton candy and grinning like the cat who ate the canary.

"You coming?" he asks, so I sigh dramatically and roll my eyes and walk into the building.

# EIGHTEEN

## SILAS

KAT IS INSUFFERABLE. She's prickly. She's haughty. She won't give an inch on anything, ever.

And the sundress she's wearing takes up most of the available real estate in my brain. It's green and soft, ends right above her knees, leaves her upper back bare except for a lattice of crisscrossing straps that might as well be a net to catch any thoughts I manage to have.

"There's not that much upside-down time," she's saying, her eyes on an abomination called The Zipper. Its acrobatics make me feel a little lightheaded. "And the restraints hardly ever come undone."

"You're more than welcome to go by yourself," I point out for at least the third time. "I'll be down here so someone can call 911 when the whole thing walks away or topples over."

"It's no fun to scream alone," she says. Her hand's in mine, and she tightens her grip on it as she looks up at me through her glasses and blinks.

Is she... batting her lashes at me? Suddenly, the ground

179

feels less stable under my feet. First the sundress, and now this.

"I need a big, strong boyfriend there to... scream next to," she says. The end of the sentence has considerably less bravado and volume than the beginning.

"And you were being so normal."

"Shut up," she mutters, but her mouth quirks like it does when she's trying not to laugh.

"You didn't even mention my strapping abilities of very manly protection," I go on. "Or the very affectionate affections I might bestow upon a terrified girlfriend."

"Okay, okay," she says. "Look. I tried something, it didn't work."

"How about the haunted house ride?" I go on, cheerfully ignoring her. "Right before the end you can pretend to swoon into my arms and I'll carry you out of there like I rescued you from King Kong my own self."

Kat glances around quickly, her dark braid sliding over her shoulder, then flips me off. I laugh. Her lips quirk again, the corners of her eyes lifting with the smile stuck behind them.

I'm not even surprised that I'm having a good time. This time last week I would have been surprised by that but Kat, for all her over-acted prickliness and staged grumpiness, is the best date I've had in years, probably because she cuts me no slack whatsoever.

Truth is, I can get away with most things from most people. It's not as if I've tried to charm my way out of a murder, but parking tickets? Sheila at the County Courthouse is married to my high school football coach and has, more than once, discharged fines while telling me about her grandchildren.

I've never gotten away with a single thing from Kat, who

seems equally immune to flattery and goodwill, and who seems to consist entirely of knowing, sharp looks. Kat, who's been harassing me for the past five minutes about my dislike of carnival rides but who seems to think nothing of the breakdown I had the night before last.

*She's humoring you*, that old, ugly voice whispers. *Now that she knows how easy you are to break, she's handling you with kid gloves and waiting for the month to be over.*

"What about a Ferris wheel?" she asks, looking up at it, twin circles of light reflecting on her glasses. "Is that also a death trap, or is it not fast or spinny enough?"

That gaze slides over to me yet again, because for all my claiming that my dislike is a safety issue, she saw right through it.

I sigh, pushing my hand through my hair, tangled with dried sweat from the day. With the sun down it's just cool enough that I only feel like I'm in a swamp, not a sauna.

"I'll go on a Ferris wheel for you, babe," I say a little too loudly as we keep strolling, hand in hand. "If that's what you want."

"I love the way you humor me," she says, and she glances up at me but then something else catches her attention. It catches it so much that she turns her head and keeps watching it behind me, and something clenches behind my lungs.

Meckler?

But I follow her gaze and don't see him. I don't see anything besides the slow-moving flow of people down the midway, strolling between flashing lights and carnival barkers. I look back at her and follow it again, then frown.

Then I do it again.

"The bear?" I finally ask, looking one last time because

I'd bet a thousand bucks she's staring at a man carrying a pink teddy bear the size of a small horse on his shoulders.

"What? No," she says, and snorts.

"You want a giant bear."

Now she's trying a *how could you even think that look on me,* and it's not working.

"I do not want a giant bear," she says, and rolls her eyes. "Where would I put a giant bear? *Why* would I want a giant bear?"

"Babe, I can get you a giant bear," I say, and I'm grinning because at last, I get to give her shit about something. "You only had to say the word."

"What about me says *please, win me a cheesy giant stuffed animal?*"

"Besides the fact that you very obviously want a giant fucking bear as a prize to take home?"

"I do not," she says. "Besides, there's no way you can actually get me one, these games are—oh come *on.*"

I'm already pulling her the way we came, back to the flashing lights of the midway. Of course I can win her a bear from one of these terrible games. If she wants I'll win her every damn bear from every damn game until we can't fit them all in the back of my truck.

"Which one you want, babe?" I ask, gesturing at all the games. "You want that giraffe? The frog with a top hat? Maybe that giant Mr. Peanut, seems like he could keep you warm at night."

"I'm sorry I implied that you might lose a rigged game," she says.

"I kinda like that shark," I say, pointing across the way.

"The whole point is that they're impossible to win."

"How about that gorilla with a gold chain?"

"Silas."

"There's a Pikachu over there that looks pretty good. You like Pikachu?"

She ducks a little closer to me, her bare shoulder touching my bare arm, as she looks between two other game stalls.

"That's Jigglypuff."

"That the one you want me to win you?"

We've come to a stop between two stands, both blindingly-bright and loud, looking at the tent beyond.

"No," she says, like she's trying her best to sound reasonable, but then she stops. Glances over at the Jigglypuff, then back at me, and I can't help the grin that takes over my face.

"You sure?"

"Of course I'm sure."

She doesn't sound sure.

"You can admit you want a Jigglypuff," I tell her. "I don't judge."

Kat closes her eyes and sighs.

"Fine," she says, as if I'm about to drag her to her doom. "I want the Jigglypuff."

"Was that so hard?" I ask, and we move toward the game stall. It's one of those games where you've gotta toss a ball into a basket, and even though I'm well aware that these things are rigged, they can't be that rigged.

"Wait," she says, and grabs my forearm with her other hand, and even though it was a hot day and now it's a hot night, her fingers are cool. I flex my forearm against them, because I can't help it. "Do you have your phone?"

I pull it from my pocket and hand it to her. She looks around again, like she thinks we're being followed, then pulls me into the shadows between two stalls, already Googling something.

I slide a hand around her waist, my thumb on the seam

of her sundress, the fabric soft and pliable, and I force myself
not to twist the folds between my fingers. Kat stiffens for an
instant, then relaxes.

"Since these are all rigged," she says, scrolling. "You may
as well know the tricks."

"Sneaky," I tease, and she snorts.

"Everyone does this."

"Then why are we hiding?"

She glances up, like she hadn't realized she dragged me
into shadows.

"We're not hiding, we're out of the way."

"Sure."

My thumb's moving over her waist, and I force it still
while she flicks through video after video, the phone screen
making her glow blue in the semi-darkness. I step in closer to
look over her shoulder and this time she doesn't tense at all.
If anything, she sinks a fraction of an inch back into me
before she finally selects one.

"Here," she says, and holds up my phone.

· · · · · ★ ★ ★ · · · · ·

"YOU HAVE TO *LOB*," Kat says, voice low and tight. She
makes an extremely unhelpful underhanded throwing
motion that does nothing to help me get this damn ball in
this damn basket.

"You're more than welcome to take over," I tell her,
offering the softball.

"I'm not the one who made the All-State Baseball team."

"That was in high school," I say, sizing up the basket
once more.

"Is that why you brought it up twice?"

I brought it up twice because as we watched videos on

how to win midway games, she leaned her head back against my shoulder and let my hand slide further around her waist. I didn't even mean to bring it up once, but here we are.

"You ready for this?'" I ask, running my thumb over the stitches on the softball, staring down the basket. "I'm about to *lob*."

I swear she holds her breath as I pull my arm back and gently release the ball toward the basket, then makes a noise when it barely clears the lip.

Then it stays, and Kat exhales, a smile creeping across her face.

"Told you," I say, picking up the last softball.

"You've still got one more, hotshot," she teases, her gaze flicking to the Jigglypuff suspended from the ceiling of the tent.

The lone Jigglypuff, bobbing and swaying gently, like it's taunting me. There's only one left, and I'm not the only one gunning for it.

There are three stations set up at this game. Two are in use: one by us, the other by a guy fifteen years my junior who's wearing a baseball hat even though it's dark out. We've been exchanging tense looks for the better part of ten minutes as we keep throwing balls and they keep bouncing out of these goddamn baskets.

I've already spent at least four times what the Jigglypuff is worth trying to win it, but we all know that *having* the prize isn't the point. It's how you get the prize: preferably through a stunning display of athleticism and physical prowess.

The other guy throws a ball and to my dismay, it stays in the basket. My fingers tighten around my final softball.

"*Silas*," hisses Kat, who's no longer smiling, just glaring at this other man who wants the prize. Her prize.

Our prize.

"Don't worry, babe," I murmur, tossing the ball once in my hand, trying to clear my mind. "I've got this."

I'm vaguely aware that the other man and I are winding up at the same time, but this is my element. I've got the perfect, crystal clarity that comes with adrenaline and competition.

The softball leaves my hand. It arcs across the space, past the bored man running the game, and into the basket.

It bounces once, then stays as the other man's ball bounces out and he swears.

"YES!" shrieks Kat. She launches herself at me before I'm expecting it, both arms going around my neck as she whoops and laughs. I'm almost caught off balance and take a step back, already laughing, my arms going around her waist.

I hoist her the last inch from the ground and spin her, still laughing, and I get an undignified squeak as she pulls her arms tighter around my neck.

"Told you," I say in her ear, putting her back on her feet. "Nothing to—"

Kat grabs my face and kisses me. It almost surprises me out of kissing her back—I wasn't expecting this, somehow didn't think that after Friday night she'd want to be seen again with her mouth on mine—but then I do, both of us breathing hard, her teeth hitting my lip as her fingers curl through my hair and I turn my head to get my sore nose out of the way, our lips sliding against each other, wet hot friction on a summer night.

It has the allure of danger, of a rope bridge over a gorge: safest to keep your feet, but who doesn't want to fly?

Her dress is still under my hands, still on her waist, and I hold on tighter and flick my tongue along her lip, but I don't bunch the fabric in my hands to draw the hem up the backs of her thighs. Stay on the bridge, don't jump. There are rules, goddammit, and I know the rules even as she stands on her toes and presses even harder against me, as her tongue brushes against mine and I let my fingers skim her jaw. She sighs. My lip is between her teeth and everything feels white.

"Y'all still want this?" a voice says. Kat jolts away from me like she was stung.

The guy who ran the game is standing there, still looking bored, the Jigglypuff aloft in one hand and it's all I can do to collect the shreds of my mind, remember what I was doing here, and nod.

"Thanks," I say as he hands it over, expression never changing.

Jigglypuff is monstrous, even bigger up close: a pale pink circle three feet in diameter, with a permanent slight smile and massive blue eyes staring into the distance as if it's seeing untold horrors, but its face only has one expression.

It's creepy. I feel like it can see my thoughts. I wonder if it can hear the blood pound through my veins, feel the tiny indentations her teeth left on my lip as I run my tongue over them.

Kat pushes up her glasses with one knuckle and pulls her braid back over her shoulder, looking everywhere but at me until we've turned away from the booth. She clears her throat.

"Sorry," she says, then clears her throat again. "I, uh. Got carried away. Thought maybe I saw Evan."

I can still feel her skin under my fingertips.

"That's all right," I say, adjusting the stuffed animal under my arm. "I think you convinced the guy at the booth, at least."

"Does he count as the wider community?"

"Sure."

I hope Meckler's here. I hope he saw Kat leap onto me with wild abandon. I hope he watched her kiss me and I hope it hurt, because he deserves to hurt.

I thought, for a while, that I'd been to enough therapy to stop being angry with him. I thought I'd done the work and found the forgiveness, had come to the understanding that everyone has their own pain to deal with and sometimes they do it in ways I hate, but then Kat showed up and the anger came roaring back. I can forgive my own shit, but I can't forgive hers.

I don't want to. I want her to stay angry, to get her slow, subtle revenge, because Kat is all sharp edges and shimmering heat, and it's beautiful. I know she'll draw blood, and I know it'll be mine, but I don't care. I've been wounded before. What's a little more wreckage?

It's not a way I ever thought I'd feel, and I do my best to ignore that. I also ignore the small sliver of worry that asks, *why does she want him to beg her to take him back?*

"So, babe," Kat says, still meandering. "Uh. Did you want to go home, or are you up for something else, or...?"

I can feel the vibration of her nerves from here, like someone's plucked a high-tension wire.

"I thought we were going on the Ferris wheel, babe," I say, and smile over at her, like a boyfriend so besotted he won her a Pokémon. "Don't tell me you're going to back down now."

"*Me?*" she asks, and gives me an indignant look. "You're the one who—oh, fuck off," she mutters, and something loosens in my chest, and I start laughing.

# NINETEEN

## KAT

THE GATE SWINGS shut and the car bobs gently, rocking side to side like a boat on an ocean as I smooth my skirt over my legs. I sit opposite Silas, who's got one arm slung over the back of the bench seat. Next to him Jigglypuff stares at me with unnerving good cheer, its eyes wide, its smile faint.

I should've gone with the gorilla, because I think Jigglypuff can see into my soul and I don't like it. I'm half horrified at how I kissed Silas a few minutes ago—in front of people, for no reason, where everyone could look and see and judge —and half so desperate to do it again that I don't trust myself to sit next to him.

The Ferris wheel swings gently upward, far enough for people to get into the next car. It's not a big car, our knees maybe a foot apart. I cross my legs just as Silas slides a foot across the floor, our ankles resting together.

His is warm, bone under skin against my own. It feels oddly dangerous, like we could hurt each other if one of us moved wrong, if we somehow rubbed at cross-purposes. I stare at the tilt-a-whirl and pretend that I can think about something besides this single point of contact.

"You never did answer my question," he says, voice low, barely rising over the hubbub of the fair below. The car swings upward again and now we're above the tented roofs of the Midway, almost level with the two-story Haunted House.

"What question was that?"

He looks out of the car for a moment, the lights of the Ferris wheel strobing across his face. Jigglypuff stares at me, knowingly.

"What you're gonna say when Meckler's on his knees," Silas finally rasps, but there's a smile on his lips. Always a smile, like everything is a joke. "I keep asking and you keep dodging the question."

"Have you ever considered that I don't want to answer it?" I say primly, tapping my fingers against the car, heartbeat accelerating.

"I did," he says, that same small smile still there. I wonder if he knows. "And I did consider what answer could possibly be more revealing than *I want my ex to crawl to me while he begs.*"

He leans forward, elbows on knees, the bulbs from the Ferris wheel an arc in his eyes, obliterating the blue and God, the way he looks. The way he is. He has to know. There must be a waiting list of women, each one jockeying for first position. I'm sure he could call one every night of the week if he wanted.

Why he needed me, why he needed to *pretend*, I can't begin to understand.

I should tell him the truth: in the fantasy, I turn Evan down and walk away. That's it. I want him to beg so I can say no.

Instead I say, "What if it's a weird sex thing?"

One side of his mouth hitches, but he holds my gaze.

"I'd say I try not to judge what's weird and what's not."

"You'd definitely judge this."

There is no sex thing. Not in this scenario, not with Evan, but I can't shut myself up.

"I doubt that. What is it, he licks your shoes and calls you mistress?"

Silas shrugs demonstrably, as if that's just a Monday night, and while being called *mistress* isn't my thing, Silas shrugging it off like it's no big deal apparently is.

"I wouldn't do that to my shoes," I say. I push up my glasses, glance away. Silas is still there, the lights still in his eyes as we jolt higher: above tree level now, above nearly everything.

"Human furniture," Silas offers. "You use him as a footrest while you and Anna Grace watch *Game of Thrones*."

"That's been off the air for years."

"*Lord of the Rings*."

"I don't want to use him as furniture," I say. "Worse."

"Again, with the judgement."

"I want," I say, slowly, watching Silas's face, "to turn him down and walk away."

Silas looks at me. For a long moment he looks at me, like he's seeing me for the first time, like I'm some new and exotic species that he's not sure he can communicate with.

"I'm not sure that's worse than being a human footrest," he finally says.

I feel myself smile, and I don't know if it's at his words or the way he's still looking at me.

"It is if you're the one begging," I say, softly.

"I can't believe I survived crossing you, once upon a time."

"You're not out of the woods just yet."

He drops his head for a moment, and when he looks back at me he's smiling, one curl of hair across his forehead.

"Have mercy on me, Kat," he says, and between the rakish smile and the lock of hair and the tiny friction of my ankle against his and the lights in his eyes like ships on a midnight sea, I have no idea what to do.

So I freeze.

Then I roll my eyes. I push up my glasses and look away, over the side of the car, and tug at the end of my braid over one shoulder and drum my fingers on the arm rest and snort like that's the dumbest thing I've ever heard.

"Quit it," I say. "We'll be free of each other in a couple weeks and I promise not to tear your head off before that."

It's sharp and bitchy and I hate it as soon as I say it, but I'm flailing and I don't know what else to do. Silas is warm and friendly and kisses me with tongue and sometimes looks at me in a way I find mildly terrifying, but I also know that this is explicitly fake. That there must be a waiting list and every entry on it more appealing than me. That he's here at all because we can't stand the same person.

And he let me wash his hair that night. And I woke up with his head in my lap.

"Sorry," I say after a long moment, still not looking at him. "I meant—you know. I won't use you as furniture."

I finally look back at him, and the rakish grin is still there. Does it ever go away?

"What if I ask real nice?"

"You're a little mouthy for a footstool."

"Was that a compliment, Kat?"

And I'm smiling back, despite myself.

"Was it?"

"I think it may have been," he says, and then he stands

192

and swings himself around the pole in the middle of the car and sits next to me before I'm even finished gasping.

"There, now it's romantic," he says, and puts his arm around me.

"Don't stand up!" I hiss, several seconds too late.

He ignores me to stretch his neck, looking out at the night sky as the Ferris wheel starts rotating, heavy and slow.

"All right," he says, and points past me. "That over there is Orion."

I follow his gaze, but I don't see Orion.

"Are you sure?"

"Right next to it is the big dipper," he goes on, pressing into my side. I can feel him breathing and I don't know what to do with my hands. "And then we've got the small dipper, and the seven sisters, and... I dunno, pick a zodiac sign. How about Gemini?"

None of those things are true, but his voice is low and rumbly and the plastic bench seat is slippery and the car is rocking again as the wheel moves, pushing me back into him.

"Are you making this up?" I ask, looking at the sky like my life depends on it. Otherwise I'll look at him.

"Course not," he says smoothly. "Keep snuggling, make it look good. And then over here, in this part of the sky, we've got Ursa Major and Capricorn Minor."

"That's not what either of those things are," I tell him, my voice perfectly light and casual. He leans forward and now his chest is against my back, the rumble of his voice shivering through me.

I put one hand on his thigh. For show. To make it look real. His swallow is audible.

"And of course that one is Andromeda being eaten by the Kraken," he says, continuing his nonsense as if I just agreed with him. "She was chained to a rock and it came back every day to eat her liver, again and again."

I'm a mess of warring impulses: to laugh at his mythology mashup and to collapse against him like lovers in a complicated Renaissance painting. To follow my own damn rules and to move my hand an inch higher on his thigh, just to see what happens.

"What about that one?" I say, nodding at a random section of sky.

"So glad you asked," Silas says, shifting against me, somehow drawing me closer. "That's Triton, king of the mer-people. And naturally, over there—" he points past my face, "—is his arch-nemesis, the Minotaur."

His lips are practically touching my ear again, and my eyes slide closed. I swallow hard.

"Remind me why they're enemies?" I say, hoping I don't sound like I feel.

"Something to do with twelve tasks, I think."

"Silas," I say, turning to face him. "Have you ever read a single—"

It's a breathless rush of a kiss: his hand gripping my jaw, his mouth on mine, my sentence unfinished on my lips. It's hot and needy and insistent, the day's stubble scraping along my lip as he turns his head, parts his lips, sinks his hand into my hair.

I feel like a knot, unraveling. His thigh flexes under my hand and I move it into his hair, twisting toward him, the bench underneath us slippery, the kisses open-mouthed as the Ferris wheel spins and the car rocks and we lower to the hubbub of the fair, to eye-level and he pulls back for a moment, his fingers tangled in my braid. Our faces an inch apart.

"Take it out," he rasps, his fingers trailing down the

plaits. I can feel the puff of his breath on my lips and I'm half in his lap, dress hiked too high, his shorts against my bare skin.

"Say please," I whisper back, but Silas grins and nips at me, catching my lower lip between his teeth as his fingers find the hair tie at the bottom.

"You do like when men beg," he murmurs, and then he's pulled it loose and we're rising again, his fingers sifting through my hair and his mouth back on mine before he wraps the strands around his fingers and gives a light pull.

Pleasure runs over my skin like water, even though I resist. I bite his lip in return and I swear he laughs, the sound low and earthy. Then he pulls again, fractionally harder, and this time I let my head go back and his lips trail down my neck.

I make a noise. I swear in a desperate, breathy whisper, and in response I get the sharp scrape of teeth against the skin of my throat. I bite my lip so I don't beg him to keep moving down.

He doesn't. He stops and works his way back up and I clench my teeth against a moan before his mouth is back on mine and he lets my hair loose and God, I want to climb into his lap and rub myself against him. I didn't think to make dry-humping against our rules.

Then the car swings to a stop, the din of the fair at a full roar, and we pull apart. My breathing's too hard, my glasses are askew, and I'm way too turned on for pretending that he's my boyfriend when my intended jealousy target isn't even here.

I feel like my lips might be bruised from how hard I kissed him. I feel like my ego might be bruised for the same reason, and I stare into his blue eyes with mounting anxiety that I just gave myself away, that somehow Silas can tell I wanted every second of that and more.

So I take my hand off his leg and clear my throat and the Ferris wheel car we're in swings lower, people entering and exiting the ride, and I smooth my hair and cross my ankles.

"Good show," I say, politely as I can. "I think they bought it."

There's a hesitation on his face, a flicker in his eyes like something wild nearly surfaced, but then I get that easy smile as he runs a hand through his wild hair and makes a show of relaxing.

"I think they did," he says, and then it's our turn to disembark.

· · · · · ★ ★ ★ · · · · ·

LATER THAT NIGHT, I'm standing in my bathroom, brushing my teeth, when I spot something in the mirror.

I lean in, mouth frothy and toothbrush clenched in my teeth, until I'm three inches away and I can see it properly without my glasses: a light purple bruise on my neck, ringed with red.

"Mother*fucker*," I hiss, spraying toothpaste flecks onto the mirror.

# TWENTY

## SILAS

MONDAY MORNING, I'm back to my routine, and it's a relief. I'm up at five, feed the cat, grab my gym clothes, get to Chillacouth Crossfit for the five-thirty workout. Go home and shower, dress, make a smoothie, drink it in the car on my way to the office between seven-thirty and eight.

A routine means I don't have to think, only act. It gives my day structure. Whatever else happens, by seven in the morning I've already accomplished something good for myself.

Not to mention that I haven't thrown my back out in nearly five years, which I attribute to all the gym-going but also to paying some damn attention when it starts feeling off. In my twenties I'd push on through any twinges but was only ever rewarded with a day spent on the floor, swearing, wondering who I could call for the real pain meds.

But the problem with a routine is that I don't have to think about it. Muscle memory means that as I feed Beast, I'm free to think about yesterday and Kat's game of cotton candy keep away. As I drive I'm free to think about the bead of sweat I watched slide from the back of her neck down her

197

spine as we looked at quilts and she finished the cotton candy. I do burpees and consider the flash in her eyes when she admitted she wanted a stuffed Pokemon.

And it's in the shower, eyes squeezed shut with a hand on my dick, that I think about how she swore in a whisper when I pulled her hair and kissed her neck. That's not usually part of the routine, but sometimes you've gotta be flexible.

I'm walking from my truck to the office, freshly showered and smoothied and ready for a great day of lawyering, when I get the text.

**Kat:** WHAT THE FUCK, SILAS?

I stop in my tracks, because that's a lot, even for her. The picture comes through before I can text her back.

It's a distinctly mouth-shaped bruise on one side of her neck, mottled purple and red, her collarbone at the bottom of the frame and at the top corner, her mouth barely visible, lips parted.

My face heats. My whole body heats. I'm overwhelmingly grateful for the morning's quick shower session to take the edge off because Jesus Mary *fuck* that's pretty. More than pretty. The sight of it opens something deep inside me, some long-forgotten hatch that heaves up from the floorboards to reveal a staircase into the dark. I. Just. *God.*

A car drives toward me, and I realize I'm standing in the middle of a parking lot, staring open-mouthed at my phone. I wave and keep walking.

**Silas:** sorry, didn't mean to
**Kat:** are you fifteen?!?

I bite back a smile even as I scroll up to the picture again for one last look—say please, she said, and I never did and she gave it up anyway, fuck, fuck—and then I close my texts and put my phone away and hum running cadences to the beat of my footsteps until I'm in the office.

· · · · ★ ★ ★ · · · · ·

NINETY MINUTES later she's in the doorway of my office, a perfunctory knock on the open door, giving me a wide, sarcastic smile.

"Morning, babe," Kat says, with more teeth than necessary.

I lean back in my chair, loop my hands behind my head, a tedious contract on my monitor in front of me.

"Morning, babe," I answer, eyes on her neck. I don't see it, and the disappointment is more than a twinge.

"I just wanted to drop something off," she says, her voice shiny and bright and far too cheerful for her at this hour. "The county fair reminded me of it."

She walks right up to me, propping herself against my desk, ankles crossed in gray slacks and a deep green sleeveless shirt that comes up past the hollow of her throat, hair pulled back.

I stare at her throat, searching, until I realize she's handing me a manila folder.

Inside is a single sheet of paper, and it simply reads:

### ADDENDUM
#### NO LOVE BITES.

I read it at least ten times.

"Love bites?" I finally ask, still leaning back in my chair.

199

"*Hickey* is a gross word," she says, arms crossed over her chest.

I swivel, purposefully, so our knees are touching, and she doesn't move away.

"Are you secretly my grandma, back from the dead?" I ask, looking at her neck again. "Because you've really got the buttoned-up, prim-and-proper thing down."

In daylight, anyway.

She pushes her glasses up and glares at me, her lips moving the way they do when she's trying to stay mad and not smile.

"Yes," she deadpans. "I am, in fact, a deceased hundred-year-old white southern woman and I've donned this clever disguise so I can tell you to mind your manners, open doors for ladies, and wait until marriage because they won't buy the cow if they can get the milk for free. Want my recipe for cheese grits and... what's that thing you claim is a vegetable?"

I bump my knee into hers again, grinning.

"Collards *are* a vegetable."

"Sure."

I lean forward in my chair until my elbows are resting on the desk and my arm is touching her hip, a single escaped strand of hair moving with my breath.

"Did it work?" I ask, searching for it.

"Yes, it worked," she says. "Did you see the picture? I look like I lost a fight with a vacuum cleaner."

I grin, and our gazes meet as she tries not to smile. I lower my voice further.

"Did Meckler hate it, I mean."

"He doesn't know it's there," she says. I'm leaning further in and she's not moving, just standing there in this perfectly casual pose, the only giveaway to her state the tension in her shoulders. "I put a pound of concealer over it because I'm not walking into my workplace with that visible on my neck, no matter how jealous it might make him."

Finally, I see it: a splotch on her neck that's not quite the same shade of tawny gold as her skin, and beneath it the faintest suggestion of a bruise, so faint it might be my imagination.

*Say please*, she said, and instead of saying it I pulled harder and she made the quietest groan and swore in a whisper and now she's here, all sharp and spiky and pretending to be angry about it.

I stand before I do something else stupid.

"Sorry," I say, even though I'm not sure I am. I rest my hands on her bare shoulders, feel her muscles like high-tension wires.

"Are you a teenager?" she asks, matching my voice, giving me a look upward through her glasses. "Am I your first girlfriend and you're so excited for the whole football team to know you're dating a real live person that you've gotta do *this?*"

"It's pretty good proof," I agree. "They'd be impressed."

She glares. I grin.

"I'm sorry," I tell her. "I'll respect the addendum. It was an accident."

I don't tell her why it was an accident, that I got lost in the sounds she was making, in the hot velvet of her skin. That all I wanted was for her to keep making those noises and I didn't think about one single consequence.

For fifteen years now, everyone around me has been dating, falling in love, settling down and embarking on new, coupled lives. They've been getting married or not, having kids or not, but by now most people I know are coupled off and heading down a path I can't follow. The only people who aren't are the other Wildwood guys, but that's a matter of time, too.

I thought it would be me, of course. I thought I'd follow the same pattern as anyone, that I'd get over my issues and find a nice woman and settle down, probably get married and have some kids, but then I didn't. I tried. I met people and went on dates and had relationships, but I could never make it work out.

It was a relief to stop trying. It was a relief to accept a life alone. It was a relief to stop looking for romance and start looking for other kinds of love in other places: the family I was born into, the family I've made, the people as important to me as any romantic partner.

It was a relief to accept sex as a means to satisfaction, an occasional and pleasant experience with no strings attached. Something I liked and enjoyed, but wouldn't make a fool of myself for.

And then Kat showed up, glittering and sharp and angry, and I've been staring at hickeys and jerking off in the shower before work.

She nods once, her stance softening.

"Thank you."

"We still on for coffee later?"

"It's on the schedule, isn't it?" she says, and I swear she's looking at me through her eyelashes. "Of course we're on for coffee. We've got a mission."

A mission. Yes. A mission that doesn't include love bites or her hand slowly working its way up my leg or her lips whispering curses when I lick her neck.

I lean in and give her one quick, chaste kiss on the mouth, a perfectly respectable *girlfriend came to say hi kiss*, and she slides off my desk and waves goodbye.

· · · · · ★ ★ ★ ★ · · · ·

**Monday, 3pm:** Mountain Grind Coffee Outing
**Activities:** get an afternoon pick-me-up together
**Objective:** display enjoyment of one another as a couple
to coworkers and town busybodies; caffeinate

"IS THAT ENOUGH SUGARS?" she asks, as I toss the
empty packets in the trash.

"Yes."

"You know if you use the simple syrup you don't have to
deal with—nope, you're not doing that anyway, all right
then."

I grin at her as I swallow my iced coffee.

"I like the sugar grits," I say, and Kat makes the perfectly
blank face that means she's hiding a smile. "Makes me feel
alive."

"Gross."

"I watched you eat a whole cone of cotton candy by
yourself yesterday."

"Not all by myself, sadly," she says, giving me one of her
pointed looks.

"Close enough." I take another sip and crunch the sugar
between my teeth this time, just to watch the way her
eyebrows rise.

"You like the weirdest shit," she says, but a corner of her
mouth twitches, and we turn to walk for the door.

"I'm not the one who sleeps with a Pikachu."

"It's a Jigglypuff, and what makes you think I slept
with it?"

"So you did."

Kat shoots me a glance that's supposed to be annoyed,

probably, but isn't and pushes the door open. I catch it behind her.

"I had to put it on the couch," she admits when we're outside, on the sidewalk, heading back to the office building. "It's got this unnerving... stare."

"Yeah. Right into your soul," I agree, and without thinking I slide her hand into mine as we walk.

· · · · ★ ★ ★ ★ ★ · · · ·

**Tuesday, noon:** Benny's Soup & Taco Lunch
**Activities:** consume food to fuel continued existence
**Objective:** eat soup and/or taco, look convincing to coworkers who go there every day

"THAT'S the wrongest opinion I've ever heard in my entire life," Kat's saying, the taco paused on the way to her mouth. A small chunk of tomato falls out, onto her plate.

"Opinions can't be wrong," I point out.

"The hell they can't, because that one sure is."

Benny's Soup & Taco is pretty small, little more than a hole-in-the-wall, and that earns her a disapproving glance from the woman at the next table over.

"I'm just saying, the guy with the double lightsaber was badass, and the movie was enjoyable," I tell her, and calmly take a bite of my own taco.

She watches me for a long moment, her eyes narrowed. It takes everything I've got not to crack up.

"Are you fucking with me?" she asks, keeping her voice low enough that she doesn't earn another look from the next table.

"Of course not."

"Did you even see that movie?"

"Yes, I saw that movie," I say, trying to keep my taco ingredients in my own taco. "All those movies stayed in heavy rotation at Bagram. There was nothing to do *but* watch that movie."

And, you know, fight an ugly, awful war, but I skip that part.

To my surprise, she laughs.

"That explains it."

I raise an eyebrow.

"Of course you liked it if that's where you saw it," she says. "Fine, you can have your bad opinion."

If there weren't a lady at the next table watching us, I'd flip her off. The taco hides my smile.

· · · ★ ★ ★ ★ ★ · · ·

**Wednesday, close of business:** Walk to Car
**Activities:** convene in office; sojourn to vehicles
**Objective:** bother Meckler

"IS IT RAINING YET?"

"I'm not answering that."

"You can't tell me whether or not it's raining?"

I lean back against Meckler's desk, facing Kat, and fold my arms over my chest.

"You have the exact same view out the window that I do," I point out.

For the record, it's not raining yet, but I like it when she gets huffy with me. Gives me a reason to prod back at her.

"But babe," she says, and she looks up at me, and there's that slight quiver around her eyes that means she's deliberately not laughing. "I love it when you tell me the weather."

"You just love making me do things you could do yourself, babe."

Meckler's not here right now, but he'll be back any second.

"Because you're so cute when you do them."

She bats her eyelashes. A week ago I had no idea she could pull that off, but when she looks up at me like that, dark eyes behind her glasses, my IQ drops by about three points.

"Mhm," I say, and push myself off Meckler's desk to put my palms on hers and lean in. "When else am I cute?"

"You're always cute," she says, sitting behind her desk, also leaning in. Trying not to laugh. "A total cutie."

Kat boops my nose, and it takes every ounce of self-control I've got not to laugh.

"I think you mean *ruggedly handsome*," I say. "Maybe *possessor of rakish good looks*."

"You think you're *rakish?*"

I try out my sauciest smile on her.

"You think I'm not?"

Now she does laugh, and I'd swear she blushes, too.

"If you looked up *All-American Golden Boy* in the dictionary, you'd find your picture," she says. "Rakes are charming and *devious*."

*Is that what you like?* I think, then stuff the thought away.

"I'm charming."

"But not devious."

We're leaning closer to each other. Where the fuck is Meckler? Did he leave for the day? I'm in here, flirting with Kat as rain starts to pelt the glass and the sky outside growls, and I don't know why we're flirting or who we're doing it for.

"So I *am* charming."

"If you were charming you'd tell me whether it was raining or not."

I'm silent for a moment, just as a barrage of raindrops hit the glass loudly and I look right into Kat's eyes.

"Nah," I tell her.

"Okay, that was a little rakish," she admits. "Hold still."

I can't even raise my eyebrows before she kisses me, eyes open and lips closed. I lean in, across her desk, and her eyes slide shut but her lips stay sealed and so do mine because since Sunday, it feels like we've tacitly agreed that the fair was... too much.

There's no need for it, is the thing. We can get our point across just fine with flowers and chaste kisses; Meckler hasn't seen the mark I left on Kat's neck and he never will. Sunday was fueled by the strange, half-dreaming night we spent together on my couch, by the sunrise arguments on Saturday morning, by the renewal of vengeance agreed upon in the truck ride to the fair.

Things got away from us, but now they're back to normal, exactly as they should be, and Kat slides her hand into my hair and I push against her and the kiss stays shallow.

"Jesus, get a room," says Meckler's voice behind me.

I pull away from Kat slowly, like I can't bear to go.

"Sorry, didn't realize you were still here," I tell him. "Thought I had her all to myself."

"We're just going," Kat says, voice cool as an ice pick.

"You ready for tonight, babe?" I ask her, catching a sideways glance at Meckler.

"What's tonight?" she asks, pushing a strand of hair

behind her ear. We don't have anything on the schedule, I'm just winging it.

"You know," I say, suggestively. Meckler stalks behind his desk, lips pressed together, shoulders stiff with anger. "That thing I suggested we try?"

She shoots him a quick glance before looking back at me.

"Oh," she says. "*That* thing."

Her voice lowers on those last two words and for a split second, I'm desperate to find out what *thing* she thinks we're talking about. Even though I know it's nothing.

"Exactly," I say with a grin. "You ready?"

"Sure am," she says, and walks around her desk. "See you tomorrow, Evan!"

His head jerks up, and he watches her go with his eyes blazing.

"Hey babe?" I call out. "Don't forget your umbrella, it's raining."

Before she covers it with a smile, Kat gives me a look that could crumble brick.

"Thanks, babe," she says, a little too chirpily.

# TWENTY-ONE

## KAT

"AND HE WANTS *me* to do the bridal shower for Leah," Anna Grace is saying later that night, a mass of lo mein held between her chopsticks as she sits on her couch. "Why would anyone in their right mind think that I should organize a bridal shower?"

"Because you can herd cats," I say.

"I can't herd in-laws," she says around a mouthful. "That requires things like delicacy and tact."

"And you're pretty good at organizing things," I go on, ignoring her previous statement. Anna Grace has plenty of delicacy and tact, just sometimes chooses not to deploy them.

"Not bridal showers," she says, plopping the takeout container back on the coffee table. "And I like Leah, but definitely not *her* bridal shower. She has... aesthetics and shit."

The briefest of glances at Anna Grace's home would reveal that she, too, has aesthetics and shit, but I don't bother making the point. She's making excuses for why she shouldn't organize her future-sister-in-law's bridal shower, but we both know the real reason she shouldn't do it.

"Can you tell him you don't want to?" I ask, even though I know the answer.

"Of course not," she says. "He'll tell her that I said I didn't want to, and she'll want to know why I don't want to, and even though I just don't want to because I don't like bridal showers, no one will believe me because we all know women love organizing bridal shit and the real reason I don't want to is because I don't like her and don't approve of his decision to marry her, and then our relationship will be weird for the rest of my life."

Anna Grace's family is considerably more traditional and conservative than Anna Grace herself, a fact that's caused her no small amount of friction over the years I've known her.

"Tell him you're busy with work."

"Not good enough."

"Tell him you're allergic to..." I wave one hand in the air, trying to think of something to be allergic to at bridal showers. "Champagne."

"Then I could never drink champagne in front of them again," she points out.

"Tell him you're busy that weekend."

"It's not scheduled yet."

"Then tell him you're busy *every* weekend."

"God, I wish," she says, tilting her head back against the couch. In theory, we're at her house to watch *The Bachelor*, which we do every Wednesday night, but in truth the sound is down too low to hear and neither of us have watched more than thirty seconds of it yet this season. "I'm gonna get roped into this, aren't I?"

"Okay," I say, picking up my beer and taking a sip, as I

think, staring off into space. "How about you make a vision board for the worst bridal shower you can possibly imagine —the worst one for *her*—and then you act really excited about it."

She rests her hands, fingers interlocked, atop her head and looks at me, thinking.

"Go on," she says.

I pull both legs onto the couch, fold them under myself, and stare into space. On the television, a brunette cries through fake eyelashes.

"First, call her excitedly and tell her that you can rent the high school gymnasium for a really good price, and even though there's no AC, they'll include use of those giant fans for free," I say.

"Oooh. Okay."

"Tell her you can't wait to see who wins the Bridal Shower Keg Stand," I go on.

"Yikes."

"Or the Bridal Shower Beer Pong."

"She might like that, you never know."

"And that you hope everyone brings a good contribution to the Bridal Shower Jungle Juice."

Anna Grace snorts.

"The other activities include monogramming tube socks for the groom and..." I push my glasses up, thinking. "Crafting bridal night lingerie from fabric scraps and googly eyes."

Now she's laughing, the sound booming through her living room, and I'm grinning at her.

"That might work," she says. "Will you help me make a mockup bra so I can show her what she's getting herself into?"

"As long as the googly eyes go on the nipples."

"Duh."

"Let me know where and when."

We drink beer in silence for a few minutes, both half-watching the TV, though if there's a plot, we've both lost track of it. All I know is that, for some reason, all these attractive women want to date this very boring white man, and I don't know why.

"Speaking of men who aren't worth it, have you murdered Evan yet?" she asks, as if she can read my mind.

Now it's my turn to tilt my head back onto the sofa and groan dramatically.

"That bad?" she asks, petting my hair away from my forehead.

"Anna Grace, he is *such a dick*," I say. "He never shuts up. He mutters to himself all day, probably because he knows I hate it. He's always on the phone when I'm trying to concentrate and I get that it's his job, but every time I take my headphones out and listen for a few seconds he's talking about golf scores or some shit. He CC's Greg on every email he sends me, like I'm not gonna do my job otherwise. And he's being a fucking asshole about—"

About Silas. For three mornings now he's walked in at ten and asked *how's Silas doing*, in the most condescendingly concerned voice possible, then gone on to make "helpful" suggestions that he knows are dickish concern trolling.

*Maybe he could use a mental health day. Maybe he needs some time off. Is he talking to anyone? I hope he gets the help he needs.*

If I thought he meant it in kindness, it would be fine. It would be nice, even, but he says it with a snide edge to his voice and his lip curling in that way that I've come to hate, so I know what he really means.

I'm starting to think that making him crawl won't be good enough.

"—everything," I finish, because I suddenly don't want to tell Anna Grace that Evan being a dick about Silas bothers me.

There's another silence. Some women on the television are presented with roses. Some are not. The roseless women seem sad.

"What did I see in him?" I ask.

"Mmmm. Nope," Anna Grace says. "Not going down this road."

"I know, I know."

"You can't blame yourself for wanting to see the best in someone when that's all they showed you, right up until it was too late," she goes on, despite her previous statement.

"I *know*."

Anna Grace thinks Evan's a narcissist and a sociopath. I think she's not a psychiatrist. We've been over this a thousand and one times, but the truth is that I still can't believe all the tiny clues, signs, and signals that I ignored right up until he dumped me in front of everyone I knew.

"Is he at least mad about Sir Suction?" she asks, smirking.

"Jesus," I mutter.

"The man really commits," she goes on, still grinning. "A hundred and ten percent."

"I should've never told you about that."

"At least one of us is getting hickeys," she says, still laughing. "I'm over here going on dates with men who think that a *Fish Fear Me, Women Want Me* shirt is a good look and women who turn out to only be there because their boyfriend wants a threesome."

"What, you're not that adventurous?" I tease, because

213

despite everything, Anna Grace is traditional in her own way.

"I might consider it a little more if the opening ploy weren't *so my boyfriend loves watching girls fool around.* Like, damn, at least tell me I've got nice tits first, then tell me you're there in service of some dipshit getting his rocks off."

"You've got nice tits."

"Thank you. I'd still turn down your threesome offer."

"Fair."

I want to touch the spot on my neck, but I don't. It's faded a tiny bit as of today, but I've still got a few layers of concealer over it and have to touch it up every few hours. It's gross, and ugly, and obnoxious, and I can't believe Silas gave me a hickey in the world's most obvious spot.

And yet every night when I wash my face, I find myself staring at it in the mirror for way longer than I should as I replay how I got it: the tug on my hair, his mouth on my neck. I think I made a noise. I think I made a lot of noises, and none of them were for show.

"Evan's pissed about Silas, and Silas takes every chance he can to bother him," I say, circling back to that. "I feel like I'm watching two moose circle each other and make weird bellowing sounds before they smash their heads together to establish dominance."

"Gross," Anna Grace says, matter-of-factly.

"Yeah, super gross," I agree, and I make an effort to watch this bland white man talk to this other bland white man about how he thinks he could consider the possibility of maybe falling in love with one of the remaining contestants, because otherwise I might start thinking about how I don't hate watching Evan and Silas square off quite as much as I should.

I might admit that I've come to enjoy Silas's cheerful

sniping at Evan, his knack for getting under my ex's skin and doing it with an aw-shucks smile.

And I might admit that I kind of wish he were doing it for reasons beyond our agreement.

"Is there still ice cream in the freezer?" I ask Anna Grace.

"All I've got is the weird low-carb coconut stuff," she says without looking over at me. "Couple derby girls came over after the last match."

"How weird is weird?"

"Try it," she says with a shrug, so I head to her freezer.

· · * * ★ ★ ★ * * · ·

**Thursday, 7pm, Hank's Hideout:** dinner
**Activities:** consume nutrition necessary for continued survival
**Objective:** appear publicly as dating couple

TWO NIGHTS LATER, Silas and I are in a booth in the back of Hank's, a burger joint, when everyone in the place starts shouting. I jump and glance over my shoulder to double-check that it's still about sports and not, you know, a murder or something.

Seems like just sports.

Across the table from me, Silas grins.

"I didn't realize they'd be this worked up about the preseason," he says. "I'd have picked somewhere quieter."

I take the top bun off my two-thirds-finished burger and pick off a piece of bacon, because I'm pretty much done but I'll always eat bacon.

"Why?" I ask, crunching it between my teeth. "Isn't crowded and loud the point?"

"It can be one without the other," he points out, and I make a face. *Crowded and loud* is far from my favorite kind of place, but it's not like anyone is looking at me here, tucked into a booth against the wall and peacefully minding my own business.

This whole week, we've followed Silas's schedule and my rules down to the letter. All the PDA has been normal. The kisses have been brief and polite. Evan's been in a terrible mood. My revenge-fake-dating plan is going exactly according to specifications, and that's great and I don't wish that anything were different, even a little.

"You into football?" I ask as there's a minor roar behind me and Silas's gaze flicks to the screen for a few seconds.

"Not much any more," he admits, still watching. "I used to be but I got too busy to really follow it. You?"

I lean back, bacon finished, and pick up my beer.

"Oh, yeah, I love sports," I say. "I'm a total... sports head, over here."

"You say that like no dork has ever watched football," he teases.

"Did you just call me a dork?" I ask, honestly surprised, but he grins it away.

"You know what I mean," Silas goes on. "As if there's no one on the planet who likes both *Doctor Who* and Monday Night Football."

"Fine," I say, straightening my shoulders. "No, I don't follow football. Thank you for asking. I'm sorry that your lifestyle no longer allows for viewing frivolous competitive events."

"Don't be, I don't mind," he says. "Watching's been a habit since I played in high school."

"Football?"

"Isn't that what we're talking about?"

"I thought you played baseball."

Silas laughs. I almost do, too.

"You want to know a secret? Lots of people play both. In high school, anyway."

I roll my eyes at him, still trying not to smile.

"You gonna brag about making all-state in that, too?"

His grin tells me everything I need to know.

"Oh, shut *up*," I say. "What, were you the star quarterback?"

"Why do you keep asking questions you don't want the answers to?"

"I have no idea," I answer honestly, and drink some more beer. I look away from Silas and at the wall by our table, which has a rusted railroad crossing sign hanging on it, and for once I'm grateful for the Asian glow that hides my blush.

It's weirdly thrilling that the kind of guy who wouldn't have looked at me twice in high school is here, now, with me. Sure, he's pretending because I sort of forced him into it, and yes, he'll probably go on lots of dates with blondes who used to cheerlead when we're done, but for right now it's... satisfying. Like I got the last laugh, somehow.

"You didn't play sports?" he asks, still watching me.

I scoff.

"Is finding used tampons in my locker while half the school stands behind me and laughs a sport?" I ask, half-laughing.

Silas's face changes, his brows coming together, the sparkle in his eyes going out.

"Jesus," he says.

Oops, I've horrified him. Fuck. I shake my head and

wave one hand in the air, like I can chase away what I just said.

"That only happened once," I say, which is technically true. "But yeah. No sports."

He's still frowning at me, strangely concerned. I glance at him and then back at a television, where men in uniform are doing stuff with a ball.

I wish I hadn't said that. Why the hell did I say that? Why, of all the shit that happened to me in high school, did I tell him about *the tampons*? This is why they were in the locker in the first place, because I'm an awkward dork who brings up things like disgusting locker tampons.

"Are you okay?" he asks, after a moment.

I have the presence of mind to smile.

"What? Yeah, of course," I say, gesturing with the half-empty beer. "It was like... twenty years ago. I think I've moved on."

He doesn't answer right away, leaning back on his side of the booth, those eyes scanning my face like he's concerned. My face gets hotter. My heart gets faster.

"Right," he says. "That's still fucked up, though."

I swallow against saying *that wasn't even the worst.*

"Like you never tortured nerds," I tease.

"Not like that."

"You never gave some glasses-wearing dork a swirly?" I go on, forcing myself to sound lighter than I feel. "You never, like, stuck some short kid on top of a really tall cabinet and then left him to get down on his own?"

"No," he says, starting to sound defensive.

"I'm sure you were an angel."

I don't know why I'm pushing him like this, because it's not like we went to high school together. It's not even like the jocks at my high school were the ones who made my life awful—they mostly ignored me. It was the kids a few rungs down the social ladder, who just needed someone to step on, who did.

"I didn't say *that*," he says now, and he runs a hand through his hair like he's a little embarrassed. "But I never did shit to anyone who didn't deserve it. And especially not the dorks. Levi would've killed me, for one."

"The same Levi with the crows?"

"The same."

"I gotta meet this guy," I say, offhandedly, because this conversation has gotten more personal than I meant for it to, and I've gotta say something.

Across the table, Silas shifts slightly, then cocks his head.

"You should," he says, thoughtfully. "You'd like him."

I drink more beer and don't know what to say, so I look at a screen. Still sports, only now they're running down the field, presumably with a ball. I wonder if an offer to meet the best friend—who's apparently been the best friend for a very long time—is part of the fake relationship show, or whether Silas and I are also... friends?

*Friends* is fine. Actually, no: *friends* is great, given my opinion of him two weeks ago. *Friends* is a monumental change and a small miracle. I like *friends*.

Except it didn't feel like friends when he kissed me on the Ferris wheel and that small discordant hitch in the pattern has been tickling at the back of my mind ever since, like an uncomfortable tag in a cashmere sweater. Ever since there's been polite hand-holding and light standing-with-an-arm-around-my-waist and gentlemanly hand-on-the-back-while-I-go-through-a-door and perfunctory, quick, closed-mouth kisses and none of these things has stopped me from getting myself off every night this week imagining that my hand is Silas's mouth.

I know it's simple frustration. There hasn't been anyone since Evan, a little over a year ago, because the idea of finding a person to have sexual contact with was off-putting at worst and exhausting at best, or at least it was until—

Nope.

Maybe I should do it anyway. Maybe when this weird pretend thing with Silas is done, I'll drive a couple of towns over and find some country western bar and endure some funny looks while I do a line dance and pick up some redneck for sex purposes, because that *totally* sounds like something I could do without having a panic attack or three.

Or I'll buy myself another fancy vibrator. One of those two things.

"You got any insider info for Saturday?" Silas asks.

I stare at him for a minute, trying to remember what we were talking about.

"Our TBD date?" he prompts, a slow smile crossing his face. "You said you'd gather intel if you could."

About what Evan's up to, he means, and about where he'll be so we can piss him off.

"Oh! Right," I say, pushing my glasses up. "Actually, he's gonna be out of town, so if there's somewhere that's better for you to run into your coworkers, we could do that."

"Where's he going?" Silas asks, still smiling. "He's not leaving yet, is he?"

"I wish," I say, and push my glasses up again. It's habit. "Olivia's coming down and they're going to some hotel for the weekend."

Silas looks at me, perfectly still, relaxed against the back of the booth. He's still got on the button-down shirt and slacks that he wore to work today, the sleeves rolled up to the elbow, the top button undone. I ignore the way his forearm flexes as he taps his beer glass with one finger.

"Which one?" he asks, and I shrug.

"I don't know, I wasn't really listening," I say.

"You were supposed to."

"They'll be gone! What does it matter?"

Now he reaches across the table and steals my last pickle spear from my plate, taking a bite. That teasing half-smile never leaves his face, like everything he says or does or thinks is some kind of secret joke, and I'm in on the secret.

"Well, what did he say about it?"

There's a nervous flutter behind my ribcage, like eels wrestling in the mud. I keep my spine straight.

"That it's nice?" I say, shrugging with an insouciance I don't feel. "That it'll be a break from this backwoods town and his incompetent coworkers?"

Silas's face darkens at *incompetent coworkers*, and I don't find a small twinge of satisfaction in that as I lean my own elbows on the table and take another drink of my beer.

"I think there's hot springs," I go on, trying to remember much beyond *babe I can't wait to get out of here and spend a whole weekend with you.* "And a river, maybe?"

"Was it Ironwood Springs?"

I narrow my eyes.

"That sounds right," I say.

For a moment, we look at each other.

"Why?" I finally ask.

In answer, I get a slow smile. Silas takes his time settling his beer on the table in front of us, rubbing his hands together, then leaning in until he's leaning on his elbows, a wickedly conspiratorial look on his face.

I didn't know Silas could look *wicked*. It... works for him, in a way I didn't expect, his eyes flashing and a lock of red-brown hair falling over his forehead. My stomach flips.

"Silas," I say, slowly, enjoying the way my tongue curls around his name. "Are you thinking something devious?"

In the low light, his eyes have gone gray-blue, the dark spokes shot through them deep navy. His almost-freckles are invisible, and his eyes search my face with a long, lingering look before that charming smile chases all the wickedness away like shadows at high noon.

"I bet we could ruin their weekend," he says. "You in?"

# TWENTY-TWO

## SILAS

THE IRONWOOD SPRINGS RESORT HOTEL hasn't changed in at least twenty-five years. It might not have undergone a deep clean in twenty-five years, because everything is exactly the same as I remember it being when my grandparents took my sister and I here for a weekend when I was in middle school: animal heads on the wall interspersed with kitschy metal signs, a massive stone fireplace, green and yellow pendant lights hanging over the front desk.

The hotel bar is even kitschier. It's designed like the interior of a log cabin, and everything that isn't rough wood is a day-glo color straight out of 1975. There are vintage hubcaps covering one wooden wall, an ancient Pabst Blue Ribbon neon sign, a lava lamp in one corner, and George Strait playing loudly over the speakers.

I love it.

It's Friday night, so the bar's in full swing: not crowded, but not not crowded. As we walk in from the lobby, I can practically feel Kat tense at the number of people, her silence radiating outward. Sixty seconds ago, back in the room we're sharing, she laughed at the fact that I brought slippers with me, but now she's quiet and upright, alert.

I put my hand on her lower back and stroke my thumb along the valley of her spine. She's strung like a suspension bridge. I keep an eye out for Meckler and his new girlfriend, but there's no sign.

"Gin and tonic?" I ask her when we get to the bar, but she's already picked up a cocktail menu and is scanning it.

"Too boring," I can barely hear her say.

I lean down and get my lips closer to her ear.

"What's exciting, then?"

Kat doesn't answer right away, just cocks her head slightly in a way that makes one shoulder come up a little, shifts her hips toward me. She's still got on the dress she wore to work though she's taken off the blazer she had on over it: deep red, v-neck, and made of something soft that outlines her thighs when she walks.

"This one," she finally says, and she arches her neck back so she can talk into my ear, voice buzzing against me. My hand is still on her back. I press my thumb in a little harder into the dip between two vertebrae.

"A Backwoods Bourbon Sour?"

"Please."

"What should I get?"

"Depends on what you like."

I look at the list longer than I should, but Kat's relaxed a little, her shoulders down from around her ears and pressed softly against mine.

"Should I get a Thunderstorm or a Hot & Humid?" I ask her, just because I get to put my mouth near her ear.

"Will you regret tequila more than rum?"

"It's one drink. I won't regret anything," I tell her, which is true.

"Get the Thunderstorm. I want to try it."

I could point out that I wanted to try her cotton candy last weekend, but instead I order our drinks and when the bartender goes to make them, I lean an elbow on the bar and turn toward her. Kat pushes her glasses up and glances around, lips pressed together, like she's nervous and trying not to show it. The song on the radio switches to Johnny Cash, and I lean in.

"Want to hear a joke?" I ask, settling my fingertips on her hip.

Kat gives me a very skeptical look.

"Do I?"

I can't help but grin.

"What happens when you play a country song backward?"

Kat considers the question carefully, her eyes narrowing, her lips moving as she thinks.

"You summon a country demon?" she finally guesses, and I laugh.

"Not quite," I tell her. "You get your wife back, you get your dog back, you get your truck back..."

Kat snorts and then she's smiling, even though we're in this crowded bar looking for Meckler, and the thrill of victory zips through me.

"You think of that all by yourself?" she teases.

"Of course not."

"It's not bad."

"That means you're gonna use it?"

"Sure, I'll put it in my standup routine," she says, and then the bartender's back, sliding two drinks across the bar to us. Kat's has a maraschino cherry on top, and for a moment, I wonder what she'd do if I stole it.

"Don't you fucking dare," she says, voice low.

"Dare *what?*" I ask, mock-offended.

"Take my cherry," she says, grabbing her glass protectively. "Don't even look at it. It's mine, I'm going to enjoy it after I finish my drink, and if you so much as make an attempt at it, I will *end* you."

God, it's fun to rile her up, especially when I can do it to get her out of her head.

"Just a nibble," I bargain.

"Ew. *No.*"

"A lick?"

And now her eyes dart up to mine, pure black in the dark bar, and there's a heat behind them that makes my mouth go dry.

"No, Silas, you cannot lick my cherry," she says, with remarkable calm, and I'm the one left needing to look away and take a sip of my own, cherry-less drink.

"Fine, it's safe," I grudgingly give in. "Patio?"

Kat nods, relief on her face, and we leave the bar.

· · · · · ★ ★ ★ ★ · · · ·

"I MIGHT HAVE GOTTEN IT WRONG," she says.

We're outside on a second-floor deck, sitting on an outdoor couch with an unlit fire pit in front of us and the wall to our backs, lights strung overhead. Past the railing of the deck is the resort's pool complex: a swimming pool currently lit with shifting underwater colors, smaller hot tubs dotted up a slight hill, each cleverly surrounded by rocks and foliage. According to the brochure I read earlier, each one is a slightly different temperature from the hot springs.

"I hope we're at the right place," I agree.

"You're the one who said it was here," she points out. "I just said hot springs and river."

"I'm ninety-five percent sure," I say, and take a sip of my almost-finished drink. "Maybe ninety-six."

Next to me, Kat sighs.

"Do we have a strategy?" she asks.

Her legs are crossed under the soft red skirt of her dress, and I've got one arm slung around her. The condensation from her glass trickles over the knuckles of her hand, leaving wet spots on the fabric, and her hair whispers against my skin as she turns her head.

One might have been the wrong number of drinks. A couple more and I could numb this out. None and I'd have a little more willpower, but one drink dulls my judgement exactly enough that I can't quit looking at her but also won't do anything about it.

"When we find them, we hang around and call each other babe a whole lot," I say.

"That's the activity. What's the objective?"

She takes another sip, and I watch her swallow before I answer. The damn cherry is still in her glass and God, I want to grab it, just to see what she'd do. Right now I feel thirteen all over again, a mess of warring impulses and urges that I can't quell and can't satisfy.

"Ruin their good time?" I say, swirling the dregs of my own drink. "Annoy them until they leave the resort early?"

"Hmm." She leans her head back onto my arm. The cherry's still there, her glass pretty much empty.

"His girlfriend's not an innocent victim in all this, is she?" I ask, the thought suddenly occurring to me. I've been so wrapped up in Kat's vengeance that I kinda forgot there was someone else involved, too.

"His girlfriend who was fucking my fiancé behind my back?" she asks dryly. "Nah."

"Did she know?"

I realize it's a bit late to ask, but still.

"She was his assistant," Kat snorts. "Yeah. She knew."

"Jesus."

She shrugs and drains her drink until there's nothing but ice and a single maraschino cherry left, bright red in the dark, fucking *taunting* me to steal it from her. Fuck. I don't even like cherries that much, but I do like riling Kat up.

"Any idea what they're planning on doing here?" I ask her, after a long silence because I need to say something, to have a plan.

"I don't know, Silas," Kat sighs, exasperated. "It's a resort. There's a pool. There's hot tubs. There's a river and some trails and some tennis courts, I think."

"Do they play tennis?"

"I half-listened to a phone call, I didn't record them and memorize their plans," she says. "I'm not even sure we're at the right place, remember?"

I finish the last watery dregs of my own drink, then put the empty glass on a side table, fighting a grin at the edge in her voice.

"I'm starting to think you lured me out here for the pleasure of my company," I tease her, and Kat huffs out an explosive little laugh.

"Definitely not."

"You sure?" I ask, eyeing the cherry in her glass. It is *calling my name.* "Because it seems like—"

I grab for the cherry. It takes me a second, because everything in her glass is wet and slippery and I'm trying for the stem but I get the fruit instead, and the second Kat realizes what I'm doing she yelps and tries to stop me.

Her glass spills to the couch, getting freezing water and ice over both of us, and she's got one hand around my wrist, hauling my hand forward, and with the other she's trying to dislodge the cherry but we're both slippery.

"You asshole," she hisses. "Goddammit, Silas. Give me that."

"You weren't eating it."

"I wasn't eating it *yet*."

"There's gotta be some sort of time limit," I point out as her fingers slide around mine. We're mangling this cherry and I can hear her breathing, feel the heat of her hand locked around my wrist. She's surprisingly strong.

Then she stops and looks at me, eyes narrowed. I grin back at her.

"You could say please," I say, my voice comes low and scratchy as tires on a gravel road.

Then her mouth is on my hand and I don't have another thought, because as she sinks her teeth into the cherry they scrape my fingers and then there's the hot heat of her mouth against them, the slide of her tongue on the pad of my thumb, her hand still holding my wrist, and then she's got the cherry but her lips close around my fingertips and there's a flutter of teeth and tongue and she's sitting up straight, plucking the stem from her mouth and chewing her prize and looking at me like she won the Superbowl or something.

All I can do is watch her mouth and listen to my heartbeat crash against my ribs. I wait, breathless, for her throat to move in the dark. It does. She licks her lips.

The next second my mouth is on hers.

Kat is hot and sweet, soft and sharp. Kat tastes like maraschino cherry and rum and she pushes back against me, hard, threads her fingers through my hair. Kat slides her tongue against mine and makes a noise when she does and she trails her cold fingers down my neck until I gasp into her mouth, grab her wrist, pull it away.

"Quit it," I growl, but she laughs and bites my lower lip and then we're kissing again and she's half on my lap, her cold hand splayed open on my chest. I grab her waist, her back, her hip. I want to dip my fingers under the hem of her dress. I want to see if the red mark I left when I fell asleep on her is still there. I want to leave five more marks on her neck and I want her to suck the cherry juice from my fingers and look at me with her sharp dark eyes while she does it.

But I settle for this kiss, for her hands on me, for my fingers in her hair and the sound she gasps into my mouth when I wrap it around my fingers and tug just hard enough.

That's within the rules. So is the kiss I plant on her jawline, on her throat, careful and closed-mouth this time. Kat made rules and God knows I've memorized them, the creases in my printout worn thin, every boundary respected with military precision. That, at least, I'm good at.

But Kat pulls back before I can say something, her lips flushed deep pink in the dark. Her eyes look like they're all pupil and she swallows again, breathing hard, and her gaze flicks over my shoulder, her spine straightening.

*Don't look at him. Look at me,* I think, and I want to take her face in my hands and kiss her until we've obliterated everything else, but I don't. I put on a smile and I turn, and exactly as I expected, Meckler's standing there with a pretty blonde and they're *watching* us.

"Hey, Meckler!" I call, like I didn't just have Kat half wrapped around me. "Fancy seeing you here!"

He nods and raises a beer, his eyes on Kat before they turn away.

# TWENTY-THREE

## KAT

I LAY flat on my back, head sinking into the too-fluffy hotel pillow, arms atop the covers, and stare at the ceiling. Next to me, I can hear Silas breathing steadily. I'm pretty sure he's in the exact same position I am, both of us on the edges of this massive king bed.

It's weird. It would be weird no matter what, but at least for me, it's about three times weirder because not too long ago, I *ate a maraschino cherry from his hand* and then we made out on a couch while Evan and Olivia apparently watched from across the patio and honestly, what is even happening? Why is this my life?

I'm pretty sure there are people out there who make reasonable, rational choices at every turn and not... whatever the hell I've been doing for the past year. I can't even tell when I went wrong to begin with. Was it when my hot coworker asked me out three years ago, and I said yes? Was it when I threw my life into disarray and moved to Sprucevale, where I knew precisely one person? Was it when I told Evan that Silas was my *lover*?

On the other side of the bed, Silas heaves a deep breath

and crosses his arms over his head on the pillow. I push myself up on one elbow to look at him. After a moment, he opens his eyes.

"Are you watching me sleep?"

"You're not sleeping."

"I was working on it."

"How was that going?"

He rolls onto his side to face me, a blurry shape with his head pillowed on one bicep, and my heart stutters a little. I could touch him. Right now, I could reach out and touch him. In the dark. In this bed. Maybe he'd kiss me back where no one could see.

In other words, if I wanted to, I could make it weird.

"Are we being creepy?" I blurt out.

"Watching me sleep? Yes," he says, and I can't see the smile but I can hear it.

"Looking at you to see if you're awake isn't watching you sleep," I point out. "If I were going to watch you sleep I'd pull up an armchair or some shit and really make an evening of it."

"So you've made a plan?"

I narrow my eyes at the blurry shape in front of me.

"Are you disappointed that I don't want to watch you sleep?" I ask. "If you want it that much, I guess I could arrange something. As a favor to you."

"Sure. To me," he says. I sigh, then flop back onto my pillow.

"We followed my ex-boyfriend on vacation," I tell the ceiling, and if Silas listens it's okay.

"Fiancé."

"Let me forget one bad decision."

I can hear him chuckle in the dark.

"It would be creepy if we followed them around all day

tomorrow and started dry-humping every time they turned to look at us," he says, voice so low and slow I can almost pretend Silas didn't just say dry-humping. "But we happen to be hanging out at the same resort."

He sounds so confident that I nearly believe that my actions are not those of a madwoman.

"Maybe we won't run into them again," I tell the ceiling.

"Running into them is the point, Kat."

He's right, of course. Never mind that earlier, I wished they weren't there so we could keep making out on the patio. Maybe we'd be naked in this bed right now instead of wearing pajamas and discussing our business deal.

I tighten my hands in the comforter and chase the thought away.

"Right. I know," I say, and we lapse into silence for a while.

Eventually, Silas clears his throat.

"It probably won't happen, but sometimes I don't sleep well," he says.

I look over. He's on his back, staring at the ceiling, one arm over his head, not looking at me, something set and determined in his blurry form. It doesn't take much to figure out what he means.

"Nightmares?"

"Something like that."

I roll my eyes in the dark and move onto my side again, trying to get comfortable.

"You can just say *yes*, for fuck's sake."

"Yeah. Nightmares," he says, voice flat. "Hardly ever any more, but I wanted to let you know."

The pillow is so squishy that I can only see him with one eye, still staring up at the ceiling like he's made of stone, and something about it makes me bite back whatever sharp retort I was going to make and just see him.

Silas, with eyes like lakes and secret freckles. Silas, who talked me down from a panic attack. Silas, who has nightmares and agreed to come on this impulsive, creepy vacation and share a bed with me anyway.

Silas, who's mended with gold and still staring at the ceiling like he can't bear to look at me.

"How do I help if you do?" I finally ask.

"Just wake me up and go back to sleep," he says.

"That's it?"

"That's it."

I want to push him into a real answer, here, in the dark, in this bed we're sharing, on this vacation we're taking together for reasons that are starting to feel so snarled that I'm less sure what they are with every passing moment. I want to slice through the layers he's put up around himself, and press my hand against whatever's underneath.

I want to tell him he can trust me. That he can use me however he needs me.

I want to kiss him again. I *really* fucking want to kiss him again.

But instead I look back at the ceiling and wish there were two beds. I wish there were two rooms. I curse my bravado last night, when we made these plans and I was so sure that two mature adults sharing a single king bed wouldn't be a big deal.

I should have never done this. All this pretending is fucking with my head, and God knows my people-reading ability was shit to begin with as evidenced by my entire relationship with Evan. With Silas it's constant, branching possibilities of *is this desire or agreement,* of *are we pretending and how much are we pretending?*

Is there a percentage? Is ten percent of every kiss true? Twenty? How much of a kiss is true between actual romantic partners, and can it ever be a hundred percent or does every human on earth always hold something back?

These are not useful thoughts, and I know it. Silas is silent. I close my eyes. I count my breaths.

# TWENTY-FOUR

## SILAS

I WAKE up in the dark. There's something soft in my face and something else soft under my arm and I freeze, stare wide-eyed into nothingness.

Then, of course, I remember: that the soft tangle in my face is Kat's hair, that the softness under my arm is Kat herself. I'm on my stomach and she's on her back and despite the vastness of the bed, we both migrated to the middle during the night.

There must be a dip in the mattress or something.

I lie there, awake, and don't move. I didn't set my alarm but it's not like I need to bother anymore; get up at five in the morning for a couple of years and that's what happens. So I lie there, still, in the deep quiet dark of early morning, and Kat breathes, her body shifting under my arm.

And oh, this is nice.

*God*, this is nice.

Fuck, this is so fucking nice, to be warm and sleepy and comfortable, to be sprawled against another person. It feels so good that I can't even believe how good it feels. I had almost forgotten how good, because the last time I woke up with someone was...

I don't remember. It doesn't matter. I lie there, perfectly still, until Kat rolls over on her own and my hand spills off of her, and then I get up and head to the hotel gym.

· · · · ★ ★ ★ · · · ·

I'M STANDING at the door to our room, two coffees from the lobby balanced in one hand as I swipe the keycard with the other, when the door to the room next to ours opens and I glance up.

My friendly *good morning* dies on my lips, because Meckler steps out.

Neither of us says anything, but I can still feel us circling like rival wolves.

Then he walks away, and I let myself into the room.

# TWENTY-FIVE

## KAT

SILAS HEAVES himself out of the pool, and I look back at the book open in front of me so I can pretend I haven't been ogling him for the past fifteen minutes. At least I'm wearing sunglasses, and he's been busy hitting a beach ball back and forth with some kids, so he probably hasn't noticed that I haven't turned a page in a very long time.

Fifteen seconds later a shadow falls across my feet, and I look up.

"You gonna come in?" he asks.

I put one hand on the top of my hat and gaze up at Silas, dripping wet in nothing but blue swimming trunks with bright pink flamingos, the early afternoon sun lighting him up like it was created for exactly this purpose. He's smiling down at me, running a hand through his wet hair, and I fight the urge to look behind myself to see who he's *really* looking at.

"I'm not really a... wet kind of person," I tell him, honestly.

"You could change that."

"I'm having a very nice time being dry, is the thing," I

238

say, and cross my ankles, holding my place in the book with a finger. "Due to being, you know, *dry*."

"Hmm," Silas says, and nods, then glances around for a moment before looking back at me, arms folding over his chest. "Well, the thing is that it's better if you go in voluntarily."

My heart kicks, the soft wings of anxiety unfurling in my chest. I freeze and can't help but glance around the crowded pool, at the dozens of people who'd be watching me make a spectacle of myself if Silas threw me into the pool.

Before I can say anything, he's sitting sideways on the end of my lounge chair, leaning back on his hands, still sunlit as anything.

"Sorry. Kidding," he says.

"Good," I say, trying for a lightness I don't quite feel yet and pull my feet back so he's got more space, curling one under me and propping one up.

Still leaning back, Silas grabs one foot and strokes his thumb over the knob of my ankle, and even though it's hot as anything today, a shiver runs up my leg.

"You really should come in, though," he goes on. "It's refreshing."

"I'd be blind as a bat," I point out, because pools and glasses don't really mix.

"I'll hold onto you."

It's not unappealing.

"Maybe in a while," I demure, and for no reason at all I extend my leg until my toes are touching his side, right under that long scar he's got across his ribs. I wiggle them and his smile gets wider.

"What are you reading?"

I hold up the book, finger still stuck in the middle.

"*The Wind-Up Bird Chronicle?*" I say, making it a question for some reason. "My sister's been after me to read it."

Silas nods.

"Is that good?"

"It's odd," I say, flipping it back around so I can look at the cover. "And sort of... soothing? I don't know."

We both sit in silence for a moment, my toes against his hip, his thumb still stroking my ankle.

"One of the characters spends a lot of time sitting at the bottom of a dry well. It sounds kind of nice," I admit.

"Why are they in a well?"

"It's complicated."

Silas doesn't answer. He tilts his head from side to side, like he's getting the kinks out of his neck, then tilts his face back into the sun. The light gleams off his hair, off the divot in his throat, off the slippery muscles of his arms and chest, the hair there slicked down from the pool until it disappears under his swim trunks.

Sitting back in the shadows, under a giant hat and sunglasses and an umbrella, a floor-length voluminous coverup over my swimsuit, I watch him looking like the sun exists simply to shine on him.

Then he looks over at me, a playful smile on his face, head still cocked to one side.

"Move," he says.

"*You* move," I start but he's already pushed my foot aside as he crawls up the chair toward me and before I can do anything he's draped over me, his back to my chest and his head on my shoulder, one hand on my thigh.

"Oh. Hi," I say, stupidly, panic fluttering in my chest for no reason at all. I put the book down. "You're still wet."

He grabs my ankle and crosses it over his thigh so we're tangled together, this chair clearly meant for one person, his skin water-cooled against mine. My heart's beating so hard I wonder if he can hear it.

"It's a nice day, you'll dry soon enough," he says, voice lazy like sunlight.

"Hmph," I say, but I realize that my hand is already trailing through his wet hair, the slight curls wrapping around my fingers. Silas sighs and sinks into me a little more, his fingers drawing slow shapes on the inside of my knee.

Evan and Olivia must be here, somewhere. Silas must have seen them and come over to ostentatiously cuddle me because running into them is the point, after all, but I don't ask. I don't even look.

Instead, I drape my other arm over his shoulder, flatten my palm against his chest, feel it rise and fall as he breathes. He puts his hand over mine like it's second nature.

It takes a long time, but he's right. We dry eventually.

· · · · ★ ★ ★ ★ · · · ·

I TAKE another sip of my drink, leaning back against the balcony railing, watching the glass doors to the lobby and bar.

"What was that story you started telling me?" Silas asks. We're facing in opposite directions and he's leaning his forearms on the railing, his drink already finished, looking out over the pool with its technicolor lights.

"I told you a story?"

"In the alleyway, outside karaoke," he says. His forearm's against my waist, warm through the thin jersey of my maxi dress. His voice is warm, too. "Something about everything but tin being illegal."

"Oh, God," I say, huffing out a laugh.

"What?" He's grinning, those eyes dancing like I've told a joke.

"It was..." I look at him, then away, and lose the words. "Nevermind."

"Do you think saying *nevermind* is gonna call me off?"

I sigh, stretching my neck backward, closing my eyes. The day's finally cooled off and there's a slight breeze out here, just enough to move my hair around.

"I don't think a legion of tanks is gonna call you off."

"That's not what you call a group of—"

"Sorry, a gaggle of tanks."

Silas snorts.

"A flock?"

"Quit arguing and tell me already," he says. "We both know you're gonna."

I sigh, then take a sip of my nearly-empty drink. It's the same drink I got at the bar last night, because that drink was good, and because it had a cherry. This one does, too, and I haven't eaten it yet.

Not because I'm hoping Silas will steal it again. I just... haven't.

"It was a D&D campaign I did in college," I tell him. "I used to run them. That's how I met Anna Grace, actually."

"Seriously?"

"Yup."

"I wouldn't have guessed."

"About her, or about me?"

That gets a quiet laugh.

"About either of you," he says, and I think his arm might move a little more solidly against my side, and I can feel his heartbeat on my skin like I'm wearing it. "Used to. Do you still?"

"Nah," I say, tracing a finger through the condensation

242

on the outside of the glass. "I have some friends from up north who still do it, and I try to get on Skype with them every so often but it's hard to schedule, you know?"

Silas nods. He shifts slightly and then I'm leaning into him a little more, the outside of my knee pressing against the outside of his. Arm notched in my waist. I've had one drink and I feel like I'm made of night air and fireworks.

This afternoon after the pool we took the nature walk along the river, and we held hands without even talking about it. It ended at an overlook by a waterfall, and when we stood at the railing he put his chin on my shoulder and his arm around my waist, and the mist floated onto all the parts of me that weren't touching him, and despite everything I was too nervous to say kiss me.

I'm still too nervous. That's why there's a cherry, I guess.

"You didn't finish your drink yet," he points out.

I roll my eyes and take the last swallow of rum-flavored melted ice, condensation dripping on the front of my dress as I do.

"There," I say.

"You're not gonna eat the cherry?"

"I'm saving it."

One eyebrow lifts.

"For what?"

*For you to steal it.*

"The right time," I say aloud, and Silas nods. He looks away for a moment, surveying the pool below us before he looks back at me.

"How about now?"

"Not yet."

He glances away again, a smile tugging at his mouth.

"How about... now?"

"How long are you gonna do this for?" I ask, fighting back my own smile.

"Until you eat it. How about now?"

I give Silas a long, dramatic sigh, then reach into my glass. I pull the cherry out by the stem, tap it gently on the inside of the glass. My heart thumps wildly, and before I can stop myself I hold it out to Silas.

And he smiles but God, the way his eyes darken. He shifts against the railing and then slides his hand across my stomach until he fits it over my hip, the heat of him soaking through the fabric. I can't breathe. I have never breathed.

"This a trick?" he asks, voice soft and low.

"Just a cherry," I answer, not much above a whisper.

With that he grabs it in his teeth and I hold onto the stem until it pops off. We don't break eye contact until he chews and swallows.

And then, finally, he leans in and kisses me. His mouth is hot and he tastes a lot like cherry and a little like whiskey. It's slow and unhurried, my fingers in his hair, and for once I let myself enjoy it without wondering who's watching or if the right people are watching or if this is happening because of our ulterior motives or if, for some reason, Silas just wanted to kiss me.

He doesn't let me go when we pull apart, still standing by the railing of the huge balcony, off to one side but still visible from everywhere.

I want to stay here forever. I want to drink a bottle of whiskey. I want to get high and go swimming. I want to run back to the waterfall and tame it, grab the stars out of the sky, fight the wind.

I want to kiss Silas again, to shove him down on one of these couches and climb on top of him. I want to strip him and feel his skin on mine.

"Thanks," Silas says, and it pulls me back. I realize I've still got a hand on his chest, lightly dragging my knuckles up and down his sternum.

"You seemed like you wanted it more than I did," I say.

And then, because I can never leave a nice moment alone: "Any sign of them?"

Silas glances around. Something shifts in the air between us and I curse myself, my anxiety, this need I have for everyone around me to be unwilling to get close.

"Thought I saw them a few minutes ago," he says, nodding down at the pool. "Maybe they'll be back."

"Yeah," I say, and nod, and swallow hard, and don't quite look at Silas. "Probably."

# TWENTY-SIX

## SILAS

WE'VE BARELY GOTTEN BACK into the room later that night when the shouting starts next door, loud enough to cut Kat off mid-sentence, for us to both glance at the wall besides the bed.

"Yikes," she says. "I thought old buildings were supposed to have *thicker—*"

Then she stops and frowns, still staring at the wall, and I remember something.

"Meckler and his girlfriend are next door," I say, leaning back against the dresser, my hands in my pockets. "I ran into him coming back from the gym this morning. Forgot to mention it."

The lie comes out casually as anything, and Kat doesn't seem to notice. I didn't *forget*. I couldn't forget that even when we came back here and fell asleep across the bed from each other, he'd be haunting me. That he'd been haunting me this morning, when I woke up, stretched across her even if I didn't know it yet.

I wanted to forget because today was... good. Great, maybe. My life is pretty good these days but today felt like walking on sunbeams and relaxing on clouds, like I was in an untouchable bubble with Kat who stroked my hair while I dozed off by the pool.

All I had to do was ignore how sometimes her eyes would dart away from me, like she was looking to see if someone else was there. The way she kissed me on the balcony and then wanted to know where he was.

So, no, I didn't mention that Meckler is next door to us because I wanted to think about him as little as possible.

"Olivia," Kat supplies, her eyes still on the wall. "The girlfriend is Olivia."

She's perfectly still, her floor-length dress barely rippling with remembered movement, eyes narrowed behind her glasses.

I don't want to know the girlfriend's name, either. I don't even want to know his. He doesn't deserve anything but a tossed-off designation: ex-fiancé.

"Sure," I say instead as another raised voice floats through the wall.

Kat looks at me, raises one eyebrow, and then heads into the bathroom. When she comes back a second later, she's got a glass in her hand, and she holds it up to the wall, her ear to the open end.

"That's not how you eavesdrop," I point out, voice low.

"Sure it is."

I settle on the side of the bed, leaning back on my hands, a few feet away from where she's standing.

"It goes the other way. The sound travels through the glass."

Kat shoots me a skeptical look, but flips the glass around. I sit back and watch her, eyes unfocused on the middle distance, listening.

I swear I can still taste the cherry. I swear I can still taste her and the sensation's got me halfway hard, even as we hear the raised voices from next door. Even as she stands here with me and listens to them.

I want to touch her. I want to pull her to me. I want to hold her until I leave finger marks on her skin and I want to kiss the bruises in the morning. I want her to bite me and leave teeth marks.

For the first time in so long I want, and I'm dizzy with it.

"They fucking?" I ask, my mind single-track.

"I hope not," she says dryly.

I raise one eyebrow. I could probably make out some of the words if I cared to, but I don't.

"I think they're fighting about work," she goes on, after a moment. "They sound pretty drunk."

"Should we worry?"

"I don't think so."

Then she looks right at me, one eyebrow raised, and now she looks amused.

"She's pissed that he's sharing an office with his ex," she says, and even in the low light of the bedside lamps, I can tell that all the skin I can see has flushed bright pink, even pinker than she was a minute ago and I want to push my face into her neck, feel that pretty heat all over me.

"His ex meaning you?" I ask, eyes on the hollow of her throat.

"She thinks I'm scheming to get him back."

That gets a small eyeroll, even as my stomach tightens.

"Apparently he complains about me a lot? Shit, they're moving away from the wall," she says, scrunching up her face. "Ugh."

That means it's working. Great. Soon the girlfriend whose name I don't care about will be gone and Meckler will be on his knees and Kat will have her revenge and that will be mission accomplished and we can be done with this weird fucking charade. Finito, The End, That's All, Folks, and good because it's not like cherry kisses and poolside cuddling was going to work out anyway.

Not when she's always looking for him. Not when the moment we're alone, she starts asking whether I have nightmares. Not when we only like each other for the purposes of the mission.

Kat sighs and plunks the glass down on the table. Through the wall, the voices fade a little.

And then I get a brilliant idea.

"Want to make them even more jealous?" I ask, voice low so they can't hear it.

"What, by knocking on their door and then making out when they open it?"

"Have some subtlety," I tease her, and she rolls her eyes at me. Smiling, though. "Like this."

I reach a hand out to the headboard and shove, hard as I can. It knocks into the wall with a loud, dull *thunk* that's definitely audible from the other side.

Kat frowns, her arms folded over her chest.

"Okay, how is that—" she starts, and then stops. "Oh."

I do it again, working into a slow rhythm. Every inch of Kat's skin that I can see turns dull pink under her gold.

"I see," she says, after a moment. She takes a deep breath, looks at me like she's thinking something.

"Yeah?"

"You can't *just* have headboard slamming," she says, voice quiet. The light's low in here—the two bedside lamps, nothing else—but I'd swear she's blushing harder. "I mean. That's not..."

I lift one eyebrow and hit the headboard into the wall again.

"Satisfying?"

"Everything," she says.

"How ungentlemanly of me," I say, and I stop banging the headboard. "You're right, it'll sound better if there's some foreplay."

"Right," she says, and she nods tensely, not quite looking at me. "We should probably, like, rustle the sheets some first—"

"How loud can you moan?"

Kat closes her eyes and scrunches up her face, and I swear I can see her fight with herself: the part of her that doesn't want to make loud sex noises versus the part of her who suggested this in the first place.

Finally she takes a deep breath.

"Ohhhh," she shouts. It sounds like she's at a sporting event, booing the opposing team.

"Nevermind," I tell her, leaning back on my hands. "We're fucked. They're gonna think we're over here watching baseball."

"I'm not good at sex noises, okay?" she hisses.

Embarrassing, how that phrase makes my cock stir.

"Come closer if you're gonna try again," I say. "We can't sound like we're shouting at each other from across the room."

She walks over to me, her long dress flowing around her legs. It's sleeveless and crisscrosses in the back, made of something flowy and stretchy and soft. I curl my hands into the comforter behind me so I don't grab it.

Which is the right thing to do, because when she stands in front of me, she rests her hands on my knees, fingertips tapping a light dance that sends sparks through my brain.

"Let's hear it again," I say, voice soft, and she closes her eyes again.

"Ohhh?"

"Better," I say, and swallow against a mouth that's suddenly dry. "Again."

"Ohhhhh."

I sit up straight and reach for her, put a hand around her back, pull her in between my knees. The bed is pretty high, and standing, she's only a couple inches taller than me, my eyeline at her throat.

"Louder," I say. I'm raspier than usual. "Let them hear it."

"Ohhhh!"

Now her hands are gripping my thighs above my knees.

"More. Like you're begging me."

It slips out, and the moment it does I'm expecting her to shove me away and roll her eyes, inform me that she'll do no such thing as beg.

"*Ohhhhh,*" she gets out instead, her head slightly back and her eyes still closed. A desperate sound with a raw, pleading edge, wild and ragged.

I lick the hollow of her throat. She makes another sound, a barely-audible groan that goes straight to my dick. I'd tease her for it but my mouth is too busy on her neck, tongue tracing up the tendons of her throat, finding the spot right below her jaw.

"Again," I say against her skin. "Please."

Kat swallows, the muscles moving below my lips. My teeth scrape her skin, and I lick the hurt away.

"*You* moan," she says, and she'd sound annoyed if she wasn't breathless.

I laugh against the side of her neck, her body against mine now, her hands on my thighs inches from the erection I'm not bothering to fight.

"So you can hear how it's done?"

"So you quit giving me notes on my fake sex noises," she says, and there's her pulse under my tongue. I press harder, feeling the thrum.

Then I take a deep breath and groan as loud as I can, closing my eyes and trying to channel every porno I've ever watched. The sound comes out desperate and raw, a rough low edge to it that I didn't intend.

Kat's skin pebbles into goosebumps. Without thinking, I lick it back down, curling my tongue over those tiny raised hairs. Now her hand is around the back of my neck. Her breath hitches.

"You like that?" I ask, voice low.

"Yes," she murmurs.

"Louder, for fuck's—"

"*YES*," she shouts, her head thrown back, the word echoing around the room. "Yes, *fuck*, I like that—"

And then I'm on my feet, hauling her backward until she's pushed against the shared wall with a thump. She looks up at me through eyelashes and glasses, lips parted, half challenge and half invitation as we press together. Her knee goes between my legs and her thigh brushes my already-hard cock, and I don't do anything but kiss her.

"Tell me what you want me to do," I say when I pull away, loud enough to be heard.

Kat clears her throat, our faces nearly touching.

"I," she starts. Clears it again. She's breathing hard. "I, um."

I laugh and grab one hand and pin it over her head, against the wall, lightly enough that she could pull away if she wanted to.

"Right, I forgot," I say, and let my lips brush the shell of her ear. "You're shy."

I bite her earlobe and she hisses, hand clenching in mine.

"You just shout my name," I murmur. "I'll take care of hollering dirty."

"Thanks," she whispers, and I pull away a bit, tilt my head back.

"God, Kat, just like that," I shout. "Yeah."

"Silas!" she gasp-yelps, and now I'm fighting a laugh and my erection all at once.

"God, that feels good," I holler at the wall.

"Ooooh, Silas," Kat adds, and I have to bite my lip.

"Love the way you feel, babe," I tell the wall.

"Babe! Silas! Yes!" she gets out.

Fuck, I'm running out of Generic Dirty Phrases.

"I can't wait to taste you," I say, and it comes out too quiet so I take a deep breath and remember to project. "You wet? Show me how ready you are for this."

There's no response, only the sound of her breathing. My body pinpricks.

"You're supposed to moan," I murmur, dipping my head to her ear, letting my lips brush the shell. She gasps, barely audible, and I run my tongue along the outer rim.

"Sorry," she whispers, breathless, and then head thrown back: "*Fuck*, Silas!"

It comes out raw and ragged and I crush her mouth under mine the second the words have escaped, control slipping, but she kisses me back hard and fast and frantic. Someone makes a small, desperate noise, and then Kat hooks her ankle around the back of my leg and pulls me even harder against her.

"Jesus," I hiss, the sound half-lost in her mouth. I've got one hand locked around her wrist, next to her head, and she's got my shirt in her other fist, pulling me in.

"What?" she whispers back.

"Say my name again."

"Why?"

*So they can hear it* is what I should say, because that's what this whole charade is about: convincing the people on the other side of the wall that we're currently having sex.

"Because I fucking like it, Kat," I manage to get out.

"*Silas*," she growls and we kiss again, open-mouthed and wild, bodies pressed together against the wall.

Something slides against my side, rough and soft in a way that makes me bite her lower lip and then lick it. It takes me a second to register that it's Kat's hand, under my shirt, skin on skin. I grab her wrist and push her hand higher, desperate to feel her, and she digs her fingers in.

"Oh," she whispers, the word half-lost against my lips, and in response I hoist her against the wall.

There's a soft *thump* and they probably heard it next door, if they're even listening, but there's also a surprised gasp and there's the way her long skirt rides up to her thighs as she wraps her legs around me and leans her head against the wall, arms slung over my shoulders as I put my mouth back on her soft, hot skin.

I know there are rules. I know. I *know*. They've been humming through my head for the past two weeks, invading my dreams.

"Does this count as a full-trunk embrace?" I murmur.

"What?"

I nip at her skin with my teeth, get another gasp out of her.

"We're not supposed to unless there's a reason," I say, even as I push her into the wall with my hips. I'm hard as a rock and I know she knows.

"I don't fucking care," she whispers, and her thighs

tighten around me, my fingers digging in where I'm still holding her.

"No?"

"*No*," she hisses.

"You care about any of the rules?"

"I don't even remember what they are," she says, and I push her even harder against the wall, rocking against her. "God. *Fuck*."

I kiss her harder until her lips are swollen and her glasses are crooked, my hands under her thighs. There's an armchair to our right and I push her into it and then plant a knee between her legs, already bending down for her mouth.

She gives it to me, my hand on her jaw, hers sliding through my hair as we devour each other before she grabs my shirt again, hauls me toward her, hooks her foot around the back of my thigh and I grab the back of the chair to steady myself.

"You good?" she whispers, face suddenly inches below mine.

I swallow hard, nod.

"Good," I rasp out, and I'm about to ask the same when her mouth is on my neck and all the words dissolve before they make it to my lips.

When she pulls me down to kiss her again I slide a hand up her thigh to the top, and she arches into me.

"Yeah?" I murmur.

"Yeah," she whimpers back. Her eyes are closed, head back, lips parted. I rub my thumb over the top of her thigh, right where it meets her hip, and she makes a soft, pleading noise that bypasses my brain completely.

I kiss her again and she grabs my hair, panting. I bite her neck and then lick it, scrape my teeth over her collarbone, listen to her gasp. My knee slides from the chair and I'm kneeling on the floor in front of her as I guess where a nipple is and bite it through her dress. Judging by her hiss I'm at least close and then my hands are under her long skirt, lips on her stomach, her hand still in my hair.

I grab her panties without thinking but before I pull them off I look up at her, and I mean to ask *yes?* again but she looks at me with lust-drunk eyes, lips parted, her hand still in my hair, so I don't ask. I just fling her panties somewhere else in the room and pull her toward me as she drapes one thigh over the side of the armchair, skirt rucked around her hips.

I find the spot on her thigh where I fell asleep on her last week and bite it, sucking her soft skin into my mouth but, I swear to God, Kat growls and writhes, her hand tensing in my hair.

"Say please," I murmur.

"Goddamn it," she whispers, her breathing rough. "Please."

I push her thighs wider and give her a long, slow lick that makes her gasp and swear, fingers curling in my hair. She's hot and wet, my mind flooded with her taste and the way her skin feels under my hands, the way she tenses and then jolts as I keep exploring with my tongue.

My mind's blank, a whirlwind of lust and desire and sensation: her hand in my hair, tight enough for me to *feel* it; my dick hard as a rock and straining against my zipper. I don't bother trying to tease her. All I bother with is finding her clit and figuring out how she wants me to lick it.

Good thing she's not shy right now. I watch her as I explore, swiping, circling, teasing, and she arches her back and closes her eyes and grabs the back of the chair over her head as she whispers half-garbled instructions: *left. The other left. A little more—oh fuck yes. That. Fuck.*

Kat swears, jolts, grips my hair hard enough to bring tears to my eyes before whispering *fuck, sorry* and relaxing her fingers. Then she does it again, and again, and before I know it I'm groaning with every tug, almost as desperate for this as she is. My cock is out, in my hand, my strokes almost as haphazard as my tongue.

When she makes a desperate, high-pitched noise I look up at her because God, I want to see this. I need to see this because at least half of me thinks there's no way it'll happen again, so I've gotta save it for later.

Her eyes are closed. Her back's arched. She's pushing my face into her with a desperation that makes me moan even as it also makes my eyes water, but now she's gasping and whimpering and swearing, and as I watch she jams a fist to her mouth and bites down.

Then she comes. There's no fucking question: she rocks herself into my face, whimpers into the hand she's biting. Her whole body shudders. One thigh muscle jerks. I moan again, right into her clit, because I want to say *God yes please, give me this*.

"Stop," she suddenly hisses, and pulls at my hair again. A leg jerks. "Ahh. Stop stop stop stop—"

I do, of course, and look up at her, hand still on my dick.

"Sorry," she says, and then she's lurching forward, legs coming off the arms of the chair, and she leans down and kisses me, her hair falling in a curtain around my head.

I groan again. I haven't even wiped my mouth off but Kat doesn't seem to care, just finds my tongue with hers and leans in more, steadying herself on my shoulder before suddenly sliding off the chair and landing half on my lap where I'm still kneeling, dressed except for the fact that my dick is in my hand and hard as fuck.

"Oh," she says, and laughs.

Then she wraps her hand around my cock, and I make a *noise*. It's rough and low and loud as all hell, and when I make it I grab one of her thighs in each hand where they're spread over me, and I hold on.

"Shh," she says, and I swear to God she's laughing.

"No," I grit out, just in time for her to put a hand over my mouth, and I moan against it.

I don't last long before I'm pumping myself into her hand with every stroke, groans muffled. I barely cover myself in time before I come, coating our fists and gasping raggedly against the hand that's still over my mouth, the edges of my vision prickling white.

After a moment, Kat takes her hand off my mouth, and the second she does I kiss her. It's less frantic now but soft and deep, broken apart by the fact that neither of us can catch our breath. When it ends I rest my forehead against hers and for one more second, I ignore the mess I've made and the fact that my knees feel like hell, and I just... bask.

"Yeah?" I finally ask in a whisper.

Kat huffs out a laugh, and her other hand strokes my hair, gentler than I've ever felt it.

"Yeah," she says.

# TWENTY-SEVEN

## KAT

WHEN I WAKE UP, Silas is gone and I can hear shouting through the wall. For one brief moment of alarm, my tired brain thinks it's Silas shouting next door, but it's not. It's Evan. Shouting at eight in the morning about... the Dulles Toll Road? What the fuck?

It takes about two seconds for me to go from sleepy and lazy to rigid with anxiety in this very comfortable bed, eyes wide and staring at a very blurry ceiling as the events of last night—last weekend? Last month? Last *year?*—come crashing down around me like chunks of plaster.

I make out *waited* and *don't even care* from the other side of the wall as Olivia shouts back at Evan. I cover my eyes with my hands, because maybe they're about to pipe down and stop shouting and, I don't know, do a meditation or something together because it sure sounds like they could —

"—For *work*, you know that."

"It was a request!"

They're closer to the wall now. Maybe five feet away

259

from me, and I pull the blanket over my head as if that'll help. It does nothing. My blood pressure spikes.

"They gave me two options!"

"And LOOK AT WHAT YOU CHOSE."

Holy fuck, someone's gonna call the cops.

"Keep it the fuck down, you know the walls are thin."

"Yeah and you know WHO'S ON THE OTHER SIDE?"

I put a pillow on my face for good measure, and curl into a ball on my side.

"Olivia, shut the *fuck* up."

"Why, so you can hear better? Maybe I should —"

Her voice fades as she moves away and for one terrible, panicky lightning bolt of a moment I think she's going to come knock on my door and start shouting at *me*, because that is something that makes sense in my just-woke-up-and-already-dialed-to-eleven brain right now.

I'd hide in the bathroom. No fucking question.

But then they're fighting again, the shouting not as dramatic, and I take the opportunity to leap out of bed and put on my glasses and the first clothes I pull out of my suitcase.

Then I heave a deep breath that's supposed to be relaxing and use the relative quiet to worry about where Silas went. Not that I was expecting to wake up to, I don't know, a hand gently brushing my cheek as he murmured sweet nothings until I awoke with a blissful smile on my face, but I did think he'd be... *here*.

Not... wherever he is. Getting coffee? Taking a walk?

He didn't panic about what happened last night and just leave without—no, his suitcase is still here.

Unless he was *so* panicked that he bolted with nothing but his wits and the clothes on his—

"You think you can do that? Just go?"

Evan again. I swear I am going to lose my fucking mind, all my panic alarms ringing like mad, not least because this is completely alien to me. When we were together, sure, we had arguments and disagreements and even raised our voices once or twice, but we never had a full-on, hear-it-through-a-wall shouting match.

*Maybe we didn't care enough about each other.*

What a fucked up thought. I grab my room key, shove my feet into flip flops, and make my escape, relieved that there's no one outside the door, inexplicably demanding to be let in, and power-walk toward the lobby. The hallway is a vulnerable area because there's nothing to duck behind and until I can get around the corner, at any minute someone could—

Behind me, a door opens. Without looking, I somehow *know*, deep in my soul, which door it is. Probably because as soon as it does, I can hear arguing.

Obviously, I shouldn't turn and look. It's another ten feet to the blessed neutral ground of the hotel lobby, where I can duck around a corner or hide under a desk or smear complimentary yogurt on my face so they don't recognize me, and of course, I should scamper in there and leave them to their own devices.

So, of course, I do. I look in time to see Olivia angrily yank her suitcase over the threshold, her blond hair in a droopy ponytail, her face bright red, wearing cutoffs and flipflops. She shouts one last thing into the room, then turns on her heel as well as one can in flip-flops, and storms off toward the parking lot, suitcase bouncing behind her.

I stand there, staring. Every nerve in my body is singing with alarm, but I can't help watching the drama because *I did this*. My ex who fucked me over and one of the girls he did it with are having a meltdown more appropriate to a trailer park than a nice hotel, and it's at least in part because I made their unhappiness my business.

I thought I'd enjoy it more.

A moment later Evan—shirtless—leans out of the door. He hollers something after her. When Olivia reaches the exit, she turns and shouts something back.

Then she sees me. Standing there in the hallway, so obviously watching the two of them that I may as well have a recliner and a bucket of popcorn. We lock eyes. Evan follows her gaze and now he's *also* looking at me, so all the adrenaline left in me dumps into my blood, and my entire body flushes with heat.

I... wave.

I think my hand is shaking. Evan and Olivia *stare* at me, and I can't even blame them.

Oh: they could also shout, which Olivia does, something like "ALL YOURS!" echoing down the hallway before she manhandles her suitcase over the threshold to the outside and disappears into the hazy sunlight.

Finally, I turn around and pretty much run for the lobby.

# TWENTY-EIGHT

## SILAS

WHEN I COME in from my run, Kat's standing in the lobby with a cup of coffee in her hand, staring out at the river so hard it looks like she's trying to lift an X-Wing out of it with the power of her mind. Her knuckles are white around the mug, her shoulders practically by her ears, her whole body strung like piano wire.

Something unpleasant tightens behind my ribcage. I'm still breathing hard and every part of my body feels sticky with the heat and humidity, but the pleasant, loose feeling I had this morning evaporates into the air conditioning as I watch Kat play statue by the window.

*This is because of last night.*

*Because we crossed a line we said we weren't going to cross, and now Kat's freaking out.*

I pull the bottom of my shirt up to wipe sweat off my face and turn away from Kat to grab some water and some coffee because suddenly, for once in my life, I'm not sure what to say. Things have a way of looking different in the morning when it's bright outside, and when you haven't spent an entire day being turned on and frustrated, and

263

when you're not faking sex noises so someone you don't like can hear it through the wall.

Yeah, why would anyone feel weird about *that*? Jesus.

I chug about ten tiny paper cups of water, then pour myself a mug of coffee. Kat stands perfectly still the entire time. She doesn't even drink the coffee she's holding, she just... stares. God, I hope she's not having a panic attack. Here, in the middle of the lobby, with everyone milling around and eating muffins. She would hate that, but there's nothing to do but go over there and act like everything's fine, so I do.

"Morni—"

Kat yelps and jumps and almost drops her coffee, splashing it all over herself and the rug, a few droplets getting on me.

"Dammit! Shit. Sorry, I'm—I don't know."

"Sorry," I tell her, already grabbing a napkin from a stack on a nearby table. "I didn't mean to sneak up—"

"—you're fine, I should be able to handle it when people say good morning—"

"Here," I say, hand her some napkins, and take the mug. The coffee's already soaked into the lobby carpet, and I'm certain it's not the first coffee to do so. "I'll get you more."

I refill her mug, and when I come back the soaked napkins are on a coffee table and she's staring out the window again, all the cords in her neck standing out. I remember the noise she made when I bit them.

"Incoming," I call, and she turns her head. Doesn't smile, but takes the mug and nods a thank you.

And once more, I'm lost for words. It's the strangest feeling. I know, in the back of my mind, that I should start chatting about the weather or the coffee or the drive home or the ugly fabric pattern on the couches in here, but Kat's watching me, her whole body singing with tension, and I can't think of a single thing to say.

"So," I finally manage, and then stop, and what the fuck? *So?*

"So," she echoes. Clears her throat. "You worked out?"

I look down at myself, like I don't know my shirt is soaked through with sweat, salty rivulets drying on my neck.

"Yeah," I agree. Great conversation. "I woke up early, and went for a..."

Her eyes flick to something behind me and Kat stands up a little taller, lips tensing.

"...run."

She doesn't answer and doesn't look at me, so I watch her dark eyes go sharp behind her glasses.

"Don't look at him," I hear myself say before I even mean to say it. "Look at me."

She does, with the same flinty, light-something-on-fire glare.

"Quit giving him the satisfaction."

"Quit telling me where to look."

But she keeps her eyes on mine, and I sip my coffee slowly, deliberately.

"What's going on?" I finally ask, some kind of spell broken.

"Nothing."

She glances down again, back at me before I can say anything.

"Bullshit." We're speaking low enough that the people around us probably can't hear, but we're getting looks anyway: the couple having a weird, awkward, intense conversation over morning coffee.

"Not here," she says, and looks away, out the window again. "It's getting late. We should head back. Go shower."

"*Kat.*"

"*Silas.*" Echoes of how she said it last night. I shiver, all sweat and air conditioning and memory.

I want to push her into the truth, for her to *tell* me what's got her like this. Whether it's something I did or something she wishes she hadn't. Whether last night was really so fucking terrible that now she'd rather stare at the river and her ex than look at me, or *what*.

When we finally collapsed into the bed and she let me tuck her into my side, I didn't think it was terrible. When I woke up this morning before sunrise with her hair in my mouth and her leg splayed across my knee, I didn't think it was so terrible. Maybe she did.

"Come back to the room with me," I say, meaning *can we please talk there* but she shakes her head. Doesn't even bother with words and I can't help but think: *even after that, this is what she's like.*

"All right," I say, and I try to sound lighthearted and care-fucking-free, but it doesn't come out that way. It comes out angry and sarcastic, and good riddance.

# TWENTY-NINE

## KAT

WE DRIVE BACK to Sprucevale mostly in silence. I try. I swear to God I try to be normal and make small talk with him about, I don't know, the cows on the side of the road, but I'm wound tight and my brain is spinning too fast for me to get words out of it. Silas keeps trying to start conversations, but I keep giving him one-word answers and after a while he gives up.

I feel like I ruined something.

No: I feel like I ruined *everything*, like the world will now crumble around my ears because I made some sex noises and made Olivia mad enough to drive off.

This sort of thinking is called a *cognitive distortion*, which I know because I've been in therapy for a million years now. I can see clear as day that I'm catastrophizing, thinking of all the ways the world could end because of something I did that had consequences I didn't really consider. I *know* that this won't result in Silas suddenly diving out of the car, or in me getting fired, or in Anna Grace no longer speaking to me, or my parents suddenly disowning me from the shame, but knowing and feeling are two different beasts and only one has its teeth in my throat right now.

When we're back in Sprucevale, I suddenly can't stand it any more. The thought of going to Silas's house to drop him off feels like ice in my veins, and the thought of inviting him to my house makes me break out in a cold sweat, so I do the first thing I think of and park.

This street has houses on one side, trees on the other, the river invisible beyond them. There's a bike path between the road and the trees. It's very nice. Silas is watching me from the passenger seat, and I swear I can *feel* it, like his eyeballs are rolling over my skin.

"Am I walking home?" he finally says.

*Wow*, I have fucked up if he thinks that. I shut my eyes and put my head back against the seat, dimly aware that I've made everything worse by being so anxious about it.

"Evan and Olivia got into a huge fight this morning and Olivia stormed out and I waved at her," I say, pushing all the words out in a rush.

Silas is quiet for a moment.

"You waved?" he finally asks, and fuck, I have to get out of here. The car's getting hotter by the second, the August sun beating down, and it's small and it's cramped and I've been in here for too long and it's a glass box and *anyone* could come along and just *look* at me and—

"Hey. I need a couple minutes," I tell the steering wheel, because I can't look at Silas right now. I can't. "Maybe ten? I'll be back. I need—yeah."

My seatbelt nearly hits me in the face as I fumble it but I shove it back and get out of the car and the air out here is a little cooler by comparison, and at least there's a breeze.

I cross the path and keep going, shoving a bunch of plants out of the way, until I can't see the car or the road or any part of Sprucevale any more, just some rocks and a lot of water and the bright green jungle I'm supposed to be calling home these days.

It makes me feel like I might have fucked up even more than I thought.

I miss concrete. I miss ugly big box stores stretching for miles along the highway. I miss four-lane suburban roads and shopping centers; I miss manicured lawns and wide sidewalks and sprawling subdivisions and commuter parking lots. I miss all the familiar parts of suburbia that I never liked before.

I miss *home*, and I never should have let Evan drive me away from it to this half-wild place where I've let things get so fucked up and tangled I'm not sure I'll ever untangle them.

I tromp through some more plants until I find a wide, flat rock overlooking the river. It's shaded by a huge tree, and I sit crosslegged and watch the river, sluggish and red-blue-brown in the late summer, the rock warm underneath me.

*What the hell did you do?* everything whispers: the river, the trees, the birds chirping. *What were you thinking?*

The panic bubbles up until it's overflowing, and I let it because I can, and because it'll be worse if I don't. It's a different flavor of anxiety than the one that brings on a panic attack, at least for me; that's a tsunami, this is a tide that comes in too high, only builds and builds until it's flooding the shore. A panic that I can't stop, only reckon with.

I got what I wanted, and it's terrible.

All I really wanted, all along, was to hurt him. Making him crawl was just something to tell Silas; the real goal was to make him feel as bad as he'd made me feel. I wanted him devastated. Preferably because of me.

It feels *awful*.

Like I'm the worst person on earth. For orchestrating this stupid scheme for the sole purpose of emotionally harming another human being. For dragging Silas along, into it; for using him, no matter how much he swears he agreed to the terms.

I don't know how long I sit there and feel shitty before the tangle of trees and vines and plants behind me rustles, and Silas steps through. He doesn't ask permission, just sits right next to me, legs stretched in front of him. If I leaned a little, I could touch him. I don't.

He sits there for a while, watching the river with me, before he says anything.

"I got your keys."

Oops. "Thanks."

We're both quiet for a while as I try to fit the words together in my head. Sentences feel like Tetris when I'm like this: all pieces that could easily fit together if only I had enough skill and speed to make it work, which I never do. Finally, I take a deep breath and wing it.

"The fight was over me. Us."

"Evan and Olivia?"

"Yeah." I take a deep breath, press the palms of my hands into my knees. "This is so fucked up."

Slowly, I give him a rundown of what happened, and he doesn't say anything. I don't look at him, but I can feel Silas watching me the way I can *always* feel it when he's watching me, like his attention is a sunbeam. When I finish, he's quiet for a moment and I take a deep breath, shift so I'm sitting with my hands behind me and my legs in front, the same position he's in. Our legs nearly touching. The knowledge of it prickles through my whole body, and I close my eyes, tilt my head back.

"I can't believe I did this," I say.

"We."

I look at him, and he looks right back. Serious and steady, with deep blue eyes and barely-there freckles, so close I swear I can feel warmth radiating from his skin.

"If you're gonna have a crisis I at least want credit," Silas says.

"*We* lied and deceived and manipulated our way into fucking up someone else's life," I say, looking at the river again. "*We* basically stalked my ex, and we clearly made his girlfriend uncomfortable enough that she stole his car to get away from him, and—"

I inhale, close my eyes, try to think of some words besides *fuck* to get across the gravity of the situation. All I get is the faint scent of sweat and hotel shampoo, and it makes me want to bury my face in his neck and sniff and it makes me want to jump into the river to get away. Good to know I can always come up with ways to make things more awkward.

"What the fuck was I thinking?" I ask the universe. "Who does this? What is *wrong* with me?"

"There's nothing wrong with you," Silas says, and the angry edge in his voice makes me look at him.

"I just stalked someone—"

"We."

"*We* just stalked someone and made sex noises until his girlfriend left him," I say. I'm positive I'm bright red. "Because—why? Because he broke up with me in a way I didn't like? Because—"

*Because he treated you like dirt*, I think, but the words die on my lips in a flash of anger.

"He didn't *break up with you*," Silas says, and even though he's in a casual pose—leaning on his hands, legs out in front of him—I can feel the tension humming through

271

him. "He lied and cheated and then did something he knew would humiliate you, and he deserves to be miserable and alone."

"I didn't have to be the one to do it."

"*We*."

"*I* didn't have to drag you into my stupid revenge scheme, either," I go on. "Sorry."

That gets a disbelieving laugh out of Silas, and I finally turn to look at him again.

"You're sorry *now*?" he says, voice low and cutting and shining with anger, though I can't even tell where it's directed. I can't even tell where mine is directed, only that it's there, pumping through my veins, glittering like broken glass next to panic and shame and regret, all borne along by adrenaline.

"Well, I can't be sorry yesterday, can I?" I snap back.

I swear the whole world falls into a dead silence as Silas and I stare at each other and I feel like something is going to burst through my skin.

"Would you be?" he asks. I can barely hear him over the river, and I swallow, my mouth suddenly dry despite the humidity.

*No*, I want to say, but I can't make my mouth form the word.

"I'm sorry I got you involved," is what I say instead. Silas's face is perfectly blank, and I turn away again, close my eyes. "We can stop. If you want. Mission accomplished."

The silence that follows is somehow even more silent. A black hole for sound, drinking everything down.

"Kat," Silas finally says. I close my eyes, take a deep breath, back ramrod straight.

"*Kat*," he says again.

"What?"

He doesn't answer, so I finally turn to look at him. I realize my knee is almost touching his thigh, that my fingernails are digging into my palm, that Silas's eyelashes are the same deep reddish brown as his hair.

"Are you breaking up with me?"

There's a space where there's nothing but sun and river and trees, the terrified thump of my heartbeat. The rough rock gouging my ankle.

Up close in the sunlight, Silas's eyes are every shade of blue: azure and lapis and cerulean. The midnight blue of the night sky and the dusty blue of twilight; the bright blue of a clear sky and the iciness of a glacier and sitting there, staring at him, thinking of the ways I've fucked up I suddenly feel like I'm the only one who knows. It feels dizzy and heavy as a secret that I never want to tell.

And then I know something else, too: whatever I've fucked up and ruined in the past year, I couldn't handle ruining *this*. Whatever *this* even is.

"No," I answer. "I don't know what I'm doing."

And then the space between us is gone, lost to desperate open-mouthed kisses. I grab his hair in my hand and hold his mouth to mine, suddenly starved for sensation. I need this, need the scrape of his teeth along my lip, need the slide of his tongue along mine, need the way he wraps a hand around my thigh and pulls me until I'm half in his lap, bare leg scraping along the rock below us.

It hurts. It might even draw blood. I gasp into his mouth but I don't mind at all, the pain nothing but a quick sizzle along my nerves. He's got his other hand in my hair and I let him tilt my head back, making a low, feral noise as he bites my neck. His thigh's between my legs, and I rock against the hard muscle.

And God, it feels good. There's no one here but us,

nothing but river and trees and birds, probably. There's the possibility of people—the road not fifty feet off, the river trail, kayakers, anything—but that's all theoretical and Silas's tongue in my mouth and hands on my hips are so, so real.

Soon enough I tear myself away with a parting lick to his lips, just like I wanted to do the day at the fair. It gets a smile and a noise out of him, looking up at me from where I'm straddling him on the ground, one knee pressed into the rock. It hurts. I almost like it.

"You gonna ask me about last night or not?" he says, and he looks wild as he says it: lips red and swollen, pupils pinpricks in the bright day, hair mussed where I've been grabbing him.

Because I can, I slide the pad of one thumb over his mouth, then press it in. Silas wraps his lips around it, bites down, swirls his tongue over the pad. The corners of his eyes crinkle with a smile and my mind goes completely blank.

I kiss him before I remember to take my thumb out and accidentally bite myself. His mouth tastes a little like stone and dirt and leaves, and then I can't tell what's Silas and what's not. I wonder if my thumb was dirty from being on the ground, but I can't be bothered to care.

"Not one tiny question?" he teases, then nips at my lower lip. I make a noise, and not a cute one. "You're not gonna ask hey, Silas, did you eat me out for fun or for revenge?"

I pull back and stare at him: grinning, eyes crawling over my face. He hooks two fingers into the waistband of my shorts and tugs hard enough to rock me forward and the jolt on my clit makes me close my eyes.

"Sure," I manage to murmur, words coalescing and dissolving like smoke, faster than I can grab them.

He tugs again and the friction is delicious.

"Come home with me and I'll tell you," he says.

I skim my fingers along his cheekbone, like I can brush away the faint freckles, along his jaw, down the tendons in his neck to the dip in his throat. I'm above him, right now, and I'm never above him. He's beautiful from this angle, too.

"You're not as charming as you think you are," I say.

"You thought I was charming enough last night."

I don't have an argument for that besides hauling him up for another ferocious kiss, my hair spilling around his face. When it ends, I'm breathless.

"My place, then?" he says.

I nod, and he helps me off the ground.

# THIRTY

## KAT

WE BARELY TALK on the drive back, and then Silas pushes me against the door as soon as he closes it. It's pure relief, a balm for the buzzing ache that's taken over my skin. His mouth is hot against mine and the door is cool against my back, the heat of the day still leaking from our clothes. Our tongues slide together and I swear I can still smell the river on Silas: dirt and rock and the heavy green tang of leaves in August, peppery and blunt.

I thread my fingers through his hair and pull him against me like I can devour him, like if I try hard enough I can sate myself with his mouth on mine and he's just as desperate, kissing me with teeth and tongue like he can press me through the door.

Silas is hard as fuck against my hip, and someone gasps. Groans. There's a surprised, throaty noise and I think that one's me but I could be wrong, because now his teeth are running along my jaw and it's hard to keep track of things.

"You taste like salt," he says, mouth working its way down my neck, my head thrown back against the door.

"Sweat, I think," because my mind is dissolving and I

can only think of the truth. He nips again, harder, and I gasp. "Sorry."

"Mmm." A long lick, slow gentle pressure. Someone makes that noise again: me, maybe. "Don't be. I like it."

I get a leg around his hips and his big hand wraps around my thigh, my other thigh, lifts them both until I'm against the door, again, like I was last night but this time I hook my feet together behind his back and drag him in with a slow, hard grind.

This time the noise is his, and it makes me dig my fingers into his shoulder.

I don't feel better, not exactly; still feel tangled and fucked up over this morning, over this weekend, over all my decisions of the last year, but the way Silas's muscles flex under my hands helps me forget. Silas feels like a wall I can hurl myself against. He feels like the rocky shore where a wave breaks and falls back, like I can do my worst and he'll laugh and tell me to really *try*. He feels like he could take the wrenching heartbreak and aimless anxiety and twist it into pleasure.

I want to take my bad year out on him. I want to see what he looks like spread out on his sheets, that come hither look in his deep blue eyes. I want to plunder their depths. I want to know what he sounds like when he begs. I want to know what it feels like to have him above me, over me, seeing what I can take.

I make another noise at that last thought and he shoves me harder against the door, grinds himself against me so hard it almost hurts so I pull his shirt over his head and dig my short nails into his back until he hisses.

"Fuck, Kat," I think he says but he's grabbing at my hair, pulling my head back, his teeth on the sensitive skin of my neck until I whimper. My tank top comes off and he pulls my bra straps down over my shoulders, chasing them with his mouth. I haul him in harder with my legs, grind my hips against the unmistakable hardness of his cock until I don't remember how I ever had doubts about his desire.

Silas groans and bites my shoulder so hard I gasp, sparks of pain shivering from his mouth over my skin as I bite my lip and hope he leaves a mark. He lets go, licks the spot, kisses it. Runs one hand over my nipple, bra still on, and when it hardens at the contact he rolls it between his fingers and I swear into his mouth.

When he pulls back, he's breathing hard. Lips red and swollen, his cheeks flushed, his hair wild. Those deep blue eyes are hazy with lust, and he looks at me, nipple still between his fingers. He doesn't break eye contact as he pushes my shirt and bra down, the air hitting the nipple, as he dances his fingertips over it and I watch him through half-closed eyes, breathing hard.

"God, look at you," he murmurs, and I don't have a response because he's got my nipple between two fingers, the pad of his thumb sliding over it, and I can barely breathe, let alone think. All I can do is put a hand on his face, brush my thumb over his lips as my brain blinks and flickers like the lights during a thunderstorm.

All at once he heaves me up, higher against the wall, every muscle in his body flexing and straining at once. I make a high-pitched breathy noise and my hands go around his biceps like they're magnets, and fuck, muscles like that should be illegal but then his lips are around my nipple, tongue sliding over the flat surface, and all I do is make another noise.

I swear Silas laughs with my nipple between his teeth, then puts me down, practically boneless against the door.

"C'mon," he says, and gives me one more hard, deep kiss

before we're stumbling to his bedroom, kissing and shoving and stumbling. I lose my shirt to the living room, my bra to the stairs, my shorts somewhere outside his bedroom. My panties fall right inside the threshold and then we're both naked, the door slamming as I push Silas against it and sink my teeth into the muscles over his collarbone.

He groans, digs his fingers into my back. I do it again, harder; I lick it, kiss it better. I fit my tongue to the divot in his throat and he's also salty, also somehow tastes like river and forest and summer. I learn his muscles with my hands: the hard peaks of his nipples, the soft chest hair, the ridge of the scar on his ribs, the way I can dig my fingers into him.

God, this man could be art. I pull his head down to mine again, kiss him like I need it to breathe as I wrap my hand around his cock and this time he moans right into my mouth, full-throated and loud enough to make my teeth buzz.

"That," I say, the word lost to the kiss. "Yes. *That.*" There's a trail of wetness down the underside of his cock, and I run the pad of my thumb from root to tip, swipe it across the head as he makes another noise.

Then I pull away and suck my thumb into my mouth without thinking, lick the salty tang off. His eyes are wide and his lips are swollen and parted, his cheeks pink, his hair wild. He looked half-debauched and the only thing I want, the only thought in my mind, is that I want him all the way there.

I slide to my knees before I can think any more, grab the hard muscles of his thighs in my hands, and lick another drop from the head of his cock and listen to the way he groans like I've broken him. He's hot and heavy in my mouth and I go slow, using my tongue on the head and the under-side of his cock before finally taking him in my mouth, one hand anchoring the base.

"Christ," he hisses, and one hand slides into my hair and stays there. Not controlling, just touching, as I work my mouth up and down his shaft, listening to his breathing hitch and the noises he makes, coming from somewhere deep in his chest. When I look up, he's looking down at me like he's in a daze and I run my tongue right over his slit, just for good measure, and he swears, his thigh muscles trembling.

"Fuck, Kat," he rasps. "I'm gonna—"

And that's my cue to let him go with one last, long lick. His hips jerk and he tilts his head against the door, swearing, so I kiss him on the hip and then suck the soft skin there while he pants for breath.

"Up," he growls, after a minute, and then he's kissing me again and pushing me back toward his nicely made bed, sending us both sprawling onto it as he covers his body with mine and this time we both groan.

Silas is taller than me and wider than me, and he pushes me down onto the bed without even trying. He pushes my legs apart with his knees, mouth desperate on mine. When I try to wrap my legs around his hips he bites my lower lip and growls, one arm anchored next to my head, the other hand like iron around my thigh, pushing it down, his tongue still in my mouth.

I whimper. It's a pleading, desperate noise, and I rock my hips as hard as I can but he's holding me down, cock sliding a wet trail along my thigh. I have to practically bite my tongue off so I don't beg him to fuck me, but he dips his head to my other nipple and sucks it into his mouth, hard.

I arch off the bed and make a noise, hands sinking into his hair as his hand lets my thigh go, his palm sliding inward until his thumb is stroking my lips and now it's his turn to make that noise because I'm pretty fucking wet right now.

Then he's sliding his slick thumb over my clit and I make a noise that's part grunt and part sigh and part barnyard animal, and I swear to god he laughs against my nipple.

Then he releases it with a lick and looks up at me, and even in the sunlight his pupils are huge, eyes dark with lust.

"There?" he says, grinning.

"Yeah," I whisper and he keeps rubbing, circling, driving jolt after jolt through me.

He shifts slightly, the rhythm pausing for a second, and then his fingers are knuckle-deep inside me and after a second my whole body jerks as he finds the right spot and then his whole hand is moving with the same rhythm and I swear to God, I'm going to dissolve. Just turn into goo, right here on this bed, because Silas is very fucking good with his hands and I had no idea.

He kisses me again. My lips, my neck, bites my nipple and then swirls his tongue around it. I'm thrusting back toward him, one hand around his cock, one leg half-wrapped around his hips. I want to shout and beg and plead, and I can't even form enough thoughts to figure out for what. Just more. Of this. More and more and more.

But then his lips are at my ear and his fingers are slowing and I'm fighting another whimper by biting my lip so hard I can taste blood.

"Can I fuck you?" he asks, thumb still lazily circling my clit.

My mouth is dry as the desert, and I swallow.

"Yes," I whisper. A single brain cell flares, briefly, back to life. "Condom?"

"Of course," he says, but he's already pulling his fingers out of me, wrapping his hand over my thigh again, opening the drawer of his bedside table and rooting through it.

And rooting through it.

"Goddamn it," Silas mutters as he pulls the whole thing out, haphazardly tossing it onto the mattress and digging until he finally comes up with a foil packet. He holds it up, grinning at me, and for some reason I laugh. He shrugs, rips it apart with his teeth, and rolls it down his long, thick cock. When he sees me watching he strokes himself a few more times, hips thrusting toward his hand, and fuck. *Fuck*.

"Yeah?" he says, and his voice is slow and teasing and gravelly, a smile tugging at his lips even as he holds himself over me with one hand and slowly fucks his other fist. I watch, brainless, almost happy to let him come this way.

Almost.

I get a hand and a knee under him and in one hard, fast motion, I shove Silas onto his back, locking my knees on either side of his hips as he lets out a surprised huff only now he's grinning, his cock bobbing in front of me.

I grab it, stroke it. I lean over, one hand next to his head, press my mouth to his and swallow his moan.

Then I sink onto him, and I swear to God Silas *shouts* and I probably would, too, if I could make any noise at all because fuck, he rocks up into me, pushing even deeper and I grab the headboard, the air rushing from my lungs, my eyes sliding shut.

"Oh," I manage to say, and Silas instantly stills, fingers digging into my hips, breathing harsh.

"Are you o—"

"Yes," I grit out as I push back onto him as hard as I can because holy fuck, I need this. It's been a long time since I was with anyone and there's no sex toy in the world that can substitute for another person gasping and swearing between your thighs while you ride them as hard as you can. At some point my glasses slide off and everything goes blurry, Silas gripping me so hard it'll probably leave bruises, his hips rising off the mattress to meet me.

It's hard and fast and so, so good. I swear a lot, probably say *please* a couple of times, and definitely leave fingernail half-moons in Silas's shoulders as he buries himself deep as he can in me, over and over again.

When I move one hand to my clit, Silas groans. His hair is stuck to his forehead with sweat, the muscles standing out in his arms and shoulders as he holds onto me, eyes wild and lips parted.

"God, Kat," he gets out. He's staring at my hand on my clit like he's mesmerized. "Yes. *Fuck.* Show me how you—"

I come before he can finish his sentence, pleasure opening and swallowing me before I even know it's coming. I bite my lip and whimper, gasp. Silas arches up into me and holds me down as I grind my hips into him, helplessly, dragging his cock against those hyper-sensitive spots inside me while my vision goes white around the edges.

"Holy shit," Silas whispers, like his voice is about to break. "Jesus, that was—you're—"

"Good," I manage to say, somehow slurring that one word.

Then he's sitting up. His hand is in my hair and he's dragging me toward him for a desperate, messy kiss, his tongue in my mouth and his cock still buried in me. I'm boneless as he rolls me over onto my back and I barely manage to wrap my legs around his hips as he thrusts, one elbow next to my head and one hand on the headboard before he comes with a garbled stream of *oh God fuck yes yes more Jesus good yes*.

We don't move. Silas rests his head in the curve between my neck and shoulder, my hand in his hair, as we both try to catch our breath. I think I'm trembling. I'm definitely sweaty as hell and I feel kind of high.

After a moment, Silas pulls out and rolls off and I take a deep breath, utterly wrung out. I can feel a drop of under-boob sweat slide off my ribcage and onto the bedsheets, and I have never cared less about anything in my life, ever.

When I finally turn my head to Silas, he's staring at me. He looks as dazed as I feel, and *I* put that look on his face. Me, Kat Nakamura, anxious mess and dedicated wallflower.

Neither of us says anything for a while, and I stare at him, close enough that I can mostly make out the details of his face: the flush underneath his barely-there freckles, the way his eyes have spokes of sky blue and navy blue running through them at the same time, the stubble on his chin glowing deep gold in the light through the curtains. The soft pink of his lips against his sharp jaw, strangely delicate.

Finally he reaches out with a look of total concentration on his face and runs one finger along the side of my face, pulling back a strand of hair stuck to me with sweat, then settles his hand there with his thumb on my cheekbone.

It's soft and silent, and I try to suspend myself in the moment. I flatten my hands on Silas's sheets and think about his almost-freckles and enjoy the small weight of his thumb on my cheek like this, but the truth is I'm going to panic. I can practically see it on the horizon, gathering like storm clouds, thundering in the distance.

Not now. Not for a bit, probably, but I'm not so optimistic that I think an orgasm will make me feel all the way better, even if it did basically reboot my brain. Because I think I know what we're doing, but I've been wrong before. I think I know what the way he's touching me, the way he's staring at me right now means, but I've fucked that up before, too.

Finally, Silas says, "I think that's all the rules."

"Is this romantic-style face touching?" I ask, and he grins.

"Yeah," he says. "I think it is."

The way my heart stutters, just then.

"No weird PDA," I point out.

"You fed me a cherry."

"That's very normal."

He taps his thumb gently against my cheek, and I roll onto my side to face him.

"You bit a cherry out of my hand," he says. "I've probably still got the marks on my fingers."

I take his hand off my face, hold it in front of my eyes. I can't see any teeth marks, but then again, my glasses are... somewhere, so instead I kiss his fingertips one by one.

"Kat," he says, low and scratchy, and curls his hand around mine.

"That better?"

He says, "Breaking all the rules renders our agreement null and void, right?"

"You're the lawyer. Is that how these things usually work?"

"This was the first time I negotiated pretending to date someone to piss off her ex," he points out, and there are crinkles around his eyes that say he's enjoying himself.

"That's what you want then? No more agreement?"

I have to bite the inside of my lip to keep myself from smiling. Not that it works.

"I'd rather date you for fun."

"Oh, I'm fun now?"

"This was real fun and I think we should do it again," he says, that relaxed, cheerful grin on his face. "And I suspect you feel the same way, based on my observations."

And yup, I'm blushing.

"Sure," I say, after a moment.

It gets a disbelieving look out of Silas.

"*Sure?*" he says. "Like I just asked you if you want another slice of pie?"

"You have pie?" I ask, trying not to laugh. We both are.

"Not for people who tell me *sure* when I'm being very romantic."

We're closer, somehow, our faces mashed into pillows, our linked hands between them. He's just inside the space where I can see more or less clearly: rumpled and lazy, smile lines around his eyes, the hint of freckles across the tops of his shoulders, that long, faded scar wrapping around the side of his ribcage.

I take a deep breath, sigh it out, pretend to be annoyed. He's not falling for it.

"Yes, Silas," I say, over enunciating. "I would like to date you for fun."

"*Thank* you," he grumbles, and then he's pulling me in for a kiss and his hand's in my hair and the panic on the horizon stays away, just a little longer.

· · · · · ★ ★ ★ · · · · ·

"I KNOW WHAT YOU'RE DOING."

Evan's voice cuts through the office, breaking an hour of very nice silence. I blink at him, not even sure he's talking to me.

Then he finally looks up from his monitor, and gives me a flat look like he's expecting an answer, so yeah, I guess it's me.

"Answering emails?" I say, pointedly. "Was your first clue that you're receiving way too many emails?"

For the past week, Evan's had me CC him on every work email I send. All of them. Even the ones that say "yes" or "no, let's hold off on that," or "sure, I think that font is okay."

All. Of. Them. Not to mention how many times he's asked me what, exactly, my job description is, or whether I really have the right amount of experience for it, or maybe someone with a computer science degree instead of a geology degree would be a better fit?

"With Flynn," he says.

Silas, he means, and I deliberately type the last line of an email and hit send before I look up again or let myself panic. Which I do, a little, that ever-present flame flickering higher while I hope it won't catch this time.

"Yes. We're dating," I say, trying to match his tone. "Lovely that you've noticed, I guess."

"Stalking me."

I roll my eyes, even though my heart rate spikes. *Don't react*, I tell myself. *Just don't react.*

"Evan, I promise I'm not trying to spend *more* time with you," I lie. Well, it's not exactly a lie, only... a truth that's sort of complicated.

"What did you tell her?"

"Tell who?" I ask, even though I know exactly what he means.

"Olivia."

"I didn't tell her anything."

"You told her something to make her leave."

The anxiety's catching, like a match held to paper, and it doesn't matter how straight I sit or how deeply I breathe right now.

"You think she needed me to tell her anything?" I ask,

voice soft and demure even though I want to shout it. Like Olivia did, yesterday morning.

"I think you said something to her, yeah," he says.

"Not a word," I say, which is close to true. "She knows exactly who you are. She's always known."

Evan doesn't say anything, just glares at me and I force myself to stare back even though my anxiety's in full flame now, flickering through my body. It's dangerous, because even though he's not the one making hiring / firing decisions, he's advising the guy who is. I should know better, and I don't.

"Maybe she stopped being dumb enough to ignore it."

He opens his mouth, but at exactly that moment a meeting reminder pops up on my screen, and I practically leap out of my chair.

"Colchester Mountain project," I say, grabbing my work iPad. "Gotta go."

I walk out of my office and do my best to pretend that there's not a trickle of sweat dripping down my back.

· · * * ★ ★ ★ * * · ·

WEDNESDAY MORNING, I'm minding my own business at work when a calendar invite pops up on my screen. I'm not even done reading the first one when another pops up.

They're both for Thursday, a week from tomorrow, and I'm shot through with panic before I even finish reading them.

The first: 4pm, a meeting with Evan, Gregory, and Rachelle Lipscomb, the head of human resources at B&L. Fuck.

The second: from Evan, who's sitting five feet away, for 7pm, same day, La Cabaña Mexican Restaurant.

I take some deep breaths and accept the first meeting, because what else am I supposed to do? Even if everything about it screams *you're getting laid off in a week* and the anxiety is already making me dizzy.

I close my eyes and try to breathe and focus on... something else, but I'm also trying to panic-breathe quietly enough that Evan can't hear me, and he keeps making little noises that remind me of his existence and the fact that he's probably responsible for me *losing my goddamn job* and I want to explode and crawl out of my skin.

A few minutes later I open my eyes and make myself look at the second invitation. To dinner. After this meeting of doom.

"Did you mean to send me a calendar invite to dinner?" I ask.

"It's to go over any questions you might have," he says. I feel like my skin is too small for my ribcage, a sickly, shimmering feeling.

"At dinner," I say, proud that my voice doesn't shake.

"Oh good, you can read," he says.

I do not throw my stapler at his head.

"Am I getting overtime for this?" I ask my monitor, because I still haven't bothered to look at him.

"You're salaried, you don't get overtime," he says.

"No, then."

There's a faint creak as he turns around in his chair, then pauses.

"I also wanted to talk," he finally says, and somewhere, distantly, I know I should be happy. That he might be taking me out to dinner to beg for me to come back, or apologize, or at least acknowledge how shitty he was. I take a deep breath and also turn around in my chair, finally facing him.

"We could talk now," I point out.

"I'd rather do it over dinner and not in the office."

He's leaning back in his chair, legs wide, twirling a pen between two fingers.

"About what?"

"I'd like to clear the air," he says. "You've spent weeks angry with me and I'd like to help you resolve that before I leave."

I freeze, because if I don't I might do something I really regret. Like throw my stapler. Or my chair. Or my whole desk, because I'm pretty sure right now I've got the rage-strength to do it.

I don't want to *resolve* my anger at Evan. I want him to leave. I want my anger to fade away with lots of time and plenty of distance.

"Maybe we could work through whatever part I've played in your anger issues," he goes on, like he's not in danger of a keyboard to the face. I swallow hard.

"Having to CC you on every email might have some-thing to do with it," I point out.

"That's necessary."

"Could be that every time you've sat in on a meeting, you've interrupted me at least twice."

"I don't think that's true," he says, frowning.

It is absolutely true.

"You keep pulling my programmers into long, impromptu one-on-ones and then asking me why they're behind with their projects," I say, and my voice still doesn't shake at all, somehow.

"I'd rather talk about this over enchiladas and margaritas on the company tab," he says.

We stare at each other for a little too long, and Evan finally takes a deep breath, then sighs.

"Please?" he says.

You know what? Fuck it. If I get laid off that afternoon, I won't show up at dinner. Maybe I won't show up anyway, but if I accept now then I get to pretend that I'm *interested in building bridges and maintaining relationships* and *invested in alternate methods of conflict resolution and communication* and shit.

"Fine," I say, and suddenly, he smiles.

"Thanks, Kat," he says, and turns around before I can do or say anything else.

I go back to my job and try to pretend that my hands aren't shaking.

# THIRTY-ONE

## SILAS

I'M POURING tortilla chips into a bowl at my kitchen island when Wyatt comes down the stairs, then leans on his elbows across from me and grins. I stop, mid-pour, because that's suspicious.

"What?"

"Looking good," he says.

"Thank you."

"*Glowing*," he goes on.

"I moisturize."

"Is that it?" he says. "Come on. Who's got you smiling like that, baby?"

"Wyatt," Gideon says as he comes into the kitchen. "What the fuck? Leave Silas alone. And don't call him baby, you know he hates that."

"No, *you* hate that," I remind Gideon, because he does. "I'm neutral on Wyatt's weird terms of endearment."

"You shouldn't be."

"They're not weird. *Baby* is an extremely standard form of affectionate address, and I feel affectionately about you

292

assholes," Wyatt says as I grab the chips and salsa and walk into the living room.

"Maybe if you were sleeping together," Gideon points out as he crouches in front of my fridge. "It's a little weird as friends."

I shoot Gideon a glance, but he's very involved in my crisper drawer. We both know that Wyatt and Lainey have a habit of calling each other *baby* after a few drinks, though I'm not sure I feel like bringing it up right now.

"Fine," Wyatt says, parking himself on my couch. "Who's got you smiling like that, *bro*? Oh, hello there. You're looking fluffy as ever."

"Thank you," Gideon says, and Wyatt snorts as he gives Beast chin scritches.

"Barry sends her affectionate regards," he tells my cat, and Beast *mrrps* in response.

"You think they remember each other?" I ask as Gideon comes into the living room and hands me a cherry soda.

"Probably," says Wyatt, who's now vigorously scritching with both hands, chips forgotten. "I mean, she's her mom."

"Cat memories aren't that good," Gideon says as he puts another soda down in front of Wyatt. "It actually creates inbreeding problems in feral colonies, because once a cat reaches adulthood it won't necessarily remember who its mother was, so the males will often mate with—"

We're saved from further details of upsetting cat incest by Javier coming through my front door like a hurricane, already talking at top speed, waving around a plastic bag in one hand and a baking dish in the other. He's got holes in the knees of his jeans and paint on his shirt, dots freckling the deep copper of his arms.

"Sorry I'm late," he says, and holds up the dish he's got

in one hand. It wobbles, but he lowers it before full disaster can strike. "I brought brownies."

"Did you remember the sugar this time?" Gideon asks, and Javier sighs dramatically.

"I try to do one nice thing for you people, and it backfires forever," he says, walking into my kitchen and putting the brownies right in the middle of the counter that I specifically cleared off so I could use it for food prep later.

"Javi," I say, and point at him. He freezes next to the breakfast bar, one eyebrow raised. "Come on."

Javier blinks at me.

"His thing about counter space," Wyatt calls around a mouthful of chips.

"Right. Sorry," Javier says, then carefully slides the pan all the way over to one side of the counter.

It's... an improvement, I guess. He grabs a cherry soda from the fridge, twists the cap off, and is drinking it as he heads into the living room and joins Wyatt on the couch in front of the snacks.

"That's the spicy one," Wyatt says around a mouthful, pointing at a container of salsa, and Javier digs right in.

Then he looks up at me for a moment, and from here I can see the circles under his eyes, shading toward his cheekbones, the slightly restless way he moves as he tilts his head to one side as if he's contemplating.

I don't worry, but I... notice.

"You look different," he says, and I sigh.

"Gideon, you got an opinion on me?" I ask.

"Solid seven," he says, as Beast jumps into his lap, head already held back for chin scritches.

"Thanks."

There's a brief, suspicious silence. Wyatt's grinning. I don't like it.

"Silas got laid," he finally says.

"The fuck?"

"Your fake girlfriend know?" asks Javier, eyebrows up.

I scrub a hand over my face.

"Bet she does," says Wyatt.

"Jesus Christ, why am I friends with you guys?" I mutter.

I was going to tell them, like a normal fucking person, but apparently I don't get that.

"Explains the joie de vivre," Javier grins.

"I've always got joie de vivre."

"Since when do you know French?" grumps Gideon.

"I'm fucking sophisticated," Javier says, cracker in hand as he crosses one knee over the opposite ankle and flops back against my couch. "Didn't you see my art review in the paper of record? The Pilot-Dispatch's art critic called my Bigfoot Zeus, and I quote, *extremely interesting*."

"Isn't that the same lady who said your painting of that baby goat had Satanic overtones and was probably for use in the occult?" Gideon asks.

"She wasn't wrong," Javier says. "I bet we could use it to summon a demon."

We all consider this for a moment, the silence broken only by Beast's incredibly loud purring.

"Maybe the demon would tell us why Silas looks so happy," Javier says.

"Do I still?" I ask sarcastically.

"You think it took a deal with the devil to get Silas laid?" Wyatt says, faux-surprise on his face. "He's not *that* bad looking."

"I can have sex without Satan getting involved," I say, glaring at Wyatt.

"Good to know," Gideon deadpans.

"And you are in my house, eating my snacks, so shut the hell up and let me get my glow on for any reason I like," I go on.

The three of them look at me, like they're waiting for something. I make them wait a little longer, because they're assholes.

"Kat and I are dating," I finally say, and even though I'm trying to sound annoyed with them, it doesn't work.

Wyatt gives Javier a very obnoxious *told you so* look.

"*What,*" Javier says, rolling his eyes. "I didn't say you were wrong, I just said you were fucking nosy."

"You didn't believe me."

"You thought Gideon was dating his sister."

"What?" That's Gideon, suddenly paying attention again.

"No, I thought Gideon was dating someone he didn't tell us about, I didn't know she was his sister."

"You've *met* my sisters."

"There are like... six of them!"

There's a brief, silent moment during which everyone counts Gideon's sisters, including Gideon.

"Right," Gideon finally says.

"How am I supposed to remember all of them if Gideon can't even keep track?" Wyatt says, as though it's the most ridiculous thing ever asked of a person.

"I was double-checking I didn't include Reid," Gideon says.

"You can't remember six people?" I ask Wyatt.

"All of you fuck off," Wyatt says. "Anyway, Silas, there's condom wrappers in the trash can in your upstairs bathroom."

"Why were you in my upstairs bathroom?"

"Because Gideon was using the one down here and it's

never been off-limits before?" he says. "Just get a trash can with a lid."

"Yeah, Beast doesn't knock it over?" Javier asks. "Zorro's a trash can maniac. Laundry hampers, too."

"She'd rather make sure nothing ever stays on a table," I say, looking over at the enormous cat currently lounging on Gideon. Not for the first time, I wonder if he wears catnip cologne or something.

"Dolly just steals rubber bands and knocks them under the couch," Gideon offers. "Anyway, good. I like Kat."

"Me too," I say.

· · · · · ★ ★ ★ · · · · ·

LATER, I find Javier in the kitchen, washing off the cheese board while Wyatt and Gideon are in the living room gossiping about whose cousin's aunt twice removed says her friend from church saw the mailman kissing the next door neighbor. They'd both deny that they're gossiping, but if it walks like a duck and quacks like a duck...

"I'll get those later," I tell him.

"I don't mind."

I knew what the answer would be, so I lean against the counter next to him and cross my arms over my chest.

"Everything okay?" I ask, as nonchalantly as I can, but I can still see the moment of tension the question gets, like he's bracing for a fight.

But then it's gone, replaced by a quizzical little smile and a shrug.

"Sure. Why wouldn't it be?"

I hold out my hand for the wet cheese board, grab a towel, and dry it without saying anything else. After a moment, Javi sighs.

"My dad's been calling."

I put the cheese board away, let the silence do some work.

"I haven't picked up but he keeps leaving voicemails," he goes on, and now he's staring at the water running into the sink, down the garbage disposal. "He wants to see me when I go visit my mom next week, but..."

He leans on the sink and stares out the window over it, knuckles white, a muscle in his jaw flexing. Javi's a little shorter than me and he's sort of pretty in a way I'm not: dark hair pulled off his face, wisps floating out and framing high cheekbones and dark eyes. Between that and the art, he's the kind of guy who'd have gotten made fun of in my high school locker room.

Javier sighs.

"I dunno."

"You can say no."

"Yeah. Of course," he says, and I know he's thinking: *but can I?*

We both stand there for a moment, and I let Javier think in silence.

"Maybe he wants to apologize this time," he says, and there's a hopeful note in his voice that hurts to hear.

"Is Bastien still gonna be there?"

Javier snorts. Fondly.

"Yeah, he still thinks I'm a damsel in distress who needs a brave knight to ride to the rescue by getting into a shouting match," he says. "Which, historically, has solved nothing but is sometimes good entertainment."

Javier's got a sister, Thalia, and a brother, Bastien. Bastien's seven years younger than Javier but he's gregarious and athletic and traditionally masculine in a way thoughtful, artistic Javier isn't, and he's decided that anyone who wants to get to Javier is going to have to get through him.

He's also gay and not out to their father. According to Javier, he's saving that revelation for the time it'll be most useful as a distraction.

"You don't even have to go," I point out, even though I know he knows already. "Cancel and head to Wildwood for a few days."

"Maybe," he says, with a little half-shrug. "I did want to see my mom, though. And my obnoxious brother, I guess."

I nod as he shuts off the water, and I hand him the towel to dry his hands.

"I'm here," I tell him, and it gets a warm, quiet smile.

"I know," he says. "Thanks."

# THIRTY-TWO

## KAT

I KNOCK on the door and try not to feel like I'm cracking apart, or like I'm desperate, or like I'm desperate and cracking apart and suddenly co-dependent on my boyfriend of—let me check my calendar—approximately three days.

I should be meditating instead of at Silas's house. I should be talking to a friend instead of at Silas's house, or re-watching *Cowboy Bebop* for the millionth time, or doing yoga, or going for a run, or one of the other thousand Ways To Deal With Anxiety that I have a literal list of on my phone.

But when he opens the door and sees me, he smiles so hard I almost forget to be nervous.

"You didn't text," he says when he kisses me before the door's even shut.

"Sorry," I say, and I can feel my heartbeat in my throat so instead of saying anything else I push forward into him, kiss him harder. When it ends I've got one hand around the back of his neck and I'm breathing too hard. So is he. Good, this is why I came.

"You okay?" he asks, and there's a frown in those pretty

blue eyes, his thumb sliding along my cheekbone. I told him earlier about the meeting and dinner, so he's got a good reason for asking.

"Yeah. Of course," I say, and make myself take a step back, though I don't stop touching him. "I just... wanted to see you."

I don't say *I feel like the work half of my life is spinning out of control*. I don't say *the stress of not knowing is going to undo me*. I don't even say *please make me feel better*. I'm here because I'm selfish. I know it's not fair to Silas.

"Here I am," he says, softly. "Ta-da."

"Right. Hi." I try to smile and I'm not sure how it goes, and God, how have I already made this so awkward? I've seen him every day for weeks. He put me on his kitchen table and ate me out two nights ago, and now I can barely look him in the eye?

We step back, and I toe my shoes off. I suddenly don't know what to do so I walk into the kitchen, stand in the middle, stop. Silas walks in, rests both hands on the countertop behind himself and gives me a long, assessing look. I look away.

"Kat," Silas says, slowly. "Are you sure you're okay?"

"Fine," I lie. He's not buying it. "I..." Have no idea how to finish that sentence, for one, without blushing myself to death.

"You showed up at my house at ten o'clock at night to say hi?" he asks, his voice gone low and teasing, his head cocked a little to one side. "There's a word for this, you know. Two, actually."

I sigh and close my eyes.

"Shut up," I say, step into his space, and kiss him. He's warm and solid, the front of his shirt damp in spots because I think he was doing dishes when I got here, and I give him a long, slow, open-mouthed kiss, let my hands roam a little. I can feel the ridge of that scar under my fingertips, and for some reason, it makes me push against him a little harder.

"You didn't come here to talk, you mean." Both hands on my back, under the jacket I'm still wearing, up over my ribcage.

"No," I say, braver when his hands are on me and my eyes are closed. "So quit it."

"Bossy," he says, but he says it into my mouth as he pulls me against him. "Get this off."

I tug my jacket off my shoulders without breaking the kiss, toss it onto the counter without looking too hard, push both my hands into his hair and bring his mouth down to mine. I let the kiss turn feral, almost savage; I know I'm shoving him into the counter, that the edge is probably in his back, that I'm grinding my hips against him and pinning him there, but it feels so good I don't care.

He feels good. His mouth feels good. Having control again feels good, so I curl my fingers through his hair and slide one hand to the back of his neck, my thumb on the hinge of his jaw.

He pulls back for a moment, blue eyes gone dark, cheeks flushed, lips red, and I steady myself with a hand on the counter next to his waist while he looks at me, letting his gaze drift down my body until suddenly, he grins and I can feel my face go red.

"Fuck, Kat," he says, and he's still grinning but his voice is all low and gravelly as he puts one thumb right on the hard point of my nipple, swirls the cotton fabric of my dress around it, because I showed up to his house in a dress made of t-shirt material with no bra on. That's why I needed a jacket. In case I got pulled over or had to get gas or something.

"Tell me this is why you came," he rumbles, his thumb still moving, the rasp of the fabric against my nipple so delicious that I'm having a little trouble thinking.

"Of course," I say. I'm trying not to make a weird noise.

"Just this?" he asks, and has the nerve to pinch my nipple gently.

I nod.

"What else?"

*I don't know, do some sex things*, I think, but I can't say that out loud. I can't say anything out loud because I am absolutely, completely sure it'll sound ridiculous. Like *do some sex things*.

"I don't know," I breathe.

"You don't know?" he says, slowly. He hasn't stopped what he's doing but he's not doing anything else, either. "You have no idea what you want?"

There's a long pause where I try to think, half mortified and half horny as fuck.

"Tell me what you need, Kat," he says, in that low, scratchy, teasing voice he has. "I'll give it to you if you ask."

"The other one, too," I finally say, and I'm immediately rewarded with a hard pinch on my other very prominent nipple. The weird noise I've been trying not to make comes out, and Silas gasps in response.

"Tell me what else," he rasps, so I grab his head and haul him down and get a long, slow kiss while I feel like I'm shivering apart. I nip at his lower lip with my teeth and pull back when the kiss ends, listening to his shuddering breath. He hasn't stopped swirling his thumbs over my nipples and he hasn't done anything else, either.

I stare at him for a long moment and let the small, delicious friction flow over me until it's blocking out everything else. I've got goosebumps everywhere. Silas watches me, eyes dark, and something else untangles deep inside me at that look.

"Use your mouth," I say, the words oddly loud in the quiet kitchen.

"Where?"

I grab one hand and press it into my breast, letting his palm slide over fabric and over my nipple, and that gets another grin out of him. Silas spins us around, pushes me into the counter, my hands automatically finding the edge as he lowers his head to that nipple and bites it, still through the fabric.

"Oh," I hiss, the word half-swallowed. Silas looks up at me. Runs his tongue across the nipple between his teeth and as I make another noise, he's on his knees and I'm watching him do exactly what I just asked for.

I have to force myself to take a breath.

When he looks up at me through his eyelashes, from his knees, I want to take a picture. I want to paint a portrait and hang it next to my bed, because Silas is beautiful and kneeling and gazing up like he's completely at my beck and call and oh, fuck. *Fuck.*

"Other one," I say, to see him do what I say and he does: bites my nipple one last time, drags his tongue over the other and my eyes flutter closed. The wet spot that's now on my dress goes cold and I exhale, hard, try not to think about how that's a little gross and just enjoy it.

It's not difficult. I sink my fingers into his hair, let the waves curl around my fingers. He looks at me again and I brush a thumb over his cheekbone, turned on as hell and feeling a little drunk with sexy power.

"So pretty," I murmur. I don't mean to. It just comes out and the second it does I think *oh God what the fuck* but the corners of his eyes crinkle like he's smiling and he sucks at my nipple through the cloth and I make another noise because it has no right to feel that good, but it does.

"Put your hands under my dress," I tell him, and both his hands find my knees, slide up until he's got one knuckle under the hem, and stops. He's still looking at me, like he's waiting for something. Toying with me, maybe.

"*Higher*," I growl, because of course I don't mean *touch my knees*. "All the way up."

He does, and when his fingers reach my hips his breathing hitches and his tongue stops for a moment, and then he rests his head right on my sternum and laughs.

"Kat," he says. "Goddamn."

I am, uh, sort of not wearing panties either because I was feeling both pretty brave and pretty horny when I left my house.

"You mind?" I ask, mock-demure because I know the answer. I'm standing here against the counter with my legs apart, the straps of my dress falling off my shoulders, and nipples visible as fuck through the two giant wet spots on my dress. There's a huge bulge in his shorts. I know he doesn't mind, I want to hear him say it.

"Fuck no, I don't mind," he says, his thumbs stroking the crease between my hip and my thigh. Then he looks up at me, lust written all over his face, and says, "Tell me."

I have to remind myself to breathe, my brain shorting out a little, when he looks at me like that, and still the words stick in my throat. God, I'm bad at this.

"Are you right-handed?" I ask.

"Yes."

I can't get the words out but I grab his right hand by the wrist, splay his fingers on my lower belly. Run my own fingers along them, not really caring that it lifts the hem of my skirt.

"You look good like that," I tell him, and I barely recognize my own voice.

"So do you," he breathes. "Holy fuck, Kat, this view."

I find his thumb and he lets me bend it down, between my legs, and I shift my hips and he moves his hand until suddenly the pad of his thumb finds my clit and I make a small, soft noise.

"Like that?" he asks, and thank God, his thumb makes a slow circle without me having to tell him.

"Yeah," I gasp. I realize my head is back and my eyes are closed, my other hand clenched on the edge of the counter. I realize I've got his wrist in my hand again and I'm moving my hips against it as he circles, chasing pleasure, letting it build. After a bit, I nudge the strap of my dress the rest of the way down, watching Silas's face, the way he looks up at me when the cloth comes off my nipple. When I slide my fingers into his hair I barely have to nudge him before his mouth is where I want it again and we both groan.

I can't stop staring at Silas. This time he's using just his tongue and I'm still half-rocking against his hand, thumb drawing slow circles. Every so often he flicks a glance up at me and there's a teasing smile around his eyes. I might be making noises. I might be making a lot of noises. I don't care.

"Stop," I finally say, and he stills his hand, his tongue. Looks up at me, his hair falling a little in his eyes, lips parted, cheeks flushed. Lust-drunk, and I move his hand to my thigh, pull my dress back up.

"Stand up," I say, and he does. One knee clicks, and I look down, suddenly guilty that I made him kneel on the tile floor. "Sorry," I say. "Are you—"

"I'm fucking fine, Kat," he says, and then he's pushing me into the counter, the line hard against my lower back, and his hands are in my hair and his mouth is hot and greedy against mine. He wedges a thigh between my legs and I can feel the iron of his cock against my hip. "Completely fine."

"Good," I breathe. Our tongues slide together and I grab his hips, pull him against me. It gets a groan, an exhale. He pulls back a little, hands in my hair, thumbs on my cheekbones.

"Tell me," he murmurs, low and teasing. "What you want now."

"Take your shirt off," I say, and he steps back, pulls it over his head and because I can, I reach out, slide my hand down his chest. Through the chest hair, over that ugly scar, through the line of fur that dips below his belt. He watches me, one eyebrow raised, and I raise my eyes to his. Deliberately dip two fingers under the waistband of his shorts and I'm pretty sure I can see his cock twitch even from here.

I give him one long, hard stroke with the palm of my hand through his shorts, and I keep my eyes on his face. Watch his eyes go hazy, his lips part, his breathing stutter.

Then I pull my hand back, hop onto the counter, crook a finger at him. He steps forward between my legs and I give him a hard, slow kiss, fingers wrapped in his hair. After a moment he pulls back and presses his mouth to my neck.

"Tell me," he murmurs, his voice buzzing through me.

Slowly, I push his head lower: my collarbone, my tits, my stomach. He keeps peppering kisses and licks, both his hands around my thighs, pushing them wide and pulling my ass down until it's on the edge of the counter and my head is against his cabinets.

Then he pauses. I've got my eyes closed, head back, one hand in his hair and the other on the edge of the counter, and I'm about to say something like *come the fuck on you know what I want*, but then he flicks the tip of his tongue against my clit and my entire body jolts.

"That it?" he has the nerve to ask.

"Again."

He does it exactly one more time.

"*Silas*," I growl, and I'm trying not to pull his hair out but God, I want to, I want to mash his stupid face into me until he makes me come but he laughs, and then he's licking me again and I forget I was ever annoyed.

Silas eats me out like he's practically taking notes on every jolt and shiver and gasp I make, and everything I like he does ten more times. It doesn't take long before I'm gasping and swearing, gripping his hair too hard and then whispering apologies.

"Fuck," I hear myself whisper. "Silas. I'm—"

He stops. Not completely but he moves his tongue from my clit and slides it between my lips, presses it into my entrance, laps at me slowly as I arch my back and try to get my breathing under control. When I look down, he's watching me.

"What the hell?" I gasp out.

"Hm?"

I grit my teeth, tilt my head against the cabinets again, gather my nerve.

"Make me come, dammit," I grind out, and then, "Fuck!" because he's back at it, harder and faster and in seconds I'm back where I was and then I'm over the top, a sound exploding out of me that's half moan and half gasp as my fingers curl against the countertop.

I keep holding his head there. I feel half out of my mind, but I don't let him go and he doesn't stop and... yeah. Yeah, I'm gonna come twice on his kitchen counter, it turns out, because the second one happens pretty fast and this time I whimper and arch my back as it rockets through me and finally, I let his hair go.

Silas stands. He hauls me up from where I've melted, his hands still on my thighs, pulls me in and kisses me, mouth musky and sweet and fuck, it's hot.

"What now, Kat?" he murmurs. I push him back slightly, hop off the counter. Lean back against it and kiss him and pull him in, brush my hand over the bulge in his shorts.

"Did you like that?" I ask. I know the answer, but I want to hear it.

Silas huffs out a laugh, one thumb stroking the inside of my thigh.

"I did," he says, voice all sandpaper and gravel. "I fucking loved it."

"How much?" I say, and suck in a breath, my hands on his shoulders. "Show me. Touch yourself."

Silas roughly palms the bulge in his shorts, his hips rocking forward. He grabs the counter next to my waist and his eyes slide shut. His head goes back. He groans, long and loud, fingers half-curled around his erection, and all I can do is stare at his hand as he strokes himself, feel his breathing in his shoulders.

Finally, he looks at me, and his eyes are pleading and teasing and asking all at once, and I remember myself. I remember that right now, I get what I want and what I want is Silas, desperate for me, at my beck and call.

"Go into the living room and take your clothes off," I say, and it comes out nearly a whisper. "Then stroke yourself and don't come."

My pulse is pounding and despite everything, I'm half-convinced he's about to laugh at me but he doesn't. He covers my mouth with one quick, hard kiss, and then walks away while I stand there, trying to collect myself.

This is... not what I thought was going to happen tonight. I'd envisioned throwing myself into his arms and

Silas carrying me upstairs and ravishing me so hard I forgot everything for a few minutes. Not this, where I get to name my desires and he gives them to me with a smile.

I had no idea I'd like it this much.

When I walk out of the kitchen toward the stairs, he's on the couch, thighs wide, head back, slowly working himself. I pause for a moment, one hand on the railing of the stairs, and just watch.

"How am I doing?" he asks, voice husky and dark, eyes watching me.

I don't answer right away, just keep watching: the way his hand moves up and down. The way his hips flex into his fist. The way he strokes the head with his thumb.

"Good," I finally say, mouth dry.

"Where are you going?"

"Wherever I want," I say, and he grins. Then gasps. Then lets his head tip back even further against the back of the couch, eyes shuddering closed.

"You're fucking killing me, Kat," he says.

"I think you'll live," I say, and head up the stairs before I can say anything else. I head into his bedroom and grab a condom from the new box in his bedside table. Glance at myself in the mirror, run my fingers through my hair. Straighten my dress. Stand there for an extra few moments and breathe.

When I get back, Silas's hand is moving even slower, his breathing ragged.

"Thought you got lost," he teases, mouth smiling, eyes hooded.

I walk up to the couch and straddle him on the edge of the couch, my knees outside his thighs. Close but not close enough to touch him, and Silas makes a half-strangled noise, his hand pausing.

"Don't stop," I murmur, leaning in to kiss him. There's another noise and a shudder goes through his whole body and then his other hand is buried in my hair, gripping, pulling me in. I brace my hands against his hard shoulders and give him a long, slow, deep kiss and don't touch him anywhere else even though God, I want to. I want to hop on his dick this instant and ride him as hard as I can, make Silas shout my name before we're both spent, but that would ruin all my hard work.

So instead I say, "Stop," and he does. I pull back and he's panting for breath but grinning at me like he's having the time of his life, and somehow, I find myself smiling back.

"You like this, huh?" he says.

And I... sort of laugh?

"Yeah," I say.

"Good. Me too."

"You sure?" I ask, and glance at his very hard dick, a single bead of moisture rolling down the underside of the head.

"I like you telling me what you want," he says. "I like giving it to you."

I hold the condom out with two fingers. "Put this on," I tell him.

"Can I touch myself again?" he asks, and I nod.

Silas rips it open with his teeth. His breathing catches as he unrolls it over the head and when he slides it all the way down and then stokes himself his hips buck up like he can't control himself and he makes a soft oh noise, looking at me from half-lidded eyes.

"What do you want now, Kat?" he asks. "Anything."

And oh, God, I want everything. I want him to bend me over the coffee table and rail me. I want to tease him like this until he begs me to let him come. I want to tell him to start doing jumping jacks, just because I think he would.

But one idea is better than the rest. Besides, I don't really want the jumping jacks. I'm only curious, so I tumble off of him and lay on the couch, head on the armrest, my foot against his side. The skirt of my dress is half hiked up, the top still more or less in place.

"C'mere," I say, crooking my finger again, and I barely have to ask before Silas is over me, between my legs, one hand next to my head on the arm of the couch.

"Here I am," he teases. "This all you—"

"Get on your knees."

He does it and I arch up, toward him, hook one knee over his shoulder. He grabs my thigh so hard his fingers dig in and he's grinning, almost laughing, his other hand on my hip as his eyes drift over me, splayed on his couch.

"Fuck me," I say before he can ask me anything, my voice quiet and rough and barely recognizable. "Make it good."

He exhales hard, strokes my hip before leaning in. Nudges the tip of his cock over my clit before he lines himself up. Then he pauses. He looks at me, and then he slides in without breaking eye contact.

I make a noise. It sounds a little like *nnnggghh* and it comes out through clenched teeth but it's a good noise because this feels fucking *good*. Because Silas, somehow, knew exactly what I needed when I turned up stressed and horny on his doorstep.

"Good?" he rasps as he sinks deep, and he's got a look on his face like he's trying for that charming, cocky smile he's got but it's not working and all he can manage is raw, disheveled lust.

"More," is all I say. I reach under myself, find his knees below my hips, grasp at them for some reason.

Silas starts moving, slow and firm, his breathing ragged. "Tell me—"

"I can't," I whisper.

A quick, hard gasp. He moves a little, adjusts the angle and then his next stroke drives straight into a spot that drags a noise out of me I've never heard before.

"*Fuck*," I hiss, eyes closed, head back. "Do that a—"

Of course he does. Of course he does exactly that, again and again. He does it fast and he does it slow; hard, gentle. Silas fucking experiments on me until I'm a breathy, incoherent mess who couldn't give him a single instruction if my life depended on it, and he watches me through half-open, sex-drugged eyes like he's memorizing everything he can about this.

"Kat," he says, and it comes out a strangled whisper. "Tell me when you're close."

I just kind of whimper, because I'm close now. I've *been* close, floating on the heady cloud of getting well-fucked, pleasure sparkling over my skin and surging through my veins in exactly the way that will never be quite enough.

"I'm close," I tell him, and before I can reach for my clit myself, he does.

"Yes. That," I manage to get out, and now my hands are clenched on the arm of the couch, next to my head. "Fuck, Silas."

And then I'm nothing but noises and swearing, maybe, and I grab onto his couch and come so hard I can't breathe, I can't think, only hang on until it's over.

"Jesus, Kat," Silas whispers but I've already got him by the wrist and I'm pulling him down. He lands on top of me and I wrap my legs around him, shove my hands into his hair. Give him a hard, messy kiss and then he buries his face in my neck and in a few more thrusts he's growling *fuck, Kat, yes* and slowly, he goes still.

We stay there, and even though my head is halfway off the arm of the couch and my back is at a weird angle and my glasses are slowly falling off, I don't move. I can feel Silas's breath against my neck, the sweat in his hair when I move my fingers through it. His heartbeat in his neck when he turns his head and tucks it under my chin.

Silas who's here, like this, lazy and gentle after fucking me out of my mind. Silas who's nothing like I thought he was, who's marshmallows on the outside and iron on the inside.

Silas who is, inexplicably, mine.

# THIRTY-THREE

## SILAS

"YOU WANT TO TALK ABOUT IT?" I ask later. We're still on the couch, cleaned up now, my shorts on and her dress decent-ish as she leans against me, our feet on the coffee table. The last time we were like this, she'd just washed my hair and I woke up hours later with my head in her lap.

Kat sighs, pushes her head back into my shoulder.

"You already know," she says. "That's all there is. Just... the specter of getting fired from a job I like in a town with nothing much else going on because I got mad enough to stalk my ex and make sex noises at him."

My brain snags on *nothing much else*, and I slide a strand of her hair between two fingers, watching Beast sleep in the armchair across the room.

"Sprucevale's got plenty going on, you know," I finally say, trying to sound light.

"I meant—shit," she says. "I didn't mean that. I meant in terms of, you know, tech jobs. Not a ton."

"Of course."

I don't want it to bother me, but it sticks in my brain,

lodged there like a sliver of glass: her tenuous connection to this town. The truth that she's only here for a job and because we were far away from her ex, and one of those things might not be true much longer.

"You staying?" I ask, still playing with her hair because I can't help it: dark and ribbony, sliding through my fingers like water. Soft and pliable. Everything I thought she usually isn't.

Kat sighs.

"I don't think tonight's a good idea," she says, and looks down at her dress.

"You can't wear that to work?"

"It looks like I just got fucked in it," she says, her head tilted back, her eyes laughing behind her glasses, and I grin. I grin at the fact that she's right, and because I got to do the fucking. I grin because I love that she's saying that at all. Laughing about it. Looking happy like this, like it's something I did. Like I got her to lower her spikes and let me in for a little while.

"Later, then," I say.

· · * * ★ ★ ★ * * · ·

FRIDAY MORNING, after my usual gym-and-shower-by-seven routine, I stand at the sliding glass door in front of my deck, holding my coffee and staring at nothing.

*You shouldn't,* I remind myself. *It's been forever since you pulled shit like this.*

When was the last time? The golf cart?

Okay, but the golf cart was fun as hell, and now I can't stop grinning. Was it stupid to put on night vision goggles and drive a borrowed golf cart around a fancy wedding venue? Hell yes.

Do I regret it? Hell no. I didn't even get caught.

And this isn't borrowing a golf cart. This is only... an outing.

I text Kat before I can think better of it.

**Me:** Call in sick to work today. I'll be at your place at nine.

I grab myself another mug of coffee while I wait for her to respond. It's only seven-thirty, so maybe she's not even awake yet, and so Beast and I do a little bird watching from the door while I wait for Kat to text me back.

**Kat:** I can't.

Thought so.

**Me:** Sure you can.
**Kat:** I can't just call in sick whenever I want.
**Me:** You literally can.
**Kat:** I'm trying not to get fired!
**Me:** They've already decided whether they're going to fire you or not. A little food poisoning won't change their minds.

I feel a little guilty about talking her into this, but I know I'm right. I also know that another eight hours in a room with her ex today isn't going to do her anxiety any favors.

**Me:** You've been stressed. It'll be fun. Come on.
**Me:** Please?

There's a long, long pause. Dots appear, then disappear.

"I think I won," I tell Beast, who doesn't even look at me. There's a bird outside.

**Kat:** Fine. What are we doing?

"Told you," I say to Beast, who still doesn't acknowledge me.

**Me:** Wear sturdy shoes.
**Kat:** For WHAT

I look at my phone and, for a moment, debate telling her. Then I decide against it.

**Kat:** FOR WHAT, SILAS

I send her a single winking emoji.

· · · · ★ ★ ★ ★ · · · ·

KAT IS STANDING NEXT to me on the riverbank and looking at me like I've just told her she'll be jumping to the moon.

"On foot?" she asks, incredulous. "Over rocks. On foot."

"Yes, you've grasped the nature of our expedition," I say.

"You had me call in sick to work to cross a whole river on foot. Over rocks."

I glance at the Chillacouth River, in case I've somehow missed that it's forty feet high or a mile across, but it's not. It's the same pretty mountain river it's always been, low in the late summer, a veritable rock causeway stretching to the opposite bank.

"I can try giving you a piggyback ride, but you're more likely to fall in that way," I offer, because I'm a gentleman.

"Are you at least going to tell me why we're crossing a river on rocks when there's probably a bridge somewhere?" she asks. This on rocks thing is really getting to her, and it's getting harder not to laugh.

"Because I want to show you something."

Kat's been acting strange since she left my house Sunday night. Unusually strange, I mean; formal and brittle when we're together, at our appointed dates, like she didn't fuck my brains out over the weekend. More anxious than usual.

Then she showed up Wednesday night, fucked my brains out again, and didn't want to stay over. I think she needs to get out of her head, so here we are. On an adventure, and she's taking it super well.

Right now, she's frowning at the river, like it's displeased her personally. I do my best not to roll my eyes, because it's not even a big river, and she's acting like I want her to scale El Capitan.

"I'll go first so you know where to walk," I tell her. "This time of year, it's maybe two feet deep in the middle. Worst that'll happen is you get a wet knee."

"The worst that happens is my glasses fall off and break in the middle of *a river*," she says.

"I promise not to leave you stranded."

"Is this even legal?"

"Of course it's legal," I tell her.

Actually, I have no idea. I've been coming here since I was a teenager and I've never thought to ask that question before.

Kat's skeptical look doesn't change, though it's hard to tell how much is honest skepticism and how much is her love of giving me a hard time. Might be about equal, so I put my hands on her shoulders and grin down at her. She relaxes as soon as I do, and I'm way too pleased about that.

"I promise you won't fall in," I tell her. "And you won't drown, and if your glasses fall off and break, I'll heroically carry you back to dry land and drive you to the glasses store myself."

"If my glasses fall off and break you'll be leading me around by the hand until I get my new ones," she says.

"Then I won't let you trip or walk into traffic," I promise, bend down, give her a light kiss on the lips. "Come on."

· · · · * ★ ★ ★ * · · · ·

UNSURPRISINGLY, Kat makes it across the river just fine. I think she even starts having fun by about halfway over, once she realizes I wasn't kidding about the lack of danger. When she accidentally dunks one foot into the water, she laughs.

Then she rolls her eyes at me and pretends to frown, but it's too late. Her laugh feels better than it should, soft and bright. Thrilling to think I can do that for her.

At the other riverbank, there's a cliff. Not a huge one, maybe six feet high, made of crumbling red dirt and held together by tree branches, but high enough.

"Don't tell me you're gonna give me a boost," she says.

"Of course not," I tease. "You could fall. There's a path this way."

It's not much of a path, but it's better than the cliff. By the time we reach the tree line at the top, both her knees are covered in leaves and dirt and I've got a scrape on one shin from a stray branch. I brush it off, a few droplets of blood trailing across my leg.

"You okay?" she asks.

"It's nothing," I tell her.

"It's bleeding."

"I've had worse," I point out. "Almost there. C'mon."

When we reach the chain link fence, she stops again. She gives me a look, and I can't help but grin.

"What?"

"There's a fence," she points out, helpfully gesturing at the fence. "Where are we going?"

"It's not much further."

"That's not an answer."

"Technically, it is. It's just not the answer you wanted."

Kat takes a deep, patient breath. I think she's trying not to look amused.

"Are you going to make me scale this fence?" she asks.

"Would you?"

She gives it a long, considering look, like: maybe. I watch her face as she considers trouble, surprised by how much I'm enjoying myself.

"It's not that high," she admits.

"Well, hopefully," I say, and trail off, walking along the fence line. "There's still a better... ah. Here."

There's a spot in the fence where a small oak tree's grown into the links, and behind it, the metal is cut. I bend it back for Kat to go through, but she's ten feet away looking at a sign.

It is, technically, a NO TRESPASSING sign.

"Silas," she says, still staring at the sign. "Where are we going?"

"The sign's just kidding," I tell her.

"Looks serious to me."

"It's only for show."

"All signs are for show, Silas, they're *signs*. Am I gonna get arrested?"

I run one hand through my hair, damp with sweat, and lean against the tree.

"Probably not," I tell her. "I never have been."

Finally, she looks over at me, annoyance and curiosity and something else playing out across her face.

"You'll like it," I tell her, and open the chain link again. I feel the thrill of victory when she squeezes through the hole, and then we're on the other side and I take her hand. She looks down at them, then up at me, and laughs.

"What?" I ask.

"What the hell am I doing?" she says.

"Having an adventure."

"I'm gonna get arrested for river crimes in a weird forest," she says. "Why did I let you talk me into this?"

"Because you needed to do something besides stress out and follow rules."

"I do lots of other things!"

I have to let her hand go when we walk through the underbrush, but after another fifty feet, we come out into a gravel-lined clearing with a huge brick building in the middle, and we both stop. There's no one else for miles, nothing but the forest, the river, the fence, this ruin. No one to perform for or worry about, just this secret place where I used to come sometimes in high school to smoke weed.

"Here we are," I say, and Kat looks up at it, lips parting slightly. I take her hand again.

"Where's *here*?" she asks.

# THIRTY-FOUR

## KAT

"AN OLD WAREHOUSE, as far as I know," he says, looking up at the dilapidated building he's brought me to.

Over a river, on foot. Through a sketchy forest. Past some very clear signage and through a literal fence.

"The river's about twenty feet that way, through the trees. There used to be a lot of logging here," he goes on, like this is a history lesson. "This is the only warehouse left. Probably because it's brick. You coming?"

I am. I've got more questions and even more reasons that I shouldn't let Silas take me inside a ruined building made of bricks, but I've got the odd feeling that I'm being led on an adventure by some sort of mythical elf-person, so I go with it.

Even though when I check back, it's still Silas holding my hand, pulling me toward a doorway. Silas, pushing aside the vines and letting me through first; Silas, who's grinning at me like he's got a secret he can't wait for me to see.

He lets my hand go and I look around: high brick walls, holes where the windows used to be, gaps in the brick where there were floor beams and a second story. The floor down to dirt, the corners of the walls uneven and crumbled.

No roof, only sky, and it's made this crumbling building into a jungle. A secret garden, trees branching upward from between piles of brick, vines covering the walls that get the most sunlight. It's strange and abandoned and *pretty*. It feels like a secret, a world self-contained.

And it's very, very quiet.

"Last weekend," he says, as I take it in, "you said you wanted to sit at the bottom of a well for a while, in the quiet."

"You remembered that?" I ask, and I turn to him because he's next to me again, hands in his pockets, looking pleased.

He shrugs. He looks at me, and his eyes are laughing, the corners crinkled, and I can't stop staring: all the shades of blue threaded together, this close. The almost-freckles on his nose and cheekbones, exactly one shade darker than the rest of his skin. A few strands of gray in his hair, messy with sweat and dirt. There's a leaf stuck in it, and I pull it out gently. Hold it between my fingers. I wonder how long I can stare at him like this before he minds.

"What else do you remember?" I ask, and my voice is nearly lost to the wilds around me.

"I remember you told me a story about a kingdom at war when I was having a breakdown outside a karaoke bar," he says.

I glance away because Jesus, what a nerd, but Silas puts his fingers under my chin and guides my face back. My heart might stop.

"I remember you can't see the words on a shampoo bottle from three inches away without your glasses," he says.

"I was pretty sure," I answer. My voice comes out in a whisper.

"I remember," he says, and then stops, and now he looks away. He pushes a hand through his hair.

"What?"

"I spent way too much time thinking about you in college," he says, and there's an odd, bashful smile on his face. Like he's embarrassed to admit it.

I have no idea what to say, and I think my face shows it, because he laughs.

"I think I've finally figured out why," he says. "I remember I felt pretty bad when you cried in that meeting with the dean."

"Oh, God," I say, and can't help laughing. "Fuck you for that."

We find a spot next to a wall in the shade, sit down. The dirt sticks to the back of my legs and I can feel the damp through my shorts, but we crossed a river and went through a fence to get here. I don't care.

"I could have been nicer," I admit, eyes closed, face tilted toward the sky.

"Could you have been?"

"Fuck *off*," I say, eyes still closed, but I can feel myself smile. "I could have been... less interested in making you follow every single rule to the letter and more interested in helping you actually learn earth science. I mean, who cares if you re-take a quiz as long as you learn the material?"

There's a silence, and I finally open my eyes to see him staring at me.

"What?"

"Nothing. Just strange," he says, eyes playing over my face. "I didn't realize you were an undergrad back then."

"Oh, was that the problem? If I'd been a grad student or an adjunct, your bullshit would've been okay?" I tease.

"I think you'd have had a better handle on me."

325

"I can't imagine having a handle on you," I tell him.

It gets another pause, another look.

"You can't?"

"Not at all," I say in a rush of honesty. "I think you're a selfish dick and then you hold my hand through a panic attack and skip the dinner party you came for. I think you're a macho meathead and then you let me wash your hair in the shower. I think you're too charming and too friendly and too outgoing to notice anyone else, and then you bring me here, and you're so much sweeter than I deserve—"

"Stop."

I swallow, hard. My heart thumps and this place is so quiet it feels like the only sound.

"Everything we've done together was so we could emotionally manipulate someone else," I say, quietly.

"Everything?" he asks.

"Most things," I say, but that's not right either. My heart keeps thumping. "Some things."

"Not still." It's not a question.

"No."

I take a deep breath against a sudden weight in my chest. I look up at the sky past the tops of the crumbling brick, feel the quiet around me. The way it smells of leaves and dirt. The way the sunlight pulses and shifts, clouds moving overhead, tall trees waving in and out of view.

"I had," I say, and I have to stop because suddenly I'm about to cry so I bite my lip, take a deep breath. "Such a bad year."

Silas doesn't say anything and I squeeze my eyes shut, swallow twice in a row because I can't believe I'm doing this. Here, now, when he brought me to this nice illegal place because he thought it would make me happy and here I am, fucking it up and crying—

But then he's got his arm around me and he's pulling me in. Tucking my head under his chin. Warm and solid as anything, and he just holds me tight.

"I know," he says, his voice a rumble into my hair.

And God, I fucking lose it. I shove my face into his chest and try to drag a breath into my lungs, but it doesn't work and I sob, ragged and gasping and ugly.

"I should have seen it coming," I manage to get out, my voice high-pitched and trembling. "Evan wasn't—I don't know. He was nice to me and did things for me and looked at me and I was stupid and shy and I thought it was love because he'd chosen *me*. But then he didn't. And—"

I breathe in for the first time, eyes still closed.

"—he must hate me," I say, shaky. "Why else at our wedding? Why not ten minutes earlier? What did I do?"

Silas's arms just tighten, his stubble digging into my scalp a little.

"It felt like he took everything," I say. "Or—I let him have everything. He got our apartment. He got our friends, because even the ones who called me, I stopped calling back. He got our jobs because I couldn't stand to be around him any more and then he got our lives because I moved down here to be closer to Anna Grace, because she felt like the one thing he couldn't touch. And then he fucking came here and all I wanted was to make him suffer."

I take a long, shaky breath, and exhale.

"What kind of monster wants that?" I whisper. It was fucked up of me and I know that, know that if I were the bigger person I'd forgive and forget and move on, but I couldn't. I've never had it in me.

"One I wouldn't fuck with," Silas says after a moment. He's got one arm slung over my chest, his other hand playing with my hair a little, tiny soothing tugs on my scalp.

"What?" I ask, after a minute.

"He backed you into a corner, what did he expect?" Silas says, so calmly it's... surprising. "Of course you came at him, all teeth and claws. Who did he think you were?"

It's a question I don't have an answer to, a way I've never considered this before.

"You think I have teeth and claws?" I ask, after a moment.

His fingers sift through my hair, mindlessly soothing.

"Teeth. Claws. Spikes. Horns, probably," he says. "Razor-sharp, too."

I close my eyes and take a deep breath, trying not to cry more at this particular revelation.

"Sorry," I say, and Silas laughs.

"Please don't be," he says, and his voice is gentle as rain. "You wouldn't be you if you were all softness and rounded edges. I like the teeth and the claws, even when it's my throat they're in."

I look up at him, and then wriggle a little until I'm on my back, head in his lap.

"That can't possibly be good for you," I say.

"Fuck good. This is better," he says, and he's smiling down at me, happy and relaxed, like he's never wanted to be anywhere else but here, an abandoned warehouse that's crumbling apart, crying girlfriend in his lap. "You know I haven't had a girlfriend for... six years, I think?"

"Don't tell me I interrupted your vows of celibacy," I say, dryly. "Not that I'm sorry."

"Not quite," he says, and tilts his head back against the wall. Fingers still in my hair, probably splayed into the dirt and leaves below us now. I don't give a single fuck. "There were people, sometimes, but there wasn't *someone*."

I just watch him. It's a strange angle, from below like this, but right now Silas looks like an angel with the blue sky stretching above him, backlit, sunlight picking out copper and gold in his hair.

"There's a lot wrong with me," he starts.

"Sil—"

"Please don't," he says, so I don't. His hand is on my ribcage so I slide my own over it and stay quiet. "I felt like everyone wanted to fix me, or put me on some pedestal, or convince me I was fine so I could be who they wanted."

Then he smiles, eyes still closed.

"And that gets old," he says. "So I gave up. And then it turned out I didn't want sympathy or sweetness. I wanted someone with teeth and claws who could see my cracks and not go all soft. Someone who could destroy me."

I watch him, and wait, sliding my fingers into the valleys between his.

"I can be soft," I point out when I'm sure he's done.

Silas looks down at me, the sky behind him like a halo, his eyes dark in the shadow.

And he starts laughing. After a minute I start laughing, too, even if I'm not totally sure what the joke is. I think it might be at my expense.

"You want to know when I started falling for you?" he asks, and I want to say, *you fell?* But I don't.

"I think you're gonna tell me no matter what I say."

"You see?"

"Yes," I tell him.

"Driving home after you had a panic attack," he says. "You were still so damn prickly. It was—I don't know. I couldn't help it. I felt like you wanted to cut me to pieces and I wanted to let you do it."

The breeze shifts the leaves overhead, making shadows play across my face.

"When you got Melissa to stop bothering me about karaoke," I say. I don't say: *I fell, too.* I let it hang there, between us. "When you acted like it was her problem that she wanted me to sing, not mine that didn't want to."

"It never occurred to me."

"Well, there you go," I say, and pause for a moment. Thinking. "And when you said you'd make Evan crawl."

"Of course," he teases. "We still haven't."

"I don't want him to," I say, honestly. "I just want to never have to think about him again. But I liked how invested you were."

"Let me know if you change your mind," he says. "There's still time."

Then he flips his hand over in mine, brings it to his lips, kisses it. We stay there, like that, in the dirt, in the silence, for a long time. Let the vines grow around us. Let the building crumble. Let the world spin, passing us by.

· · · · · ★ ★ ★ ★ · · · · ·

"STRATIFITE," Levi says slowly. "Is that the 'safe fracking' startup?"

It's Saturday night, and we're at Loveless Brewing because Silas wants me to meet his friends. I tap my fingers on the table in front of me and kind of wish that Silas had waited, like, five more minutes before heading off to get us beers. He seemed to think that Levi and I would get along well enough without him, but this already feels off to a bad start.

"No," I say, pushing my glasses up and flicking at my bangs, like either of those things can shield me. "Well, not really. We've done a couple of GIS projects related to fracking, though. For other companies, we don't actually have, like, drills ourselves. We're mostly programmers."

Levi doesn't say anything for a long moment. I think he's glowering. Fuck. Is he glowering? We're at one of the outdoor tables at Loveless Brewing on Saturday night, and even though there are lights strung all over the place, Levi's face is a little hard to read.

Not that I'm spectacular at reading people to begin with. Where the hell is Silas? He couldn't give me five more minutes of gentle conversational guidance?

"We also work with companies in geothermal energy, which is starting to catch on down here," I say. "And has a way lower carbon footprint and all that. It's not evil or anything, it's just data."

Levi nods. I am not impressing Silas's best friend, and I'm starting to wonder why on earth he was so sure we'd get along. Because we're both weird and quiet?

"I only manage the people who do the coding," I go on, because why not keep talking? "And sometimes do the coding. Uh. What do you do? Not fracking, I guess."

Great segue.

"I work for the National Forest," he says, nodding at the nearby trees. "I'm an arborist."

He clears his throat and looks at his hands for a moment.

"So," he says. He does not follow it up with another statement, even though I wait.

Okay. I've read, like, a million self-help books called *How to Not Be A Fucking Weirdo In Public*, I can do this, no matter how anxious I am right now.

"What's your favorite tree?" I ask.

Levi looks very thoughtful, and I'm about to apologize for the question when he answers.

"My favorite tree species, or my favorite specific tree?"

"You have a specific favorite tree?"

"The huge magnolia outside City Hall. When we were kids we used to climb it and then throw—"

"Are you seriously talking about *trees?*" asks Silas's voice behind me. A second later, he puts three beers down on the table, then slides two toward Levi and I.

"You didn't give us any guidance," I say. "That's your whole job."

"You're adults!"

"You could have given us *something*," I go on, because Silas is grinning like he's absolutely delighted and I can't help myself. "You know, you're gonna meet my best friend Levi, he has a favorite tree, he's married to my sister, he has a..."

"Weird mole?" Silas supplies, at the same time that Levi says, "Dog."

Levi gives Silas a very patient look.

"I was thinking more along the lines of *dog*," I tell Silas, and I'm still sort of nervous but also enjoying this. "Why would you say weird mole?"

"Why *would* you say that?" Levi joins in, and that's when I realize he's enjoying this, too. "June tell you about that?"

Suddenly, Silas has nothing to say and takes a long drink of his beer instead. I glance over at Levi to find him looking at me. Then, after a moment, he smiles.

I get a warm, fuzzy feeling I can't quite decipher.

"Where's everyone else? They're late," Levi says, after another moment.

"I told them eight-fifteen instead of eight," Silas says. "Figured you two might need a few minutes to get used to each other."

Then he gives me a sweet, almost shy look, and his foot nudges against mine and my heart speeds up and my mouth goes dry. Across the table Levi is giving him a very strange, thoughtful look, like he's seeing something for the first time.

"Oh," I say, and I can feel myself blushing. "Thanks."

# THIRTY-FIVE

## SILAS

"IS THAT LEGAL?" Kat is asking. It's an hour later and we're all at a table together: Kat next to me, Wyatt on her other side, Levi, Javier, and Gideon across the table from us.

"Of course it's legal," I tell her. "I wouldn't build a whole cabin if it weren't legal."

"I feel like you might, actually," she says, and everyone else at the table exchanges some looks.

"We have a lease," I say, pretending to be offended. "For ten years, from the Forest Service. It took months of detangling red tape to make it all legal, thanks very much."

"You know, the rest of us never saw that paperwork," Wyatt says, leaning around Kat.

"I watched you sign it," Gideon says.

"You did?"

"Did I sign it?" asks Javier, idly swirling the last of his soda in the bottom of his glass.

"Yes," says Gideon. "You, me, Wyatt, and Silas all signed leases. And, frankly, we did the Forest Service a favor because we had to dismantle the old cabins that were there before we built ours."

"And that was legal, too?" Kat asks.

"They weren't historical or anything," I say, and can't help grinning at her.

"That's not what the lady asked," says Wyatt.

"They were a hazard," I say.

"So you tore down cabins and built your own without telling the Forest Service?" Kat asks, still teasing me. "I can't believe you didn't get a permit."

"You can't?" says Wyatt.

"They're up to code," I tell her. "Totally safe, well-maintained. Much better than the crumbling fire traps that used to be there."

"Technically," Levi says, and everyone turns to look at him. "Those cabins weren't there. The paperwork never mentioned them. Maybe it got lost, who knows. The files on Wildwood were a mess."

It's true. When I started looking into Camp Wildwood—a small clearing on the side of a mountain in the national forest with a handful of old, rundown cabins—it was almost impossible to find anything about it, almost like it didn't exist. Levi offered to help, and eventually we wound up in a dusty basement in Roanoke, going through faded carbon copy forms, though they only said that First Baptist of Sprucevale had had a lease on the camp that ended in 1972. It took a while to convince anyone that it was worth the time and effort to write up more lease paperwork, but we did, and now it's ours. More or less.

"So it's semi-legal," Kat says.

"It's plenty legal," I say, and take another drink from my beer.

Next to me, Kat laughs, and I can't help but grin at her.

We talk like that for a while. Kat's mostly quiet—she's Kat—but she's relaxed and happy and even joins in teasing me every so often, which everyone else *loves*. I get a lot of looks, and I don't care.

"I like her," Levi says a while later. We're still at the table while Kat is playing shuffleboard with the other three, standing next to Wyatt at one end of the long table while Gideon and Javier are on the other side.

"Yeah?"

"No, I said that to get your hopes up," he says, rolling his eyes.

"Fuck off."

"Yes, I like her," he says. "She gives you a hard time."

I start laughing, and that gets a big, honest grin out of Levi, the rarest of all facial expressions.

"That's your criteria?"

"I'm not the one who likes it so much," he says, and we lapse into silence for a while because it's Levi, who's not in the habit of saying something if he doesn't have anything to say. It's a silence like a favorite sweater: warm, soft, welcoming.

I watch them play shuffleboard for a while. Kat's a little stiff at first, quiet, but she seems okay. Wyatt cheerfully trash talks her, their drinks on a table off to one side, and after a while she starts trash talking back. When she knocks his puck off the board, she throws her head back and laughs gleefully as Wyatt throws his hands in the air and shouts.

"She's killing me," he calls over his shoulder at me.

"Good," I call back.

Their game finishes, and the brewery is filling up since it's Saturday night. Wyatt and Kat are still at the shuffleboard table, Wyatt animatedly telling Kat something that involves a lot of hand motions. Gideon's wandered off, and as I watch, Javier heads over to where Wyatt and Kat's beers are.

Then he picks one up—Wyatt's, I think—and takes two long hauls before putting it down and walking away. It happens so quickly that I don't react, just freeze, a faint alarm bell going off in my head.

"What?" Levi asks. He's looking at me curiously. Not a lot gets by him.

I lose Javier in the crowd. He's probably seen someone he knows, since half the people under thirty-five in Sprucevale are here tonight.

"Nothing," I say, and shake my head, because that's what it was. A couple sips of beer. He probably just wanted a taste.

I wonder if his father's kept calling him, but then Wyatt's there, leaning over the table between Levi and I, orange hair falling into his eyes.

"You guys up for a game?" he asks.

· · · · ★ ★ ★ ★ · · · ·

I STAY LATER than I mean to, playing shuffleboard and then darts. Sitting by a fire pit with my arm around Kat, listening to Wyatt complain about work.

When we finally leave, I can't find Gideon.

"Maybe he went home," Wyatt says, shrugging. "You know how he is."

"Hates fun?" says Javier. "Thinks muttering *bye* from across a crowded room counts as a proper farewell?"

"Pretty much," agrees Wyatt. "It's not—"

Wyatt frowns.

"Is that him?" he asks, hands in the pockets of his jacket.

Javier, Kat, and I all turn at the exact same time, following Wyatt's gaze, and find Gideon standing in the light of a fire pit. Animatedly talking to a woman with long blond hair, rings on every finger, and a flowing skirt that moves in the breeze.

Then he says something to her. She laughs, and he grins, looking a little sheepish.

"*What*," whispers Javier.

"Don't stare, you're being super obvious," Wyatt says, staring. Super obviously.

"Is he... hitting on her?" I ask, the words feeling a little weird in my mouth when I say them about Gideon. I've known him to go on dates, that sort of thing, but I've never once seen it in action.

"Maybe?" whispers Wyatt. "I feel like I'm in a nature documentary."

I open my mouth to tell Wyatt not to be a dick, but then something extraordinary happens: Gideon hugs this woman. She hugs him back. It's a long hug. There's back rubbing in this hug. He says something into her ear while they're hugging, and when they pull away, he smiles at her for the second time in a few minutes.

"What the hell," whispers Wyatt.

Kat glances between the three of us, looking confused.

"Not a hugger?" she asks, and all we can do is shake our heads.

· · · · · ★ ★ ★ · · · · ·

IT ALWAYS STARTS the same way: a dirty couch in a disgusting living room. The cracked TV against the far wall. Two overflowing ashtrays on a half-destroyed coffee table. The orange glow of the streetlight outside slashing through broken cheap blinds.

I stand up, barefoot. The carpet is more dirt than rug,

crunching under my feet as I walk: out of the living room, past the dark, dirty kitchen, toward the hallway.

I can't stop myself. I can never stop myself, can never do anything different: touch the ragged edge of the hole in the drywall, glance into the bedroom where there's a bare mattress on the floor, a single blanket on it. Up ahead, the hard white line of light beneath a door.

The smell is always first: iron and smoke, then the surge of adrenaline that always follows. The hallway wavers, like it's suddenly uncertain but it stays: the light under the door, the cool metal knob under my fingers, the crunchy carpet under my feet and then finally, the adrenaline pulls me out.

I'm already sitting up. Gasping. Sweating. Everything tilts because I'm half here and half there, stuck somewhere between my own bed and the filthy couch; between the tidy organization of my bedroom and the crunchy carpet. I can still smell that scent and I feel like it'll never go away.

Something touches my shoulder and then I'm half out of bed and Kat's wrist is in my hand, and I'm holding it so tight I can feel her pulse under my palm, my own skyrocketing. I let it go just as fast.

"Silas," she says.

"I'm fine."

"Silas."

"Go back to sleep," I tell her. My heart's pounding so fast I'm dizzy, my skin cool with sweat. I'm buzzing, everywhere. I should get up and go downstairs, have some water or something but I need another moment to stop feeling that carpet under my feet, that light under the door—

"I'm gonna touch your shoulder again," she says. I think I nod, and she does, her hand so warm against my skin I shiver. "This okay?"

I swallow and make an affirmative noise. Slowly, she sits

up until she's behind me, on her knees, and her arms across my chest.

"You're here," she says, slowly, her voice like a dream of its own. "In your bed. In your house. It's two-thirty in the morning and there's a three-quarter moon outside."

Something dark hurtles onto the bed and I flinch, but Kat doesn't let me go.

"Your predator is here," Kat says, and I hold out a hand to Beast, who butts her head against it.

"Hey," I tell Beast, and my voice sounds strange, far away as I push my fingers through her thick fur. I pet her for a while, let Kat hold me.

"Is your wrist okay?" I ask, after some amount of time. A minute. An hour. I don't know.

"I'm fine," she says.

I let her hold me. After a while, we lie back down. I listen to her breathing.

· · · · · ★ ★ ★ ★ · · · ·

I MUST FALL ASLEEP, because I wake up. I've slept later than usual—almost seven—but Kat is still asleep, on her side, dark hair fanned around her head. Glasses on the nightstand next to her, neatly folded. I feel like they're watching me.

I'm downstairs, drinking coffee at my breakfast bar and mindlessly scrolling my phone, when Kat comes down in one of my old t-shirts and her own shorts. Her hair's a little funny on one side, and there are pillow lines on her face, behind her glasses.

"Hey," she says softly, and drops a kiss on my temple.

"Hey," I answer. "There's coffee. Mugs are—uh, next cabinet over."

She grabs one out and then looks at it for a moment longer than necessary.

"Did you go to Dollywood?" she asks.

"Gideon's obsessed," I tell her. "We went last summer."

She turns, frowns at me.

"Gideon?" she says. "Dolly Parton?"

I shrug, and she gives the mug a very considering look.

"Huh," she finally says, and I go back to my phone. I know I probably should have offered to get her coffee, or at least show her where the cream and sugar are, but I don't. There's a part of me that wishes she'd leave so I can be alone with myself right now, not that that ever helps either.

Finally, she sits across from me. Sips coffee. Waits until I put the phone down. I know what's coming and I look away, torn between the urge to leave so I don't have to face this and the urge to tell her everything and see if she stays.

"If you want to talk about it, you can," she says, and it makes my chest tighten. My heart pound. I have the same urge as ever: smile and laugh and tell her it's nothing. That I don't even remember the dream, sometimes this happens, it's not a big deal.

But Kat's here, and she's not flinching, and it makes me brave.

"It's not what you think," I tell her.

"I don't think anything."

"Of course you do," I say, the words coming out before I can stop them. "You think I have nightmares about firefights and IEDs and bravely fallen comrades and rescuing civilians from bombed hospitals. I don't even have good nightmares."

"There are good nightmares?"

"You know what I mean," I tell her, pushing a hand through my hair. "The ones you earn by doing heroic shit."

341

Kat frowns a little, and I brace myself: here it comes. The pity, the sweet soft *oh you poor thing*.

"I need your therapist's number so I can tell him you said that," she finally says. "Because you two need to unpack it."

I open my mouth, then close it. Stare at her, lost for words.

"Fuck. Sorry," she says, and puts her face in her hands. "I just woke up, that was—"

"No," I say, and she peeks at me through her fingers. "It was—where the fuck have you been all my life?"

"You blew your first chance," she says, faintly pink.

"What a terrible idea that would have been," I say, and she snorts.

"You can still tell me, if you want," she says a moment later, and yes, her voice is a little softer now, a little less sharp but I don't mind.

"It's a bathroom door," I start, and then stop. I realize I'm waiting: for her to scoff and say *that's boring and stupid*, for her to roll her eyes and realize I was right about good nightmares.

But she doesn't say anything. Just waits.

"I'm drunk, in the dream," I say, and I lean my elbows on the counter top. I don't look at her. "I'm walking through a filthy apartment, and I know I just heard something, but I don't know what. It's quiet, but there's a light on under the bathroom door. And when I reach it, I wake up."

I inhale, exhale. "All that for just a door."

Kat extends her hand, palm up, on the countertop. After a moment I put mine in it, her fingers warm from the coffee mug.

"Tell me you don't think I'll believe it's just a door," she says, so gently it's soothing.

"I hardly ever open it any more," I say, and in that moment, I know. I'm picking the second option: seeing if she stays. "I didn't last night. Usually I can wake myself up first." I swallow, stare at our linked hands. "Usually I don't have this dream."

I look away from her at that, at the twin echoes of guilt: that I still have nightmares, all these years later. That if I were a better person, I'd be unable to forget and have them all the time.

"But sometimes I open the door," I hear myself say. "And Mike Hernandez is in there, and the floor is covered in blood, and the gun is still in his hand."

"Jesus, Silas," she whispers. Squeezes my hand so hard it hurts, and I revel in it.

"It was my fault."

"I doubt that."

I look away again, instead of at her. I've got my other hand to my mouth, the knuckle of my thumb against my lips, the edge of my teeth sharp, grounding me.

"I hadn't seen him for... a year. Maybe two," I tell her. My memory from the first few years after I left the Marines is hazy and full of holes, huge gaps where I know time passed but I've got no recollection of it. "So when he called me up and wanted to go drinking, I didn't realize—"

What, that his problem was quite so bad? That Hernandez was calling me out of the blue because he'd destroyed every other relationship he had? That this wouldn't be his first attempt, only his last?

"—how far gone he was," I finally say, which doesn't do it justice. "So we got drunk, went back to his place. I passed out on the couch. And he shot himself in the bathroom."

A million things have slipped through the cracks in my brain, but that night couldn't be one of them. It took so long:

343

the walk from the couch. Opening the door. The distance between seeing what was inside and understanding it.

What no one tells you is that tragedy doesn't strike, it slithers. It's slow and steady and takes its time with you. It felt like I stood there, door open, for an hour while I put the clues together: the noise that had woken me up. The blood. The smell of gunpowder. Mike, unmoving.

"We weren't even that close any more," I tell her. "I always wondered if it was something I said to him."

Kat says nothing, and finally, I look back at her.

"You're supposed to say *of course not, there was nothing you could do, things happen, blah blah blah*," I say.

"You already know," she says. "You're here because you know."

Here's what I don't tell her, not yet: that Hernandez wasn't the first, just the loudest. That the guys who killed themselves by getting loaded every night until they drove off a bridge, or who overdosed, or who died some other *accidental* death were tragic but Mike Hernandez was shameful. That his death was an admission of weakness that everyone wanted to sweep under the rug so they could blame anything but the truth that he'd been failed.

I don't tell her that I've never wondered why Mike couldn't live with himself anymore. I've only wondered why I can.

"Two weeks later I went to a combat PTSD support group for the first time," I say. "And I felt guilty. Like I was taking advantage of him, somehow. That's where I met Gideon."

Kat nods, and looks at our hands for a moment. I bite my lips together, wondering what she must think of me right now. But she stayed.

Holy shit: she stayed. She's here, holding my hand, the

two of us together in a silence that feels like being wrapped in clouds. I don't know what I wanted her to say, but maybe it was this. Maybe it was nothing.

"Can I tell you something kind of terrible?" she says, after a little while.

"God. Yes. Please," I say, my thoughts getting too loud.

"I'm kind of glad that Earth Sciences 101 wasn't your rock bottom," she says.

"You're glad that things got worse from there?" I ask, and her eyes go wide.

"That's not what I'm—oh, shut up," she says when I start grinning. "I'm glad I wasn't the worst thing that happened to you. For completely selfish reasons."

"I wish you'd been my worst problem."

"You used to come to class black and blue," she says, and our hands are still joined, and she's absently rubbing the pad of her thumb over my knuckles. I want her to do it forever. "I don't think I was even your worst problem that semester."

"No," I admit. "I had a bad habit of getting blackout drunk and starting fights."

She takes a deep breath and rubs her eyes under her glasses with her other hand.

"Yeah," she says. "That's exactly as bad as I always suspected."

"I've got a nasty scar from being slashed with a broken bottle," I tell her. I don't know why now, except it feels right: here in the morning sunlight, Kat leaning across the breakfast bar, wearing my shirt. Looking nothing at all like she might leave. I want to hand over a list for inspection, say: here it is, everything that's wrong with me. Do your worst.

"The one on your ribs?" she asks, and doesn't even look surprised.

"Oh, come on," I tease her. "Have some mercy and tell

me you thought that one was from knife-fighting to save an orphan."

"If you had a scar from saving an orphan you'd never stop telling everyone about it," she says.

"Sure I would. I sleep sometimes."

Kat squeezes my hand one more time, then releases me to walk around the breakfast bar. I turn toward her on my stool and she comes up to me, standing between my legs, suddenly so close that I feel like she's washed over me.

After a moment, she takes her glasses off and puts them on the counter. She seems so vulnerable like this: her armor gone, her eyes wide. The faint pink marks on the sides of her nose where they usually sit. The smooth gold of her skin. The heavy silk of her hair.

"Can you see?" I murmur.

"From here, yeah," she murmurs back, and she's looking at me. Skimming her fingers along my jaw, up over my cheeks, across the bridge of my nose. She ruffles them through my hair and my eyes close.

"Don't," she says, and I force them open again.

"Kat," I say, barely aware I'm saying it.

She says, so softly, "I'm glad it wasn't you," and she takes my face in her hands and kisses the tip of my nose.

And I want to say, *this is why it wasn't.* I want to say, *I didn't know it but I held on so we could be exactly here, doing exactly this.*

I want to say, *for so long I didn't think this feeling existed.*

But I don't say any of that, because how could I? Ridiculous, probably, to feel like this, so instead I take her face in my hands, too. I kiss the tip of her nose, soft and sweet as anything.

I say, "Me too," and we kiss in my sunlit kitchen.

# THIRTY-SIX

## KAT

"KAT," Anna Grace says very, very patiently. "You're not gonna get fired."

I jab at my chocolate shake with my straw, chin on my hand, and sigh.

"Okay, but what if I get fired?"

Anna Grace deliberately dips two french fries into her strawberry shake and then eats them without ever breaking eye contact. We're in a booth at Debbie's Diner, a Sprucevale institution that looks like it hasn't updated one single thing since 1955. There's formica countertops, vinyl in the booths, and over-the-top banana creme cakes in a rotating display case. I've never gotten one, and I probably never will, but I'm glad they exist.

"You're so weird," I say.

"First, B&L is absolutely one of those corporations that has a whole bullshit philosophy on, like, maintaining morale through layoffs and having pizza parties while lives are destroyed, so they'd fire on you Friday, because that's the *good morale* firing day, not tomorrow," she says.

"Thanks?"

"And two, you're not getting fired," she says again. "Gregory thinks you're great, and so does everyone you work with who isn't your sociopathic ex."

"He's probably not a—"

A french fry hits me in the face.

"Ow!"

"Sorry."

I grab it from the table and eat it.

"They're really good if you dip them in the shake," Anna Grace says, mouth full of strawberry shake and french fries.

"No, they're gross if you dip them in the shake," I say.

"How do you know?"

"I try it every time we come here?"

"Maybe you'll like it this time."

I sigh dramatically and blow my bangs away from my glasses. I need to get them trimmed, but I've been too scattered this week to make an appointment.

I've also been too busy figuring out which surfaces in my apartment are good for sex and which aren't. Couch: yes. Kitchen table: too wobbly. Bed: obviously. The stairs: surprisingly, yes, though I think I tweaked my back. I'd be happy to try it again, though.

"I'd have to move if I got fired," I say, looking through the plate glass window at the parking lot. There's a quick, weird twinge in my stomach when I say that, which is... okay. Interesting.

"I could throw another one," Anna Grace offers.

"Ahh," I say, opening my mouth. She makes a face, aims, and it bounces off my glasses.

"Ow," I say, and she snorts.

"Worry about getting fired if you get fired, which you won't," she says. "You're anxiety spiraling."

She's right, which doesn't really make it better. Except it

does, maybe, a little bit, having someone else point out what's happening. Talking to Anna Grace is like watching the flight attendants during a turbulent flight: if she's not worried, maybe I shouldn't be either.

Except what does she know, really? Of course she thinks I'd never get fired, she's my best friend who doesn't even work with me, she has no actual—

"Oh hey, it's Lainey," Anna Grace says, and she's already waving. "LAINEY!"

"Where's your volume control?" I ask, as everyone in this entire diner looks over at us.

"Busted," she says, scooting over on her side of the booth. "Hey, looking good at practice today."

"Thanks," says Lainey, as she slides into the booth next to Anna Grace. "My knee's still feeling it. I don't think I get to ditch the brace yet. How are you guys?"

Lainey's Black, short, and petite, so she and tall, white, built-like-a-linebacker Anna Grace always look like someone designed two opposite humans. Her locs are pulled off her face, a couple of the ends bleached to copper and gold, and her nails are electric blue. They play roller derby together with the Blue Ridge Bruisers, which Anna Grace keeps trying to convince me to try out for. It might be the worst idea I've ever heard.

"I'm great," Anna Grace says. "I'm trying to convince Kat she's not gonna get fired."

"Why would you get fired?"

"The startup I work for got bought by a much larger conglomerate," I say, leaving out all the *antagonized my evil ex* parts.

"Ohhh," she says, leaning on one hand. "Have they laid anyone off yet?"

"No," supplies Anna Grace.

"Are they going to?"

"No," Anna Grace says again.

"Is there a reason you're worried?"

I shoot Anna Grace a glare for getting a whole third person involved in this, but I also like Lainey even if I don't know her very well, so I can't be too mad.

"I have a meeting tomorrow," I say. "With higher-ups."

I don't mention the whole *and then dinner with my ex* thing. It's too much information, and also, if I have to go into the whole story right now I might actually implode instead of just feeling like my chest cavity is filled with eels.

"That sucks," she says, shaking her head. "Can we help?"

"I need to quit thinking about it."

"Hmm." Lainey goes quiet for a moment, then narrows her eyes and glances slyly at Anna Grace. "You want to hear a story?"

"What?" Anna Grace asks, suspiciously dipping more fries.

"You remember the time you had to get a tetanus shot because Nathaniel Sloan dared you to push over one of Judy Belmont's beehives?" Lainey asks, grinning.

Anna Grace puts her face in her hands.

"She was *so pissed*," Anna Grace mutters. "I was *so dumb*."

"Tell me everything," I say. "The more embarrassing details, the better."

· · · · ★ ★ ★ ★ · · · ·

AT 3:45 on Thursday afternoon, there's a knock on my open office door, and I jump a mile in the air.

"Sorry," Silas says, walking in. "I wanted to come see

350

how you were doing."

"Great," I deadpan. "Super great and super relaxed."

Silas sighs, the hint of a smile at the corner of his mouth. He's got both his hands in the pockets of his gray pants, the sleeves of his shirt rolled up to the elbow. No tie. I guess he's lawyering casually today, and he glances through my office door, rocking back on his heels.

"He in meetings?" he asks, still looking through the doorway.

"Yeah," I say. My face is now in my hands, as I remember too late not to fuck up my eyeliner.

Silas reaches out and silently nudges the door until it's one inch open, only Evan's desk visible from outside, then comes around my desk. I spin in my chair until I'm facing him, and he leans his hips on my desk, feet crossed in front of him.

Then he reaches out and slides his fingers over my hair. It's back in a low bun—my most respectable hairstyle—and he's gentle enough not to mess it up.

"You're worried," he says.

I take a deep breath, eyes closed.

"Yeah. I'm sorry. I know it's probably nothing, and I'm just doing this to myself and getting all worked up for no reason, but it's—you know," I say, all one fast breath.

"It was a bad year," he offers, still gentle.

"Mostly."

I swear, I can hear him smile.

"You found me at the worst time," I tell him. "Usually the meds work a lot better and I'm only half a mess, not the whole thing."

"Month's almost over," he points out. "Then Meckler will be gone and you'll be calm, cool, and collected at all times."

351

That makes me snort and finally open my eyes. I have to tip my head back a little to look up at him from where I'm still sitting in my office chair.

"Silas," I say, seriously. "I've got terrible news for you about that."

"You mean you're anxious all the time?" he teases.

"Afraid so."

Then he gives me a long, slow look that starts at my glasses and travels down my body: button-down white shirt, long chain necklace dotted with freshwater pearls, gray pencil skirt, knees crossed, black pumps. By the time he finishes, I'm blushing a little.

"I can live with that," he says, and then he leans in and kisses me.

At first I freeze, because kissing for real in my office feels... wrong. I don't know why faking it to piss Evan off didn't and this does, but I'm not interested in splitting hairs.

But the door's basically closed and it's just a quick, gentle, *relax it'll be fine* kiss, so I kiss him back, quickly and gently. Then a little harder. Then a little deeper and suddenly it's not that kind of kiss any more: now it's open-mouthed and exploratory, headed toward filthy. My chair creaks as he puts his weight on one arm, leans in. My fingers find his hair. His skim down my thigh and find the hem of my skirt and he draws a line along it that feels like a question.

"Silas," I say, pulling back enough to talk.

"I came to distract you," he says. Brushes his lips against mine again. "Is it working?"

"We can't do this in my office," I remind him, even though *yes*. It is working. I am currently very, very distracted, even though I glance at the clock behind his head.

"Hm," he says, like he's thinking, and then his thumb is on the inside of my thigh. Half an inch above the hem, which is nothing—it's basically my knee—except he's stroking it back and forth and it. Is. Working. "Is there a copier room?"

"Yes, and someone's probably making copies in it right now," I say.

"A supply closet."

"More like a cabinet."

"There's always the stairwell," he says, all low and suggestive and rumbly. "No one ever uses it. Except Linda when she needs to get her steps in."

"We're not going to any of those places right now," I say, and I'm torn between breathless and laughing, because this is ridiculous and hot and I have to turn down these delicious offers and I don't want to. I'd much rather get railed in a stairwell than go to this meeting, that's for sure.

"You'd be very distracted," he points out, but he stands up straight, takes his hand off my leg.

"I know," I tell him, and I squirm a little bit in my chair for... reasons. Silas watches me, leaning against my desk.

"I can distract you some other way," he offers, laughing a little. "Linda's best friend's granddaughter is on a competitive dance team in Blacksburg and you wouldn't believe the backstabbing."

I rock back a little in my chair, drumming my fingers on the armrest, and try to smile even though I feel like fifty pounds of pigs in a ten-pound sack, or whatever that phrase is. Anna Grace used it once and it sounded pretty good.

"I'm not sure I can hear about teenagers fighting over meaningless prizes right now, but thanks," I say, and Silas snorts.

"The dancers are seven," he says. "The parents are the ones backstabbing."

"Oh, God, that's even worse," I say, eyes closed. "Tell me about... fishing or something."

"The most boring thing in the world?"

I sigh, half-distracted because I can still practically feel his thumb on my inner thigh and I'd much rather go back to that instead of talking about fish or going to this goddamn meeting in ten minutes.

"It can't be the most boring," I hear myself say.

"It's close."

God, we *could* go fuck in the stairwell right now. It's the worst idea in the world but it's technically possible, and right now I'm the kind of anxious so desperate for an outlet that I'm... kind of into it.

Then I get the second-worst idea in the world. It's an all-time great in the Kat Nakamura Hall of Fame of Bad Ideas, but I'm ten minutes away from possibly getting fired and I'm not sure I give a fuck.

"If we went... somewhere else," I say, my mouth suddenly dry. "Tell me what we'd do."

"Somewhere else," he says, words careful, one eyebrow lifting. "Like where?"

"Like the stairwell."

His face changes, from teasing to heated, in half a second and he gives me a long, slow, assessing look. Like he's wondering if he should talk me out of this but mostly thinking of what to say.

"If we were in the stairwell right now, nine minutes before your big meeting," he says, slowly. "We wouldn't have much time to waste."

Oh fuck. Oh *fuck*. Silas glances at the door again. Pushes a

354

hand through his hair. Swallows hard. Grips the desk next to his hips. Thinks for a moment, and I swear there's a faint blush on his cheekbones that makes his eyes look even sharper and bluer.

"So, I'd push you against the railing, right inside the door," he says. "And you'd gasp the way you do when you're surprised and turned on at the same time."

"We wouldn't go down to the landing?"

"No time," he says.

"Someone could come in," I point out, heart racing.

Silas raises one eyebrow.

"I'd kiss you first," he says. "Find that spot on your neck you like, and I'd suck on it until I left a mark."

"You liked that, huh?" I ask. My fingers are on the spot where the bruise was, and I swear it tingles.

"I did," he says. "I liked how you let me. I liked how it looked after."

"Is that all you'd do?"

We're so quiet it's a miracle we can hear each other, but I've never listened harder in my life.

"Of course not," he says. "Next I'd push your skirt over your hips and spin you around, and you'd lean over the railing and grip it until your knuckles turned white."

He swallows.

"And you'd try not to make a noise, but you would, and it would echo. Anyone in the stairwell would be able to hear you, trying not to moan."

I am bright red and very, very still in my office chair, embarrassed and turned on and terrified that someone will walk through the door all at once. Even though there's nothing to see here.

"I'd want to tease you," he goes on. "I'd want to draw it out. I'd want to get on my knees and lick you slowly until you begged me to make you come, but there's probably not enough time for that, is there?"

I glance at the clock. Five minutes until four.

"No," I say.

"Then I'd pull your panties down and leave them around your thighs," he says. "Hopefully no one else opens the door, because you're really putting on a show. You even wiggle a little, the way you do when you're too horny to be patient."

He pauses again, like he's trying to regain control.

"When you want me and can't remember how to ask for it."

I meet his eyes, and I can't stop the next question.

"Does it work?"

"I'd make you do it," he says, softly. "I'd use my fingers in you, and then stay still while you rock back and forth. I'd make sure you feel good and watch you work yourself up until you can't think about anything else."

Fuck. What the fuck am I doing? *Fuck*.

"And it would be so fucking hot, watching you," he goes on. His voice is shaking. I might be dying. "Knowing that anyone could come in and find you, fucking yourself on my hand, forgetting to be embarrassed. You'd be breathing hard. Swearing the way you do to keep yourself from begging me."

Now I'm staring at his hands, imagining. I can't breathe. I can't move. If I do either of those things I'm in serious danger of actually dragging him into the stairwell. What the hell was I thinking?

"So I'd get on my knees, put my tongue on your clit, and you'd use me to make yourself come."

My eyes are closed and I'm counting my breaths, because this was the worst idea I've ever had. The worst, hottest, *worst* idea, to ask this of Silas. For him to go along with it. I'm so fucking turned on right now that there might be a wet spot on the back of my skirt, and I cannot go into this meeting that way.

"Fuck," I whisper.

"Then you'd pull your skirt down and get back to work," he says, and there's the cocky little smile, the light in his eyes, as if we didn't just do... that.

I take a deep and somewhat shaky breath.

"So, now I have to go to a meeting with my ex and my boss," I say.

"Shit," Silas says. "Right."

"Yeah."

Then we look at each other. He starts laughing first but I join in, pinching the bridge of my nose between my fingers because honestly, what the fuck?

"It was distracting," I say.

"Jesus," he mutters through laughter. Then: "Come over tonight?"

"Yes. Definitely yes," I say. "God. Okay. I can do this."

I stand and he starts to lean in, but I hold up both hands to ward me off.

"You *cannot* touch me right now," I tell him, and something feral sparkles in his eyes.

"Good luck, Kat," he tells me.

"Thank you."

He glances at the door again, then back at me.

"Do you mind leaving first?" he asks. "I could use a few minutes."

Yes. Yes, he definitely could. I nod and step away, walking all the way around the other end of my desk because I. Cannot. Touch him.

"Kat," he says, right before I leave, and when I turn, he blows me a kiss.

# THIRTY-SEVEN

## SILAS

I DON'T ACCOMPLISH shit for the rest of the afternoon, and not for lack of trying. It's because every time I try to focus on the discovery documents for a water-rights case about orchards on a tributary of the Chillacouth river, after twenty seconds I'm thinking of Kat saying *tell me what we'd do* and it's extremely unproductive.

It was a terrible idea. Her door wasn't even closed. I could hear her coworkers right outside: typing, talking, laughing, walking. Anyone could've walked in. It was stupid and shortsighted and reckless and holy shit *hot*.

The way she asked for it like she did, sitting with perfect posture in her office chair, behind her desk. White button-up shirt with long sleeves and a high collar. Knee-length skirt. Glasses. There's something about Kat looking impossibly prim and proper while I talk dirty to her that unravels my entire being. Something about her knowing a risk and taking it anyway because it turns her on that does me in.

I'm staring out the window of my office, watching the sun lower over Sprucevale, when my phone buzzes.

**Wyatt:** Anybody going up this weekend?

**Gideon:** I was thinking about it

**Me:** I can't, I've got a work thing Saturday night

**Wyatt:** Who the hell has a work event the Saturday of Labor Day weekend?

**Me:** Law firms. It's the annual Lawyering Awards

**Wyatt:** You up for Best Lawyer?

**Me:** No

**Wyatt:** Come up Sunday, then

Sunday I've got every intention of waking up with Kat in my bed, having a lazy Sunday morning, and then maybe doing something disgustingly cute like brunch. As much as I love Wildwood—it was my idea and my doing, after all—the twin bunks in my tiny cabin aren't good for much besides sleeping.

**Me:** I'll see

**Wyatt:** Fuck you, that means no

**Wyatt:** Javi, are you gonna be back from VA Beach?

**Wyatt:** JAVIIIIIIIIIII

**Wyatt:** Did he throw his phone into the ocean again?

Before I can tell Wyatt to chill out, there's a knock on my open door and Kat steps in, grinning from ear to ear, looking relieved and almost relaxed for once.

"I didn't get fired," she says.

"Can I say I told you so?" I ask, coming around my desk toward her.

"Absolutely not."

"Then congrats on not getting fired," I say, and give her a kiss. Right inside my office, the door open to everyone else who's still here a little after six. I can hear someone typing, someone else talking on the phone. They could walk by. They could come in.

But Kat's here and she's kissing me in her excruciatingly proper outfit. She's wearing heels so she's taller than usual, the angles of us a little different, and I flick my tongue along her lower lip, not expecting anything. Just to see what happens.

What happens is Kat opens her mouth under mine and steps closer, one hand on my chest and the other around the back of my neck. What happens is I barely bite back a groan and push my hand into her hair, where it snags because she's got it back in a knot and she bites my lower lip, laughing.

"Sorry," I murmur, my lips moving against hers.

"You're not."

I swallow hard, my other hand on her lower back, fingers moving in slow circles. I take one more kiss and then force myself to pull away, clearing my throat because there are people. Coworkers. Come on.

"You got a minute?" I ask, as if I'm not half-hard right now.

"A few, then dinner," she says, and makes a face. She's pulling pins from her hair, then runs a hand through it and shakes it out, falling in loose dark waves past her shoulders.

I. Uh. Fuck.

"Then I'm finally free of all this bullshit," she says, then wrinkles her nose and glances at the door. "Bull... crap."

"Linda went home," I tell her, leaning against my desk. Linda doesn't exactly have a swear jar or anything—though she probably would if she could get away with it—but she Does Not Approve of cursing and has a whole arsenal of glares to get the point across.

Kat perches on the arm of a chair, kicks her shoes off,

nudges them together with her toes. I nearly point out that she's welcome to sit in the chair the normal way, but she probably knows about chairs, so I don't say anything.

Instead, I say, "You look nice," which is such a fucking understatement.

"Thanks. It's a nice place," she says.

"La Cabaña is an okay place," I say, because it's true, and because I'm not giving Meckler credit if I don't have to.

"Look who's a restaurant critic," she teases.

"I'm not saying it isn't good. I'm saying don't be too impressed."

"I wasn't planning on it," she says, still wiggling her toes against the carpet. They're painted deep red. I wonder if she ever paints her fingernails. She sighs and tilts her head back, looking at my ceiling. Her hair swishes back. I look at the sharpness of her jaw from this angle, the line of her throat, the curve of her neck. None of it's helping.

"You really do look good," I say, and my voice is lower now.

"Thanks," she says, head still tilted back. "It's just armor, you know. And camouflage. The more I look like I'm supposed to, the less anyone notices me."

I don't say anything for a moment, because I can't imagine not noticing Kat. Even when I didn't like her, I noticed. I resented that I noticed, but I always did.

"You nervous?" I ask.

"Of course," she says, and gives me a half-smile. "Have you even met me?"

"You could stand him up."

Kat snorts.

"And let him win? No. I want to—"

She stops, and I wait a moment.

361

"Watch him crawl?" I ask, voice going even lower. I glance at the door, hoping no one can hear us.

"I regret telling you that."

"No, you don't."

"You're way too taken with it," she says. "You know I didn't mean it literally."

I think she did. The way she said it is carved into my brain: her sharp, dark eyes; how she nearly whispered; how it sent a chill down my spine.

"I just liked the way you sounded when you said it," I tell her instead.

"How was that?"

"Angry," I say. "Dangerous."

She bites her lip like she's trying not to smile.

"I think it would be too weird if he crawled across the floor of the restaurant," she says. "I'd settle for an apology."

"Is that what you're hoping for?"

She pushes herself to her feet, thoughtlessly smooths her skirt. Starts pacing.

"I don't think I'll get one," she admits. "I think he's gonna... honestly, I have no idea."

Kat turns, keeps pacing, arms folded in front of herself.

"I know it's nothing," she says. "Maybe some misguided attempt to 'clear the air'"—she uses sarcastic air quotes—"between exes before he leaves, but mostly, I think it'll be nothing and then I'll never have to see him again. Hopefully."

"You don't have to go," I point out.

"I know. But I'm going to."

I stay still and watch her pace back and forth across my office, angry and anxious and stubborn as hell. I know she doesn't want to have a public conversation with her ex and I know she's going to anyway, to prove to him and God and

362

everybody that she can. She's sharp and alluring and dangerous as a dagger, and woe to anyone who doesn't understand that.

I don't let myself think about what I do next.

"Close the door," I tell her. She stops pacing, looks at me. "Please?"

There's a moment where I know she's going to refuse. She *should* refuse. We both know why I want the door closed.

Then Kat closes the door, turning the knob so it doesn't click.

"Lock it," I say, voice already rough. "Turn out the lights."

She does. I pull the shade on the windows behind my desk and suddenly my office doesn't look like my office anymore: shadowed and dark, the sunset trickling in around the blinds. It feels like an alternate version of the world. I feel like an alternate version of myself: a reckless, mindless one who's all impulse and desire. A version I thought I'd buried ages ago.

Then we're kissing again, my hands locked in her hair, and it's slow and soft and filthy, all at once. Her teeth sharp against my lip. Her tongue curling against mine, the softest sigh escaping her.

"There are people still in the office," she murmurs, but she's got one hand fisted in the front of my shirt.

"You're right."

"I'm supposed to be there at seven," she says.

"Are you telling me to stop?"

She tugs on my shirt, pulls me down. Presses a kiss to the corner of my mouth, the spot right under my jaw.

"Just hurry," she says.

"I wouldn't want you to be late," I say, and now her

363

other hand is in my hair and she's pulling me in two directions at once, like she might split me open, her teeth scraping along my neck. "I wouldn't want you walking in with your hair wild and my name practically still on your lips."

She nips at me, and I gasp.

"That," she says. "Would be terrible."

"You wouldn't want," I start, "to still have teeth marks on your neck."

She bites me a little harder, then jolts. I've backed her up against the side of my desk without even realizing it.

"I wouldn't want to still be thinking of you at all," she says, and licks the hollow of my throat, the frame of her glasses bumping the underside of my chin.

Suddenly, I understand: this is armor, too. It's stupid, and it's reckless, but I can give her this. Let me be her armor against a bad year. Let me give her what she wants because she gives me what I need.

I take her mouth again, because I can. I grab her hips and push her against the desk because I can, and because I like the way she bends slightly backward when we kiss.

"Kat," I say, very quietly. "You know you're the brightest thing in every room, don't you?"

I slide one hand under her skirt, draw a circle on her inner thigh with my thumb. When we lock eyes I raise one eyebrow, and she swallows. Then nods and in half a second, her skirt's around her hips and she's sitting on my desk, legs around my waist.

"We *are* in a hurry," I remind her, and brush my fingers against her clit through the thin fabric of her panties.

"Fuck," she whispers, glancing at the door.

"Don't look at that. Look at me," I tell her. "C'mon."

Kat rolls her eyes, so I slide my thumb harder over her clit and her eyes go closed, her hips jolting.

"You're so brave," I murmur. "So determined. Hardly anyone knows it, but you're reckless."

"I'm not."

"If you're gonna moan your disagreements, you're gonna have to do it quietly," I tell her, thumb circling.

That gets her eyes at half-mast as she leans back on her hands, legs wide, skirt around her waist, shirt pristine.

"Fuck off," she says, and I grin.

Then push my hand under her panties. She's warm and slippery and her breath catches when I do.

"You're completely fucking impossible," I tell her. She swallows, her throat working. "You tell me to fuck off when you're half-clothed on my desk and I'm plotting ways to make you come."

That gets a sound that's part laugh and part moan.

"You wouldn't like me otherwise," she says.

"Probably not. I like you too much this way. Come kiss me again."

She does, her fingers tangling in my hair. I keep stroking her clit slowly, and after a few moments she whimpers into my mouth.

"God, I love when you do that," I tell her.

"Make weird noises?"

"Yeah. It's the fucking best."

She kisses me harder, pulling me against her. Bites my lip, makes a strangled sigh, and I groan in response.

"It feels good," she murmurs, like she has to explain herself, so we keep going until the noises get desperate, and then I stop.

"Hey," she says, but I pull her off the desk and tug her panties down.

"Off," I tell her, and for once, she doesn't argue with me. "Turn around."

"Why?" Okay, that didn't last long.

"Please, Kat?" I ask, one hand on her bare hip.

She gives me one of her looks, but she does and she braces herself against the desk, looks over her shoulder at me with her hair spilling everywhere. Her breath catches when I stroke her again, sliding my fingertips between her warm, slippery lips. She knows what's next. I told her earlier.

"Go ahead," I tell her, waiting at her entrance.

She does, and I gasp as she envelops me. When I'm buried in her up to my knuckles I crook my fingers and she hisses and pushes back harder, flexing around me. I'm hard as iron but I ignore it. I'd hate to do anything to distract myself right now.

"Keep going," I tell her. "This is perfect."

"Fuck," she whispers again, and she does. After a few more strokes I add a third finger and she swears again, swears a little louder when I stroke her inner wall and she works into a rhythm.

"You're beautiful," I tell her. "I love watching you take what you want. Love letting you make yourself feel good."

I don't think she's going to come without me touching her clit, so I don't. It takes everything I have to hold still and let her do this, but it's worth it because every time I tell her how incredible she is, how fucking sexy, how fucking perfect, she swears back at me in a whisper that's somewhere between angry and ecstatic until finally, I don't think either of us can take much more.

Somehow, I gather the concentration to grab my wallet and pull out the condom I put there earlier this week. Kat looks at me over her shoulder, throwing off her rhythm, eyes hazy behind her glasses. I hold the condom out.

"Open this for me," I tell her. "My hands are busy."

That gets one of her *don't tell me what to do* looks, so I

follow it with, "Please?" and slide my thumb over her clit once.

Kat swallows a noise and unwraps the condom. Somehow I get my own pants undone and out of the way with only one hand, and I give myself one left-handed stroke before Kat hands the condom back over her shoulder. I bury my fingers in her, flexing them one more time, before I take them out to roll the condom on, breathing like I've been sprinting.

She looks over her shoulder at me, face flushed, lips bright red like she's been biting them to stay quiet. I give myself another long, slow stroke, and watch her watch me do it.

"Well?" she says, and it's teasing and impatient and impossibly sexy, so I lean forward and kiss the back of her neck before sitting in my office chair.

Kat half-turns toward me but I grab her hips, turn her back, guide her down. She grabs the arms of the chair as she sinks onto me, and it feels like the world shrinks to nothing more than this room, the two people in it.

When I bottom out she flexes around me, hot and tight and perfect, and I can't help myself.

"Good girl," I murmur into her shoulder.

It just comes out, and I clench my jaw to keep from saying it again, but then Kat whispers, "Oh, God," so quietly I can barely hear her and I'm done for.

"You feel so good like this," I tell her. I brace myself, rock my hips. "I fucking love it when you take me this deep."

"*Fuck*," she hisses, and this time her head goes back and she flexes around me again, and now we both groan.

"God, look at you," I say, even though I feel like my brain is dissolving. "Fucking glorious like this."

We keep moving. It takes a little maneuvering and a

little experimenting to find the right angle and the right rhythm, because I've definitely never fucked anyone in my office chair before, but once we get it right I wrap an arm around her and go slow, my face buried in the back of her neck.

I don't know what I'm saying but I can't stop saying it: how good everything is, how perfect. Before long she grabs my other hand and shoves it toward her clit, and I laugh and tell her she's impatient, but I stroke her anyway. I put my hand over her mouth with seconds to spare because when she comes she tries to be quiet, but she doesn't quite make it. I follow her seconds later, my face against the back of her white shirt now damp with sweat, and bite my own tongue trying not to shout.

We stay like that for a minute. I wrap both arms around her in the near-dark of my office and she leans her head back against mine, lets her breathing slow.

"Shit," she finally whispers. "I'm gonna be late."

I grin against her shoulder, kiss it, and then help her stand.

"I look respectable, right?" she asks as she slips her shoes back on, her face flushed, skirt wrinkled, hair mussed.

I'm still in the chair, trying to figure out how to deal with the condom, and I look up at her.

"Perfect," I say, and she laughs.

# THIRTY-EIGHT

## KAT

THE MINUTE I walk into La Cabaña, I can tell Evan is drunk. He's sitting alone at a table in the middle of the crowded room, staring vacantly into space. There's guacamole and two margaritas in front of him, one half-finished. I wonder what else he's had to drink. I wonder why he's at that table instead of one of the empty booths along a wall, but I probably know why.

I take a deep breath and cross the room toward him, spine straight, heels clicking along the floor. There's the familiar prickle of attention, real and imagined: the sensation that everyone here is looking at me and everyone is wondering why I walk so weird or have these glasses or didn't wear lipstick today. It's better now than it used to be, because meds and therapy help, but simple shit like this is what I've always hated the most. I've always wanted to walk through a crowded room without feeling like there are eyeballs rolling over my skin.

"Hey," I say, when I get to his table. "Sorry I'm late."

I'm not, but it's the polite thing to say. There's another table two feet behind me where a family's sharing nachos, a table behind Evan with four women drinking margaritas. I know better than to think any of them care what I'm doing, but it never feels that way.

"I was about to start on your drink if you didn't show up soon," he says.

I push it toward him, and he snorts.

"C'mon. Might help you relax. God knows you need it."

He takes a long pull from his own margarita, then picks up a chip.

"Evan," I ask, quietly. "Why am I here?"

He leans forward, and his light brown hair falls into his eyes. His face is flushed, and he rubs a hand along his jaw, smiling at me. The academic part of my brain notes that he's still handsome, and it's still a nice smile.

"I thought I could comfort you after you got laid off," he says, because apparently he's had enough tequila to be honest. "Figured I'd come here, tell you how I was the one who fought for you to keep your job, buy you some margaritas, make you stop hating me quite so much. But that didn't work, huh? Gregory actually thinks you're good at your job."

I'd love it if I were surprised right now, but I'm not. I'm bolt upright in this chair, trying to ignore the noise of all these people, telling myself that no one is paying us any attention. If I left, how much attention would that draw? Would it be worse than staying?

"Is this because of Olivia?" I finally ask, since he's in a mood to tell the truth. Figures that he'd be upset enough about her to take it out on me.

First, he finishes his own margarita.

"It's because everyone hates me now and it's your fault," he says, a little louder than he was. Not quite loud enough to be noticeable, but loud enough to make my skin feel a little tighter. "All you had to do was cry all over the office and it got everyone on your side. Oh, for fuck's sake, don't give me that surprised look. Why do you think I'm here? You think I wanted to be the guy who has to go to some podunk town for a month and talk a bunch of hillbillies through a merger?"

He grabs another chip, stabs it into the guacamole like he can kill it.

"It was punishment because everyone took your side, even after you were gone."

I open my mouth to tell him that it never felt that way to me. It felt like he moved on instantly and everything except me moved with him—our friends, our coworkers, the company we both worked for—but then I close it. I don't care if he knows or not.

"Go ahead," he says, waving a chip. A chunk of guacamole falls on the table. "Tell me I'm wrong. Tell me how I deserved getting shuttled off to this dead-end position because I hurt your feelings."

"You slept with your assistant," I point out, as politely as I can.

"And you ruined that, too," he says. "You and fucking Flynn. He's a condescending asshole. Used to act like he was everybody's dad back in Afghanistan. I swear he almost punched me once over a Snickers bar," Evan says, and snorts. "Then a couple years later, he told *me* to go to therapy."

"Oh *no*," I say.

"He's as bad as anyone," Evan says, and he's suddenly vicious. "We all did the same shit. We had to. He just couldn't handle it."

I stare at him. My brain's frozen, and that's nothing new. It's nothing new that there are tons of people in here and I'm certain they're all looking at me, even when they're not. It's nothing new that there's anxiety stuck in my chest like a sea

371

urchin in my lungs, spikes dug deep into flesh. It's nothing new that I can't think of a single thing to say in response, that my brain has the same deer-in-headlights response as ever.

But it's new that in the middle of all that, I feel... *bad* for him. He seems pathetic right now, drunk in the middle of a Mexican restaurant on a Thursday night, telling his ex-fiancé that he tried to get her fired and it didn't work.

I don't remember why I came here. Something about not wanting to let him win, whatever that means. Maybe I thought he'd apologize, and we could be... not friends, but people who existed a little easier in the same universe. I thought that might be nice, but I'm past caring. I'm past anger. I'm past ever wanting to think about him again.

"Hi there!" a voice says, and I jump. "Sorry for the wait, can I get you anything to drink?"

"Yeah," Evan says, before I find my voice. "She'll take a Cadillac—"

"Actually, I was leaving," I say, and smile at her. I think I smile. My face feels a little weird and my heart's beating so fast it's hard to pay attention to other body parts. "Sorry for the trouble."

"She's not leaving," Evan says, but I stand and grab my purse. The waitress is standing there, eyebrows up, notepad out, looking between us.

"I am," I confirm. "Sorry for the trouble."

With that, I turn and walk away. Evan shouts something behind me and this time I know people are looking at me, because I can see the heads turn and that sickly, sticky feeling washes through me but I keep walking without looking back.

# THIRTY-NINE

## SILAS

I MAKE myself wait until 9:05 before I knock on the door of Kat's office. After she called me last night and told me about dinner, part of me wanted to march in there the moment I got to work so I could plant myself between her and Meckler, but I know better. Kat can handle herself and might kill me if I tried to handle anything for her.

Which doesn't mean I wouldn't finish anything he started. Just that he'd have to start it.

"Morning, babe," I say, when she tells me to come in. "Happy Fri—"

Meckler's desk is empty, the only thing left of him is a monitor sitting on his chair, the cord wrapped around it like a sad tail.

"If you need help hiding a body..." I say, and raise an eyebrow at her.

"I'd have asked a month ago instead of waiting until now," she says. "They were taking the computer out when I got here this morning. I guess he's taking an extra-long weekend."

Kat is grinning at me. Grinning. She's happier and more relaxed than I've ever seen her at work: spinning back and forth in her office hair, hands laced on top of her head, pleased and carefree and I just want to drink her in, like this.

"Month's up," I say, and lean against the desk that used to be his. "How does it feel to be free of contractual obligations?"

Kat laughs, and something warm flares behind my ribcage.

"We've still got that thing tomorrow," she points out. "Then we're free."

"Just until the Christmas party," I say, and she scrunches her nose at me. "Look, you're the one who kept sleeping with me. I don't make the rules."

"Fine," she says, but she's laughing and spins all the way around in her chair.

"You can skip the party tomorrow if you want," I tell her. "It's fine. They know you exist."

"You RSVP'd for me."

"I'm a lawyer. I promise I can get you out of it if you want."

Her eyes narrow behind her glasses, and she stops twisting back and forth in the chair.

"Is this because I freaked out at the last one?"

"No, it's because you've had a bad month in a bad year and I don't want small talk with lawyers to be the rotten cherry on top," I say.

"Ew."

"Sorry."

"It wasn't all bad," she says, and now she's back to twisting, a devious smile playing across her lips. "Some of it was actually pretty good."

374

"Yeah?" I ask, and I can't stop looking at her: glasses, loose hair, blue wrap shirt over jeans. I want to kiss her and see if she tastes happy. "Like what? Tell me."

Could be my imagination, but I think she blushes.

"We are *not* doing that again," she says, voice low.

"Not ever?"

Kat glances at the door, then back at me.

"Not now."

"If you insist," I tell her, and cross my legs at the ankles. She spins in the chair one more time, then looks at me suspiciously.

"Do you not want me to come tomorrow?"

"Of course I want you to come," I say. "Everything's better when you're there. But you don't have to."

Kat shrugs, looks thoughtful.

"I get better with practice," she says. "And now I sort of know Linda, and some of your other coworkers, and I know what to expect. And you'll be there to tell me who's who, so long as you don't leave me to the wolves."

I put one hand over my heart, as if wounded.

"I would never," I say.

"It'll be like *The Devil Wears Prada*," she says, and I laugh. "There's a scene where—"

"Anne Hathaway has to whisper names to Meryl Streep," I say.

"You've seen it?"

"I heard it was good. Don't be sexist."

That gets another laugh out of her: here, in her office, glowing like sunlight.

"You're right," she says. "Sorry."

Then she glances at the door again and stands, walking over until she's right in front of me.

375

"Hey," she says, suddenly serious.

"What?"

"This was a weird month but I'm glad it happened," she says, and there's that glow again, the way my heart feels like it sparkles or something.

"It's not over yet," I tell her, and Kat rolls her eyes, trying not to smile.

I try not to wonder too much at this: that after everything she's here, laughing, telling me she's glad it happened. That I was set for a life alone and then she crashed in. I know better than to question gifts, but it can be hard not to think they weren't really meant for me.

"I'm still glad it happened," she says, and kisses me. It's chaste and sweet and quick but yes: she tastes like sunshine.

"Get to work," I tell her when she pulls back. "I hear you almost lost your job."

"You're such a dick," she says, laughing.

"You wouldn't give me the time of day if I were too nice to you."

"Get out," she laughs, and I do, blowing her a kiss. I feel a million pounds lighter.

· · · · · ★ ★ ★ ★ · · · · ·

"COME ON," I say. "Those are important."

Beast stares at me, unrepentant, two paws on the keyboard of my work laptop.

"I'm not petting you while you're on my computer," I tell her. "Ear scritches are for well-behaved cats."

"MRROWP," she responds. She does not move, so I sigh, then lift my enormous twenty-pound cat off my lap and onto the couch cushion next to me.

Instantly, there's a paw on the computer again.

"For fuck's sake," I tell her, and shove it off. She frowns, but I scratch that spot behind her ears and her eyes slowly close. It's Saturday afternoon and I'm watching college football while answering emails, since Kat's at some board game thing with Anna Grace and I may as well catch up on work.

I've just hit send on another one when my phone buzzes and Beast mrrrps, because she's half lying on top of it.

"You know there's the entire rest of the couch, right?" I ask, but she bats half-heartedly at my hand as I retrieve the phone.

**Wyatt:** Have you guys heard from Javi?

I frown at my phone for a moment, then take a second to go through my texts.

**Me:** Not since Tuesday
**Gideon:** Tuesday was the last time
**Gideon:** Have you?
**Me:** You?
**Wyatt:** No
**Wyatt:** Fuck. Hold on.

A swirl of dread curls through me, like I've just swallowed something cold.

*It's nothing*, I tell myself. *He lost his phone or forgot to charge it or threw it in the ocean as an offering to the gods of the sea or something.* Javier's kooky. He's forgetful. He does things like that sometimes and then shows up a day later with ink stains all over his hands, sand in his pockets, and a grin on his face.

But a day, maybe. Not—*fuck*—five days that none of us have heard from him.

I'm already shoving my laptop off my lap and standing. Beast protests and I stop long enough to scratch her behind the ears again. Where's Zorro? Someone's taking care of Zorro, right?

I call Wyatt, but his phone's busy. I'm pacing. I head into the kitchen, get a glass of water, stare out the window, try to get my thoughts into order, but all I can think is: Wyatt's worried. Wyatt doesn't worry, but he does have an uncanny sixth sense about his two best friends in the world: Javier and Lainey.

Fuck.

I need to do something, so I make myself useful and call Javier's sister Thalia, who lives a couple hours away in Ochreville. She hasn't heard from Javier either and she doesn't believe me when I tell her that it's nothing and she shouldn't worry.

*Fuck.*

I call a couple other people Javi knows, but no one's got any useful info. I'm standing in my kitchen, wondering if he's a missing person yet, when my phone rings with a FaceTime call from Wyatt.

"His sister hasn't heard from him," I say. On the bottom of the screen, Wyatt looks pale and tired in a tiny screen, and Gideon's jaw is clenched.

"Bastien said he left Wednesday night," Wyatt says. "Out of the blue. Bastien was out, got back, and Javier was putting his suitcase into his car. Said he was coming back here."

There's a long, silent pause as we all stare at each other.

"You talk to his mom?" I ask, and Wyatt shakes his head.

"Bastien said he would. Seemed better."

I've only met Javier's mom once, but I know she's had a rough few years, mostly thanks to her estranged husband.

"I assume he told you about his father," Gideon says.

"He told me he'd been calling," I say, and Wyatt nods.

"Fuck," Wyatt hisses, one hand over his mouth.

Gideon blows out a breath, running his hand through his dark hair.

"I'm gonna head up to Wildwood," he says. "I'll let you know."

"Where's Zorro?" I ask, watching Beast stand and stretch on the couch.

"I've got him," Gideon says. "He's fine."

Then he closes the call, and it's only Wyatt and me. I fight the temptation to say something pointless, like *I'm sure it'll be okay* or *Javier's grown, he's fine.*

"He's never been gone this long," Wyatt says. "Thirty-six hours, maybe."

I swallow against the cold dread in my chest, the adrenaline pumping through my veins. I want to run five miles and punch through a wall and charge through a river and fight a bear. I want to find Javier's dad and scream in his face.

"He'll turn up just fine," I say, and I hate myself for the platitude. "He always has before."

Wyatt presses his knuckles to his mouth and looks away and I know it means *no, he hasn't,* but he doesn't say that. Instead he says, "I'm gonna make some calls."

And I say, "Yeah, me too," and then we both hang up.

I make more calls. No one knows anything.

An hour later, Gideon calls back.

"Sorry it took me so long," he says, his voice fuzzy and crackled. "Had to get back down to Deep Creek before I had any signal."

For Gideon to get from his house to Wildwood and back to Deep Creek he must have been driving like a bat out of hell, but I don't say that.

"His car's there," Gideon says, and cold dread clenches my stomach. "He's not."

"I'm coming up," I say, and grab my keys.

# FORTY

## KAT

I GLANCE around the parking lot of the Blue Ridge Country Club again, but I still don't see Silas's truck.

**Me:** I'm here
**Me:** Are you inside yet?

Still no response. I first texted him five minutes ago, when I first pulled in, but he hasn't answered any of my texts yet, so I look at myself in the rear view mirror and tap the steering wheel and hope that no one drives past me and wonders what I'm doing, sitting here in my car.

God, I hate this, the part of any social gathering where I don't know what to do and any move I could make seems awkward as hell. Stay in my car: now I'm the weird car girl. Go inside: why is Silas's girlfriend here without him? Hover expectantly near the front door, neither in the parking lot or inside: is she a vagrant, trying to score free food?

Is one the right option? Is it possible for all the options to be wrong options?

Where the *hell* is Silas?

I stay in my car a little longer—I was early, it's fine—but the minutes slowly tick past five and something else becomes apparent: I have to pee.

I give it five more minutes. No Silas. No text from Silas, and now I really fucking have to pee. The bushes around the parking lot are a no-go. I consider leaving, finding a gas station, and coming back, but that's probably even more awkward than peeing in a bush.

Shit. I'm gonna have to go inside.

I manage to smile at a small group of people who look sort of familiar just inside the front door, and they don't immediately kick me out, so that's good. In what can only be an act of mercy from the gods, the bathroom is right past them.

When I'm finished, I check my phone again. No text. No call. I text him again because now he's fifteen minutes late and Silas is never this late. It stays unread.

I lean on the sink and try not to panic. It's a nice sink. Marble, probably, and the mirror in front of it is fancy with a gold frame, and the wallpaper in here is a *choice* but it's clearly a well-done, expensive choice. I've been here a bunch of times with Anna Grace but it's never felt quite so foreign before. I've never felt quite so much like I don't belong here.

*He's blowing you off*, says a small voice in the back of my head. *He found something else to do and couldn't be bothered to remember to tell you, so now he's leaving you alone to make small talk.*

It's ridiculous, and I know it's ridiculous, and it doesn't matter that I know. It doesn't matter that it's *his* work event and every single thinking part of my brain is calmly reminding me that present-day Silas is the mostly-responsible man who distracted people at karaoke and took me to an abandoned building.

I'm panicking because he's not here—not even texting me back—and his coworkers are practically hovering outside the bathroom door and I can't sprint past them and drive away because the whole point of me right now is to show up and act right.

Oh, God, I'm gonna throw up in this sink.

I don't, but it's close. I'm nauseous and a little dizzy, and I almost wish I would puke, but I don't. Instead I take some deep breaths. I name some things I can see and touch and hear. I check my phone five more times and wonder where he is and if something is wrong, but I also know he probably got caught behind a tractor or something and can't text.

Finally, I pull myself together and look at myself in the mirror. I've got all the good armor on: the expensive eyeliner and new lipstick. My hair's in an extremely classy low chignon. I'm wearing a sleeveless, knee-length black dress—classic—and I'm even wearing pearls, for fuck's sake, because nothing screams *lawyer girlfriend* like pearl earrings and a pearl necklace.

"Okay," I mutter at the mirror. "Let's do this, Nakamura."

· · · · ★ ★ ★ ★ · · · ·

FIFTEEN MINUTES LATER, Silas still isn't here, and I'm starting to panic for different reasons. Not that I've stopped panicking for my initial reasons; there's plenty of panic space in here to panic for every reason imaginable.

"Annie Mae's is fine if you want somewhere in town," Linda is saying to the small knot of people gathered at this end of the hall. "But for my money, the best apple cider donuts are at Jackson Orchard. They make 'em fresh right in front of you and mm-mm-MMM, they're good. They only do it for September and October, though."

I pull my phone out of my purse for the thousandth time in the last several minutes. Silas is now thirty-five minutes late, which is way too much. I already called him once, and nothing. The *he abandoned you to the wolves* part of my brain still hasn't shut up.

"We took the kids up there last year, they had a blast," someone else says. I should know his name and don't. Should I start calling other people? Will Anna Grace know where he is? Will Levi? I don't have Levi's number, but I bet Anna Grace either does or knows someone who does, or I think Lainey is friends with—

"Darlin', you okay?" Linda asks, her cool hand suddenly on my shoulder. Everyone in the small group—five people— look at me and I know I turn stoplight red.

I force a smile anyway and take a breath past the tightness in my chest. It's not a panic attack yet, and I don't think it's going to turn into one, but I'm watching it warily anyway, like a tiger across a river.

"Fine," I say, even though the way I'm gripping my phone probably gives me away. I should've taken the free wine. "Just wondering where the heck Silas is!"

Wow, apparently I'm a person who says *heck*.

"I'm gonna try calling him again," I tell them, waving my phone like it's proof that I am, in fact, going to make a call using it. "I'll be right back."

"Hope everything's okay," Linda says, and I keep smiling and say something normal and then walk through the room full of people without tripping and back into the foyer and then, for good measure, through some French doors and onto an empty patio overlooking a dark golf course.

I've just hit the call button when my phone buzzes in my hand, a text message from a strange number.

**Unknown:** Kat? Are you at the lawyer thing?
**Unknown:** Sorry this is June
**Unknown:** Silas's sister

Oh God. Oh fuck. My hands are shaking.

**Me:** Is he okay?
**June:** Fine! He's fine. Shit, sorry
**June:** I should have led with that

I do not type *YES YOU SHOULD HAVE FUCKING LED WITH THAT*.

**Me:** Yeah, I'm at the lawyer thing at the country club. What happened? Did he get in an accident? Did something happen? Is he okay?

I swear, she types forever. I walk over to a bush and start tearing leaves off of it because I have to do something with my hands.

**June:** No accident, but nobody can find Javier. They're all up at Wildwood. Can you make some excuses and I'll pick you up in fifteen minutes?
**Me:** God yes.
**June:** Ha. I'll be the lady in the Forest Service truck.
**Me:** Thanks.

I spend the next ten minutes out there, alone, watching

the golf course and the forest beyond fade into darkness. Venus is on the horizon, and I watch it for a while. God, it feels good to be alone. I wonder if I can walk around the outside of the building back to my car without having to say goodbye to anyone.

*Two more sentences, Nakamura,* I think. *Come on.*

I make myself walk back in. Smile pleasantly at everyone. Re-enter the group I was in before, and when the conversation pauses, say that I am so sorry but something's come up, and need to leave. Silas is fine. He sends his regrets. Thank you for a lovely night.

I'm pretty sure I say most of that, at least. I might thank them for regrets and say that Silas sends a lovely night, who fucking knows.

But then I'm outside again. There's a guy in a vest at a valet stand, and we nod at each other as I lean against a brick column, kick my shoes off, and lean back. It's done. It's over. I didn't say anything incredibly embarrassing, I didn't have another panic attack, I didn't throw up on anyone's shoes. I didn't throw up at all, even though I thought I might at least twice.

Wait. What did she mean *nobody can find Javier?* I was so busy being glad I got to leave that I skimmed past that part, but standing here with my shoes off and relief washing over me like a cool shower, it suddenly hits me.

A few minutes later, a dark pickup truck loops around the parking lot, then pulls up. It's got dings in every door, needs to be washed, and has clearly seen better days.

I put my shoes back on and open the door.

"Kat?" says the woman inside.

"Hi. June?" I ask.

"Careful of the running board," she says. "It's a little

wobbly on that—yeah, there you go. Sorry. This is the worst car for that outfit, probably."

"It's fine," I say, as I heave myself into the passenger seat in the most unladylike manner possible. I probably didn't even flash anyone, mostly because there's no one out here to flash.

When I finally settle in and buckle up, she's looking at me, across the cab of the truck. I'm not sure how, but my stupid brain manages to dredge up just enough adrenaline to get nervous about it. God, I'm tired of myself sometimes.

"Hi," she says, after a moment, her face serious. She holds out a hand. "I'm June, Silas's sister."

Even in the dark, June looks like a smaller, female version of Silas. I can't see if she's got the same almost-freckles, but they've got the same eyes, the same eyebrows, his features softened and smaller on her face. I think her hair's darker. Also, she's visibly pregnant, somewhere in the 'cute bump' stage of pregnancy.

"Kat," I say, shaking it. "I'm. Uh. Silas's girlfriend."

Still a weird thing to say out loud, but June laughs.

"I've heard all about you," she says, and practically peels out of the parking lot. "Sorry. This thing either stalls or does that."

We reach the main road, and June almost stops before turning right.

"So, I heard you nearly made him drop out of college?"

I've got my head back against the seat, mind still racing.

"Not quite," I say without thinking. "I heard you slept with his best friend?"

That gets silence.

"Oh, my God," I say, the second my brain catches up with my mouth. "Pretend—"

June's laughing too hard to even hear me, I think. The truck wobbles a little on the road. I clear my throat.

"Sorry," I say, but now I'm trying not to laugh, too.

"No wonder he likes you," she says, still giggling. "That asshole needed someone with a spine."

I blow out a breath, then reach back and start undoing my hair since it's uncomfortable in the car and I think I'm about to go on some sort of deep woods adventure.

"I'm glad we're on the same page about him," I say.

"That he's an asshole, but we love him anyway?"

I glance over at her, profiled in the dark, dashboard lights giving her face an eerie glow.

"Yeah," I say, and don't elaborate.

"He's sorry for ditching you with his coworkers," she says, and then rolls her eyes. "Probably. He should be, I've met them before."

She blows out a breath, runs a hand through her hair the exact same way Silas does sometimes.

"No one knows where Javier is," she says. "But his car's up at Wildwood."

"Oh," I say, the only thing I can think of. I remember Javier at the brewery: the easy way he laughed, the paint that dotted his knuckles. Floppy black hair that he kept shoving out of his eyes. The casual way he moved, like he was in communication with all his limbs but couldn't always tell them what to do. Mexican, I think he said. A pretty kind of handsome.

"The guys are up there right now," she goes on. "They were looking for him earlier but it's probably too dark now. No point in getting two people lost. I think now they're just hoping he comes back."

"Okay," I say.

"We're going for moral support. Javi..."

June thinks for a minute, like she's being certain of getting her words right.

"...Struggles with addiction," she finishes, and takes a sharp curve about ten miles an hour too fast. I grab onto the sides of my seat.

"Oh," I say again.

"He's been sober for about three years," June goes on. "But. You know."

"Yeah," I say, even though I don't really. I know as much as anyone who reads the news or watches documentaries, but there's no one in my life who's struggled.

It's a long, dark drive, and June and I lapse into silence. We go from a main road to a smaller road and then, finally, a steep narrow road right up the side of a mountain, gouged with cracks and potholes. At the top there's a gravel parking area with a few other cars in it and a wooden Park Services sign that says CAMP WILDWOOD.

June turns the truck off and it's suddenly very, very quiet, the only sound is the keys still jangling from the ignition.

"Kat," she says, the word loud in the dark. "Listen. I know Silas is... a lot, sometimes."

"Is this an 'if you hurt my brother I'll kill you' speech?" I ask, because I've run through my capacity for thinking much before I speak, but June snorts.

"God, no," she says. "I'm way too late for that shit. If I was gonna kill something I'd kill, I dunno. The military industrial complex?"

I take a deep breath and push my hands through my hair, and I think we're both sort of laughing and sort of tired and sort of frazzled and confused and worried and scared.

"Yeah, he's kinda fucked up, huh?" I say, and it's the

kind of thing I could only say to his sister here, in the dark, after that drive. Lucky for me, June breathes out a laugh.

"He really is," she says, and then turns to look at me. "You're here anyway."

I don't know what to say. I never do, but especially not now, because *I'm in love with your brother* seems awkward and *of course* is trite.

"Yeah," I finally say. "I am."

# FORTY-ONE

## SILAS

IT'S GETTING TOO dark to be in the creek. The water's cold. The rocks are slippery. It's not deep—maybe two feet in the middle—but it's easy enough to drown if you find yourself face-down in it, and I don't know what the current would do then. I know water's always surprising. I know it takes less than you'd think, sometimes. I know how well easy, bucolic beauty can hide horror.

I slip on a rock and nearly fall in myself, wading a little further. I'm still in the gym shorts and an old tie-dye t-shirt that says Denim Jocker's Good Time Jug Band on the front —probably got it for free somewhere—but at least I put on hiking boots before I left my house hours ago. The one useful thing I did today.

There's a noise from somewhere, a crunch that's direc-tionless with the sound of the water rushing around me. It's soothing, like I'm in a box of noise and nothing else can get in, even though I know I'm wrong about that and something else can always get in. I turn and face upstream: the flat, placid dark of the creek. The hulking dark of the forest around it. The endless, deep dark of the sky above, faint stars like pinpricks.

Somewhere to my left is the path back to the cabin. I know I can find it if I want to, but that desire seems hard to reach right now. I should have done something. I should have called him more, checked in, made sure he had someone to talk to. I should have driven across the state and punched his father in the face.

Then there's a light bobbing through the trees, and all the dark gets darker.

"Silas," Levi calls. "Come back."

I stand there, unmoving, water up to my shins.

"What if I don't?"

"Silas."

"Yeah. I'm here."

"I know."

Levi waits. I don't know how long he waits, but he stands there on the bank, the light like a beacon. There's something ancient, solid, immovable about him, as if Levi could still be standing there tomorrow, next week, next year. Even though I know he can be swayed.

Finally, he puts the lantern down and steps into the creek. Wades until he's standing in front of me, his face half-lit and half-shadow from the light on the bank.

Then he puts his arms around me and then my head's on his shoulder and I nearly cry, I'm so grateful. The water is cold but Levi is warm, and he just holds me. Silently. Like always.

"We should go back," I say, after a while, and stand up straight again. Levi just nods and holds out one hand, and I don't even think before I take it and let him help me back to shore.

We're nearly back to the cabins when he says, "I think June went to go get Kat."

I slam to a stop so hard I almost fall over.

"Fuck," I say, and reach for the phone that's not in my pocket. I left it in my cabin because there's no signal up here. "*Fuck.* What time is it? I'm meeting Kat at that goddamn lawyer thing—"

"Silas. It's almost nine," Levi says.

Of course it is. It's dark out, of course it's late and oh, God, I left Kat to the wolves just like I said I wouldn't. I fucked this up, too.

"Thanks for thinking of it," I tell Levi.

"You asked me to," he says, and sounds faintly amused.

"I did?"

"Mhm. When you called me on the way here you went through a whole list of people who could help and at the end you said *and Kat* right before your signal cut out. June figured out where she was."

I don't remember that at all. I don't remember saying much of anything to anyone, even though I know I did; all I can remember is the descending fog of worry and panic, two things that make the holes in my brain worse.

A while later I'm sitting with Wyatt, leaning against Javi's cabin. Someone's made a fire in the fire pit, and across it I can see my own cabin: basic, one room, two bunk beds, a small porch with two plastic chairs. Sooner or later I'll make better chairs, but it hasn't happened yet. Next to it is Gideon's cabin, then Javier's, then Wyatt's. The corners of a square.

"I shouldn't have let him go," Wyatt says, miserable. His head's on my shoulder and I've got one arm around him. His hair smells like smoke.

"You know it wasn't up to you," I tell him, even though I have the exact same thought.

"I should've gone with him," Wyatt said. "I should've at least offered, I knew his brother was gonna be there but his parents can be so bad for him—"

He breaks off and takes a deep, ragged breath.

"Shhh," I say, as much to him as to myself because even though I know the right words to say to him—it wasn't up to you, it was out of your control—I feel the exact same way.

I have the urge to sing Wyatt a lullaby, but I don't know any. Maybe I should learn some before Levi and June have their kid.

We're still there when Kat appears. It's so sudden I'm afraid I'm hallucinating: one moment I'm staring into the fire and the next she's stepping around it, the light moving across her skin like she's something dangerous and other-worldly.

"Oh," I whisper, to no one at all. Wyatt sits up.

"Go," he says. "I'm good."

I do, and then she's in my arms and I've got my face buried in her hair that smells like citrus and flowers and hairspray or something. I want to tell her she shouldn't have come. I want to crumple at her feet.

Instead, I say, "I'm sorry."

"It's okay."

Now she's looking up at me, and behind her glasses her eyes are smudged with black and her hair is wild, strands picking up the orange glow of the fire, giving her an infernal halo. I'd never have her any other way.

"I swore I wouldn't leave you to the wolves," I say. "I know how much you hate—"

"Silas," she says. "*It's okay*."

Kat reaches up, thread her fingers through my hair, pulls my head down until our foreheads are touching.

"You must hate me right now," I murmur. "You should." But then her hands are on my face, fingertips skimming over my jaw, a thumb brushing my cheek. It doesn't feel like hate.

"You're being very dramatic," she says, voice low. "This isn't a soap opera."

For the first time in hours, I smile.

"Do you ever take a break from being the way you are?"

"How else would I be?"

"Good," I say, and kiss her, and then we stand there for a moment. The fire crackles and I can hear people talking: Levi and June, Gideon, Wyatt.

"I'm here," she says, a little later. "What do you need from me?"

# FORTY-TWO

## KAT

WHEN I FIND HIM AGAIN, Silas is sitting against a tree, twenty feet behind his cabin. Not hard to find but not easy, either: his head back, eyes closed, feet bare, legs in front of him. It's deep into the night now, not that time has meaning here: it's dark or it's not, the moon is somewhere, crickets chirp.

He opens his eyes but doesn't move when I crunch toward him in the sneakers I borrowed from June, wearing sweatpants I borrowed from Wyatt under my dress.

Silas watches me, his pupils blown in the dark. There's a look on his face like he's holding something back: a word, a sentence, a sob, an embrace. Like there's a canyon between us that only he can see.

The thought of it makes me feel like I'm exploding inside, the anxiety like broken glass. I wonder if he's about to end things. Tell me I shouldn't have come. Tell me that I've got it all wrong and this was him faking it all along, could I please go home now.

I'm afraid he'll tell me something that isn't about me at all, and I wonder how many of his secrets I can hear. I want the answer to be *all of them*, but I also know I'm human. My capacity isn't unlimited.

But right now he looks at me, brave and lovely in the dark, and I try to quell myself as I kneel next to him.

"Can I touch you?" I ask, and he nods. There's a curl of his deep auburn hair stuck to his forehead, so I reach out and brush it off. In the pale moonlight I can see a strand of gray threaded through it, and I let it sift through my fingers, falling away from his face.

When I comb my fingers through the rest of his hair, his eyes flicker shut and his lips part, head back against the tree. He swallows convulsively, throat working in the dark.

"I used to think about doing this all the time," he finally says.

"Sitting in the woods?" I ask, and slow my fingers, pull them out of his hair. He doesn't open his eyes.

"Just... disappearing," he goes on, his voice low and slow. "However Javier broke, I could break, too. Get in my car one day and just drive. End up somewhere no one knows me and no one cares."

He breathes, and I want to tell him that there's no place like that, but that's not helpful and he's not done.

"Pitch a tent in the forest," he goes on. "Live off the land. Go to the rundown part of some city and scrape by on under-the-table jobs. Find some cave and stay there."

Silas pushes both hands through his hair, eyes open and focused on nothing. The gray strand catches the moonlight for a moment and then disappears, and I want to kiss it as proof of how far he's come.

"I still do, sometimes," he says. "Not much. But I will always have killed people and hurt people and caused suffering because I was following orders. And there's always a part of me that will want to walk into the woods. Like if I could leave everything and everyone behind, maybe I'll finally fix myself."

I bite my lips together, take his hand, put it on my knee. *I want to disappear forever* is the first step on a long path down, and I know that.

"I wanted that for such a long time," he says. "To fix myself. But turns out there's no fixing me. There's only living with the damage."

So many meaningless platitudes crowd into my brain that they start punching each other for space: from *you're not damaged* to *broken is beautiful* to *everything is fixable if you believe in yourself!*

I don't say anything, but his hair's fallen onto his forehead again and I brush it back.

"What if it's me, Kat?" he asks, voice quiet and rough as tree bark. His eyes open, endless as the horizon.

"If you disappeared?" I ask.

He nods, barely.

"I'd look for you."

"What if you couldn't find me?"

"I'd keep looking."

"What if I told you not to look?"

His hand is covered with mine, and I'm in uncharted territory. All I can do is hope I understand what he needs.

"I'd ignore you and look anyway. Until I found you."

Finally he looks away, his eyes tracking upward. He's looking at the moon, I think.

"I thought about telling you I didn't want you any more," he says. "Saying that this had all been fake, the sex was great but nothing special. That this was fun but it needed to be over, because you deserve someone who's never gotten drunk and driven home and the whole way thought about how fast and which curve and what tree."

398

He looks at me again, and his voice goes softer.

"I haven't in years," he says, then swallows. "But you know it never goes away, just fades."

"I know," I say, and take his hand.

"I'm too selfish, Kat," he says, and a weird, broken laugh comes out of his throat. "I want you here. I want you with me. I want to keep you, in all your sharp, angry glory, and it turns out I can't sacrifice all that on the altar of thinking I know what's best for you."

I don't feel sharp and angry, just then. I feel soft as a feather mattress.

"You don't know what's best for me," I point out, and it gets the first smile from him I've seen all night.

"That was the other reason," he says. "That's some condescending, patriarchal bullshit and if anyone here found out they'd light me on fire."

"I'd be first."

"You'd have to line up behind my sister, I think she's got dibs."

"I like her."

"You would."

I turn our hands so our fingers can twine together, and Silas gives me a long, slow look.

"You know, I got ordained on the internet and performed their wedding ceremony," he says, and his voice is quiet again, rough like velvet rubbed the wrong way. "And I lied through my fucking teeth the whole time."

For some reason I glance over my shoulder, back toward the cabins where Levi and June are somewhere, huddled together, worrying.

"I said all the right things, up there. Marrying my best friend to my sister," he goes on. "About love and happiness and two souls intertwined and blah fucking blah. You know the deal. You've heard people talk about soulmates and shit. And I did not believe one fucking word of it."

"About them?" I ask, because even though I've seen them together for about thirty seconds, they seemed genuine.

"About anyone," Silas says. "I thought they were all lying and saying what they thought they were supposed to say, that they'd all agreed on a set of parameters for some feeling that didn't exist but that everyone thought they were supposed to feel. I mean, I thought that maybe poets and songwriters were telling the truth, sometimes, but I didn't really think that most people fell in love. I thought they all settled and said a lot of nice things about it."

He looks at me, and I think my heart stops.

"Because if it was all real, why not me?" he goes on, softly. "So I figured it couldn't be. And then."

He's silent for a moment, like he's trying to decide what to say.

"And then I saw you tonight and I was *happy*. This stupid, miserable night, and you showed up and my heart just... sang. How fucked up is that?"

"It's not," I tell him, and I move closer, until I'm practically in his lap. I'm sitting off-balance on some roots and my butt is damp and Silas is half-twisted toward me in a way that can't feel good on his back, but this is all I want. I thread my fingers through his hair and bring his face to mine until our foreheads are touching. Until we can't see anything but each other.

"I love you, too," I whisper.

He swallows, his eyes closed, and his hands find mine. There's a terrible moment where I think he's going to pull me away, shove me off him, but he doesn't. He skims his hands along mine, my arms, shoulders, my sides. Like he's checking that all of me is here.

"You shouldn't," he says, when he's done.

"Don't tell me what to do."

And then Silas smiles. I'm too close to see it but I can feel it in the way his face moves, in the way his breath catches, in the way it feels like my heart splits open and light pours out.

"Fuck, Kat," he whispers, and now he's laughing and kissing me and it's a terrible kiss, all teeth and lips and bad angles, but it's also the best kiss.

We don't say anything else. We kiss. I stroke his hair, watch his eyes close. After a while I wedge myself half between him and the tree and Silas slumps, leans his head back against my chest. I hold him and feel his breathing. Watch the fire flicker through the trees. Watch the moon arc above the trees. I'm dirty and damp and I'm pretty sure my pelvis and spine have fused with this tree, but I don't move.

Finally he turns until his head is in my lap, more or less, and looks up at me.

"Are you staying?" he asks.

"Of course," I say.

· · · · · ★ ★ ★ ★ · · · ·

EVERYONE ELSE IS around the fire: Wyatt flanked by Gideon and now Lainey, who waves hello. Levi and June together on a log, even though I've seen plenty of chairs around here. As if everyone is afraid of comfort, of settling in. Like we're all on edge and the thought of feeling better is impossible.

"I meant to tell you earlier," June says, eyes still on the

fire. "Search and rescue guys are coming up tomorrow, early."

"They listened?" Silas says.

"I had to ask very nicely," says Levi, who doesn't sound happy about it. "I think it's mostly a favor."

Sitting on the grass, Wyatt cracks a knuckle, his nostrils flaring.

"He's disappeared before," Silas tells me, voice low. "Not for this long. Never for this long, but... you know."

"Oh," I say. I feel hypnotized by the fire. I think we all do.

"When you call out search and rescue and then the missing person shows up five hours later saying he just wanted to see what Bloodroot Meadow looked like under a full moon, they're less excited about coming out the next time," Silas says.

"He told us, after that," Wyatt says. "He always told us."

Lainey gives him a side hug, pulling his head against her shoulder.

"We should all go to bed," Gideon says. "No use being awake. May as well get some rest. You two staying with me?"

"If you don't mind," says June, and Gideon snorts.

"Of course I don't mind," he says. "Why do you think I asked?"

Then there are hugs. Everyone hugs everyone else, maybe more hugs than I've received at once in my entire life, and normally it might be overwhelming but here, in the fire-light, in the circumstances, it's nice.

I hug Levi last, and when I do, he holds on for an extra second.

"Thank you," he says, so quietly that no one else can hear.

"Of course," I tell him, and when he pulls back he gives

me a quiet, secret smile, like he's pleased by my response.

Back in Silas's cabin, he clicks on a lantern on a crate next to the bunk beds. It makes the small space look oddly bigger, makes shadows loom, makes it feel like this one room is the only place that's real and everything outside is dust and fog. Like we're together at the end of the world.

He falls onto the bottom bunk, lying on top of a blanket, then covers his face with his hands.

"No," I say, and he groans. "Come on. Up."

He stands again. With the light at this angle, from below, he looks different than I'm used to, almost like he's someone else: shadows and angles going the wrong direction, but he looks down at me and gives me the ghost of a smile and lets me pull his shirt off before getting his pants and shoes himself.

I do the same, turn off the lantern, and then crawl into the same bed as him. It's even smaller than a regular twin, I think, and I'm crammed between Silas's broad back and the wooden wall of the cabin, but I wouldn't be anywhere else. I wrap one arm around him, feeling the raised edge of his broken bottle scar. My face is buried in the base of his neck.

I think he's asleep, but then he speaks.

"I don't know what to do if we don't find him," he says into the dark.

"We keep looking," I say.

There's a long pause, and I wonder again if he's asleep, the darkness in the cabin so deep I don't know if my eyes are open or closed.

"I love you," Silas says. "I didn't say it before."

"It's okay. I knew."

He takes the hand that's wrapped around him, raises it to his lips, softly kisses my palm, and I breathe into the silence.

# FORTY-THREE

## KAT

"WHAT THE HELL?"

Silas nearly falls out of the tiny bed. I grab his arm, not that it would help, and blink because everything is blurry, someone's shouting, I'm mostly naked, and I've got no idea where I am.

"The police?" the shouter shouts, and I swear it sounds like he's right outside the door of... right, Silas's cabin in the middle of the woods. That's where I am.

"Search and rescue?!" he goes on. "You called search and rescue?"

Silas is out of bed and swearing already, the early sunlight glowing in through two small curtained windows.

"Fuck. That's Javi," he says, shaking out the pants he was wearing yesterday.

"He's back," I offer, pulling the blanket over myself.

"And pissed."

"But he's back."

Silas blows out a breath, his shirt held in one hand, as he shoves a hand through his hair. Then he smiles, the relief practically cracking his face in half.

"Yeah. Thank fuck."

"You were gone for *three days*," Gideon says, outside the cabins. "The fuck were we supposed to do?"

"Not call my mom!" Javier says. "Not call my *father*, because now half the Navy is going through Norfolk and Portsmouth, hanging up *have you seen this unfortunate young man* posters!"

Silas shoves open his cabin door, shirt mostly on.

"We didn't tell your father," he says, walking out and letting the door swing shut behind him.

"Someone fucking did," Javier says. "You called the cops? You called *search and rescue?*"

"Your car was here and you weren't." That's Gideon again, sounding even more pissed off. "Tell me, what were we supposed to think?"

There's no answer as I pull on the same thing I was wearing yesterday and finally grab my glasses from the crate by the bed. When I come through the door, blinking in the just-barely-dawn, Javier's standing stock-still in the open doorway of his own cabin.

"Did you go through my shit?" he asks, his voice quieter now and twice as dangerous.

"We were hoping you'd left a note," says Silas.

Everyone's out here now: Levi and June in the middle, near the fire pit; Wyatt and Lainey in front of his cabin, looking tired. I can see the circles under Wyatt's eyes from here.

Javier steps in, looks around. There's a long, tense silence before he shouts again.

"You find anything?" he asks. "Anything at all? Some pills? A beer bottle? Did you find a fucking *Snickers?*"

"No," says Silas, who's finally raising his voice. "We also

didn't find a single fucking clue of where you'd gone for *three days* without talking to anyone."

"I don't owe you knowledge of every movement! You don't have to keep an eye on me!"

"Where the fuck were you, then?" That's Gideon.

We're all slowly moving closer to the three of them, like the circle is closing in. I sort of feel like I'm snooping and don't know what else I could do, given the volume of the argument.

"It's none of your business," Javier says.

That gets another long, tense silence, and I can feel everyone looking at each other.

"Javi—"

"Maybe next time you could put a tracker on me," he cuts Silas off. "Save yourselves the frustration."

"We're not putting a fucking tracker on you," Gideon says.

Now Silas is a few feet from Javier, in front of his cabin, staring at the other man.

"You checking to see if I'm high right now?" Javier asks, his voice suddenly soft and edged.

"No."

Javier holds out both arms, wrists up.

"I don't tell you guys everything," he says. "There. Happy? Do I still get to keep some things to myself?"

"Jesus fucking Christ, Javi, there's keeping things to yourself and then there's disappearing for—"

Gideon's cut off by Wyatt, who closes the ten feet between them and wraps Javier in a massive, tight hug.

"I'm sorry," Wyatt says, and doesn't let up.

After a moment, Javier's arms go around Wyatt's back: tentative at first, then tighter.

"Fuck," I hear him mutter. "Me too."

I watch as Silas and Gideon pile on, as well, until the four of them are standing in front of Javier's cabin in one big lump, hugging.

"These idiots," Lainey says, standing next to me, and I smile.

"Yeah," I agree. "Idiots."

· · · · ★ ★ ★ ★ ★ · · · ·

I SETTLE my back against the wall and offer the bag to Silas, who reaches in and takes out a donut.

"This was a great idea," he says through a mouthful.

"Thank Linda," I say, reaching in myself and grabbing a slightly sticky, still-warm apple cider donut. "She was very excited to tell me all about them yesterday."

"Maybe I should unleash you on my colleagues by yourself more often," he says, and I snort hard. Cinnamon sugar sprays off my donut and onto the roof in front of me.

"Don't you dare," I say. "Just because I survived it doesn't mean I want to do it again."

Silas turns and presses a quick kiss to my hair. There's probably cinnamon sugar in it now, but I don't say that. I just enjoy the moment as we watch the sun lower in the sky over Sprucevale, mouths full of fried dough.

It's been a *day*. Even after storming into Wildwood in a borrowed car at six in the morning, Javier absolutely refuses to tell anyone where he was or why he was missing for three whole days. Not even a hint.

It's fucked up of him, for sure. I spent the morning kind of wanting to shake him and shout *what the hell, they thought you were dead*, but that's very much not my job so I did some glaring and left it at that. Silas, Gideon, and Wyatt are pissed, but they're also glad he's not dead, so I think they've reached a tentative truce.

Then, after we came down the mountain and told Javier's family he's alive and called off Search and Rescue and the police and showered, Silas and I got donuts and came up here, to the roof of the Sprucevale Central Library. The key is hidden above the door frame to one of the archive rooms, and I didn't even ask why Silas knew that.

"Linda also said that Jackson Orchard has better donuts, but they don't open until September," I say.

"We should go," Silas says. "You ever been apple picking?"

"Maybe once, when I was a kid."

He grins over at me, one thumb in his mouth as he sucks the sugar off it. I wonder if anyone can see us up here.

"We'll go," he says, taking his thumb out of his mouth with a final, distracting lick. "Next month. We'll pick way, way too many apples and make apple pies and apple tarts and applesauce and still have too many apples, and by the time we finish all the apples we got we'll be sick of them."

"Sounds like you've got a plan," I say, laughing.

"I've got a lot of experience with Appalachian autumns."

I shift the way I'm sitting, pull my legs in to sit cross-legged.

"What else are we gonna do?"

Now that everything is over—Evan's gone, the month is up—I suddenly feel like I can think into the future, stretching before us, bright as the horizon. It looks *fun*.

"Before or after the orchard?"

"Either."

"Well," he says, head back against the wall behind us, the golden glow of the sunset bathing him in its perfect, gentle light, "Bountiful Farms has a pumpkin patch with a corn maze I've always wanted to try."

"You've never been?"

"I never have," he says.

"This year, then."

Our hands touch, and I lace our fingers together. I feel giddier than I should at the simple prospect of *a month from now.*

"For Halloween, a couples' costume," he says.

"Absolutely not. What else?"

Silas laughs with his head back and his eyes crinkling, happy and beautiful. I think of him, last night in the dark, saying *I can only live with the damage* and the way I heard *damage.* Now, in the sunlight, crumbs of sugar on his lips, I think: *I can only live.*

"Thanksgiving," he says. "Are you gonna want me to meet your parents by then?"

"We'll see how well you behave," I say, but I'm grinning back at him, my face practically split in half.

"If I'm not up to your standards you can come to mine," he tells me. "Though sometimes we all go to Levi's mom's house. That's a fun time. Kids, dogs. Last year there was a pumpkin catapult."

"A what?"

"It was pretty fun," he says, grinning. "I got mine the farthest. Levi's little brother was pissed."

I don't love the idea of a house full of people, but I'm... intrigued by a catapult.

"Then we can go to your parents' house for Christmas," he goes on. "Do they do Christmas?"

"Not the Jesus parts, but yeah," I say. "You think you'll be up to snuff by then?"

"Probably," he says. "Come back here for New Year's. They do a ball drop at midnight downtown. With a pear."

I'm imagining a guy in a camouflage baseball hat dropping a single pear off a tall ladder. It's not very impressive.

"A pear?"

"It's, like, a lit up pear on a pole. Not just some guy chucking it out a second-story window."

I can't help but laugh, because yeah, he's not far off.

"Do we have Valentine's plans?"

His hand flexes in mine, locking us together a little tighter.

"We could," he says. "Or not. Either way, so long as they're with you."

It's so simple but it's sweet, and true, and maybe that's what I've been missing. Maybe not a lot else matters when things are sweet and true like this, when we're holding hands on a roof where we're not really supposed to be, when the sunlight is a dusky gold, when everything feels beautiful and perfect even though I know it's not.

Even though I know there's no *perfect* when it comes to people, only endless irregularities: gaps and holes and sharp edges and broken pieces, but it all works anyway. Sometimes in the strangest, most beautiful ways.

"We should go get dinner if we're gonna," he says after a bit.

I exhale, tilting my head back against the wall, the sun right below the tree line.

"Yeah," I say. "Eventually."

"It's Sunday night, so everything around here closes at about eight," Silas says. "Small town charm."

I turn my head toward him, and after a moment, he turns toward me. Silas is ten thousand things all at once, and right now, I feel like I can see them all: faint freckles and

410

messy hair, laugh lines and stubble. Scars and gray hairs and old injuries that hurt when it rains, all earned and precious in their own odd way.

His eyes that make me feel like I could float forever in them; that maybe I belong there with my teeth and claws, happily swimming through the depths.

"Kiss me first," I say, and he smiles like he's surprised and excited, cups my face in his hand, strokes my cheekbone with his thumb.

And then he does.

# EPILOGUE

## SILAS

### Eight Months Later

"I JUST FEEL like we should be doing something," Kat says, arms crossed in front of her chest as she looks down. "Shouldn't we be doing something?"

"I can't imagine why you're asking me."

"You volunteered us for this."

"I was very specific that I didn't know what we were doing, though," I point out. "What's the manual say?"

"Nothing about what we do while he's asleep," Kat says. "Beast, quit it."

She bends down and gently shoves Beast's nose away from Nathaniel, who remains fast asleep in his carseat.

"Then I think we let this happen," I say as Beast sits down, politely curling her tail around her front paws and watching Nathaniel with an unnerving, unflinching stare. "Right?"

There's another pause as Nathaniel twitches in his sleep, one arm waving haphazardly in the air, but then he settles back down.

"Cats don't eat babies, do they?" whispers Kat. "Maybe we should feed Beast early. Should we unbuckle him? That doesn't look very comfortable."

"I don't think he minds, he's asleep," I point out. "And I don't think she has the taste for human flesh. Yet."

Kat gives me one of her looks at yet, up through her glasses, and I can't help but grin at it.

"Please don't give your cat a taste for humans," she says.

"Look, you never know," I say. "I could get a papercut, leave the room to find a bandaid, come back to find her lapping at the drops of blood on my desk..."

Kat's giving me a stern look, but she's trying not to laugh.

"Then what?" she asks. "Beast develops a thirst for blood and roams the neighborhood, lurking in the shadows as she awaits her next victim?"

As if she can hear us, Beast turns her head and looks up at me with her enormous green eyes. I could swear she's admonishing me.

"Did I ever tell you I thought she was a demon or something when I found her?"

"Only like thirty times," Kat says.

"Mrrp," says Beast.

"Well, now I know that," I tell her.

"Should we watch a movie or something?" Kat asks, still staring down at the baby. "I could keep unpacking, I've only got like three boxes le—"

Nathaniel makes a long, plaintive noise without opening his eyes. I freeze. Kat freezes.

Beast leaves the room.

"It's fine," I say, as the noise gets louder. "We can do this. It's just a baby, people have babies all the time."

Bravely, Kat nods. Nathaniel's eyes open. The noises get louder and more varied, but they're clearly all unhappy noises, his tiny fists uselessly hitting the sides of his car seat.

I take a deep breath, then crouch and unbuckle him as the volume level steadily increases. Then I pause, trying to remember all the various instructions regarding my nephew I've been given over the past four months. Do I still need to support the head? That was a pretty big deal at one point.

It's my first time uncle-ing without Levi or June around, and I'm not sure I'm up to the task.

Nathaniel confirms this when I pick him up, because the unhappy noises turn into a full-on scream: mouth open, eyes closed, face bright red.

"Oh, shit," Kat says as I try to awkwardly settle him against my shoulder. He's not having it.

"Don't listen to your Aunt Kat, she's a bad influence," I tell Nathaniel, who can't possibly hear me over his own screaming.

"I've got, like, four years before I have to worry about swearing," she says, heading into the kitchen. "I'm getting a bottle!"

"You're okay, buddy," I tell Nathaniel, who doesn't believe me. "And no, she's never met a child before."

I walk Nathaniel around some while he screams his head off. From the kitchen, I can hear Kat swearing as she fiddles with the bottle warmer that Levi and June brought over, along with the car seat, a travel crib, several bottles, five changes of clothing, a diaper pad, and what looks like a year's worth of diapers. There's easily five times as much baby stuff as there is actual baby.

"Okay!" Kat says, coming out of the kitchen with a bottle in one hand and The Nathaniel Manual in the other, open to the page about how to feed a baby. June has been very thorough, and I'm trying not to read too much into it.

Then, we stare at each other. I've fed Nathaniel a handful of times before, but again: I was being supervised at the time.

"Maybe sit on the couch?" Kat says, pointing. "And sort of, prop him up against... yeah."

"Okay, buddy," I say, hoping I sound soothing instead of panicky. Apparently my one paternal instinct is to call an infant *buddy*. "Okay. Here we go."

I take the bottle from Kat and sort of... put it on his mouth. He cries for a few seconds more, then seems to realize that something is going on in the face region, and quickly gets down to business.

Kat and I both exhale as the room goes quiet.

"See?" I tell Nathaniel. "You're in great hands."

· · · · ★ ★ ★ ★ ★ · · · ·

SEVERAL HOURS LATER, Kat and I are slumped together on the couch, staring into space. Nathaniel and all of his possessions are gone, picked up by parents who seemed really happy to have a night alone. There's puke on my shirt, and one lens of Kat's glasses is smudged to hell because Nathaniel took a liking to them.

"That was okay," she finally says. "I'd do it again. Next month."

"I'm not sure who's more damaged, us or him," I tell her, and she snorts.

"I didn't swear that much," she says. "Or drop him even once! Or let Beast eat him! Or hand him a knife!"

"Yeah, you're a natural," I tell her, and she laughs.

"You did okay," she says. "That was cute. You're a good uncle."

Even though I'm tired and frazzled, it ignites a warm,

fuzzy glow in my chest.

"Yeah?"

"Of course," she says, tilting her head back on the couch. "And you'll have a great time teaching that kid to raise hell in a few years."

"Kat," I say, putting one hand to my chest. "I would never."

"You absolutely would," she says, grinning.

"I'm not the one who hypnotized him with Pikachu."

"Jigglypuff," she corrects me as we both turn to look at it, still propped against an armchair.

It stares back, its eyes vacant, its smile alarming. Nathaniel spent a good twenty minutes on the floor staring at it, and I think we're both a little worried that we've caused brain damage.

"It can't be worse than screen time, right?" Kat says, eyes never leaving the large stuffed Pokémon.

"Probably not," I say. And then: "Is screen time bad?"

"I don't know. Maybe? I don't actually know shit about babies," she says, and I start laughing.

"Really?"

"Shut up."

"So babysitting didn't suddenly ignite your baby fever?" I tease. Once Kat stopped being so anxious, she and Nathaniel were actually pretty cute together. I think she'll be a fun aunt.

"It very much did not," she says. "You?"

"Not even a little," I say.

"Good," she says. "I like having you all to myself."

"Greedy," I say, kissing the top of her head, her hair warm and smooth beneath my lips.

"You like it," she says back, voice lazy and a little rough, and she's never been more right.

416

"Yeah," I agree, because I can't argue with that. "I do."

# ACKNOWLEDGMENTS

First, thanks to all the readers who read the Loveless series and have spent three years demanding that Silas get his own book. I always wanted to write it, but I might not have pushed through otherwise.

This book would probably not exist without my husband bringing me snacks, reminding me to hydrate, and occasionally dragging me away from the keyboard to go do something fun. Despite being mostly stuck inside a two-bedroom apartment for close to two years, I still like hanging out with you, which is probably the best compliment I know how to give.

More thanks: to Becca Hensley Mysoor, who's both an actual book genius and possibly a literal angel, for patiently telling me how to write a romance, for responding to catastrophic-sounding late-night texts with gentle encouragement, and for generally being a fun, awesome person who I like being around.

To Theresa and Julia, for all-caps texts of encouragement and absolutely unhinged voice memos that made me laugh so hard strangers worried.

To Vivian, Andrew, Kat, and Linnea, for sticking around all these years.

To Alex and Connie, who let me pick their brains and provided me with wine and couches to lie on while I shouted.

To Steph Boardman, who was kind enough to do a sensitivity read and made this book so much stronger.

And to Sarah Ferguson, who still hasn't quit. I think.

## ABOUT ROXIE

Roxie lives in California with her husband, son, and two very grumpy cats.

www.roxienoir.com
roxie@roxienoir.com

Made in the USA
Monee, IL
30 June 2023

38218615R00249